SCIMITAR MOON

Chris A. Jackson

WWW.DRAGONMOONPRESS.COM

Dragon
Moon

Scimitar Moon

pISBN 10 1-896944-54-X
pISBN 13 978-1-896944-8

Dragon Moon Press is an Imprint of Hades Publications Inc.
P.O. Box 1714, Calgary, Alberta, T2P 2L7, Canada

Printed and bound in Canada or the United States of America
www.dragonmoonpress.com

Dedication

I dedicate this book to my father:
The man who took me to sea for the first time...
and made me love it, forever.

Acknowledgments

Thanks to all my friends at Elfwood and the Herscher Project who reviewed and critiqued this manuscript, and to my editor Gabrielle, who provided the final polish. A special thanks to Sarah for inspiring the character Mouse. And, as always, my profound thanks go to my dear wife, Anne, for not killing me in my sleep for even considering being a writer, and for living on a boat, and for leaving everything to go sailing with me...

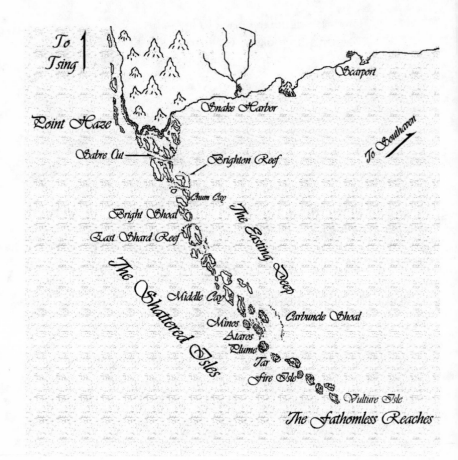

To Tsing

Scarport

Point Haze

Snake Harbor

To Southaven

Sabre Cut

Brighton Reef

Chum Cay

The Easting Deep

Bright Shoal

East Shard Reef

The Shattered Isles

Middle Cay

Carbuncle Shoal

Minos
Ataros
Plume

Tar
Fire Isle

Vulture Isle

The Fathomless Reaches

PROLOGUE

Seasprite's Bane

"LOTS OF SHIPS HAVE one, Julia," Ben Garrison argued, spearing a broiled to-mato and a slice of ham from the silver tray. "It's not like he's doing any harm. Just pranks, is all."

"This isn't a ship!" the stately woman snapped, scowling at her husband as she plucked a butter knife from the loaf of steaming bread at the center of the table. An identical knife thunked into the loaf, accompanied by a peal of impossibly high-pitched laughter. "It's my home, and no place for a seasprite to be playing tricks. He's setting a bad example for Cynthia!"

"I think he's cute, Grammy!" Cynthia chirped, giggling as a six-inch sprite in loose pants and a tiny seaman's shirt fluttered from hiding and circled her head once, before snatching up her butter knife and vanishing behind the china cabinet. "Mouse don't mean no harm. He's just a sprite."

"*Doesn't* mean *any* harm, Cynthia," the matron of the house corrected. "Honestly, I don't know where you pick up such poor grammar."

"Probably from me, Mother," Orin Flaxal said, entering the breakfast room with his usual aplomb, which was none at all, and tousling his daughter's hair. She giggled and snatched a scone from the basket, bit off a corner and grinned at him through the crumbs. "She's got a seaman's manner, sure enough."

"Cynthia! Put that down and use a knife and fork!" Julia snapped, prick-ling visibly at being called "Mother" by her son-in-law. "I won't have you acting like a sailor at this table!"

"I guess we're in trouble then, eh, Pop?" Orin said, taking a scone and slathering it with butter before sitting down and taking a bite. "Being sail-ors, I mean," he added, grinning at his daughter through his own mouthful of crumbs.

"Aye, we better start actin' like lubbers, I guess." Ben tried to pick up his cup with a pinky sticking out, but failed and slopped blackbrew on the spot-less white tablecloth. Another butter knife thunked into the bread. "Oops. Sorry, Julia." He dabbed at the stain with his napkin, smiling sheepishly.

"I don't know how you manage it, Daddy," Cynthia's mother said as she entered the room and gave her daughter a hug. Peggy Flaxal rounded the table and kissed her father on the forehead. "You can walk from poopdeck to forecastle in a full gale with a cup of blackbrew without spilling a drop. Put you on the beach and you're all thumbs."

"You know it takes me a fortnight to get my land legs, Peg." He reached for the knife sticking out of the bread, but a fluttering streak of faerie wings plucked it away before his fingers touched it. The bread was starting to look a bit worse for wear, having been impaled half a dozen times this morning. "Ha! The little bugger's quick, I gotta admit!"

"The thing is a nuisance and a bad influence on your granddaughter. I want him out of this house, Benjamin!" Julia demanded.

The recently pilfered butter knife thunked back into the bread.

"Mother, he's just a—" Peggy started, as the little sprite flew from hiding and dove for the bread.

"Out this instant!" Julia screeched, her tone rattling the dishes. She swatted ineffectually at the fluttering faerie before he snatched the knife once again and darted off.

"Careful, Julia. Don't hurt the little fella!"

"Hurt him! I'll throttle the little imp if I get my hands on him!" She glared at the plate on the sideboard where the sprite was hiding. He peeked around the gilded rim and stuck his tongue out at her.

"Take care, Mother," Orin said, his mien becoming serious. "It's dreadful luck to hurt a seasprite on purpose. Why, ships have run up on reefs for it."

"A poor excuse for drunken captains and bad seamanship, I'll warrant." She threw down her napkin in disgust. "Breakfast is ruined, thanks to that little monster! Why don't you use those vaunted *powers* of yours to banish that little wasp!"

She stormed out of the room in a huff.

The silver butter knife thunked into the loaf of bread.

"Well, at least his aim is improving," Orin said, snatching the knife before Mouse could swish back across the table to retrieve it. He buttered the rest of his scone and started breakfast in earnest.

"You won't let Grammy hurt Mouse, will you, Daddy?" Cynthia chewed on a piece of ham and turned her head to watch the little seasprite circle the table, orbiting everyone's head once before finding another butter knife to pilfer.

"Oh, he's too quick for her, Cynny. Don't you worry." Orin filled his cup and shared a concerned look with his father-in-law.

"Not to worry, Cyn," the old sailor said, patting his granddaughter's hand. "I'll talk to your grammy."

"Thanks, Grampy!" She giggled again as another butter knife hit the bread. "Wow, Mouse! That's eight in a row!"

The seasprite flew out from behind a gravy boat and landed on the lacerated loaf, striking a pose as if he'd slain it single-handedly. Cynthia clapped and cheered the little hero, and he bowed deeply before extracting

Chris A. Jackson ≈ 7

his knife and sawing off a slice as his just desserts.

The whole family laughed and smiled, even Orin, despite his genuine concern about his mother-in-law's ill intentions.

≈

"Please, Julia. Orin knows what he's talkin' about. It *is* bad luck to hurt a seasprite."

"Hogwash!" she retorted, checking the linen closet for wrinkled napkins and poorly creased tablecloths. "There's no such thing as bad luck, or good luck for that matter. There's only hard work and reward, and you should know that, Benjamin." She flicked the corner of a napkin and clicked her tongue disapprovingly. "Or laziness and due punishment. Marta! Marta, this linen cabinet is a mess. Take everything out and iron it, then see that it's all folded properly. I won't have wrinkled napkins at my table."

"Yes, Mistress Garrison," the maid said with a curtsey. She started taking out the linen as Ben smiled apologetically and pulled his rampaging wife aside.

"Julia, I'm serious about this. Orin is a seamage. He knows this isn't something to be trifled with. Seasprites are one of Odea's favored creatures, and she's a vengeful goddess when her toes are trod on."

"Then Orin better figure out a way to get the little insect out of my house," she said coldly. "This is *my* house, Benjamin Garrison. You have your ships, and you said this household would be mine to govern as I saw fit the day I agreed to marry you. You wouldn't have a single ship to your name if it weren't for my inheritance, and don't you forget it."

"I haven't forgotten it, Julia. How could I?" His tone stated that she reminded him all-too-regularly of that fact. "But I have a dozen ships now, and more than that many river barges. This house was built with profits I made with those ships. Your inheritance has been doubled, redoubled, and redoubled again."

"I fail to see your point, Benjamin," she said with a haughty sniff. "This is still my household, and that sprite is an unwanted guest. See that it is removed, or I will do so myself."

She turned to leave, but Ben's strong hand encircled her arm. Her gasp may have been pain or simple surprise. Either way, he relaxed his grip a trifle, but he did not let her go.

"I'm *not* asking, Julia," he said in the tone he used at sea, where he was sole master of life and death. "I'll see if Orin can coax Mouse down to one of the ships, but the sprite's taken a shine to little Cynthia. If he won't leave, I don't want you doing anything drastic."

Her eyes narrowed and lowered to his grip on her arm, her mouth pursing in distaste, as if his sailor's hands offended her in some way. Her gaze slowly rose, as much steel in her eyes as his.

"See that the creature is removed, Benjamin, and there will be no need for me to do so myself," she said.

He held her eyes for another moment, then released her arm. "I will see what I can do, Julia, but I warn you, do *not* bring Odea's wrath down on this house."

She turned without a word and walked away.

Ben stood for a while, wondering what had happened to the woman he'd married. Time had worn them thin, it seemed. Time he'd spent at sea building his floating empire.

"A master of ships..." he mumbled, staring down at his broad, scarred hand. *How fragile it all is*, he thought, flexing his fingers. His empire, his family and his life could all fall apart in an instant if Odea so chose.

≈

Orin Flaxal stood on the quarterdeck of the largest galleon in the Garrison fleet, the first rays of morning sun warming his face. The ship teemed with activity, but he wasn't really paying attention to the bustling crew or the shouting boatswain. The ship was *Peggy's Pride*, the gem of the fleet, and the only two things his father-in-law loved more were the woman it was named after and little Cynthia, his only grandchild. That was why Orin and Ben got along so well: they had their loves in common. Right now, he was making sure that nothing would come to harm those things he loved most, not even the source of his own powers.

The crew of *Peggy's Pride* had worked through the night to load a cargo that was probably not going to earn the Garrison family a single ounce of gold. The hold full of copra and breadfruit had been purchased hastily, and the markets to the north had been soft of late, but this trip had very little to do with making a profit. If Ben Garrison broke even on the cargo's sale and everything else worked as planned, he would count himself fortunate.

If everything worked as planned; that was where Orin's skills came into play.

He stood and closed his eyes and started humming a tune low in his throat, for all the world looking like a man simply enjoying the sunrise. Beneath that guise, he wove a gentle compulsion, a song of the sea to woo one particular seasprite into joining him for a little cruise. He wove the salt spray, the rolling swell and the steady trade winds into his song. He added the crack of canvas filling with wind, the creak of spars and the howl of wind in the rigging. He blended it all together and sent it up the hill to waft through the open windows of the estate. He sent it to the little sprite

Mouse, where he played with Cynthia on the floor of the sunroom.

He felt a little tug, not unlike that of a fish taking a hook, and he knew Mouse had taken the bait. A seasprite loved little in the world more than sailing, and Mouse had sailed with Orin many times. A smile touched his lips as he felt the tug again. His little friend was hooked.

The boatswain shouted, "All ashore what's goin' ashore! Secure the main yard! Dog down that hatch and make ready the tops'ls!"

His timing was perfect.

≈

"Where you goin', Mouse?" Cynthia cried as the little sprite leapt into the air and flashed around the room, his gossamer-crystal wings a blur in the morning sunlight. "We were just about ready to play!"

She snatched up one of the dolls she had been transforming from a little girl dressed in a frilly gown to a naked mermaid. The doll's dress had been stripped away, and her little legs were bound together with green ribbon. Grammy didn't like it when she played sharks and mermaids with her dolls, but they were *her* dolls. But just as they were ready to venture out into the yard in search of a decently sized puddle, Mouse threw off the little wooden fin that she'd strapped to his back and swooped into the air.

"Mouse! Don't go! I won't hold you underwater again, I promise!" She was honestly sorry about the last time she'd done that—who would have thought that a seasprite couldn't breathe water? But her shouts had no effect, and the next thing she knew, he'd flown out the window and vanished.

"Well, fine! I can play sharks and mermaids on my own!" She pouted and got up to look for another doll, one that she could transform into an adequately convincing shark, maybe with a strip of material from the hem of one of her mother's dresses. Daddy always said that sailors liked shorter dresses anyway...

≈

"Ship the boats, if you please, Mr. Brael. Sheet the tops'ls as she comes about and set the main and mizzen when all's secure. And well done to the boat crews." Ben Garrison smiled as the deck officer relayed his orders and the boatswain's deafening bellow drew the boats in. All was well; at least, all under his control. He cast a glance to his son-in-law and cocked an eyebrow. "Well?"

"He's coming, Ben. Don't worry."

The boats thumped aboard, and the great mainsail dropped from the yard and cracked full in the freshening breeze. Despite his worry, the sight of it made his heart rise in his chest. Ben Garrison smiled and snapped off orders for the helmsman and the deck officer. *Peggy's Pride* came around smartly and started to make way.

"There," Orin said with a smile, nodding to the silvery streak of a seasprite swooping through the rigging. Several sailors cried out with joy, for though a seasprite was an irksome presence, they were considered good luck. "We'd best be well away before he smokes out our plot, Ben."

"Aye. Set what canvas she'll bear, Mr. Brael. We've got weather coming in by my son's reckoning, and I want to beat it to deep water."

"Aye, Captain!" The deck officer smiled in understanding. He shouted orders to set additional sails, and by the time his breath was out, *Peggy's Pride* was making good headway toward the harbor mouth.

All the while, Orin looked to the skies. The officers and crew would think him concerned about the weather, but his attention focused only upon the little streak of silvery wings darting around the sailors in the rigging, tugging at shirts and ponytails.

≈

"Cynthia! What in the name of the Gods of Light and Darkness are you doing!" Julia strode off the porch and across the lawn to glower down at her granddaughter. "You've ruined your best dolls, and you're soaked!"

"I'm playing sharks and mermaids!" she said, holding up the two sopping wet dolls, one wrapped from the waist down in green ribbon, the other bound head to foot in strips of silvery cloth with the tiny triangle fin strapped to its back. "You wanna play, Grammy?"

"No, I do *not* want to play! Now come with me this instant and we'll get you some clean clothes." Julia's iron grip encircled Cynthia's arm and the child fairly levitated from the puddle that had served as her south-sea lagoon.

The girl yelped at the treatment, but her protests that she wasn't finished, and that the sharks were just about to get the mermaids (which was how most of her games of sharks and mermaids ended) went unheeded. Her feet barely touched the ground all the way to the sunroom, where Julia stripped off the girl's dress and applied towels to her muddy underclothes. The maids were called, and a pot of piping hot water appeared, as well as a cake of soap.

"But Grammy, I just took a bath yesterday!" Her determined little face began sprouting tears. First Mouse had flown away, now her grandmother was forcing her to bathe! "This ain't fair!"

"*Isn't* fair, Cynthia. And you should have thought about fair before you raided the sewing cabinet, ripped out the hem of your mother's dress, ruined your dolls and got yourself soaking wet! Now hold still!"

"No! Momma!"

"Your mother has gone to town, Cynthia, so stop your complaining." She wiped at the water on the girl's face, but more gushed from her eyes. "Now, this really isn't worth crying about. What's the matter?"

"Mouse flew away!" she shrieked, struggling free of the maids' grasping hands. "We were going to play sharks and mermaids, and he flew away!"

"Well, thank the Gods for that, anyway! Best if the little insect never came back!"

"Stop it! Stop it!" Cynthia screamed, slapping at the hands of the maids. "Lemme go! I'll go find Mouse myself!"

The girl dashed out of the circle of women, nimble as a cat, and through the door to the yard, all the while screaming in her shrill little voice, "Mouse! Mouse! Where are you, Mouse?"

The maids ran after her to the hawking cries of, "Bring her back this instant!" and "Cynthia Marie Flaxal, you come here!" which had no effect at all on the girl. It was about time someone laid down some discipline in this household.

Julia snatched up a broom one of the maids had dropped and strode after them, a jabbering juggernaut in a twenty-one button corset.

≈

"Uh-oh," Orin mumbled, just as the *Peggy's Pride* rounded the breakwater and the first swells of the trade winds took her on the port quarter. "What's gotten into the little bugger now?"

"What? What's wrong?" Ben stood beside him, his eyes searching the rigging for the elusive little seasprite.

"There's something wrong with Mouse. I don't know, but he's stopped flying about. He's sitting on the main-tops'l yard just looking around. It's almost like he hears something."

The two men looked at one another, and sudden worry passed between them. Both looked over the taffrail toward the estate that dominated the hill to the east of Southaven. There, barely discernible in the distance, several figures trundled down the expansive lawn toward the low wall that girded the estate. One, a small one in white, dodged and evaded the others, then broke for the wall.

"Oh no!" Orin said, looking back up at the rigging. Mouse stood rapt, his eyes locked onto the distant spectacle. "He's onto something. I think that's Cyn up there, and it looks like the maids are chasing her around the yard. Knowing my Cynny, she's screaming her lungs out. If he hears her..."

"I think you're right, Orin. Look." Ben pointed. Mouse had snatched a rigging knife from a sailor's belt. It wasn't much bigger than a butter knife, but it was a lot sharper. The faerie flew twice around the quarterdeck and set out for the distant cliffs and the Garrison estate.

"Damn!" Orin swore, cracking his fist down on the taffrail. He watched every hope of keeping Mouse out of his mother-in-law's way vanish into the distance.

≈

"Cynthia, you come down from there this instant!" Julia screamed, brandishing the broom and taking another step closer.

"NO!" Cynthia shrieked, stomping her feet on the top of the three-foot wall that surrounded the estate. "I won't!"

The girl was in no real danger from a fall; if she fell forward, the maids would catch her, and if she fell backward, she would land in foot-deep scrub grass as soft as any featherbed. But that didn't dissuade her from stomping and kicking and screaming every time one of the ladies tried to grab her. Her face shone red as a beet and her hair rivaled any dandelion in the realm, but her voice was her real weapon and it rose to screeching heights that threatened deafness to anyone who dared approach.

Julia had just about had enough.

"This is the result of a house with too little discipline," she explained more to herself than the three puffing maids. She withdrew a small pen-knife from a pocket and handed it to the nearest of her charges. "Lori, cut me a switch. It's just about time someone laid down the law in this household."

"Yes'm," the maid said, taking the tiny knife with wide eyes, clearly in shock that the mistress intended to meter out punishment without Lady Peggy present. But she answered to Mistress Garrison, and turned to cut a switch.

She didn't make three steps before Mouse flew in to the rescue. His little rigging knife flashed, and in a blink he'd cut the maid's apron strings and pulled the garment up and over her head.

"Mouse!" Cynthia squealed in sudden delight. "You came back!"

The little sprite landed on the befuddled maid's head, danced a little jig, sketched a bow and darted off just as Julia's broom came crashing down. The maid screamed at the blow, though she was not really hurt.

Now Mouse had his true enemy in his sights, and he darted in for the kill.

In a flash of gossamer-crystal wings and steel, two of Julia's pearl buttons were snipped off. The broom swung, but he flew like a flash of greased quicksilver, streaking in for another slash and two more buttons. A peal of high-pitched laughter followed him as he circled her head and hacked a third of the bristles from her broom in one lightning pass.

"Hold still, you little insect!" she raged, swinging the broom in a broad arc, to no avail.

Mouse snipped three more buttons before she could even swing back again. He laughed and lunged, carved a quick "M" into the broom's handle and darted away before she could even gasp.

"Yay, Mouse!" little Cynthia cheered, dancing out of reach of the maids again and laughing. The spoiled little monster was enjoying this even more than her inane little games.

Julia's corset risked rupture with every breath she drew and every button that flew, but now she knew she could not hope to hit the little sprite. She wasn't fast enough. But she was smarter than any sprite, or she would sell her good name and all her worldly possessions to any pauper for a penny!

She swung again, gasping as she missed, and the sprite darted in. Another pair of buttons fell free, and the strain proved too much for the bedraggled bodice. The remaining buttons popped free in a ripping volley not unlike a full broadside of catapults fired from a man-o-war. Julia fell to her hands and knees, gasping and crying out. Her maids were at her side instantly as the sprite cheered in its screeching little voice and flew to Cynthia.

"Wait," she told her maids, glaring them to silence as she gathered her legs under her skirts. "Just wait."

The sprite circled Cynthia once, dropped the knife and joined hands with the little girl for a spinning cheer.

"Now!" The maids pulled her up, broom in her hands and her corset flapping in the breeze. As the child and faerie spun in a laughing, dancing circle of merriment, Julia timed her swing perfectly.

Broom met sprite with a sound like a crystal goblet striking stone.

Mouse flew in a flat trajectory, trailing glittering bits of fractured wing fragments. The low stone wall stopped his flight short and he fell, leaving more bits of gossamer-crystal stuck to the stucco.

"NO!" Cynthia screeched, her voice rivaling that of any sprite. "You killed him!" She started to dash to the fallen sprite, but the two maids grabbed her arms, holding her fast between them. "I hate you! I hate you!"

"Now, Cynthia..." Julia's diatribe on the necessity of her attack fell short, however, as thunder boomed from far out to sea. No storm darkened the horizon and no lightning flashed, but the thunder continued to rumble.

"Odea!" one of the maids murmured, aghast.

"Nonsense!" Julia hefted her broom and turned back to the fallen sprite, but Mouse had managed to stand and now fluttered unsteadily into the air. He didn't fly straight, and he didn't fly fast, but he flew. He flew over the wall and vanished into the shrubbery. "Now, where did that little insect go?"

Thunder ripped again, this time closer, and still the sky shone clear.

"Perhaps we'd best move inside until this strange weather passes," Julia suggested.

The maids needed no encouragement. They took little Cynthia back to the house as peal after peal of thunder sounded from a clear sky and a teary eyed sprite sat in a shrub and nursed his broken wings. Mouse was crying, but he wasn't crying for himself, or even for his shattered wings; he was crying for poor Cynthia.

Orin Flaxal was right; there was a storm on the way.

CHAPTER ONE
Moonlight Memories

CYNTHIA'S HANDS CLENCHED THE low stone wall as the moonlight on the sea gripped her heart like a siren song. The silvery orb that was her namesake glowed three quarters full. It had invaded her study and cast its spell on her as effectively as any wizard's love potion, calling her to the sea.

The sea...

It was in her blood; as her mother's sandy hair and her father's sea-blue eyes had been passed down, so had their love of the sea. The sea had taken much from her in the years since she played sharks and mermaids in the mud puddles of her back yard, but it had never relaxed its hold upon her soul.

She closed her eyes and could almost feel the long, gentle swells lifting her, could almost taste the salt spray. Oh, to have the winds push her effortlessly out to sea, to watch the land sink and finally fade away until nothing surrounded her but the waves. She gripped the stone harder as the fantasy filled her, but the sweet dream shattered with a wavering call on the wind.

"Cynthia. Cyn-thia!"

She cringed at her grandmother's call. She should not have been out this late, and the month-end accounts were past due, but the columns of numbers, balances, debits and credits had no power against call of the sea. She looked over her shoulder at the house and smiled thinly, knowing she was safe out here. Grammy never left the house after dusk.

The Garrison home was more of an estate than a simple house. Coconut palms and frangipani lined the wide drive, and bougainvillea colored the trellises on either side of the pillared foyer. The great stone turret commanded a view for leagues, and had been Cynthia's favorite place to look out over the sea until her grandmother had discovered it, forcing her out onto the grounds.

"The old place isn't what it used to be, Grandpa," she said to nobody, unless the spirit of the old sea dog still haunted the home he'd built. Memories of those days rose unbidden: climbing the ancient banyan tree, jumping from the low branches into her grandfather's gnarled hands. Yes, it had been a home then. Cynthia had been the beginning of the third generation of seafarers to dwell here, with the hopes of many more on the watery horizon. Now all those hopes were as dead as the stone under her hands.

"Odea's toll," she muttered, remembering the tales the maids told her as a child, the curse that had been levied upon the Garrison family. She honestly didn't believe in curses, but the fact remained that the sea had taken away her parents and her grandfather. And still, she loved it beyond all else.

"You're a harsh mistress, Odea."

Despite the losses, Cynthia grew up well enough. She had never lacked pretty dresses, always slept in a warm bed and received a proper education from private tutors. Julia Garrison spared no expense to ensure that she was raised in a wholesome and healthy environment, and for a few years after the loss of her parents, that structured existence had been comforting.

But the song of the sea would not be ignored, and as the girl became a young woman she began to hear that song more clearly. The moon called her up to the tower at night to watch its beams dance on the waves, and the sun woke her at dawn when the ships slipped out of Southaven on the ebbing tide. Then one day she asked her grandmother if she could go down to the docks to see the ships come and go.

"The docks? Why ever would you want to see that dirty, smelly place, Cynthia? That is no environment for a young lady! Sailors are nothing but a lot of irresponsible drunkards! You're best off if you concentrate on your studies."

"Cyn-thia..."

Resentment swelled at the memory and her grandmother's relentless call. She whirled away from it, pressing her palms to her ears, banishing the voice that had kept her prisoner in her own childhood ignorance. With no influence but her grandmother, Cynthia had tried to live her life as she was told, learning to read and write and dress properly as well as mastering the ciphers and ledgers and account books, all boring as stale bread.

The moon emerged from a concealing cloud, casting its light onto the harbor below and the cluster of stately craft swaying at anchor. The sight banished her anger. She dropped her hands and cocked an ear, smiling as she thought she heard distant music of revelers in the local pubs.

"Not tonight," she admonished herself, as the desire to steal down to the docks tugged at her. She'd done it a thousand times since her discovery that she could disobey with little repercussion. Her first rebellion had been ridiculously trivial, refusing to attend her lessons, but her grandmother had simply talked softly to her, pleading with her never to do it again, a far cry from the harsh disciplinarian of Cynthia's childhood. The loss of her daughter had changed Julia Garrison; she viewed the world as a threat, and wanted only to protect her single remaining relative. Cynthia, on the other hand, viewed the world as a forbidden adventure.

Southaven quickly became her childhood playground.

She would steal down to the docks, the shipyards, the wharves and even the taverns that lined the waterfront, sneaking around and learning every foul word, ill manner and habit of every sailor she could meet. By fifteen she was a holy terror, and could spit, swear and drink as well as any sailor on the wharf. She showed up at home at dreadful hours, sometimes drunk, and never endured anything more than a stern lecture from her grandmother. Cynthia thought it was all a wonderful game, and would simply sneak out again at the next opportunity.

The full arrival of womanhood tempered her impetuous nature, but had not quenched her love of the sea, nor her desire to steal away aboard one of the stately craft that slid effortlessly out into the limitless blue of Odea's domain. Now, at twenty-two years of age, she watched those ships and sighed, for that was the one adventure she had never managed to achieve: going to sea. That was where the sailors' indulgence of her antics had ended. They put up with her tomfoolery on land, but they had never allowed her aboard their vessels, despite—or perhaps because of—who she was. At times like this, with the moonlight on the water glittering in her eyes, that unrealized dream broke her heart.

A patch of blackness moved around the headland to the west, and Cynthia's thoughts shifted from her spiraling self-pity. One hand wiped at her tears while the other fumbled in the pocket of her dress for the bronze spyglass that had been her mother's. Her gaze never left the ship as she extended the instrument and brought it up to her eye. She smiled at the thought of the daring captain bringing his ship in under moonlight, a dangerous practice even in tonight's calm breezes. She twisted the scope and the distant vessel came into focus.

Her breath caught in her throat at the sight of the galleon's mangled rig. The foremast was a stark pole, the yards gone and the forestays and bowsprit missing save for an improvised spar lashed to the foredeck. The mainmast sported only about half the canvas it normally would, probably in an effort to balance the sails. She could see men dumping buckets over the side at regular intervals. The ship had obviously fallen prey to the greatest threat in the Southern Ocean.

"Pirates!" she said between clenched teeth, climbing atop the low wall for a better view. "The bastards!"

Memories of a thousand stories of the pirates of the Shattered Isles surged through her mind. Those stories had been her only education about what had really happened that day her parents had fallen in a welter of blood and seawater before her eyes, for she had no clear recollection of it. Only in her nightmares did those images surface. Even to this day, visions of blood-red sails, and a deep-throated laugh plagued her sleep. Her hands clenched the telescope until the view shook in her eye.

"Cyn-thia!" came her grandmother's urgent call, snapping her attention.

She looked back at the house and judged this far too important for her grandmother to spoil. She pocketed the telescope and hopped down from the wall, drawing up her skirts and striking out at a jog for the gate. She could make the docks well before the ship if she ran part of the way, and the last thing she wanted was to miss a single word of what the sailors had to say about the pirates.

CHAPTER TWO
Tall Tales

"KATHLAN!" CYNTHIA YELLED, ELBOWING her way to the head of the quay. "Kath! Over here!"

The call jerked the sailor's gaze up like a marionette. He raised a hand and let it drop to his side. Cynthia saw the bandage on his forearm and the bloodstain on his shirt, and felt guilty for what she was about to do to the poor, tired sailor.

"Heya, Cyn, you seen us come 'round the point, huh?" He looked as if he hadn't slept in days. If the ship leaked badly, the off watches would bail to keep her from foundering. They clasped hands briefly and lightly as his exhaustion warranted.

"Looks like one of the slimy bastards got a piece of ya," she said with a wry grin, touching the bloody bandage of his forearm. "You must be gettin' old and slow since they made you third mate."

"Second mate now, Cyn," he said grimly, turning around to watch as three canvas-shrouded bundles were carried down the gangplank. "Forsee took a burnin' tops'l yard alongside her skull tryin' to get aloft to cut the flamin' canvas free."

"Those filthy bastards," she hissed. She wanted his first-hand account before a tavern full of drunken sailors amplified the facts threefold, but did not want to push him too hard. "Come on now and we'll get that arm looked at by a physicker and get some hot food into you. Was it that whore-spawn Bloodwind that did this?"

"Naw, and I couldn't be happier that it weren't!" Kathlan made a quick sign of devotion to Odea and nodded back to the ship. "If the scourge o' the Shattered Isles had been at the helm of that corsair, the *Latharnia* wouldn't be still floatin', to be sure. It's plain luck we got away, and if that bastard had'a known his arse from his rudder post, he'd a had us sure and simple."

"Well, come along then and tell me how you got away. I told Brulo I'd bring you by." She jingled her purse as much to emphasize the fact that she was offering to pay as to add credence to her claim: "I had a good night playing Five Card Mango."

"Well, I really should stay close to the *Latharnia*, in case the captain wants me..."

"Oh, you can't fill a sail with that, Kath!" Cynthia laughed and clapped a hand on the man's shoulder, ushering him through the crowd toward her favorite inn. "Besides, Brulo'll send his lad to tell your captain where you are if you like. I told him to set up a private room for us so the crowd won't bother you. You can have a bath and a pot of ale while I get dinner. I'll even pay an extra crown for that fair lass Marcia to help you scrub!"

"Well, now *that's* enough to make a man want to bathe on a right regular basis!" he laughed, quickening his suddenly less-tired steps toward the Galloping Starfish Inn.

Cynthia hurried to keep up, and began to wonder if Kathlan's injury and exhaustion were as severe as they appeared, and if *she* were not the one really being taken for a sap. If she wasn't careful, she was going to get a reputation as a meal ticket.

≈

The crippled galleon lay lashed to the massive quay like a wounded whale beached to keep from drowning. Most of the town already knew what had befallen the ship; the old hermit who operated the lighthouse had seen it come around the point at roughly the same time as Cynthia, and all efforts had been made to bring the injured vessel into a berth with no further damage.

Observers and concerned relatives crowded the wide stone quay. Some pointed and some cried and others merely shook their heads and thanked the sea goddess Odea that all hands had not been lost, but none noticed the patch of inky water fifty yards from the dock that swirled and rose into the shape of a broad serpentine head.

Red coals burned in its watery eye sockets, disturbed only by the flicking of reptilian eyelids. Not a creature at all, but magic and seawater woven into the semblance of a serpent, it lurked like a prowling crocodile and scanned the crowded waterfront. The things it saw were viewed many leagues away by the sorcerous force that had brought it into being.

The watery spy's glowing eyes watched the men leaving the ship, and then scanned the people crowded upon the quay. The great head turned, still barely above the water's surface, gauging the faces, hearing the voices and tasting the anger that filled the thick sea air, the words too distant and soft to discern.

The coal eyes turned once more, scanning the rest of the harbor, assessing the other ships as prey, ensuring its own continuing anonymity, or merely taking in the view. One last look swept over the damaged ship, then the fire within the watery thing's eyes faded and its shape melted away into the sea from which it had been wrought.

≈

"Nay, it weren't as bad as all that," Kathlan said, reaching for another roll and a slice of roast lamb. He split the roll, stuffed the meat inside and took a bite, following it with a swig of Brulo's best ale. "Some plankin' on the bulwarks, a few seams recaulked and maybe a single cracked rib replaced and she's right as rain. That and the riggin', o'course."

"She looked a lot worse when she came around the point. It must have been one of Bloodwind's ships; none of the freebooters use that flamin' tar." She tried once again to shift the conversation to her own liking. Bloodwind—the devil who had killed her parents—had become her obsession, and she scrabbled for any tidbit she could glean as to his whereabouts, how many ships he commanded, or even if he still lived. She sipped her ale carefully, smiling at Brulo when he took the empty pitcher and replaced it with a full one. The pot-bellied innkeeper of the Galloping Starfish didn't usually do his own serving, but he had known her father and she'd been his best customer for years.

"Oh, aye, I suppose it was one of his flunkies." Kathlan tapped his freshly bandaged forearm with his eating knife and said, "I'd be sportin' a lot worse'n this li'l scratch if someone with some salt had been at the helm of that corsair. Capt'n Jellis knows them waters, mind ye, and that's what saved our hides, but anyone what's passed through the Shattered Isles as many times as me knows that bar ain't passable."

"The one between Chum Cay and Brighton's Reef? I thought you could get through that cut at mean low water." She glared at him as she sampled the meat, chewing thoughtfully and hoping he wasn't lying to her just to liven up the story. "All you need to do is cut close to the reef and tack back out. Hell, you can see the sandbar!"

"Aye, you can when you're not starin' right into the risin' sun, lass." He drained his cup and poured himself another. He knew as well as any that she had never actually seen the Shattered Isles. All of her knowledge had been gleaned from hearsay and her grandfather's old charts, both of which were less accurate than first-hand knowledge.

"I told you they jumped us at first light, didn't I? The capt'n had 'im to lee-ward after we struck rails with 'em, which put us in a bad spot since our fors'l was in flames and them corsairs can beat two points sharper than any galleon on the sea. We hit hard enough to stop him dead in the water, though, and the captain made it east of the sandbar before they got their heads out o' their arses. Then he just let her ride north so it were between us and them." The man speared a roasted potato dripping with meat juices and took a bite before placing the remainder on his plate. "That corsair captain cut a line straight for us. I guess he thought we was still south of the bar."

"So he ploughed right into the shallows?" Cynthia's jaw dropped. "That's the stupidest thing I've ever heard! Did they ground her hard?"

"Damn near broke her back, is how hard!" Kathlan slammed his hand into the edge of the heavy table for a demonstration, rattling the dishes in emphasis. "Hit like an ogre humpin' a whale, I tell ya! Heard timbers crack from a quarter mile off. Mayhaps a stay give way, too, though she didn't lose any of her rig. She was still hard on the bottom when we was over the horizon."

"Lucky they didn't try to board you when they were alongside," Cynthia offered, sipping her ale again.

"How in all the Nine Hells did ya think I got this?" the sailor protested, cracking his forearm with the flat of his knife again, proving that it was less tender than he had let on. "Why, them buggers was like rats comin' over the side. I was tryin' to cut their grapple lines when I got this. The feller's aim was wide though, so I just took one prong of the hook I'd just freed and fed it to him," he paused and raised his tankard before saying, "through his eye."

"Not a better place for it, I don't think," Cynthia agreed, raising her own cup to clank with his. They both drank to the pirate's demise and she continued with, "And I think the Lady of the Sea was smilin' on you that morning to put such a dunce at their helm."

"Aye, that Odea had a hand in the feller's choosin', I have no doubt," he agreed, returning to his meal in earnest.

"Mmm, and I can imagine Captain Bloodwind will have a few particularly terse words with the fellow for grounding one if his ships so hard."

"Aye, that cod-brained captain may decide to just leave his ship grounded and call her an island instead of goin' back to face Bloodwind." He speared a slab of lamb and wrestled off a corner before saying, "Not that I'd mind if the feller was in a shark's belly, as sure as this poor li'l sheep is in mine!"

They both laughed and drank and laughed some more, and the evening wore on with Cynthia hanging on every word that passed the sailor's lips.

≈

The plink and patter of water wore on Bloodwind's nerves like a rasp on a slate shingle. He suppressed a shiver despite the torrid air; the temperature had nothing to do with his chill. His island lair was volcanically active, which had earned it the name of Plume Isle and influenced his decision to make it his home port. Its harbor—a sunken caldera—and the tar pits on the west flat were two of the three things he needed. The last was secrecy, and the deal he'd made with this cavern's denizen had ensured that for as long as he gave her what she wanted.

"What do you see, Hydra?" he asked, squinting through the haze at the flat stone bench and the shrouded figure across the chamber. "Have you found it?"

One thin finger rose from a fist like a tangle of walnut husks. It twitched once then retracted; not an answer, but enough to quell Bloodwind's impatience.

His hands wrung a short braided leather cord that rarely left his grasp. He wound it around his hand until it came taut, tugging a flame-haired girl at its end toward him. A collar of purest gold hung around her supple neck, a miniscule treasure against her flawless features. He examined her in the ruddy light, willing her smooth skin to distract him from this loathsome place and the hideous creature that dwelled here.

The slave girl stepped closer without resistance. She didn't flinch when he ran the back of his knuckles down her cheek, neck and finally her slim shoulder, brushing away the thin dew of sweat. Perhaps she gave a faint shiver, but she no longer tried to resist his touch. Yes, years of his attentions had taught her very well. Only her eyes showed that she still had a will of her own, and even that was slowly, inexorably bending under his care. He reached for her chin to pull her face around, then stopped as a wheezing rasp from across the chamber snapped his desire like a twig.

"I see..." The voice stung like black ice crystallizing in his ears. "I see..."

"You see what, Hydra?" he demanded, stepping forward against his revulsion. "Where is that blasted galleon?"

"Safe, my captain," the sorceress finally answered. The crimson glow silhouetting her form faded to the torchlight that illuminated the rest of the cavern, and when she turned and stepped forward, Bloodwind could only thank the Dark Gods for the barrier of darkness that kept her features hidden. "The *Latharnia* is docked in Southaven; its crew and cargo are both, for the most part, intact."

"Blast that incompetent Nolak!" he seethed, jerking the tether savagely and eliciting a yelp of shock from his slave.

"If you wish, my captain," Hydra said, her voice the rasp of an aged crone, "but I must rest and... refresh myself."

The hint of laughter in that comment turned Bloodwind's stomach. "It was not a request, Hydra, as you well know. The *Latharina*—is she crippled badly, or will she sail again?"

"I saw only light damage. Some minor leaking, a burned foremast." A decrepit claw covered in blotched skin twitched in dismissal. "She will sail again in a fortnight."

"Well, that's at least some consolation. If she sails again, she'll eventually pass through the Shattered Isles, and she'll pay the toll for damaging the *Blackheart*." He turned away from the tottering figure, tugging absently on the leash in his hand. "As will that useless whelp Nolak."

"What of *my* payment, Captain?" Hydra hissed, lurching forward and gripping the slim girl's arm in a vice of leather-covered bones. Black nails clawed at the milky flesh, drawing a gasp of horror from the slave's supple lips. "Forces have I wielded for you this day. Energies have I expended. Tides moved to raise the *Blackheart* from the shoal that would have kept her prisoner for days! Every harbor throughout the Southern Ocean did I delve at the cost of my own blood!"

"Not this one, Hydra!" Bloodwind snapped, jerking the line taut as if to play tug-of-war with his prize. The girl wrenched her arm free more as an act of revulsion than an attempt to join her captor, but the black nails left creases in their wake. Thin trails of blood welled from the scratches, and the pirate captain snatched a kerchief from his ornate doublet and pressed it to the injury.

"If you have marred her flesh permanently I'll hold back your payment until you rot into a pile of bones!" He peeked under the cloth at the tiny rents and glared at the sorceress.

"Give me my payment, Captain, or the apple of your eye will bear far worse blemishes than a few thin scratches!" She turned and slashed at a thick column of living stone, her nails leaving trails of molten rock. "Our continued coexistence is based on one simple premise, Captain: you feed my hunger in return for the use of my powers. Do you wish to dissolve our partnership at this time?" He could feel the festering grin within the darkness of her hood.

He glared at her openly, knowing he needed her just as much as she depended on him. If he thought for a moment he could continue his piracy with half the efficiency without her, he would kill her in her sleep. Unfortunately, two decades of raiding among the Shattered Isles had made the merchant captains wary. Yes, he still needed her, damn it to the pits of all Nine Hells.

"Stay here, Hydra. I will get your payment." At her nod, he tugged his treasure up the slimy stair to the portal of her deep cavern.

He threw the bolt, said a few words to the men standing on the other side, and exchanged the tether in his hand for a wrought-iron chain. He pulled savagely and returned to the depths, heedless of the damage his brisk pace did to Hydra's payment. When he reached the last step, he handed the chain over to her pale, skeletal claw. The gagged young man at its end was bruised and bleeding from several bad falls, but it didn't matter; his fate had been sealed the moment he'd been taken prisoner. Bloodwind had dozens like this one. Too old to be of any use, they were all kept alive at minimal expense for a single purpose: to keep Hydra sated.

"Thank you, my captain," she hissed, a faint flicker of torchlight daring to glint off the horror dwelling within that deep, black hood. "This will do nicely!"

"Find me another galleon to raid and I'll give you two more just like him," he said, turning away and ignoring the boy's frantic struggles. "But you'll only get the second one *after* we bring home a hold full of plunder! Understood?" He glanced back as he climbed the stairs, and instantly regretted it.

"Oh, I understand, Captain Bloodwind," she said, her voice rising over the muffled screams of her prey. "I understand you all too well."

The thick oaken door sealed out the noises as his guard handed over his treasure's leash, which calmed his nerves somewhat. He started up the next flight of stairs, banishing the image of the last few moments as he flung orders to his men. "Bring *Captain* Nolak to me when he arrives. I wish to discuss his future."

≈

When Kathlan's head lolled to the point where he dipped his nose in the lamb gravy, Cynthia decided that most of the pertinent details were safely in her head. She paid Brulo as the serving girl cleared the dishes, and took one more sip of ale. As she stood to leave, an older but quick-moving man entered the room. He grinned at her, his merry blue eyes squinting from beneath bushy white eyebrows.

"How was everything, Miss Cynthia?" he asked, trundling forward like a gleeful old elf, wringing his flour-sprinkled hands on his apron and patting the handles of the knives in the tooled sheaths at his hip.

"Excellent as always, Rowland," she assured the old cook, extending a hand. His grip felt like a bag full of sticks, but his hands were still strong and nimble after wielding his knives in kitchens and galleys throughout the Southern Ocean for almost thrice her lifetime. "I just wish I could lure you up the hill. Marta's a fair cook, but I hate to have to come all the way down here for a really good meal!"

"Oh, you lie like a rug, girl!" he said with smile. "Besides, you couldn't afford me. I'm chargin' Brulo twice what your old gran-dad used to pay me for sea wages!"

"Aye, and he'd be worth it," Brulo said, frowning in feigned disapproval, "if he'd stay in the kitchen and not pester the customers."

"Just payin' my respects to the gran-daughter of my former employer, *Master* Brulo. No harm in that. The kitchen won't go up in flames if I leave it for a minute now and then."

"Ha! There ain't a sailin' man in Southaven that ain't worked for Cynthia's family at one time or 'nother, you old bean boiler!" Kathlan roused from his slumber long enough to join the conversation. "If they all paid their respects every time she passed, she'd never be able to walk from West Street to the yards in a single day!"

"My point exactly!" Brulo agreed.

"Well, then consider it payin' my respects to a *potential* employer then." Rowland glared at Brulo sideways, sparing a wink at Cynthia. "I very well might follow her up the hill someday, you know. Company's better up there, and someday Cyn here's gonna be head of that family, and there'll be more ships afloat under her flag than her gran-dad ever dreamed of!"

"Not until someone takes care of that bastard Bloodwind," she said, the muscles of her jaw clenching like ropes. "He's bleedin' the whole south coast dry, and nobody even knows where he lairs."

"Aye, some say he's retired and just livin' off the cream o' what his men take in," Rowland said, his eyes squinting in a far-off glare of hatred. "They say he's got twenty ships workin' the Shattered Isles now, and a seamage of his own to hide 'em in the fog and shift the winds in their favor."

"It ain't natural, that's fer sure," Kathlan put in, slurping ale and wiping his mouth on his bandage.

"Aye, I remember the days when yer family's ships sailed without harassment through the islands, Cyn. Them days are gone, I guess."

"If I had my way, Rowland, those days would be back in a heartbeat." She clapped his shoulder. "I'd sell off every part and parcel my grandmother ever put a copper into and build a fleet of ships to rival any on the ocean! And I'd have you as my own personal chef aboard the flagship, as sure as seagulls squawk!"

"Well, now that's somethin' I'd like to see, Miss Cynthia," Brulo said with a smile and a firm clasp of his cook's shoulder, "but for right now, I'd settle for not lettin' my customers starve to death while they wait for their dinners, so I'll have to be biddin' you a good night."

They all laughed at the irrepressible innkeeper and said their goodnights. Cool night air and the scents of the harbor greeted Cynthia as she left the inn, clearing her head with one deep breath. Southaven was quiet at this time of the night, despite her grandmother's opinion that all sailors were a bunch of drunken rowdies. Only when a ship came in after a long voyage did a crew truly tie one on. No, Southaven was just a sleepy little port with a sleepy little populace. There were no dangers lurking in the dark alleys, and no slavers waiting to kidnap and sell a girl into a life of servitude or worse.

At least, that was what Cynthia had always thought.

This evening, however, a shrouded figure skulked through the alley behind the Galloping Starfish, its attention directed more than casually toward Cynthia. The shape moved to the razor edge of light created by the nearby streetlamp and watched her until she was out of sight. It did not follow, but turned its attention back toward the inn.

The figure jerked suddenly and a few tiny pebbles arced through the night air to rattle on a window of the inn's second floor. Shadows moved across the window, then the lamplight dimmed and the stout oaken frame creaked open. A shaded face peered out into the night, as a complex four-note whistle sounded from the darkness below. The figure in the window held out a slim tube and dropped it without hesitation. The window closed even before the tube popped into the hand of the shadow below. In a wink the figure vanished, and Southaven reverted to the sleepy little town that Cynthia had always believed it to be.

CHAPTER THREE

Blood and Water

THE WHITE PORCELAIN DISHES, silver utensils, serving pieces and vase with four
fresh day lilies greeted Cynthia with far more warmth than the stately
woman seated at the other end of the breakfast table. Julia Garrison sat
ramrod straight, the tiny, round mother-of-pearl buttons of her dress lined
up like double rows of precisely marching soldiers, her lapels and wrist-
length sleeves freshly pressed and gleaming white. Cynthia wondered how
the woman breathed with her corset laced so tightly.

Cynthia mumbled a good morning, but received no answer. Sighing softly, she straightened her napkin on her lap and started a mental count, wondering how long it would take her grandmother to start her usual tirade.

Steam rose from her cup as Marta poured blackbrew and lightened it
with cream—too much, as usual. Cynthia thanked her, downed half the cup
with a suppressed grimace and snatched the pot to fill it until the color was
just right. She took a hot roll from the linen-covered basket and buttered it
while Marta put bowls of fresh melon and other assorted fruit before them.
She took a bite of the roll—good, but not as good as Rowland's biscuits—
and chased it with a sip of blackbrew. She skewered a slice of mango and
had it halfway to her mouth when the lecture started.

"I really would like to know why you persist in this aberrant behavior,
Cynthia."

Nineteen... twenty, she counted silently. *She really must be mad this time.
She usually gets to thirty.* She didn't answer aloud, knowing too well that
she wouldn't be allowed a word for at least another slow count of fifty. She
just met her grandmother's steely glare and continued eating, savoring each
bite as the diatribe continued.

"I simply don't understand the lure of a tarnished reputation. I mean,
what else do you think you'll get from carousing around with drunken sailors and the trollops they socialize with?"

Cynthia raised an eyebrow at that, wondering what the barmaids and
serving girls she knew would do if she told them that her grandmother re-
ferred to them as trollops. No, that would be a bad idea. Likely they'd charge
up the hill in battalion strength and rip the estate apart stone by stone.

"Those types will only hurt you, Cynthia. I know the goings on down
there in those seedy taverns and fleshpots! You're lucky you haven't ended up pregnant, diseased or sold into slavery by that rabble. The way you

carry on, I swear. And with the month-end balances already overdue. Why, our creditors will be beating down the door of this house one day soon, and the only answer I'll have for them is 'Oh, I'm sorry. Lady Cynthia was responsible for those balances, and she felt it was more important to go out and get *drunk* last night than finish them.'"

Well, that much was true, at least, but her goal for the evening had not been to get drunk. Unfortunately, her grandmother would never even try to fathom her true goals.

"One day you'll wake up poor and alone and with nothing but a soiled reputation and a hangover to keep you warm, Cynthia. You mark my words!" The woman finally started to wind down, raising a shaking teacup for a careful sip before continuing. "I just thank the Gods that your grand-father isn't alive to see you act like this. Why, if he—"

That was *enough*!

"If Grandpa *was* alive, I'd be first mate on one of his ships by now, Grandmother!" Cynthia snapped, scraping her chair on the tiles and casting her napkin on her half-eaten breakfast. "He was a master of *ships*, not a dabbler in a dozen different losing investments that have never earned us a bent copper! We should sell off all that damned *rubbish* and lay down a half dozen new hulls, not to mention overhauling the few remaining ships you haven't given away yet."

"Cynthia! I will not have that gutter language spoken in this house!" Her grandmother's teacup rattled into its saucer, spilling amber liquid on the white linen tablecloth. "See what carousing with trash has done to you? And building new ships is far too expensive and risky a proposition to—"

"Ships *built* this house, Grandmother!" Cynthia fumed, planting her hands on the table and leaning halfway over it to drive her point home. "Grandpa built what could have been an *empire* by now with nothing but his own skill as a sailor to start with. I don't understand what makes you think shipping cargo is more risky than any other proposition. Ships *made* this family, Grandmother."

"No, Cynthia, ships *destroyed* this family!" the woman screeched, slap-ping her hand on the table with an impact that threatened to topple the flowers. "Ships took my daughter away from me and then my husband, and I will *not* let you be taken from me in the same manner!"

"Pirates took my mother *and* father from us both. Pirates that Grandpa was trying to hunt down when he was lost."

"Your father was as much at fault as anyone in that, Cynthia," the wom-an said, unaware of the daggers she thrust into her granddaughter's soul with every word. "Orin Flaxal was nothing but a power-hungry wizard, and he had no business taking his wife and daughter out on that accursed ocean. I thank the Gods of Light that you didn't inherit that curse from him, and that he died before he could pollute your mind with his poison! All that nonsense about the magic of the sea and suchlike."

As the woman's tirade subsided, she realized the damage her words had caused. Her stony facade melted, a hand rising to cover her mouth, as if to prevent the words she'd already spoken from escaping. But it was too late.

Cynthia stood stunned and staring as ice gripped her heart in a vice like nothing she'd ever felt. All the years her grandmother had held her tongue, all the hours of soft talk, mild scolding and lectures, and now the truth had finally come to light. The truth of why her grandmother was so intent on destroying everything her husband had spent his life building, and why she would never, ever let Cynthia go to sea.

"Oh Cynthia, I—"

Cynthia felt light-headed, and realized that she had been holding her breath. Never in her life had simple words hurt her so. But even as she stared back at her grandmother's stricken features, she knew she couldn't blame her for her misdirected hostility. All the anger and betrayal melted away. Cynthia felt only sad, empty, and even more alone than she had the day her parents died.

"I'll have the balances done by noon," she said carefully, trying not to let her roiling emotions show. "I'll take them down to the creditors myself."

"Cynthia, I'm sorry. I didn't mean to..." The woman's stricken voice trailed off as her granddaughter turned and walked away without another word.

≈

Swirling threads of crimson stained the azure water beside Captain Bloodwind's flagship, *Guillotine*. Long, finned shapes cut through the eddies of blood, predatory denizens of the outer reef summoned for the occasion. The turmoil of the sharks' passage dissipated the blood quickly, but more fell from above in a steady cadence of frenzy-inducing droplets. The tiny brains of the relentless killers registered only that food lurked somewhere in the water, and the longer they searched, the more maddened they became.

The focus of their hunger hung some eight feet above the surface of their world, suspended from the end of the mainsail yard. The man hung before his peers, his eyes level with theirs while blood dripped from cuts in his legs. Pity found no home among the faces of the men and women he'd known, fought with, killed with, sailed with and drank with. They were pirates; all remorse had been wrung out of them. Now it was simply a matter of how quickly the end would come.

"Some might say that this is my fault," Bloodwind bellowed from the afterdeck of his flagship. His voice carried over the heads of the amassed throng, piercing the hiss of the waterfall that fed the sheltered cove. "To that I say, mayhap. I may have put my trust in one who was not ready to bear the burden. But as you all know, the burden was accepted freely and sealed in blood, the very blood which now summons his fate."

He waved a hand at the impatiently circling predators that would soon administer the pirate captain's punishment. They had been brought here by blood and the dark sorceress standing at Bloodwind's side. Instead of the crone he'd left in the caves beneath his citadel, Hydra now appeared as a beautiful young woman, dark hair and smoldering features accentuating a sensuously shaped form. Her sultry guise fooled no one, for her lifeless eyes described her true nature. As she looked at Nolak, her hunger sent chills of revulsion down the man's spine that made the horror of being eaten alive pale by comparison.

"Give him to me, my captain," the creature said, her immaculate hand caressing Bloodwind's shoulder. "His blood would serve me better than those I have summoned for you. Give him to me."

Bloodwind spared the sorceress a disgusted stare, and then turned back to the crowded deck. "Captain Nolak! For the crime of damaging one of my ships without just cause, and without atoning for that damage with plunder taken from your intended prey, I sentence you to death."

A murmur of "Death," swept over the crowded deck, but their commander was not finished and raised a hand to forestall them.

"However, though you failed me, you did not let your failure make you a coward. You brought my ship back to be repaired, knowing it would cost your life." His piercing blue eyes fixed on his erstwhile captain's, and he nodded imperceptibly. "For that, I grant you a quick death, not at the jaws of the wolves of the sea, nor at the hands of my sorceress, Hydra, but at my own."

The sorceress sneered in contempt as he brushed past her and took the great ballista in hand. The device, a crossbow so huge that two strong men had to crank it for loading, stood on a pedestal on the quarterdeck. It had been loaded with a piercing bolt instead of one lashed with tar-soaked rags used to fire the sails of merchant vessels. The iron tip swung around until it lined up with Nolak's hands, then lowered until the doomed man looked straight down the wrist-thick bolt into his commander's eyes. The former captain's jaw tightened, his chin raised, but his eyes remained fixed upon those of the man who controlled the very last moments of his life.

Bloodwind nodded once at the other's stoicism, lowered the weapon until the iron tip pointed directly at the prominent scar on the pirate's chest, and fired. Shock passed over Nolak's features for an instant as the length of wood and iron destroyed his heart. His lifeless figure swung lazily on the end of the rope while the bolt splashed into the water some distance away.

"Cut him loose," Bloodwind ordered.

One of his men leaned out with a cutlass in hand and severed the rope. The water roiled instantly with the frenzied feeding of the sharks. The turmoil lasted until one of the larger beasts took the limbless remainder in one huge gulp. Bloodwind ignored them, turning his attention back to the mass of cutthroats crowding *Guillotine's* deck.

"The *Blackheart* is yours, Broiful," he told the former first mate of the damaged corsair. "Serve me better than Nolak."

"I will, my captain!" the man bellowed, climbing the short stair to the quarterdeck. He pulled open his tunic and knelt before Bloodwind, his face studiously firm as the older man drew a golden-hilted cutlass.

"See that you do." He passed the razor edge in a broad "X" centered over the man's heart, leaving a shallow gash that would scar nicely when the man rubbed ash into the wound. "Or meet a fate worse than your former captain's."

Hydra cackled in timely amusement. Broiful rose and stood beside Bloodwind, eyes front, ignoring the sickening sweet laughter of the woman-shaped thing behind him. Bloodwind raised his bloodstained sword and shouted over the crowd.

"By this blood, I name this man Captain Broiful, commander of the corsair *Blackheart*! Is there anyone here who would challenge his right to that name?" The deck was silent save for the roar of falling water and the distant hammering of the workmen dismembering the broken portions of the new captain's charge. "Good! Initiate him properly!" And with that he clapped the new captain on the back and shoved him off the raised quarterdeck and into the cheering crowd. They broke his fall and had a jug of rum to his lips before his feet touched the deck. Bloodwind laughed at their antics then turned back to his other officers and Hydra.

"Hydra has been told to find us some prey. Go hunting," he told the other captains, relishing the hungry grins that stretched their tanned faces.

His captains followed the sorceress to *Guilotine's* taffrail, eager to hear her counsel but wary of what lurked beneath the feminine facade. They stood out of arm's reach, attentive but mindful that she was not what she seemed. As they spoke, the pirate lord took in the view of all he had built. Blood Bay was framed on three sides by the walls of the caldera. A wide, black sand beach stretched along the northern edge of the cove, crowded by a cobbled-up shantytown. The southern, rockier crescent of the cove supported his shipyard. His abode, little short of a palace, had been carved into the lava rock face of the caldera's west wall.

The pier at which *Guillotine* rested led up the beach to a wide stone stair and the massively pillared foyer of his home. Years of slave labor had hewn the residence out of the slumbering volcano, and the plunder of two decades of piracy had gilded it with appointments more lavish than many a king's castle. With the entire island ringed with razor sharp coral, and the only channel into Blood Bay hidden in a twisting tangle of giant mangroves, his lair lay more secure than any walled city or fortress. He had truly made this his own private kingdom, and in it he wielded more power than any emperor or sovereign. And still, it was not enough.

"You think they revere you, but any one of them would put a knife in you for a fist full of gold."

"There you are wrong, my sweetling," he said with a predatory smile, turning to consider the slave girl's haughty glare.

She stood by the wheel of *Guillotine*, her braided leather leash looped loosely over one spoke like a horse's rein on a light hitch. Fear had taught her to hold her tongue when others stood within hearing; fear of punishments that left no marks on her exquisite frame, but took longer to heal than fifty strokes with a lash would. He didn't punish her for speaking her mind in private, however, for he enjoyed her caustic wit and didn't want to quash that part of her spirit just yet. In time, she would be more than his slave.

"Captain Nolak proved that today. He knew he would face death by coming back here, yet he did so. He could have taken *Blackheart* into any port in the Southern Empires and gotten a sack full of gold for her, but he came back." He waved his hand at the now pristine waters of the cove. "And for that I gave him a much easier death than he deserved."

"His own crew would have killed him if he'd tried to run away."

"Which proves my point once again, dear Camilla." He uncoiled the leather thong from around the wheel's kingpin and pulled it gently until her eyes were only a hand's breadth from his. "There is more loyalty in them than in any emperor's hired army. They know I alone give them life and can give them death if I so choose. They *do* revere me, sweetling, as you should." He caressed the exquisite line of her shoulder with his rough sailor's fingers, but she merely averted her eyes and gazed out onto the still waters of the cove.

"That could have been you luring the sharks to a feast today, Camilla," he threatened, jerking the line attached to the golden collar. Her eyes snapped to his, the smoldering hatred in their depths drawing a smile to his lips. "Or perhaps I could give you to Hydra for a plaything."

"You wouldn't," she said, more confidence in her tone than fear. "Kill me and you lose more than a slave girl."

He jerked the braided leather again, his face contorted briefly in rage. But he did not strike her. Instead, he merely smiled his shark's smile and said, "Right you are again, my sweetling." Then his thick fingers caressed the golden collar at her throat. "But I think it's time you got some more jewelry. Something truly worthy of your... slavery."

Her lip quivered, but she held her tongue as he pulled her along behind him, off the ship, down the pier and to the shack that housed his smithy.

CHAPTER FOUR

Mentor

CYNTHIA STRODE FROM THE creditors' offices feeling like she needed to wash her hands. She had delivered the balances before noon as promised, and endured a lecture on the importance of punctuality that consumed an hour of the afternoon. Consequently, she didn't feel like facing her grandmother, especially after the morning's confrontation, so she let her feet take her toward the one place where she knew she could forget the day's tribulations.

The smell of freshly cut timber, the pounding of hammers, the whisk of planes and the rasp of saws set her nerves tingling. She rounded the last corner and found herself grinning up at the dripping bulk of the *Latharnia*. Cynthia stood and watched in fascination as scrapers removed a thin dusting of barnacles and carpenters began chiseling at the cracked planks.

"A narrow escape from what I hear," a slightly slurred voice said at her shoulder. A cloud of sweet smoke announced the owner's identity more effectively than the voice, and she turned to greet the man with a smile and an outstretched hand.

"You shouldn't sneak up on ladies like that, Koybur," she said, gripping his strong right hand and turning back to the damaged ship.

"When you're marked like me, Cyn, sneakin's the only way you *can* get close to a lady."

That drew a derisive snort from Cynthia, but the statement was accurate enough, even if meant in jest. Koybur was not just marked; he was maimed. The entire left side of his body from his scalp to his toes had been burned so badly it had left him a veritable wreck. One eye was missing and his left hand hung in a twisted hook of scar tissue. He walked stiffly, dragging one foot slightly, but his good eye saw as sharply as any eagle's and there was nothing wrong with his mind. He'd smoked the same sweet-smelling pipe for as long as Cynthia had known him, and could tap it out, refill it and light it all one-handed while carrying on with instructions on how to lash this or tie that. Cynthia felt a kinship to the old sailor, perhaps from their long acquaintance, and perhaps because Koybur had received his injuries the very day Cynthia's parents were killed.

Visions of a flaming sail falling to the deck as a frothy mixture of blood and seawater stained her white stockings flashed into her mind. The high-pitched scream of a girl, the nightmare laughter as two figures fell to the bloody deck...

"Cyn?"

"Oh, sorry. Just woolgathering." She banished the vision with a dismissive shrug. That day had claimed more than her parents' lives; the burning sail had pinned Koybur to the deck like a cockroach under a boot, and damaged him only slightly less.

By the time Koybur was able to walk again, Cynthia's grandfather had been lost in a hurricane, hunting for the pirate Bloodwind, and Julia Garrison needed someone to manage the shipping business, so she offered him continued employment. Koybur had proved himself more valuable than any whole man on the payroll, and had been running the shipping portion of the family business ever since. Her grandmother didn't give him much to work with, but the four vessels that remained were managed as smartly as his meager funds allowed, and Cynthia knew he often used his own salary to replace worn items that might risk a sailor's life.

She respected him a great deal and enjoyed his company besides. It was Koybur who had finally lured her from her rebellious phase, and he'd done it by giving her the one thing she wanted more than anything else in the world. He'd taught her everything he knew about ships, sailing and the sea. Not that she ever got to actually *go* to sea, but his lessons were the next best thing.

"More luck than skill, from what one of the mates told me," she said, referring to his remark about the *Latharnia*. "The corsair captain was an idiot, or maybe just unlucky. He tried to sail his ship over a sandbar without enough water to float a skiff."

"Hmm, the one off Brighton's Reef, or so the capt'n told me." He puffed his pipe and squinted at her through the smoke. Her mouth closed before the obscenity escaped, barely. "Don't try to teach yer mammy how ta soak beans, girl. I was plyin' sailors for information when you was only hip high on a Horoway harlot."

"Humph," she said studiously, ignoring his claim. Koybur had a snappy quip for every occasion, most far more inventive or obscene than this one. She'd stopped trying to memorize them years ago, convinced that he made them up on the fly and never used the same one twice.

"It'd be interesting to compare our stories, since you got yours from the horse's mouth, and I got mine from the other end." That wasn't exactly true, but it sounded good. "Could be Captain Jellis told you more than really happened."

"Could be, but I wouldn't go callin' Kathlan a horse's arse if you expect to go on breathin' long."

"Now how in the Nine Hells did you find out who I spoke with?" she said, whirling on him, her hands firmly on her hips.

"Girl, you're too predictable." He tapped his pipe out and turned away, limping along while talking and refilling it. "Come along and I'll teach you a thing or two about close-wind sailin' while I tell ya how I found you out."

Cynthia followed dutifully, thinking that one of Koybur's lessons might be exactly what she needed to forget the unpleasantries of the day.

≈

"It really weren't that hard, Cyn," Koybur admitted, shifting the tiller of his little sloop into the crook of his ruined left arm and sheeting in the mainsail a touch. He could, and often did, sail the little smack alone, but it was nice to have Cynthia on the jib sheets. "I mean, you practically *live* at the Gallopin' Starfish. I knew you'd want to know what happened to the *Latharnia*, so I just asked Brulo who you'd been talkin' to all night like I knew you'd been there all along. You never told him to keep his mouth shut, so—"

"So he opened it," she finished for him, glaring back at him. "It's impossible to keep a secret in this damned town."

"Only when you don't make an effort, lass."

He pushed the tiller hard and hauled on the sheet without warning, tacking the little boat in the span of a half dozen heartbeats. The boom came across with a lurch, and would have cracked Cynthia smartly on the head if she hadn't been paying attention. She cursed appropriately, ducked under and moved to the other side of the small cockpit. She cursed again as her skirts fouled her legs while tending the jib sheets.

"See what happens when someone does somethin' yer not expectin'? If you wanted to be secretive, you shouldn'ta gone to your favorite inn, talked to all your friends there and left through the main room grinnin' like you'd just sold a mule for the price of a warhorse." He tended his sheet again, squinting up at the sail critically. "Now where's that ship there from?" he continued with a nod toward a low-hulled galley with brightly painted bulwark shields.

"Fornice, from the paint, but it could be Marathian." She squinted against the afternoon sun and nodded. This was a common game they played, he pointing out a ship, and she answering his questions about it. "Lateen rig with oarsmen for upwind work. This is probably the farthest north she's ever been."

"And why don't they travel farther north?"

"She's a coastal sailor, made for the southern oceans. She'd be hard pressed in the North Sea with her low profile."

"Why use them at all then? Why not just use a bigger ship like a galleon in the Southern Ocean?"

"Well, the galley draws less water, and there're lots of shallow, sandy bays in the Southern Ocean. She can also do river work, and she can make good time in calm weather, which they get a lot of in the dry seasons."

"Good. Now tend yer sheets, we're comin' 'round." They slipped off the wind, and passed quickly around the galley's carved bowsprit. "Now, are them round things just for show, or what?" he asked, nodding to the row of large round shields bound to the side of the ship.

"No, not just for show, though every ship has different colors. The oarsmen sit behind them, which makes them less likely to catch an arrow from a corsair." She waved to the swarthy bowman glaring at them from between two of the colorful shields. "They also make good cover for guys like him."

"Ontoay!" Koybur shouted to the man, smiling and nodding to Cynthia. "Ola ke batna! Umbeyo!" The swarthy man laughed and waved before he put down the bow and vanished behind one of the shields.

"What'd you say?" she asked, squinting back at Koybur suspiciously.

"I told him you wanted ta bed him. What'd you think?"

"So long as you don't offer me up for sale again. The last time you did that they took you seriously and I couldn't show my face in town until the ship left port."

"I *was* serious," he joked, laughing at her openly. "I could'a got two hundred kopeks fer ya!"

"That's not even the price of a camel, you..." She turned and kicked halfheartedly at him, then said, "I'm worth three times that!"

This was their usual banter between lessons, and it continued for two more crossings of the harbor before Cynthia changed the subject.

"Been a while since I've seen one of our flags in Southaven. What'd you do, sell all four ships and not tell anyone?" He was silent for a few breaths, and when she turned to look, his head jerked back from some distant point that had drawn his attention.

"Oh, sorry. No. Two of 'em's in the north, tradin' copra for wool. One's in the west tryin' to find a load of silks." He nodded to the south. "*Winter Gale*'s due in a fortnight or so, up from Baklanar, hopefully with some good steel. She's due for a bit of caulking and a host of new runnin' riggin'. I just hope this sale makes enough to pay for it, otherwise yer gram'll likely sell her off."

"Tell me that's a joke," she said, her jaw set in a knot.

"I wish it was, Cyn, but you know how she is. If I don't have the cash in hand to pay fer what I need, she's likely to take the highest bid and hand the money over to one of them fish-eyed bankers of hers." He cleated the sheet, pulled the pipe from his mouth and spat overboard. "Them types might just as well fly a black flag and sail the Shattered Isles as call themselves honest."

"I won't let her do it!" Cynthia said, pounding the cabin top. "Not this time. She's not going to be running things forever, Koybur, and when she's not, this family's going to be a *shipping* family again. She's damn near ruined every dream I ever had, but I'm not going to let her take this one from me. Not anymore!"

"Sounds like you two had a row," the old sailor said, the unscarred side of his face scrinching into a smile.

"More than just a row, Koybur. She went too far this time. She can't plan my life for me anymore. If she won't let me keep the shipping end of things alive until... well, until it's all my responsibility anyway, then I'll tell her to take the whole business and stick it up her arse!"

"Now, Cyn, don't be takin' that tack with her. She's been through a lot, ya know. Lucky the old gal didn't just let the whole thing flap in the breeze when the old man was lost." He tapped out his pipe and peered past the jib, eying the course he was taking. He let the little boat fall off the wind a bit and adjusted the mainsail so they would miss a three-masted galleon moored ahead. "It'll be yours soon enough, then you'll see it ain't so easy as all that."

"I don't expect it to be easy, just focused!" She watched the mooring ball as they passed it by and waved absently at the sailors on the bowsprit looking almost straight down on them. They made some predictable suggestions as to the cut of her blouse, but she just smiled and ignored them. Sailors were all alike. "I'd put every copper I could scrape together into new hulls and put them to sea. With you telling them where to go and what to trade for, we'd be sailin' downwind inside two years."

"Aye, and I suppose you'd want to captain one of 'em, too, eh?" He eyed her sidelong, grinning at her misty eyed stare.

"Well, maybe not right away, but eventually." She glared at him openly. "Why not? Other women captain ships!"

"Aye, that they do, Cyn. That they do."

He changed the subject by rattling off a dozen more questions about a lugsail junk that had arrived in port that very morning. She let herself be immersed in the details of rigs, cargos, languages and customs, and tried to forget her anger with her grandmother.

CHAPTER FIVE
Plans for the Future

CAMILLA STOOD AT HER master's side, trying to keep her new jewelry from jingling every time she moved. Wide golden bracelets encircled her wrists, each linked to her golden collar by three feet of burnished chain. Another longer golden chain led from her collar to drape over the arm of Bloodwind's chair; her gilded leash.

She swallowed and clenched her teeth, ignoring the delicious aromas of the feast and the stares men leveled at her with every jingle of the chains. She kept her eyes focused on the flickering candles and her ears attuned to the ill-played music. Bloodwind never let her partake of the feasts; she would eat her single daily meal alone in her chambers later, unless she displeased him.

Any interruption from this torment would normally have been welcome, but when the candles flickered with a sudden draft and a shout rang out from the entry hall, Camilla felt a flutter of tribulation instead of relief. The shouts heralded one of Bloodwind's messengers, and the news they brought was never good.

"Captain! Captain Bloodwind!" A scurrying servant ushered the man into the dining hall. "Word from Southaven, Captain!"

Soaked clothing clung to the messenger's gaunt frame as he stumbled forward, exhausted from his three-day trip from Southaven in one of the fast little fishing smacks the pirates used for sending messages. He fell to his knees before the table, reaching inside his sodden tunic to withdraw a waxed scroll tube.

"Probably just news about the *Latharnia*," Bloodwind said with a shrug. He rose from his seat and stepped up to the kneeling man. "Is that right? The message is news about the damaged galleon that arrived there three nights ago?"

"I know not, Captain!" the messenger insisted, his hand wavering with worry. "I deliver the message, sir. By your orders, I never break the seal on the tube! I swear!"

Bloodwind's cruel eyes narrowed for a moment before he let a thin smile lift a corner of his crimson beard. Hydra ensured the loyalty of his messengers, casting magics that would reduce them to ashes if they ever broke their vows of secrecy. None of them had ever been coerced or spelled into an assassination attempt, but one could transport a spell-trapped case in ignorance easily enough, and Bloodwind had many powerful enemies.

"Broiful!" he snapped over his shoulder at the table. "Come here, if you please."

"Yes, Captain!" The newest of his captains lurched out of his chair and strode confidently to his commander's side.

"Take the case and open it for me, would you?" His voice was strangely sweet, and it sent a shiver up Camilla's spine that made her chains jingle faintly.

"Yes, Captain!" Broiful snatched the messenger's burden without pause and cracked open the seal. He removed the cork and extended the open tube to Bloodwind.

"Thank you," he said evenly, taking the opened tube with another sly smile. "You can go back to your dinner now, Broiful. And take your pick of the wenches for tonight."

"Thank *you*, Captain!" the man said with a broad grin to his peers and a leer to several of the shy girls removing the remains of the meal.

Bloodwind waved the messenger away and unrolled the parchment to read. The pirate commander's bushy red eyebrows arched as he sank back to his chair, an amused expression stretching his bearded visage into a mask of intrigue.

"Well, well! Not about the *Latharnia* after all, but the bud of an opportunity." He shifted the pages and continued reading, leaving his captains staring at him expectantly. Camilla's eyes drifted over to the parchment, widening slightly as she recognized the sturdy block script.

"It would appear that a once-powerful shipping family could soon fall into young and inexperienced hands." He grinned over the pages then let his gaze slide toward Camilla. She caught him watching her and returned her attention to the candles, refusing to show the emotions she knew he was trying to provoke. "Our spy in Southaven says this young woman's enthusiasm for reestablishing her family's fleet is only held in check by her aging grandmother."

"Sounds like the ol' bird needs ta meet with an accident," Ethrain, the captain of the *Scarnose*, said, grabbing a clay jug and refilling his cup.

"Exactly what I was thinking, good captain," Bloodwind agreed, running his thick, scarred fingers through his beard as his eyes mirrored the murderous thoughts whirling through his mind. "If she were out of the way, the girl would put everything they had into new hulls, which could only improve our hunting. Seems like a small investment for a possibly good return, but just who would be best at this sort of thing?"

"Send me, Captain!" Broiful said with a ravenous grin. "I'll cut the old woman's throat and be back here before *Blackheart's* back in the water!"

"Your enthusiasm does you credit, Broiful, but I really think we need someone who will be a bit more subtle." He continued finger-combing his beard, saying, "Let's see, killing old ladies. Hmmm. I think we should call on Yodrin for this. It definitely sounds like his cup of tea."

Mumbles of agreement swept around the table, and Bloodwind nodded for the musicians to continue the night's entertainment. He picked up the message again and scanned it, an amused smile returning to his lips.

"Oh, and remind me to send my spy in Southaven a special bonus this month." He fingered the golden chain that lay draped over the arm of his chair, tugging on it lightly until the links jingled. "Oh, I forgot. I don't pay that spy anything at all, do I?"

His laughter raked across Camilla's nerves. She clenched her teeth against the words that she knew would only earn her bruises and glared at the flickering candles.

"That's the best kind of spy, you know," he told his men, "the kind that works for free. Or, more precisely, because you hold something dear to them." He rattled her chain again, laughing louder and longer this time.

"It's almost like having a slave. Isn't that right, my dear Camilla?" He wound the golden chain around his hand, forcing her to lean over almost into his lap, his rum-scented breath warm against her ear. "Just like having a slave."

The men laughed at her misery, which affected Bloodwind like a drug. He ran his fingers into Camilla's hair and closed his fist, pulling her face close to his own before he said, "Now, dance for us, my dear. Show us that your new ornaments don't interfere with your grace."

She straightened as he released her and began to move to the music. The chains jingled and pulled at her wrists and neck with every turn and dip, but she danced anyway. She ignored the laughter and the rude calls and danced, because she knew exactly what would happen if she did not.

≈

"Gramma?" Cynthia's knuckles tapped the door of her grandmother's study. The woman sat hunched over her ancient roll-top desk, engrossed in her unending and self-imposed toil. She hadn't heard Cynthia, so the young woman bit her lip and knocked louder, saying, "Gramma, can I talk with you?"

"Oh, Cynthia!" She turned stiffly and put her quill down, adjusting her reading glasses to look over them at her granddaughter. "I'm sorry. Sometimes these numbers take up so much of my attention that the house could fall down around me and I'd never know. Please, sit. Would you like some tea? I'll call for Marta."

Cynthia knew the woman's twittering was only eagerness to mend the injuries she had dealt a week before. Cynthia's own temper had taken that long to simmer down to a level where she felt she could open her mouth without screaming.

"Actually, Gramma, I'd just as soon we were alone. I've got some things I want to show you." She stepped into the study holding her big leather satchel before her like a shield—a purpose it could have served, since it held enough paper to stop a hunting arrow.

"Oh. Well, all right." Julia motioned to a pair of thickly upholstered chairs by the window and rose to join her. "Is there some problem with the books?"

"That's one way of putting it." Cynthia sat and placed the satchel on her lap, delving into it with both hands. She extracted a roll of parchment as thick as her leg and bound with two wide ribbons. She placed that to the side and took an additional stack of flat paper out of the bag. These she spread out on the broad, low table between their chairs.

"I think you need to see what I've done here." She took the top sheet and pushed it over to her grandmother. "This is something I learned from Koybur. Sailors use charts that have lines on them that represent the mountains and valleys under the water. I thought I might do the same with money instead of the depth of the water. This is like a picture of what's been happening to our money over the last few years."

"My goodness, dear. Why would you ever want to look at all that?" Julia glanced at the maze of dotted lines tracing from left to right, some rising, some falling. "It's not what's happened in the past that's important, it's what will happen tomorrow, and the day after that."

"But by looking at this you can see what we did wrong before and what needs to be changed. See?" She pointed out four different lines that trended steadily downward. "When the lines angle down like that, that means we lose money. When they're flat, like these five, we are breaking even, and when they are rising, like these three, we are making money."

"So you're saying we should take the money from these falling investments and put it in the ones that make more money? Well, that might work dear, but you have no way of knowing what the future will bring. Next year these lines might all change direction."

"They might, but it's not likely, Gramma. This picture covers the last five years, and these trends haven't changed much in that whole time. Besides, it's not that simple." She pulled out another sheet. "This is another picture showing how much money we put into these different investments. You have to look at how much goes in to see if you're getting your money's worth. Now, these two that were making money here, were costing us more to maintain over here. See?"

"I, uh... I suppose." The older woman's eyes flickered from one chart to the other, mystified at how the squiggly lines represented numbers, which represented gold. This was a new concept to her. All her financial advisers simply looked at columns of numbers.

"Good. So what we want to do is put these two together to see which of our investments are giving us the best return for the money, right?" Cynthia produced another sheet, this one sporting one line soaring skyward while the rest wavered about the middle, or fell precipitously. "Do you see how this works?"

"I think so, dear," the older woman said, her eyes brightening a bit. "This one shows how much money we made or lost; this one, how much money we put into each; and this one is like taking the investment away from the profits. Is that right?"

"Exactly!" Cynthia said with a smile. "Now, would you like to know which of these is the only one giving us a decent return for our investment?"

Cynthia's grandmother's face fell like a sail cut from its halyard. She stared at her granddaughter with a look of betrayal and disbelief. She stiffened in her chair and removed her reading glasses with a shaking hand. Her lips pursed, and Cynthia could tell her teeth were clenched to the point of breaking.

"I refuse to believe that the only investment we have of any value is those ships, Cynthia." Her voice was tightly controlled, on the verge of rage but held in check to prevent another unthinking outburst. "You could have made these pictures any way you wanted. They mean nothing."

"I am *not* lying to you, Grandmother." Cynthia's voice shook with anger, but she also knew it would do her no good to vent that anger right now. "These charts are accurate. You can look at the numbers I used to make them if you wish."

"I'll do that, but I don't see what that will prove."

"It'll prove that this family has been living off of nothing but those four leaky hulls that have not seen a shipyard in two years, Grandmother. They must be maintained, or they will fail us and their crews. If we are forced to pay the death settlements for sixty or so sailors, we'll be ruined completely."

"Then we should sell them directly and get out from under the burden!" the elder woman said, her fiery blue eyes shooting sparks of affirmation at Cynthia.

"Grandmother," Cynthia began, calming herself, "we can't do away with the only business we own that is actually making us money. If we do, we will run out of money in about three years. Koybur knows more about what to ship where and when than either you or I know about any of the other investments we have put money into. What we *should* do is spend some money on the ships we have and lay down a new hull to increase our fleet."

She grabbed the heavy roll of parchment and pulled the ribbons free, laying the huge pages flat for her grandmother to see. Fine lined drawings crowded the pages, the kind of drawings shipwrights used to construct vessels. Cynthia presented the designs of the sleekly lined craft she'd been working on for years to her grandmother triumphantly.

"I've learned a lot from Master Keelson and Koybur. This is a different kind of ship; it's smaller, faster and will sail closer to the wind than any galleon on the ocean. It'll only carry about half as much cargo, but needs fewer crew and it'll get where it's going in half the time. We could ship perishable fruits and valuable silks. We could even transport ice from the Northlands south in winter! This ship will make us rich, Gramma, if you'll only let me build it!"

"I realize that you want to follow in your grandfather's footsteps, Cynthia, but I don't think you realize how expensive new ships really are, not to mention hiring crew to man them. That is, if any trustworthy men can be found south of the Northern Desert." She shifted uncomfortably in the upholstered chair as if her bones preferred the hard seat at her desk. "The problem with shipping is not ships, dear, it is sailors. They are irresponsible and prone to drunkenness, and I won't trust them, ever."

"You don't *know* any sailors, Gramma," Cynthia said with a sarcastic smile. "Besides Koybur, there hasn't been a sailor in this house in fifteen years. Sure they drink, but never aboard their ships, and the money they spend is theirs, not yours. How they spend it is their business."

"I knew sailors aplenty when your mother was a girl, Cynthia, and not a one of them was worth the spit it takes to polish a spoon!" She took a handkerchief from a pocket and rubbed her reddened eyes with it. "I don't know why I ever married one."

"Don't punish both of us for something that happened years ago, Gramma." Cynthia's voice had turned soft and pleading. "Grandpa must have done something right to get as far as he did. Let me try to do the same. We're starting with more than he did."

"I'm sorry, Cynthia, but no." The soft denial was more crushing than any that could have been screamed in rage, for she knew it wasn't from anger but from careful thought. "I won't put any more money into shipping. If we cannot stay solvent with our other investments, we may have to sell the estate, but I won't have any more ships built."

"Then I *will*, Grandmother!" Cynthia rolled the plans tightly, cinched the ribbons in taut bows, and stuffed them into her satchel. She stood and flung the heavy bag over her shoulder so hard that it almost spun her around. "The day you sell one more of our ships rather than repair it properly is the day I leave and hire on as crew on the first ship that'll have me. If I have to start at the bottom, I will, but one day this family's affairs will be *mine* to govern, and that will be the day we build *ships* again!"

"I won't have you disgrace yourself and this family by hiring on as common labor, Cynthia!" The older woman sprang up out of the chair, stepping around the low table with surprising agility. "I raised you better that that!"

"I won't argue with you any more, Grandma," Cynthia said, her voice softening once again. "I've said what I'm going to do. You think of me as a girl, but I'm not one anymore. I'm a woman, and if I want to go to sea, you can't stop me. If you think I'm bluffing, *Winter Gale* is due in port in a few days. Put her up for sale and see what happens."

She turned to go, but stopped in her tracks at one last offer from her grandmother.

"I'll keep the four ships we own afloat, Cynthia. If they're lost to pirates, or if some drunken captain runs them into a reef, I'll not replace them, and I won't build any more ships. What you do once I'm gone is out of my control."

"Yes, Grandma, it is," she said, turning to give the woman a grudging nod of agreement. "I'll stay as long as there're ships sailing with our flag on them. Once they're gone, I'm gone."

Cynthia left the study and strode through the halls of the only home she ever knew, wondering what had happened to the family she'd once been a part of. She turned a corner and thrust the heavy satchel back out of her way. She didn't want the drawings ruined by the tears that dripped unchecked from her cheeks.

CHAPTER SIX
Assassins and Broken Wings

WHITE LACE CURTAINS FLUTTERED in the light, cool breezes that filled the bedchamber with the fragrances of honeysuckle and frangipani. A few early mourning doves were cooing their soothing song, but the sun had yet to lighten the eastern sky. These were the hours when everyone slept most deeply, a fact that the dark, hooded figure easing through the window of the Garrison estate house knew all too well.

The casement creaked with his weight, but his feet met the floor without a sound. He left the window like a wraith on the wind, and moved around the foot of the great canopied bed with less than a whisper from the soles of his boots. The woman in the bed breathed easily and deeply, shrouded in a gossamer veil of mosquito netting that draped from above. She slept with a peace that melted the years away from her features and hinted of the stunning woman she had once been. The intruder looked down on that face without the faintest trace of pity.

A hand clad in black kidskin brushed aside the netting while its twin drew a short leather sap from a pocket. The weapon lashed out like a black viper. The sap struck Julia Garrison on the temple with enough force to snap her head to the side, knocking her unconscious before the pain of the blow could wake her.

Her assailant took a step back from the bed and cast about the room, absorbing every detail in a single long glance. He moved to the night table and tipped over the oil lamp, then removed a bottle from inside his shirt. The cork from the bottle of local rum popped free with a twist, and he poured a good amount over the night table and the lamp, and then made a circuit of the bed, dousing the gauzy canopy. The cork squeaked back into the neck of the bottle and he tucked it under the woman's pillow. He returned to the nightstand and struck a match from the box there. Fire flared in his hand, and he paused a moment before dropping it onto the overturned lamp.

He was back to the window before the blue alcohol flames completed their circuit of the bed. The mosquito netting exploded into flames, crackling up to the ceiling in seconds. He spared one more glance back at the flaming canopy and the inferno cast a lurid light into the depths of his cloak's hood. A cruel smile flickered for an instant before he turned and vanished into the night. His stealth was complete, the murder unwitnessed...or so he thought.

≈

A tiny pair of eyes blinked at the orange light flaring through the window where the broom-wielder slept. He had watched and listened for many years, but fear of the broom-wielder, the wing-breaker, kept him from showing himself. He'd watched little Cynny grow and become a different person, but he still loved her, so he watched.

But this was something different; this was something dire. If there was one thing a seasprite feared more than a matron wielding a broom, it was fire. Fire at sea was everyone's worst fear, and even a whiff of smoke would send a seasprite into a panic. Mouse was no exception, and the first gout of rolling smoke to escape the broom-wielder's window sent him fluttering into action.

Years had not healed his wings, but Mouse had been deft with a bit of stolen silk thread and a few tiny fish bones. His wings were patched and splinted, and he could fly, after a fashion. He could not flitter about like he once had, and his speed was slow at best, but he could stay aloft and he could, mostly, avoid running into things.

He abandoned his sheltering banana frond and flew to the broom-wielder's window. Flames filled the room. He could barely see the shape on the bed, and the fire set his tiny heart racing to such a frantic pace that it matched the beat of his wings. He had seen the shadowy figure leave, had watched it slip among the darkest bits of night, across the lawn and over the wall, but finding out who that figure was right now seemed less important than finding Cynny. She needed to know about the fire.

He fluttered around the foyer, avoided the trellises of thorny bougain-villea, and made his best speed to her window. It was cracked open just enough for him to slip through.

≈

Cynthia woke as something fluttered against her face. A great moth or some other insect had managed to find a path through the netting and was tormenting her. She waved her hand and struck something remarkably solid. A high-pitched yelp brought her fully awake.

"Wha—?"

Something struggled, tangled in the mosquito netting. The flicker of gossamer-crystal wings and a white shirt and loose trousers on a six-inch frame brought her up short. It was Mouse!

"Mouse? What the hell? I thought you—" The smell of smoke filled her nostrils and her mind screamed a warning. She leapt out of bed, pulling at her nightdress and rummaging through her dresser. She knew that pausing to dress was ridiculous, but took a few moments to find a shirt and a pair of trousers anyway.

"Thank you, Mouse! By the Gods, thank you for waking me!" The sprite struggled to disentangle himself from the mosquito netting as she flung a shirt over her shoulders and burst from her room, shouting for the servants with every ounce of voice she could muster.

"Marta! Brolen! There's a fire in the house!" She fought to get her arms in the sleeves as she shouted, finally getting the shirt on.

"Gramma! Brolen! Marta! Fire!"

She dashed down the hall to the landing of the main stair. Smoke filled the air here, limiting her vision and making her cough. Figures moved below and she recognized the servants.

"Get out of the house!" she bellowed, waving Marta toward the front door. "I'll see to Gramma. Get out!"

"But Miss Cynthia!" she heard over her shoulder as she dashed down the hall. Her grandmother's rooms were at the northernmost wing, just as hers were in the southernmost tower. She could not see through the smoke here, and imagined the worst even before she grasped the handle to her grandmother's bedroom door.

Flesh hissed like a steak on a grill as her hand met the hot brass door handle, and her ears rang with her own reflexive scream. She knew even as she fumbled for the loose tail of her shirt that the room was ablaze, but she had to get in there.

Gramma's in there!

The heat from the handle baked through the thin linen, burning her hand again. She looked at her reddened palm and decided on a more direct approach. She took a step back, raised a foot and kicked the thin oak planking near the handle as hard as she could. As the door crashed open, the fire leapt outward in a billowing cloud of orange that blasted her off her feet.

The room glowed in a raging inferno.

Lying there smelling the acrid odor of her own singed eyebrows, Cynthia could see beneath the billowing smoke and flames. Everything in the room was burning. The bed was still intact, the four sturdy posts standing erect, though eager tongues of flame licked up their spirals. The form on the mattress lay as still as a headstone, blackened and blazing, barely recognizable as human. Agony stabbed through Cynthia's heart.

She tried to go to her grandmother, but heat like the inside of a kiln beat her back. She peered through the haze of flames, smoke and tears. Her grandmother could not be alive. Nothing could survive that. Cool streaks ran down her cheeks, a trickle against the inferno; she wiped them angrily. She would never be able to banish that terrible vision from her mind.

Cynthia stared in shock for what seemed an eternity. If she didn't act quickly the whole house would go up in flames. But what could she do?

Part of the ceiling collapsed onto the charred remnant of the bed. Sparks billowed out of the doorway, then were sucked back in as air was funneled into the room and up through the gaping hole in the roof. The flames being pulled back into the room, away from the rest of the house, gave her a desperate idea. She dashed down the stairs, unsure if her plan was even sane, but determined to try something. She glanced frantically around the great atrium. The towering room bisected the house into northern and southern wings. Behind the grand stair were the morning room and the patio, solid flagstones and a sparse framework of windows.

"Nothing to burn!" she shouted, looking back at the great arched stair and the two pillars that held up the ceiling. "Nothing to burn if the stairs and the roof weren't here!"

She dashed out the front and almost fell over Brolen carrying two sloshing buckets from the horse trough. She snatched the buckets from him and screamed right in his face, "Get the team harnessed! Now! We need to pull down the pillars to save the rest of the house!"

"Yes'm!" she heard from behind her as she dashed up the stairs, hoping she could slow the blaze long enough to put her weak plan into effect.

If she could pull down the pillars, and then somehow the main stair, the house would be cut in half. The north half would burn, but the south half would be saved. Her hopes dwindled, however, when she mounted the stair and dashed down the hall to her grandmother's room, for flames had already spread into the hall. She put one bucket down and splashed the other as well as she could at the worst part of the fire, but it didn't seem to have much effect. The second bucket didn't do much more, so she ran back down the stairs to get more.

Her buckets clattered to the ground and a convulsive screech of hope escaped her throat when she reached the front steps. A buckboard with a team of four stout horses was rounding the drive at a gallop.

"Koybur!" she shouted, waving her arms unnecessarily as he brought the team up short right in front of her. "Koybur, we need to pull the foyer down! The north wing is a loss! Please tell me this is the shipwright's wagon!" She vaulted into the bed of the wagon and shouted a yip of triumph at the coils of wrist-thick rope that lay beneath her bare feet.

"I'll take one end!" she shouted to him, snatching up the eye that was spliced into the end of the line and flinging an arm through it before jumping down. "Tie the other end to the harness!"

"Hang on, Cyn!" His shout stopped her for a moment. "Where's yer gram?"

"Just tie the other end!" she screamed, shaking her head in the haze of smoke and ash that was blowing down from her burning home. "It's too late for anything else!"

He stared at her in shock for a moment, then set the brake and swung around into the bed of the wagon. In a moment the other end of the heavy line was in his good right hand and he was threading it under the seat and lashing it to the harness brace.

Cynthia dashed up the steps and into the smoke-filled entry hall. Above her, ghostly gray-orange tendrils of flame crawled and quested along the alabaster ceiling, hungry tongues searching for something to devour. The entire front of the house rested upon the two central pillars, the back was an open patio behind the stair. She flung one end of the rope around the left hand pillar and flipped a quick bowline into it. The last thing she wanted now was a knot she couldn't untie. She jerked twice to seat the knot, forgetting about the blisters on her palm. Blood slicked the line and tears welled once again in her eyes, but it wasn't important. The house, her home, was the only thing that mattered now. It was the only thing she had left.

She dropped the rope and stared at the pillar for a moment. She had no idea how deeply it was seated into the flagstones. Perhaps it just sat on top and could be jerked out from under the ceiling like a weak table leg. If it was set into a foot of rock, they might as well try to pull down the tower. She whispered a quick oath to Odea, wondering if the goddess would listen to someone who'd only been to sea once in her life, and raced back out the front door.

Brolen was hitching the two bays in front of Koybur's team, and the sight of the six stout horses sent a thrill of hope up Cynthia's spine. A team like that should be able to pull the whole damned house down! She rushed up to the men and clapped Koybur on the shoulder.

"I tied it around the northern main pillar! It might take out the porch, too, if you pull at the right angle!"

"Cyn, wait! Are you sure you want to—"

"The whole damn thing will burn if we don't!" She glanced at Brolen as he stepped away from the hastily rigged team. The heavy rope was tied directly into their harnesses, and the horses stamped and pawed nervously as embers drifted down on the wind and smoke filled the air. "Drive, Koybur!"

He nodded once and pulled himself up into the driver's seat. Brolen had threaded additional reins from the front pair; Koybur wrapped one side around his maimed left hand and took the other in his right. He looked back at the lay of the coiled line leading into the burning house and eased the team forward. When only about two feet of slack remained, he lashed the reins hard and shouted at the skittish team.

Cynthia's eyes were locked onto the house. Through the open front door she could see the rope strain against the pillar's base. She saw the ornate molding splinter, watched the marble facing crack and buckle up like a rug beneath a chair leg. The reins lashed against the horses' flanks, Koybur shouted again, and the thick rope strained.

The pillar gave way.

The horses lunged forward as the massive wooden support flipped outward and smashed through the foyer. White painted splinters flew in all directions as the smaller pillar of the porch was shattered and flung aside. The rope tightened again as the pillar fell flat and half the roof chased it on its descent, but then the sturdy team jerked the massive thing right out the front of the house, dragging roof, wall, and all, along with it.

"WHOA!" Koybur shouted, reining in the team and turning them around. Cynthia was already racing to the huge pile of rubble, fighting to untie the rope and yank it free. One glance at the house confirmed that her plan would work if they could do the same with the huge sweeping stair, but flames were already licking greedily at the top.

"Take the team around back, Koybur!" Cynthia shouted, finally succeeding with the knot. "We'll pull the stairs out through the patio!" She looked at Brolen apologetically. He had spent a good deal of his life keeping this old house standing, and now they were tearing it in half. "I'm sorry Brolen, but it's the only way."

"Then we'd best get to it, I thinks!" He set his old jaw grimly and strode right into the rubble of the foyer, his long legs picking their way through the splintered wood and bent nails.

"What'll I do, Miss Cynthia?"

She turned and stared at Marta, having forgotten the woman was even there.

"There'll be more people coming up from town. Tell them what we're doing and have them douse the rest of the house with water from the well!"

She turned and dashed into the ruined house even before Marta replied. Splinters and nails threatened her bare feet at every step, but she pressed on. When she reached the stair, she saw Brolen coming back the other way with a heavy broadaxe. With a sheepish grin, he began hacking a hole in the stair's side facing. She hadn't thought about how to attach the rope to the thing, but he obviously had a plan, so she edged past and ran through the hall to the breakfast room and out onto the patio.

As Koybur pulled up, the long rope trailing out behind, she snatched up the end and headed back into the house. A ragged hole had been hacked in one side of the stair, and she could hear Brolen working on the other. A glance up confirmed that the fire was still confined to the north side of the house, but the smoke was billowing out the huge chasm left by the pillar's departure, and flames licked the roof's edge.

She knelt and peered into the dark recesses under the stair. The space was filled with crates and chests, so she shoved inside and wormed her way through and among them, trying to ignore the dust and filth. She could see a ruddy glow before her where Brolen's axe was doing its work, and nudged her way past an ancient bronze-strapped strongbox, ignoring the scrapes it left on her shoulder and stomach.

"Brolen! Here!" The hacking stopped and his face appeared in the irregular hole. She thrust the eye of the rope at him. "Take it! I'll go back and feed you slack. It has to reach back to the breakfast room!"

"Yes'm!" he said, taking the loop of heavy rope from her and pulling hard. She yelped as it rasped past her, flinging dust and lint all around as she backed her way out. She was a wreck, covered in dust and a shirt that was in tatters, but it didn't matter. They had to make this rope reach all the way around, or the plan wouldn't work.

She grasped the line and pulled, ignoring the searing pain of her blistered hand. Sparks and soot were starting to fall around her, and she knew time was short. She pulled and screamed for Koybur to give more slack, hoping he could hear her from out back. When the rope finally came taut and would yield no more, she raced through the hall to the breakfast room, only to find Brolen already tying a hasty knot.

"I hopes this'll do, Miss. I figured if we jerked all the supports out from under the thing, it'd fall and we could just drag it out. I don't know if it'll fall, but I think it will."

"It better, Brolen, or we're finished." She cringed at the knot he'd tied, wondering if anything short of a knife would be able to free it after a team of six horses cinched it tight. Koybur had the wagon backed up almost to the patio, and Cynthia hopped in and slapped him on the shoulder.

"Have at it, Koybur!" she yelled and snatched a handful of seat as the wagon lurched forward.

The staircase supports were less massive than the pillar, only about the width of her outstretched hand, but there were many more of them. The horses trod forward, churning the soft ground, and the heavy rope tightened. For a moment the supports held, but then they fractured and cracked like kindling and the framework that Brolen had chopped through collapsed in wads of crumpled wood. Furniture, glass and crockery smashed and shattered as the horses pulled the entire bundle of splintered supports through the breakfast room and the patio. When Koybur finally stopped, a hole the size of the wagon itself had been cleared right back to the base of the stairs.

But the stair itself still stood.

"What the bloody hell's holding the thing up?" she shouted, vaulting down from the wagon's bed and starting back to the house. She skirted the pile of broken lumber and peered up at the mysteriously suspended staircase. Only the cross bracing at the top held it up, and the beams on the north side were already burning.

"We've got to—"

Nails squealed free from their wooden sheaths as two strong hands grasped Cynthia by the shoulders, lifting her right off the stones of the patio. No one heard her cry of alarm over the splintering, crashing demise of the grand staircase and most of the remaining roof. Some of the mess that fell where she had stood burned lazily, but nothing like the inferno that raged through the rest of the northern wing of the house.

"Sorry 'bout that, Miss," Brolen apologized, putting her down, "but that there stair was 'bout ready to come down on your head."

"Yeah, I... Uh, thanks." She steadied herself and looked at the result of their mayhem. The fire was effectively isolated to the north half of the house, and would not reach the remnants of the fallen staircase until it worked its way to the lower floor. She turned to tell Koybur to start pulling anything flammable out of the way when shouts and thundering hooves interrupted her.

The sailors and shopkeepers of Southaven swarmed into the front yard of the estate like an army, wielding buckets, axes, shovels and rope. Men and women poured from the beds of wagons, carts and buggies. They drained the horse trough in a single pass and started flinging its contents on the blazing house. Others drove their wagons around to the back and attacked the well with similar ferocity while still more wrenched and pulled and hacked at the remains of the staircase. By the time Cynthia could find half a dozen faces she knew, a clear path shone from the patio to the front porch.

"Cynthia!" Rowland shouted above the din, shepherding Marta around the corner of the house. "What in Odea's name happened, girl?"

"I don't know, Rowland," she confessed as the shock of her ordeal finally took hold. "I woke—No, Mouse woke me!"

"Mouse? A mouse woke you?" Rowland looked at her as if he thought she'd been drinking.

"Not a mouse! The *seasprite*, Mouse! I thought he was gone but—" She looked around frantically. "Gods, I hope he wasn't caught in the fire! But he woke me! I smelled smoke, and when I went to find Gramma there was nothing in there but fire. I tried to get to her but... And then the fire started to spread, and I... I couldn't let it *all* burn!" She felt his long arms enfolding her, and realized she was bawling like a babe.

She knew she should try to collect herself, try to help the sailors fight the fire or salvage things, but the wracking sobs just wouldn't stop. She felt Marta's gentle caress, and heard Koybur's supportive words, and it was just easier to let the tears come. If only they could wash away the horrible image of the flames consuming her grandmother's bed.

CHAPTER SEVEN

Among the Ashes

CYNTHIA BRUSHED AN UNRULY lock of hair out of her eyes, leaving a streak of soot across her forehead. Ash caked her nails and saturated the bandage on her blistered hand. She felt something flutter against her hair, followed by a tug at her sooty locks, and smiled at Mouse's attempt to help. He'd shown up when the last of the flames were quenched and hadn't left her side since.

She pressed her fists into the small of her back to ease the ache. About a third of the northern wing still remained to be sifted through. They'd been at it for most of the morning, and the heat of the day was beginning to take its toll.

"Here, Cyn. You need somethin' in yer stomach."

She turned and accepted a cloth-wrapped sandwich from Rowland, smiling weakly. "Thanks, Row." She nodded toward the long table laden with food and drink that he and Brulo had set up for everyone. "Thanks for everything." She took a bite, the wonderful flavors of seasoned roast mutton, spicy mustard, tomatoes and crispy lettuce exploding in her mouth. She chewed slowly, eyes closed in bliss.

"Nothin' you wouldn't do fer us if the Starfish burned, I imagine." He pushed a cool drink into her hand. "That'll help wash it down." She nodded and took a healthy swallow of the tangy juice. Mouse landed on the opposite rim of her mug and took a healthy draught, smacking his tiny lips. That the little sprite had come to back to her, and quite literally saved her life, warmed her heart. She had no idea where he had been all these years, but it didn't matter. They were together again. Just like old times.

"It could have been a lot worse, I suppose." That had been Cynthia's litany all morning. "Koybur saved the house, that's for sure. If he hadn't seen the flames and brought that wagon, we'd have lost it all."

Rowland chuckled ruefully. "Aye, he said he'd never been so thankful for his insomnia. Couldn't sleep, so he figured he'd fetch a load of caulking twine from old Woolard, up the valley. He was on his way out of town when he saw the fire in yer gram's window."

"Damn lucky." She shook her head and finished the last of her sandwich, feeling guilty about calling anything about this catastrophe lucky. Her grandmother had burned to death in her bed. They would never know how the fire got started, not with the whole north wing reduced to ash and charred timbers.

"Miss Cynthia!"

She turned toward three men sorting through piles of salvaged junk with Marta. One waved her over. "Guess I better see what they want. Thanks again, Rowland." She swallowed the rest of her drink and handed the glass to him with a nod.

Along with the stairway, a number of crates, boxes, bags and chests had been dragged out onto the lawn. Four pitiful heaps of salvaged items lay on the grass. The largest by far was charred and useless junk ready to be carted off to the town refuse heaps. The next contained things that might be of use or could be sold at auction: clothes, jewelry, picture frames, eating utensils and the like.

Cynthia would go through all this again herself, but doubted Marta would sell anything she might want. The third pile was of things to be kept, refinished, repaired or restored. The last pile consisted only of two long trunks and a smaller metal box.

"We got the most of it, Miss Cynthia," Flaven, the sailor in charge of the detail, said with a shrug. "Marta just wanted yer okay on these last three."

"What's in them?" she asked, peering at the two open trunks. "Looks like more clothes to me."

"Yes, Miss," Marta agreed, bending down to finger the hem of a particularly lovely gown. "These are your mother's old dresses. Some of them might fit you right nicely with a stitch or two. They need to be aired out, of course, but..."

"You go through them, Marta. Pick out two or three for me. I can't imagine needing more than that. Keep whatever you want for yourself and put the rest in the auction pile." She looked at the other chest, this one full of men's clothing. "Was this my father's?"

"Yes'm. He didn't have much fancy clothes, but your mum, she'd bought a few things for him." Marta reached down and fingered the cuff of a shirt of azure silk. "Some nice things, but..."

"Put the shirts in a pile for me. I'll go through them later. Auction the rest." She toed the stout bronze box. "And what about this?" There was a good amount of corrosion on the outside, but it looked sturdy enough to have survived the entire house falling on it. Instead of a simple padlock, the lock was built right into the box. Under the dust of a decade of neglect lay thinly scrawled lines in a pattern that played tricks with her eyes. "I've never seen a box like this, and I certainly don't have a key for it."

"We could chisel it open from the hinge side," Flaven suggested.

"You're sure it's locked?" Cynthia reached for the lid.

"Oh, it's locked sure enough. I tried to—"

Something clicked, and the lid creaked open in Cynthia's hand. She looked at Flaven dubiously. "So it's locked sure enough, is it?" Mouse gave a little cackle of laughter almost too high-pitched to hear.

"Miss Cynthia, I tried everything short of prying that thing open with a riggin' knife! There ain't no way it couldn't a been locked!"

"Well, it's open now," she said, brushing her fingers over the supple suede that wrapped the box's contents. Beneath lay a number of charts and two leather-bound books. One was bound in red with gold edging, and looked to be a logbook of some kind. The other was black and about four hands tall, three wide, and several fingers thick. As she lifted them out, something slipped from the bundle and clanked into the box: a silver medallion, its crescent shape glittering in the midday sun.

"Odea's green garters! Them's yer father's books! They gotta be!" Flaven gaped, making a warding sign. Everyone backed a half step away from the box except Cynthia. Mouse gave a little "Eep!" of alarm and ducked behind her neck, peering out at the books in her hands.

"What?" Cynthia put the books down and reached for the silver crescent. "These were my father's?"

"Aye, lass, that they were." Koybur nudged through the crowd and smiled down at Cynthia. "And I think you just used up a year's worth of luck, pokin' into a wizard's things without gettin' rendered down to a puddle of whale oil."

Cynthia's fingers stopped an inch from the silver crescent. "You mean there might be a trap set on his things?"

"Oh, nothin' you might call a trap. Wizards just have a reputation as bein' a bit stingy with their secrets is all." Koybur bent down onto his good knee, peering at the items inside the box. "If they haven't hurt you yet, I don't think they're likely to. Them are sure enough his personal charts, and his journal and log. And that was the very crescent he wore the day he died. That there's the sign of the seamage." He nodded for her to go ahead and pick it up.

"It's beautiful," she said, lifting the silver crescent by its chain. The lower end of the crescent was worked into the shape of the hilt of a sword. In the hilt were set three tiny diamonds, a ruby and a sapphire.

"That's the Scimitar Moon, lass, and that you can even touch it without Odea's hand slappin' you down like a naughty child proves you've got his blood runnin' through yer veins."

Mouse leapt from her shoulder to dance a jig on the hand that held the medallion's chain, laughing with glee. Cynthia stared at the medallion, barely seeing the sprite or hearing a word from Koybur. Its surface showed tiny lines and craters, emulating the surface of the moon in bas relief. The detail was startling, so perfect and untarnished, and every gem sparkled like a newborn star. She caressed its surface with her thumb, wondering how many times her father had done the same. Without thinking, she looped the chain over her head and let the crescent rest upon her breast. It felt warm, comforting, like a part of her family that had been lost and suddenly found. Like Mouse.

"And these books. You said one was a journal, and the other his log?"

"Aye, lass, but you might be a bit more careful with them. Some of what's written on them pages could very well burn yer eyes out if yer not prepared properly."

"Prepared?" she asked, picking up the red leather log and cracking it open. "What do you mean 'prepared'?" But as she glanced at the angular script, the characters squirmed under her gaze, and her head throbbed in pain. "Oh my..." She slapped the tome shut, rubbing her tortured eyes. "That was like trying to look into the sun at midday!"

"Like I said, be careful with that one. Them letters are magic, as sure as any wizard's wand or staff." He patted her shoulder and pointed to the other book. "That, however, I think you'll find more to your likin'."

"His journal?" She lifted the black book and opened it a couple of inches, peering in carefully. Sharp letters in a precise hand greeted her... his hand, his words. She closed it carefully, knowing that she would require rest and a clear head before she could read it. "I'll save it for later."

"That's probably wise, and the same for these, though you might find them just as interestin'." He unrolled one of the charts, and Cynthia could see that they were the most detailed she had ever seen. Contour lines in black ink, current lines in blue, with depth and the set of the current logged in different colors. Dead reckoning lines cut across both in red, with bearings from critical points scrawled along them. She started to touch them before she realized that her hands were still filthy.

"Put them back for me, would you, Koybur? I'm afraid to get them dirty." She pushed herself up and took a long look around. "There's a lot more to sift through before I'll be ready to take stock of what's left."

"Aye, Ma'am."

Koybur sounded strange; he'd never called her 'Ma'am' in his life. Then realization struck: He was her employee now, and she his mistress. Their relationship had changed with this tragedy. She hoped he wouldn't start treating her with the distant deference that he had her grandmother. She would need his honest help if she had a hope to make any of this work.

"When all this is cleaned up, we'll both go over the charts, Koybur.

You've got a better eye than me. Anything you think would be of use, we'll have copied and distributed to our captains."

"Aye, Ma'am. I'll come by tomorrow afternoon. And I'll get hold of yer creditors and let 'em know you want a word with 'em, with yer permission, of course."

"The day after tomorrow would be fine. And let Master Keelson know that we'll be hauling *Winter Gale* for a refit as soon as she arrives."

"Aye, Ma'am," he said with a nod and a smile. "That'll be my pleasure."

"Right now, I think I'm going to get cleaned up and sleep for a few hours, if I can." She nodded to Marta and Koybur and turned to what was left of her home. "Wake me if anything important comes up."

≈

Moonlight shone through the open window of Cynthia's room, glittering on the tears that coursed unabated down her cheeks. So many emotions surged through her that she didn't know what to feel.

Upon the table behind her sat a lamp, half a glass of wine, a sleeping seasprite and her father's open journal. The journal entries echoed in her mind—the love, the hope and the dreams—more than she could grasp. The first entry to truly capture her dated from when he met her grandfather.

I have signed on with Benjamin Garrison, a master of ships of great repute. I met him in Tsing, and was quite impressed with both his mastery of his ship and his success as a business man. This will afford me a fine opportunity to practice my skills in the Southern Ocean. Mouse approved of Captain Garrison, and the captain tolerated the sprite's antics with good humor. I also met the captain's daughter, Peggy, who is currently serving as his second mate and is a fine sailor in her own right, although she seems a bit uppity...

The passages continued to detail his whirlwind relationship with Peggy Garrison, their marriage and even the birth of his child.

Never did I believe that anything could bring me greater joy than communing with the sea, but nothing I have ever experienced compares with this morning. Holding the fruit of my own body, my beautiful Cynthia, then watching her suckle at the breast of her equally beautiful mother, my Peggy, has humbled me beyond words. I don't know what I have done to deserve this bounty, but I shall endeavor to be worthy of this boon and dedicate my life to preserving their safety and happiness.

Passage by passage, Cynthia alternated between tears of joy, longing and heartbreaking sadness that left her emotionally exhausted. A glass of wine and a walk around the estate steeled her nerves, and she had finally returned to read the final few pages. But what she found there had left her bewildered.

The time draws near for Cynthia's voyage. In twelve days, the alignments will be correct. I'm sure we will be successful. Cynthia is such a bright child, and she has a true affinity for the sea. She watches it day by day from the garden, and her games all revolve around the sea and its denizens. I especially enjoy watching her play "sharks and mermaids", although she'll find out soon enough that merfolk are not such easy prey as she depicts. I worry that Mouse is gone; I always assumed he would be present for Cynthia's Awakening, as he was for mine. Planning is critical for this voyage. The next alignment won't occur for five years, which may be too late for Cynthia, since Odea's requirements become more rigorous with age.

Eventually, the significance of the voyage struck her: she was supposed to have become a seamage like her father, with powers over wind and water, over the sea and all that lay above and beneath her waves. Now her tears were for herself, and what she might have been.

Exhaustion, wine and the overwhelming feeling of loss mounted within her, sapping her strength. She turned away from the moonlight and slid down to sit with her back to the stone of the tower's outer wall, her tears wetting her father's azure shirt in spots the color of midnight. Her head sagged forward onto her knees as the anguish of what would never be drifted through her mind, recalling and illuminating her nightmares...

Cynthia peered out onto a scene from hell. Sailors, her grandfather's sailors, battled fierce men who leapt onto their ship from the deck of a huge black-hulled corsair with crimson sails. She flinched as cries of rage and agony washed over her like the bloody seawater that doused her stockings.

At the center of the melee her parents fought back to back. Her mother's skirts were red with blood, her long rapier and poniard drenched to their hilts. Her father stood empty handed, his lips clenched tightly, his face furrowed in concentration. Water leapt at his command, dashing against the black-hulled ship even as blasts of wind beat at the crimson sails. The grappling lines that held the two ships in bondage parted like the crack of a cat o' nine tails and the pirate ship heeled violently away until seawater spilled over its leeward rail. A shroud snapped and the pirate ship's main mast fractured at its midpoint, falling in a mass of splintered wood, twisted line, and screaming men.

The sailors cheered, and her parents clutched each other in a fierce, life-affirming embrace. Cynthia's spirit lifted even as she stood, poised to rush to them and share in their love and celebration. But with an ear-splitting crack-whistle, a ballista bolt from the quarterdeck of the pirate ship ended the sailors' revelry—and altered Cynthia's future—in one searing jolt.

Orin and Peggy Flaxal stood still, staring in shock at one another as blood pooled at their feet in a horrific torrent. Their lips parted, but they made no sound. Cynthia tried to call out to them, but could not make her voice work. Suddenly the ship rolled and her parents toppled to the deck, still clenched in their last embrace, staring into one another's eyes as the life fled their bodies.

The laughter...

The horrible laughter drew Cynthia's attention. There, standing at the rail near the massive weapon that had killed her parents, stood a man in black and red, his hair and beard the color of blood, a wide scar creasing his nose and cheek. His laughter rose and fell as the two ships diverged and the black-hulled ship disappeared into the mists, his evil mirth sparking a coal of rage in her heart.

Cynthia jerked awake, cracking the back of her head against the unforgiving stone of the tower's outer wall. Pain exploded through her skull, wrenching her thoughts from the nightmare.

"Damn it to all Nine Hells!" she swore, pushing herself up onto trembling legs. She rubbed the lump on the back of her head and banished the dream. She'd not had one so vivid in years. *It was just a dream, just a nightmare*, she insisted. She had been too young to remember that day, really.

Nightmare or memory, one element had been corroborated by men and women who had seen it: Bloodwind had killed her parents. And now, after reading Orin Flaxal's journal, she knew that the pirate had not only taken her parents from her, but had also stolen her heritage, her future as a seamage.

"I'll hunt you until one of us is dead, you bastard," she vowed, wiping away the tears that she felt would never stop. She closed the window, blocking out the moonlight, and closed her father's journal, knowing she could never block out the troubling knowledge she had found within.

CHAPTER EIGHT

Mistress of Ships

"THANK YOU FOR COMING on such short notice, gentlemen," Cynthia said as she entered the private room Brulo had prepared for her meeting with her creditors. Mouse flew in over her shoulder and settled on the back of the chair at the head of the table. He sketched a bow and leapt into the air, fluttering a wobbly path around the room. The four men rose from their seats, eyeing the sprite suspiciously.

"Please excuse my little friend, Mouse. He's been with my family since before my parents died and has grown rather fond of me. He's harmless."

Mouse made a rude noise at being called harmless as she recovered the balance sheets and charts from her satchel and took her seat. She started organizing her papers, but stopped when she noticed the four men still standing.

"Shall we get down to business?"

"Before we begin," one of them said, fingering the gold buttons on his waistcoat, "please let us express our heartfelt condolences. Your grandmother was an extraordinary woman. We are aggrieved beyond measure at her loss."

Mouse scowled at the man and fluttered the length of the table, landing on the back of Cynthia's chair.

"Thank you," she said, thinking, *You have no idea.* "I loved my grandmother very much, and I will miss her, but in matters of business she was extraordinary only in her ability to run our shipping concerns into the ground. Now if you would please be seated, I have a few things I would like to say before we start discussing numbers."

Nervous glances arced among them like lightning as they took their seats.

"Let me first say thank you for your attempts to help my grandmother manage the financial dealings of this family. I know you did your best for her, simply because the better we did, the better you did." One of them opened his mouth to speak, but she forestalled him with a raised hand. "I am going to make some changes, and I will be the first to admit that the reasons behind these changes are not solely financial, just as my grandmother's attempts to destroy our shipping interests were not financial."

"Miss Cynthia, you don't think—"

"*Mistress Flaxal*, if you please, and as much as it might surprise you all, I *do* think!" Her words were edged with temper. She'd been chastised by these men for everything from penmanship to punctuality far too many times to back away from a fight, especially now.

Mouse let out a peal of laughter, so high-pitched that it hurt her ear. She shushed him with a pat of her hand and directed her attention back to her creditors.

"I also *know* that my grandmother despised ships, sailors and everything associated with them, and that this family's four leaky galleons are the most profitable venture we've had for the last five years."

At their exclamations of denial and incredulity, she dug through her papers for the charts she'd made and distributed them.

"These pictures represent my money, gentlemen. The first one is profits, the second is expenditures and the third is the two combined, all over the last five years." She looked around at the brows knitted in confusion, and almost laughed. "It's simple, really: when the lines go up, I'm making money; when the lines go down, I'm losing money."

She let them stew a bit, their narrowed eyes analyzing the charts that they so obviously did not believe. She sipped blackbrew and buttered a hot scone. She hadn't noticed the pastries when she came in, but they were delicious. She cut off a small corner and balanced it on her knife for Mouse, hoping to divert him from the men. She had just swallowed her second bite when the dam finally broke.

"With all due respect, Miss— *Mistress* Flaxal," the boldest of them said, letting the paper flutter to the table as if it was offensive to him, "pictures do not represent money. Money can only be represented by numbers. One must look at the balance sheets, the expenditure totals, the interest payments. A few lines, rising or falling, cannot show—"

"Those lines *do* represent my money, sir. All the numbers you are so enamored with are right there for you to see, they're just easier to look at in a chart than in twenty different columns, each row in a different hand, and none of the decimals lining up. By looking at what has happened to my money in the past, I can see what will happen in the future, and plan accordingly. It's that simple."

"It is *not* that simple!" The man thrust himself to his feet and puffed up like a porcupine fish.

Mouse chirped a threat from Cynthia's shoulder and launched himself at him, but she snatched him back. She did not need the sprite's antics to provoke them; what she had to say would be upsetting enough. She planted him on her shoulder, where he sat and sulked.

"If you could predict financial interactions that easily, every peddler and shopkeeper in the empire would be rich! Things change from year to year, from season to season, and even from month to month! To think what happened three *years* ago has anything to do with what might happen tomorrow is ridiculous!"

"Why?"

Her calm retort caught him off guard. He burbled a bit then spouted, "Because it is! Like I said, things change."

"So do the weather, the tides, and the fishing and hunting, but anyone who sails, fishes or hunts can predict how they will change because they've seen them change before."

"That's something totally different!"

"Is it really?" She stood slowly, fixing the creditor's eyes with her own. "Then tell me how my man Koybur can turn a better profit than every other investment I've got? Everything you four have managed for the last dozen years has done little better than break even. You've been riding the back of our shipping business, getting a new lump of money to invest every time my grandmother sold another of our ships. I'm telling you that the free ride is over, gentlemen! I'm liquidating everything except the estate and the shipping business. I'm going to reinvest it in new hulls, as many as I can, as quickly as I can have them built!"

Cynthia managed to suppress a smile.

"You will lose money," the creditor said, scowling across the table at her.

"No, *you* will lose money." She snapped her papers into line and put them back in her satchel. "You will liquidate my holdings, gentlemen, immediately. You will get the highest value that you can, for which you will earn your usual transaction fee. After that, since you all obviously disagree with my plans, I will no longer require your services." Cynthia could not help but smile ever so slightly.

"What?"

"You can't do that!"

"Our contracts are—"

"Your contracts were with my grandmother, gentlemen. I've read them. Carefully. Only her signature is on the documents. I was *not* consulted on these contracts when I came of age, so, with her death, they are meaningless." She balled her fists and leaned onto the table, narrowing her eyes at them. "I can consult the magistrate on this, but I think he may find that I am violating the law by allowing you to earn additional fees beyond the term of the contracts."

They glared at her for a moment, but she could see the realization in their eyes: they could not fight this. If they tried, she would revoke the fees they would earn in the restructuring. Before any of them could say anything further, the door opened and Koybur limped into the room.

"Sorry to interrupt, Ma'am," he said, nodding to the men. "I can come back if yer still busy here."

"No, Koybur, our business here is finished. These gentlemen were just leaving."

"Where would you like the money to be deposited, Mistress Flaxal?" one of the creditors asked. "Our accounts will be voided with the termination of our contracts."

"I will need to draw on the funds immediately. Deposit it in my name with Master Fergus; he holds a small account that we use to maintain the estate. I'll inform him of the changes."

They filed out of the room as if they were on their way to the gallows. When the door closed, Cynthia sat down and reached for her cup. The porcelain clattered with the tremors in her hand, but she felt good, as if a great wheel had finally started to turn within her. Mouse swooped down and landed on her wrist, blowing her a kiss before jumping off to attack her scone in earnest.

"Well, that was a dour bunch," Koybur said, taking one of the vacated seats and rescuing a scone and a cup before they could be removed by the serving girl.

"Leave that, Marcia," Cynthia said, "and bring up another cup and some more blackbrew. I've asked Master Keelson to meet us. He should be here shortly."

"So what's this you got brewin', lass? Them banker types were scowlin' like a bridegroom that finds out the in-laws are comin' to stay."

"Well, I can't blame them for scowling; I just fired them." Cynthia laughed at Koybur's expression. "Do me a favor and swallow before you leave your mouth hanging open like that, huh?"

"Oh. Sorry." He washed down the bite with a mouthful of blackbrew. "Why'd you go and fire them fellas, Cyn? They been keepin' your family's books fer longer than I can remember."

"I don't need them anymore, Koybur. I'm dumping everything they used to manage and putting it into the household account." She pulled the largest roll of parchment out of her satchel and laid it out for Koybur to see. "I'm going to need the money if I'm going to build four or five of these."

Mouse let out a whoop and danced a jig on the table.

"By Odea's scaly hide!" Koybur's one good eye widened until Cynthia feared it would pop out and roll across the table. His fingers brushed the drawings as if they were sacred. "Where did you get these, girl? They must-a cost you a perty penny, contractin' a draftsman and a naval architect."

"I didn't contract anyone, and they didn't cost me anything but the paper and ink. I drew these, Koybur. I know they're not that good, so don't try to flatter me with that bilgewater about an architect."

"They're not that good, eh?" Koybur took some quick measurements with a quill and twine and jotted down numbers. After a few minutes he looked at Cynthia with one narrowed eye and said, "Damn finest set of draft plans I've ever seen! I can't say as I've ever seen a ship quite like her. The rake of the masts is, well... Damn, but the strain would be taken up by the stays, so..." He foundered a bit, speechless for the first time Cynthia could remember. "If everything's as tight as these lines say, she'll be a fine vessel."

"We'll see what Master Keelson says," she replied, still suspicious that Koybur might be blowing sunshine up her skirts just to make her feel good. In truth, she hated to admit just how good his praise did make her feel.

"You really plan to do it then?"

"You thought I was kidding?"

"No, I—"

The door opened and three men entered: Brulo brought with him a large blackbrew service. Rowland bore a huge tray of scones, rolls and other delicacies. Master Keelson, the burly shipwright, brought with him only the aromas of sawdust, oil and creosote.

"What's all this?" Cynthia asked, eying Brulo suspiciously.

"Well, I never seen them four leave so early or so sour lookin', so I figured I'd come up and see if everything was a-right."

"And I figured the good Master Keelson might want a bit more to munch on." Rowland placed the huge tray on the table, and helped Brulo pour the blackbrew.

"And I," rumbled Keelson, drawn immediately to the detailed renderings of the new ship, "see exactly why I was called here." He ran his hands over the drawings carefully, fetching a pair of dividers from a pocket and taking measurements, muttering words like, "Interesting. Amazing. Why, I never thought to..."

"Actually, Master Keelson," Cynthia began, laying more paper onto the table, these covered with blank columns, "I need you and Koybur to advise me as to the seaworthiness of this design, and lay down some estimates on just how much building one will cost me. We should also go over what materials would be best, where to get them, and anything else you can think of."

"Well, don't go looking for a cook!" Rowland grinned, clapping her on the shoulder. "At least for one of 'em."

"Damn, girl, I've never even *seen* a design like this. I wouldn't know what to call it, let alone if it'd stand up to a gale!" Keelson leaned back, scratching his chin. "It looks stout enough, and would probably be a might faster than most cargo ships. But only one square rig? The main and fores'l are right *huge*, but I guess they'd reef down well enough. And that bowsprit, why it's half the length of the deck!"

"Oh, that's with it all the way out for medium to light winds." She pointed out the pins that would allow it to be retracted incrementally. "The forestays and bobstays are adjustable."

"Well, Holy Mother of Storms, they are!" Keelson scratched his chin some more, then shook his head. "I'd be happy to build it for ya, lass, but I think you need to bring in someone else to work out the specifics."

"But I thought you could—"

"Oh, I just build 'em, lass. I could work up some estimates as to how much it'd cost ya, but I don't *design* 'em. And this, like I said, is nothin' like I ever seen before. I know a feller who'd be tickled pink to have a look at these plans, though. He's half elvish, and he's been designin' and buildin' ships since before I was born."

"Where do I find him?"

"I'll send for him if you like. He lives up north, a little place called Dog Bay. Ain't even on most charts, 'cause there ain't no town, just him and his crew. His name's Ghelfan. He's the best there is 'round these parts, but the best don't come cheap."

"If you think he's the one we need, send for him." Cynthia recovered her pen and dipped it into the inkwell. "For now, let's work out how much this monstrosity is going to cost me."

"Now *that* I can help ya with!"

They started firing numbers at her so fast that she was hard pressed to keep up, and Rowland had brought them lunch and afternoon tea before all was said and done.

That evening a fast courier boat left Southaven and struck out up the coast. Two experienced sailors were the only crew, and they'd already been paid well for the trip they were making. If they returned in less than a fortnight with the man they sought, one half-elven shipwright named Ghelfan, they would earn a tidy bonus.

When the courier boat had cleared the breakwater and turned west, and the sun dipped below the horizon, another boat left Southaven. The little fishing smack had only one man aboard, bore no hooks, no line and no bait. His only cargo resided inside a tightly sealed scroll tube.

≈

"Messenger, Captain Bloodwind!"

The servant blundered into his master's private bath with no more preamble than those three words. He knew the intrusion would be forgiven under the circumstances, but the scene that greeted him stopped him dead in his tracks. The jingle of golden chains and the low groaning of his master's voice should have been warning enough, but his hurry was such that he stood only feet away before he thought to avert his eyes.

"Who is it from?" Bloodwind mumbled between grunts of pleasure, his face pressed against a rolled-up towel on the floor.

"Yodrin, Master." The servant tried not to look at the slave girl perched on his master's backside, kneading the heels of her hands into his back while another servant drizzled high-quality whale oil over him. The filmy gauze draped over the slave girl was soaked through with oil, sweat and the humidity of the steaming bath. "Do you wish me to break the seal, sir?"

"Yes, but stand over there to do it. Stop for a moment, Camilla, I want to watch this."

The golden-chained slave girl pushed herself up and stood there panting from exertion, her eyes carefully elsewhere. Bloodwind rolled up onto one elbow, his narrowed eyes centering on his servant.

The servant moved to the corner and twisted open the sealed tube, knowing that he was being used like a sacrificial goat, but preferring the relatively quick death of a trapped message to the agonizingly slow one that awaited him if he disobeyed.

"Fine, now bring it here."

The servant complied, handing over the scroll and risking one more glance at the slave girl while Bloodwind read.

"Efficient as ever, Master Yodrin. You earned your pay this fortnight." He handed the scroll back to the servant and said, "Burn it and crush the ashes."

As the servant's hand grasped the door latch, his master's parting comment stopped him.

"And if I ever catch you ogling my possessions again, I'll have you eating your own liver for supper."

"Yes, Master," he croaked miserably, knowing that the threat was not idle. He knew it because he'd seen worse first hand. Despite that, he thought it worth the risk and stole one more glance as he closed the door.

CHAPTER NINE
Guests and Conversation

"THIS IS STUPID!" CYNTHIA muttered as she shuffled up the steps to the light-keeper's tower. She had been up these steps before, years ago, when she was thirteen years old and terrorizing every inn, dock and merchant in Southaven. She had climbed the stairs on a dare, knocked on the old light-keeper's door and run away before the ill-tempered wizard could set her britches afire.

She doubted if the last nine years had improved his temper, or his opinion of the scurrilous girl who had knocked on his door so long ago, but here she stood ready to knock on that door once again. This time, however, there would be no running away. She was here because the lightkeeper was the only person within a seven-day sail who knew anything at all about magic.

As she raised her hand to knock, Mouse leapt off of her shoulder and flit-tered in front of her face waving his arms and shaking his head so fast that his face was a blur. He knew the old wizard's temper as well as any, and the lightkeeper was a firemage; nothing scared a seasprite like fire.

"Oh, so you don't want me to, huh?" She chuckled at the little sprite's mien of horror. He pushed against her chest, flapping his tattered wings madly, but Cynthia remained determined. "Don't worry, Mouse," she said with more conviction than she felt. "He won't hurt us."

She took a deep breath, and knocked firmly three times. At the third rap, however, her knuckles barely touched the wood as the door jerked open and a gnarled old hand grabbed her by the wrist.

"Gotcha! Now, you little rapscallion, you're gonna pay fer..."

"Ahhh!" Her scream escaped before she could control her voice.

Mouse let out a piercing "EEP!" of alarm and vanished down her collar.

"Why, you're not—" The old man's eyes flung wide in astonishment at what he had caught. The white wisps of his hair stuck out at all angles, as if he'd been sleeping or actively trying to pull it out. His lips were thin, and his skin a ruddy hue. He wore a leather jerkin over a once-white shirt and dark crimson pantaloons.

"Please, Master Lightkeeper," she pleaded, her wrist throbbing in his as-tonishing grip. "I mean no disrespect, but simply seek your advice. I'm will-ing to pay you for your time."

"You're not one of those blasted children who keep knocking on my door at all hours and running away!" he snapped accusatively, not releasing his grip. "Where are they? Where are you hiding them?"

"I'm not hiding anyone, sir," she said, regaining some of her composure and trying to ignore the tickle of Mouse wiggling around between her shoulder blades. "I've come seeking your advice about a magical book, but if all you're going to do is accuse me and hurt my wrist, I'll take my questions *and* my money elsewhere!" She jerked her wrist against his grip, to no avail.

"Oh, my goodness!" the wizened old man exclaimed, releasing her wrist as if her skin was on fire. "Oh, I'm so sorry, Miss! I thought you were one of those pestering little rascals from town up here to bother me. They've been doing it for years, you know, knocking and running away in the middle of the day or night, waking me or disturbing my work. It's all I can do to get one wink of sleep with all my aches and pains, you know, and with all their interruptions... Well, I'm quite beside myself, let me tell you."

"I'm sorry I startled you, Master Lightkeeper," she said, rubbing her bruised wrist. "But as I said, I'm not here playing pranks, at least not for the past eight or nine years. I'm here to ask you some questions about this book." She brought her father's log out of her satchel and showed him the ornate tome. "It was my father's, and it's got some kind of magical writing in it that gives me a headache whenever I try to read it."

"Oh, my goodness gracious!" His wrinkled old fingers reached out to within an inch of the volume, then drew back. "That's a seamage's log! Where ever did you come by that? Why, there hasn't been a seamage 'round these parts for fifteen years!"

"Well, nearly that. My father, Orin Flaxal, died at sea fourteen years ago in summer's second month, and my mother Peggy with him." She held the book up again for him to see. "This is one of the few things he left for me, and I've only just discovered it. I can't read a word of it, and I was hoping you might be able to help."

"Oh, my goodness indeed," he uttered in a much subdued voice, his eyes flickering from her face to the tome and back several times. "You must be little Cynthia, then! Well, you better come up. Discussing such weighty matters on the stoop is hardly appropriate."

The lightkeeper ushered her through the door, his manner much friendlier if somewhat cautious, especially of the book she held. He shied away from it as if it would burn him.

The interior of the light tower proved somewhat less wondrous than she imagined in all her childhood fantasies. They wound their way to a stair through a maze of barrels, crates, boxes and thick clay jars marked with dwarvish script, and began to climb. Past two more levels similarly festooned with unidentifiable containers, her legs burning from the climb, they came to a door that opened into a room sweltering with heat and cluttered with so many books, candles, lanterns and lamps that Cynthia thought she had stumbled into a cross between a library and a chandlery.

"Sit, sit, sit," the lightkeeper babbled, fluttering his wrinkled old hands. "There's a chair right over there, just put those old scrolls on the floor. Let me get something on the stove. Would you like blackbrew, tea, spiced cider, or maybe something a bit stronger? We've serious matters to discuss, Miss Cynthia. A spot of spiced rum in blackbrew's the best nerve tonic I know."

"It's barely mid morning," she said, shifting a stack of scrolls to the floor and sitting gently on the musty old chair. Mouse ventured out to her shoulder, his eyes wide with wonder at the room. This place had enough to keep him entertained for a month, but most of it had flame attached to it, which made him uncharacteristically cautious.

"What's the time of day got to do with anything?" The lightkeeper's blank stare caught Cynthia off guard once again. "And what's that thing on your shoulder, some kind of moth? I asked you if you wanted something to drink. I've got a swatter around here somewhere."

"Uh, no. That's Mouse, and he's a seasprite, not a moth. Sorry. Plain blackbrew's fine." His changes of subject were so quick she found it hard to keep up.

"Blackbrew it is, then!"

While pots and kettles clanked and clattered around the old iron stove, Cynthia took in her surroundings more fully, astounded at the variety of flame-producing implements cluttering the walls, shelves and floor. Some were quite beyond her comprehension, and most were alight, casting a hundred shades of light and waves of stifling heat through the room. She mopped the sweat from her neck and was wondering what a hand crank on the side of a lantern could be for, when a heavy tray clattered down in front of her bearing a silver blackbrew service, two porcelain cups and a small plate of lumpy little cookies.

"Shall I pour?"

"Uh, sure." Nothing out of his mouth seemed to make sense with the surroundings or her thoughts at the time, leaving her feeling a bit doltish. Mouse started flapping his wings at her neck, and the breeze felt refreshingly cool.

"Now, that book you bear's no common log book, I'm sure you're aware," he said, pouring blackbrew as dark as a moonless night first into her cup, then his. "That you've looked into it and still have a mind to think with is proof enough that you're his daughter, Cynthia." A silver flask materialized in his hand and stood poised over the lip of her cup. "Sure you won't have a touch of the cane squeezin's with that? You look a little flustered. It'll set you to rights, I guarantee."

"Well, I don't usually—"

"Atta girl!" His wrist bent and a measure of dark rum topped off her steaming cup. "That'll set a fire in you, by the forge of Phekkar." He poured a considerably larger measure of liquor into his own cup and sat, sipping noisily and smacking his lips. "Now, about this book of your father's; I'd be a liar twice over if I told you I had no interest in what he had written in those pages, but I'd be thrice a dolt if I tried to read any of it."

"You mean you can't read it either?" Mouse bounded down to the table and sniffed her cup inquisitively. "But I thought—"

"You thought magic's magic, and since I've got a bit flowin' through my veins, I might be able to help you with your father's log." He sipped again and took a deep breath. "Well, let me tell you about magic."

He snapped his gnarled old fingers and a ball of flame erupted from his hand for an instant, then vanished. Mouse let out an "EEP!" and scuttled down her collar again.

"Just because I can do that, doesn't mean I can read another mage's incantations. There are as many different types of mage as there are gods in the Seven Heavens and Nine Hells, not to mention the ones that lurk about the middle ground. Your father was a seamage, and though I knew him and called him friend, his and my magics were very different. If I tried to read a single word of that book, my mind would be fried like an oyster on a bed of coals."

"Then can you teach me how to read it? I've tried, but all I ever get is a headache."

"Well, now, you're alive and sane, which tells me that your ol' dad was right thinking that you had enough of his blood in your veins to make a seamage, but headaches are the only thing you're ever gonna get from that book Miss Cynthia. Unless, by some tragedy, you're still a virgin?"

"Well, I usually don't—"

"Of course you don't. Of course you don't. Not that it would really matter much, not with you having nigh on a score of summers behind you."

"Oh, you mean I'm too old?" Cynthia's knuckles blanched with her grip on her father's log. "His journal mentioned that seamages usually didn't get their powers past the age of twelve or so. There was something about Odea's requirements, how they become more dangerous as you grow older."

"That they do, Miss Cynthia. That they do. And let me tell you that the requirements of Phekkar are no picnic. I could show you some of my scars, but then I'd have to— But that's neither here nor there."

"Phekkar? But isn't he one of the evil gods?"

"Evil, schmeevil, boll weevil," he scoffed with a wave of his hand. "He's the God of Fire, the Flaming One, just like Odea's the Goddess of Sea and Storms. I daresay a sailor caught in a hurricane has called Odea evil once or twice. Are you sure you won't have one of these? I made them myself!" He lifted one of the little cookies and nibbled.

"Uh, no thank you. But I don't understand what Odea has to do with it. My father was a mage, not a priest."

"Well, now that's where the lines between magic and faith get a little blurry, Miss Cynthia. And that's where your father's and my magic were more alike than not. We were both what you would call elementalists, mages that focus on a particular element. Orin's element was the sea, and mine's fire. Other elementalists direct their energies toward earth or air—or life and death, for that matter. Now, there's mages that dabble in magic that's not directly tied to any element, and they can do tricks that no elementalist can. They learn all they need to know straight from books and have a more diverse skill, though less powerful in some regards. Elementalists get their power straight from the Gods themselves, but not like priests. We don't heal, curse or bless people, for instance. Well, most of us don't. We do have the ability to bend our elements to our own will, to shape them, you might say." He took another deep draught from his cup and sighed gustily.

"But your old dad was right about one thing, Miss Cynthia: Once a boy is a man—or a girl a woman, as is your case—there is about the same chance of them becoming an elementalist as there is of pigs taking up knitting."

The words stabbed like a lance through her heart. She'd expected this, but even so, the final refusal of her dream cut deeply. Reading her father's journal, Cynthia had hoped that maybe, just maybe, she might yet inherit her father's powers. She reached for her cup with shaky hands and gulped down the fiery liquid. She coughed against the scalding heat and stood.

"Thank you for the blackbrew, Master Lightkeeper," she said, grateful that the drink helped to burn away the persistent lump in her throat. "I'm sorry I disturbed you for nothing."

"Nothing? Oh, I wouldn't call this nothing, Miss Cynthia!" He stood and smiled at her amiably, oblivious to the fact that she fought back tears. "As I said, I knew your father, and called him friend. I'd be more than happy to sit and talk with you about him any time. I don't get many visitors, and my hospitality is probably a little rusty, but mayhap I know a few things about him that your grandmother never told you, rest her soul."

"Perhaps another time, Master Lightkeeper. I—" She turned away and moved toward the door, the light from a hundred lanterns blurring in her misted vision. "I really should be going now."

"Oh, very well then. Let me show you out." He moved to the door.

Mouse flittered from her shoulder to the table, nabbed a cookie and returned, his little features confused at all the talk about gods and magic. Cynthia patted the little sprite, envious despite his tattered wings; as a magical creature, he would never know why not having magic of her own would make her cry.

≈

"Haul away!" Bloodwind bellowed, raising a tankard of dark rum in toast as the man in front of him left the deck with a strangled gasp. "Send the brave captain up to join his crew!"

The crowd of drunken pirates cheered their approval as the captain of the captured galleon kicked and struggled vainly, finally stilling to an occasional twitch. He hung beside eleven of his crew from the main yard of his own ship, all dead, all captured in their sleep and paying the ultimate price for their lack of vigilance.

"And now to see to our guests!" That brought another roar from the crowd and a bustle of activity as four figures were ushered forward. Two were women, one in expensive clothes, and another less extravagantly dressed, who clung to two young children, a girl and a boy. The finely dressed woman glared at him, obviously afraid but covering it well; attractive enough, if somewhat severe, laced tightly into her finery as if it were armor.

Bloodwind ignored her and knelt before the children, grinning broadly. "And who might you two be?"

"My husband, Count Norris, will pay whatever you ask for our safe return."

"If she speaks again without being told to, cut out her tongue." Bloodwind said without looking at her. Her gasp of horror told him that someone had produced a knife and a pair of pliers. He grinned at the children, but was again interrupted, this time by the distant call of a horn giving three long blasts. He stood and looked up at the peak of Plume Isle and saw the flag signal; a vessel approached, a friendly one.

"Find out who approaches," he told a cabin boy, who ran off as fast as he could.

"So, where were we?" he began again with the children. "What's your names, then?

"I'm Samantha," the girl said through her tears, "that's Timmy."

"Timothy!" the boy corrected with a glare at his sister. "My name's Timothy!"

"Well, there you are! Well said, Timothy." He clapped the boy on the shoulder.

"Please, sir! They're just children!" The maid knelt, bowing her head and clutching the children with white-knuckled fists. "Please don't kill them!"

"Kill them? Why would I do such a thing?" He tousled the boy's hair and grinned. "Why I'd sooner pluck out my own eye than harm a hair on their heads. This boy's got potential, and the girl's got more fire than a volcano. They'll make fine additions to our family."

"Your family? But I..."

"You're a servant, I'll wager." he said to the woman, his tone neutral.

"Yes."

"Hired or indentured?"

"I've served Count Norris all my life, as my father and mother did before me," she said, as if it were something to be proud about.

"You're a slave, then. Well, let me tell you something that might just surprise you: as soon as this ship entered Blood Bay, your slavery ended. You're a free woman now, free to seek employment anywhere on my island, and let me assure you that there is much work to be done." He wouldn't elaborate on exactly what *kind* of work could be had, but she'd find out soon enough. He grinned down at the two kids as the servant woman stared in shock. "The children are ours now, and they'll grow up under our protection and learn our ways. What do you say to that Tim? How would you like to be a real pirate? And you, too, Samantha, though we'll be callin' you Sam, I'm sure. I've many a woman crew on my ships, and even an officer or two."

The two children stared at him in shock. "A pirate?" the boy squeaked, eyes as big as hen's eggs.

"What choice do they have?" the servant woman put in, her face unreadable. "You won't let any of us leave here, ever."

"Aye, and that's the rub, ain't it?" He turned once again to the finely dressed woman who stood now crying in silence. "And that's why I don't *ever* ransom out prisoners. You'll spend the rest of your days here, or die. That's the choice you've got to make," he turned back to the servant woman, "all of you."

Silence reigned for several breaths before the servant woman said, "If I'm truly free, then I choose to live, Captain. And if you're a man of your word, I'll be free to walk off this ship and into that town and look for honest work."

"Well said! Well spoken!" He nodded to his men. "She's free to go, so long as she stays on the island."

With that, and to no one's surprise—except, of course, her noble-born mistress and the two stunned children—the servant woman released her grip on her charges and walked off the ship. The young girl whimpered a plea as her fingers were torn free from the woman's skirts, but the servant never looked back.

"Captain Rufio!"

"Aye, Captain!" The captain of the *Black Cloud* ambled forward, a tankard in one hand, the other resting on the saber at his hip.

"As part of your bonus, if you want her, I give you this woman." He nodded toward the glowering captive. "She's got fire in her, that's plain to see, but enough brains to keep her mouth shut when needs be. Keep her, sell her or give her away, I don't care. Just don't let her leave the island."

"Aye, sir!" He stepped forward and hoisted the struggling woman over his broad shoulder amid the cheers of the crowd. "Mayhap I'll see if she's got any more like these two yet in her!"

"A fine plan!" Bloodwind commended, clapping the woman on the rump as Rufio hauled her off.

He turned to the children once again, and he could see in their eyes that he had already won. They had nobody left. Only Captain Bloodwind remained, and he had promised to care for them. He'd done this hundreds of times, and the result of his successes surrounded him, for fully half of his pirate nation had once been lost children, and he their only parent left in the world. They were his family, his blood and his strength.

"So now we've got two new members of our family to welcome properly, my mates!" He hoisted the dumbstruck children into his arms and thrust them up for everyone to see. "These here are Tim and Sam. They are ours, and we are theirs. Welcome them properly."

The crowd roared, and he felt the surge of excitement, fear and wonder shudder through the children. He handed them over to two able men, knowing they would be treated properly. In three or four days, with no sleep and nothing but alcohol in them, they would be ready to swear their lives to him.

Now to business, he thought, leaving the roaring throng by way of the gangplank. As his boots clacked up the stonework quay, the boy he'd sent to scout out the approaching ship ran down to meet him.

"It's a catboat, sir!" He panted and grabbed his cramping stomach; running to the top of the south point and back so quickly had left him gasping for breath. "A messenger boat. Looks like the one what works the south coast."

"Well done, Raff!" He tossed the boy a copper, which vanished before it reached the apex of its arc. "Off with you then!"

"Aye, sir!" The boy disappeared into the throng aboard the galleon.

Bloodwind stepped out onto the long pier and strode casually to its end. He let himself wonder what news the boat might bring. His plans in Southaven were tenuous, like picking a pup from a litter of wild dogs: If you picked the right pup, it might serve you well. The wrong one could become a danger, and would have to be killed before it killed you first. But that was something at which Bloodwind was expert—killing first.

The crack of canvas snapped his musing, bringing his eyes up to the small craft as it emerged from the giant mangroves.

The catboat tacked cleanly, cutting through the turquoise water like a saber through yielding flesh. She beat a line straight for the pier, slipping downwind slightly at a perfectly calculated angle. He truly loved to watch these small boats in action—so nimble, so fast and responsive to every adjustment of the tiller. If only he could have a corsair with such responsive agility, there would not be a safe galleon on the Southern Ocean.

When the catboat was three lengths away, he extended his hand, smiling thinly at the man at the tiller. The boat was single handed, her master manning the tiller and sheeting lines simultaneously.

At the last possible moment, the tiller snapped across the cockpit and the man let go the two sheeting lines. The craft rounded up in a heartbeat and, for an instant, stood perfectly still. The helmsman took skilled advantage of that instant of calm, snatching up a small tube and stepping up onto the gunwale of the boat to hand over the scroll case. He was seated again before the craft began to drift, and he sheeted in the sail and darted off downwind.

Bloodwind stared after the small boat, marveling once again at its agility. Finally he noticed the heavy scroll case in his hand. Belaying his usual caution, he cracked the wax seal with his thumbnail, his mind still half occupied with the beauty and grace of the small catboat. His first glance at the parchment made him wonder if he was hallucinating, or if some bewitchment had been cast on the scroll in his hand. He blinked and shook his head, then he focused more closely, and he saw that he held the plans of a ship, a ship like none he had ever seen. For an instant he saw the nimble catboat jibe before the wind, agile and quick, then saw the ship in his hands jibe the same way, her great mainsail sweeping across the deck, the sheeting lines taking the strain of the huge gaff sail as she filled.

"Odea's scaly hide," he muttered beneath his breath, staring at the rough sketches. They were not proper plans, nothing he could use to build a ship, but he could see the power in the design. Any true sailor could. It was as if a smaller boat had grown, gaining the power and strength of a galleon while keeping the agility and grace of the tiny catboat.

"This is it!" he proclaimed to no one in particular. "This is what I've been waiting for." He looked at the plans more thoroughly, fighting the stiff breeze for possession of the priceless parchment. "This is the ship that will bring me the entire Southern Ocean!"

CHAPTER TEN
Flotsam and Dreams

WIND TORE AT THE shutters of the Galloping Starfish as if all the demons of the Nine Hells were trying to rip them free. The hiss of rain rose and fell with the gusts of the last storm of the season, a storm proving to be more than just a late squall. Old Kurian, the local priest of Odea, had warned of its arrival, so Southaven was lashed down tighter than a spinster's corset. There was nothing left to do but sit in the Starfish and drink spiced rum.

Cynthia chose to ride the storm out here rather than up on the hill. Good company, good liquor and good conversation were helping the storm pass quickly, while Mouse did his best to enliven the room with impromptu merriment. He wobbled around, perching on tankards and glasses, stealing sips of rum, ale or spiced wine. The more he drank the straighter he flew, and the better he danced when the sailors joined in and struck up their pipes and fiddles. The music and lively tales were distracting her from her woes, for it had been more than three weeks since the messenger left to fetch the half elven shipwright, and still no word had arrived.

When the door of the tavern slammed open everyone jumped, thinking that the storm had finally won its fight with Brulo's shutters. The gust sent Mouse right into a serving girl's tray of tankards, but she just plucked him from a pot of ale and handed him over to Cynthia.

A tall figure in a sodden slicker stepped into the light, braced himself against the door and pushed it closed against the driving wind. When the latch clicked home, he turned and stopped, every eye in the tavern on him. Only the foolish or insane ventured out in a hurricane; everyone was interested to know whether an idiot or a lunatic stood before them. Several began formulating opinions as he dropped a huge waxed canvas satchel, doffed his hat and bowed gracefully.

"My apologies for the mistreatment of your door, Master Innkeeper," the man said, divesting himself of his dripping outer garments and hanging them on pegs. He shook his head, his long, flaxen hair shedding water in a halo of tiny droplets. "I but touched the latch and the wind snatched the handle from my grasp like an eagle plucking a trout from a stream." He bent to pick up his satchel, but stopped when he realized everyone was still staring at him. "If the wood was damaged by my lapse, I will happily pay for its repair."

"Yer pardon, sir," Brulo said, rounding the bar to greet the newcomer.

"We rarely get visitors in weather such as this. Come in and have a seat by the fire. Why, the roads must be a bog in this rain." He ushered the stranger to the hearth, calling for one of the maids to fetch a towel.

"They probably are, but to that fact I cannot attest. The only road my feet have trod this day was the one from the pier to this door, and it, as you undoubtedly know, is cobbled."

"You came in on a *ship*?" one of the sailors asked, his tone skeptical.

"No ship, sir, for the *Flothrindel* is barely thirty cubits from stem to stern, and is but a wisp of flotsam alongside the great galleons that crowd your fair harbor."

"Out in a blow like this in a scrap of kindling not much bigger than a fishing smack? You must be daft, man!"

"Would that I had the prescience of wind and wave that is found in the priests of Odea. We were caught unawares by the weather as we came through the Shattered Isles. The entrance at Scarport was untenable with the wind direction, so we reefed thrice and made for deep water, then tacked for our destination when the wind shifted with the passage of the storm. It was a close reach into the harbor, but the waves were not so high as they may have been." He bowed as someone thrust a cup into his hand, breathing deeply of the steaming vapors wafting from its lip.

"You say yer destination was Southaven," Koybur said, his one good eye still appraising the slim man. "What business is so important as to bring you here in such weather?"

"I come here at the behest of one of your local shipwrights, one Morris Keelson. He sent me some designs that I found—"

"*You're* Ghelfan?" Cynthia lurched to her feet, her outburst catching the man off guard. "But it's been near a month since we sent word! Did something happen? Is the messenger boat all right?"

"Ah, and you must be Cynthia Flaxal. I am indeed Kloetesh Ghelfan, and I am at your service, lady." With this he bowed low, took Cynthia's hand and embarrassed her by kissing it. Mouse lit on her shoulder and giggled in her ear, pointing at the display.

"My apologies for the delay, but the messenger boat did come into some weather of its own, and was somewhat damaged. The crew is quite fine, but I took their small craft up for repairs before I put to sea. We sailed with all haste, and *Flothrindel* is a speedy craft, but this storm did delay us somewhat."

"I, uh... Well... Nice to meet you." Mouse tugged at her earlobe and giggled again.

"The pleasure is entirely mine, lady, for your designs have stirred a fire in me that I thought quenched fifty years ago. I would know where you came upon such a radical marriage of dhow, gaff-sloop and traditional square rig, unless you hold the impetus of your genius too dear to divulge."

"Uh, well, I've been working on the sketches for some time." Cynthia covered her embarrassment with a sip from her cup. "I thought that a ship needed to be faster, kinder to her crew, and sail closer to the wind. I've watched the different ships in the harbor for years; each had their own strong points. I put them together, that's all."

"That is, indeed, all. All that will change the way ships are built for the next half millennia." He reached for his satchel and withdrew a long chart case. "I took the liberty of making some notes and adjustments to the rigging specifications that, with your approval, I think will work well with your design." He looked around at the crowd and smiled thinly. "Perhaps a private room would be more conducive to our needs."

"Right away on that!" Brulo said, ushering the newcomer, Cynthia and Koybur away from the curious throng. Mouse danced a jig on her shoulder and stuck his tongue out at the scowling sailors as they climbed the stairs.

≈

Cynthia's breath caught at her first glimpse of the renderings that Ghelfan had made from her comparatively rough drawings. Art finer than any she'd seen spread across the table in sheets of fine cotton parchment. Ink of three colors graced the pages in precise lines and script. Footnotes explained every minute detail in flowing characters whose beauty left her eyes watering.

"Unbelievable!" she whispered, her fingers brushing the beautiful pages. Mouse trundled down her arm to land on the parchment, but she snatched him up and put him on her shoulder. "No, Mouse. No sprite footprints on these, my little friend." He sulked, but stayed put.

"I see you have the amity of a seasprite, lady. That is surely a sign from Odea that this venture is blessed."

"Mouse has been with my family for longer than I've been alive, Master Ghelfan. Whether it's a sign from Odea, or just that he likes me, I have no idea."

"Well, I welcome the presence of Master Mouse," he said, nodding at the sprite, who puffed up and sketched a sweeping bow. "And as to these plans, I must make my apologies for any liberties I have taken with your creation."

"No apology necessary," she assured him, noting for the first time that his eyes had a slight upturn, and his ears a faint point. His elven blood was disguised, but still detectable. "These are beautiful."

"Ah, the beauty is in the design itself, lady. I have but traced the lines and jotted a few crude notes." He pointed to some of his changes and their accompanying footnotes. "The design is sound, and can be put out with only slight modifications. Her profile is low, so she'll ship seas in heavy weather, but the rig can be managed by fewer crew, and in a blow, once the fore tops'l yards are housed, no one need go aloft to reef. A kinder vessel indeed, and I estimate she will sail two points closer to the wind than any galleon. That is all to the good."

He paused, and took a deep breath. "The stresses invoked by so much sail area require some modifications. Most can be taken into account with some reinforcing measures; for example, the shrouds and stays will be made of wire-rope, tensioned with triple deadeyes, and affixed to the hull by bronze chain plates."

"Won't that put too much weight aloft?" Koybur asked.

"The weight is more than made up for by strength, and this rig will need the strength. Spar and gaff ends will be whipped with chord and lacquered to handle the added load. Gaff jaws and blocks will all be reinforced with bronze. The keels can be shaped and laid immediately. Your notion of lowering the center of mass by using laminated beams inlaid with lead is masterful, lady. It will require a bit of labor, but the savings in ballast space will make up for the expense. The hulls will be cross-planked as you suggest, and those materials are fine."

"Good. Most of it's already ordered and should be here in a few days, except for the spars, of course."

"Very good, lady." He smiled at her, and she thought her cheeks would catch fire. "Now, this adjustable bowsprit design. Absolute genius. The rake of the masts can be altered with only minimal tuning of shrouds and stays, and could be done underway to adjust weather helm. I've taken the liberty of redesigning the block systems for tightening the fore, thwart and bob-stays." He leaned back with his hands on his narrow hips and grinned like a kid with a new toy. "With any luck at all, the hulls will be roughed in before winter solstice, framed, planked and decked by the spring equinox and in the water by the first of storm season."

"That's fast work," Keelson said from the door, his hair and beard dripping from the stormy trek up to the inn. "Especially since you don't know my crew."

"Master Keelson, I presume." Ghelfan bowed low. "Know that your messengers are well and that their vessel is being repaired in my yard. They will be back, I am sure, by month-end, and will bring a few indispensable members of my own crew. I know you only by reputation, sir, but that is a good reputation, and I do not think I am overestimating the abilities of your people, or your yard."

"Well, now I don't know about takin' on any of your people here, Master Ghelfan. I was under the impression that the lady here was just to contract you for some modifications to the design." He rubbed his jaw and approached the table, his eyes widening as they took in the artful renderings. "Modifications that I see you've nary well completed before any agreement as to your fee!"

"As to your fee, Master Ghelfan," Cynthia said, cognizant of her ever-dwindling funds, "I realize that you are accustomed to contracts with some of the largest shipping firms on the—"

"Please, lady," Ghelfan said, palms raised and head bowed, "an endeavor that may very well change shipbuilding for centuries cannot be demeaned by attaching a price. Let us just say that—"

"Let us just say that I will have a contract drawn up tomorrow that will reflect our discussion regarding your fee for services from this time forward." Cynthia stepped back from the table, tearing her eyes from the beautiful plans that she suddenly realized might never come to fruition. "Forgive me, Master Ghelfan, but you must know a few things about me before this entire undertaking is ruined by a misunderstanding."

"Please, lady. I wish there to be nothing but clarity between us."

"Good." Cynthia steeled her nerves and tried to banish the buzzing in her ears, the product of adrenalin and too much rum. "While it is true that I am young and have only recently come into control of my family's business, I am neither dim of wit nor particularly deep of pocket. My grandmother spent the last fifteen years trying to destroy our shipping business, and nearly succeeded in ruining us financially. I have consolidated my holdings into a tidy sum of ready capital that *should* be enough to float two, maybe three of those." She nodded toward the parchment-littered table. "Do not tell me that money is of no matter. We will discuss your fee, sir, or we have nothing further to discuss, so name a figure."

"Nothing."

Three pairs of eyes blinked in unison. Mouse slapped his knee and giggled incoherently, flopping onto his back, kicking his heels in the air and rolling right off her shoulder.

"Excuse me?" Cynthia said, blinking again when Mouse's mirth ended as sprite met floor. "You can't be serious."

"I will take no money from you for my own or my crew's services for the design modifications and assistance in the construction of these vessels."

He looked from one face to the next and smiled. "You must understand that my association with this project is more valuable to me than any sum you could pay." At their mystified looks he elaborated.

"You see this as a family venture, a few new ships, two or three for a start, perhaps as many as a dozen later, maybe even more. I see this as a chance to place my name among those of the greatest naval architects of history. I merely wish to ride your coattails, as it were, Mistress Flaxal. When you no longer need or wish to use these plans, I want the right to modify them as I see fit and produce like vessels for other shipping interests all around the world."

"But that won't be for years," Cynthia said, flabbergasted by the notion. "Decades! As I said, Master Ghelfan, I'm young, and I plan to produce a fleet of these ships if they prove to be as profitable as I think they will be."

"I have been building ships for a hundred and a half years, lady, and when your children are old and gray, I will still be building ships." His almond eyes narrowed with his smile, and he somehow looked different, as if he had grown taller, or become a thing chiseled from alabaster. "I can afford to take the long view in this. We can draw up any contract you wish, and set any time limit or other constraints you deem fair."

"Well, I— uh." Cynthia looked to the other men for support. Keelson shrugged, and Koybur looked as bewildered as she felt. "I can't imagine keeping the plans secret for too long. I mean, someone will eventually copy them." She bit her lip while everyone stared expectantly at her. "Shall we say that fifty years hence you have the right to do with the plans as you wish, excepting to sell them outright, and that I, or my surviving family, retains the right to use them for our own purposes regardless and forever?"

"Wise, fair, and totally agreeable, lady." Ghelfan bowed again. "You may have a scribe draw up a contract, and I will sign it."

Mouse whooped, flew up to the shipwright's shoulder, tweaked his pointed ear and clapped him on the neck. Ghelfan smiled at the sprite's antics and nodded to the rest of them.

"So, I daresay, we have a good deal to discuss regarding these hulls, do we not, Master Keelson?"

"Aye to that, Master Ghelfan, we do indeed." The door creaked, and the old shipwright accepted a warm towel from a maid who bore several. Rowland entered with a platter of pastries, cold meats, cheeses and a pot of steaming blackbrew, and placed the entire array out around the plans. He couldn't help but gape at them, however, and smiled at Cynthia, proud of her accomplishment. Careful to avoid dripping on the plans, Keelson bent forward to examine the points of structural modification.

"Now, these joints that support that monstrosity of a bowsprit the girl's dreamt up. I dunno if they're stout enough fer the strain..."

The conversation quickly devolved into discussions about joints, planking, framing, resins, different woods, and even what type of nails and bolts would be used. In less than an hour Cynthia found herself sitting in an armchair watching the men pick apart her designs to the last sheave, bitt and belaying pin, feeling simultaneously bored, excited and put out that the subject matter had so suddenly gone beyond her.

"Why so sour-faced, lass?" Koybur eased his maimed frame into the chair beside her and gave her his best lop-sided smile. "I imagined you'd be chompin' at the bit like a stallion in a draft harness right now."

"Oh, I am." She shrugged and sipped at her cup, pursing her lips and scowling. "I just didn't think it would be taken out of my hands so quickly. I'm feeling a bit like a fourth wheel on a three-wheeled cart, if you know what I mean."

"How so, lady?" Ghelfan stood before her, a puzzled look marring his graceful features. "You are the driving force behind this entire endeavor."

"There just doesn't seem much left for me to do." She shrugged again and sighed.

The three men looked at one another, exchanging smiles that only annoyed her, as if they knew some private joke of which she was the butt.

"What's so entertaining?"

"Your pardon, lady," Ghelfan smiled apologetically, "but our work is all lying upon that table. Your labor, as I see it, is much more difficult, and will involve quite a bit of travel and many of the skills that we do not possess."

"What are you talking about? I don't know anything about building ships."

"Aye, but you know about people and business, lass," Koybur countered. "And you know more about sailors than anyone here but me. You've also got that 'innocent-as-a-yearling-lamb' look about you that's more dangerous than any pirate in the Shattered Isles."

"I what?"

"He's got ye there, lassie," Keelson said with a grin.

"What Master Koybur is saying," Ghelfan added with a nod, "is that these ships will need crews and officers, and that you are the obvious one to hire them."

"Me?" She looked to Koybur, ignoring his horrific grin. "But I thought that you would just hire from around here. You already do the hiring for the other ships."

"No, and fer two reasons, lass. First, I only hired fer yer gram because she had no taste or talent for it. Second, you'll want to hire the best, and you don't have enough to choose from here to find it. We'll have to go further than Scarport or even Rock Harbor, I'd guess. Probably up to Tsing or south to Vonja."

"And third," Keelson put in, "it'll keep your nose out of my business for a few months!"

They all laughed, and Cynthia found herself smiling at the prospect of a sea voyage, her first since the one that had cost her parents their lives. "*Winter Gale's* still on the dry. As soon as she's refitted, we could take her north!"

Mouse whooped with glee and did a back flip on her shoulder.

"Could?" Koybur scowled at her and chucked her on the shoulder. "That's no way fer a Mistress of Ships to talk, lass!"

"Fine then!" She vaulted to her feet and strode for the door, barking orders all the way. "I want *Winter Gale* back in the water and a cargo ready to fill her holds in three days. Inform Captain Uben that we'll be sailing north to Tsing, but will stop in every decent port along the way to hire crew for my new ships." At the door, she turned and scowled, unaware that Mouse stood on her shoulder wagging a finger at them, ruining the effect.

"And tell him that he'll need berthing space for two passengers, and as many as six on the return trip. You got all that, Koybur?"

"Yes, Ma'am." He pushed himself to his feet and managed a stiff bow.

"Good." She tried unsuccessfully to suppress a smile, muttering, "I'll show you 'innocent as a yearling lamb'." Her eyes flashed at their poorly-hidden amusement. "Don't you three have shipwright things to discuss?"

"Yes, Ma'am," they all chimed together, bowing as one.

"I thought so. Make a list of anything that needs my attention, and I'll have a look at it in the morning. Goodnight, gentlemen."

"Goodnight, Ma'am."

Cynthia closed the door and grinned openly at the thought of going to sea in one of her own ships. "My ships," she said softly, and Mouse kissed her noisily on the ear. For the first time she understood all that those words meant. It was really going to happen. Her dream, living for so long only in her mind, would come true.

CHAPTER ELEVEN

Voyage

"LEAVING?" BLOODWIND JERKED THE golden chain, dragging his gilded slave up the slime-covered steps to Hydra's scrying pool. "What do you mean, crone? Why would she be leaving, and where in the name of Odea's scaly hide would she be going?"

He leaned close, peering into the bloody seawater as her clawed nails stirred its surface. The wavering image of a beamy galleon easing away from the Southaven quay drifted in the murk; a slim woman in a blousy shirt and blue skirt stood at the taffrail, gazing up as the mizzen and topsails unfurled.

"You're sure that's not some captain's trollop?"

"This is the one, my captain." She stirred the bloody water, willing the image nearer to show the woman's sandy-blond hair and, as she turned, her face. "This is the spawn of the seamage whom you destroyed. This is the get of Orin Flaxal."

"Flaxal?"

Bloodwind's attention snapped from the young woman's image to the wide eyes of his slave. He jerked the chain savagely, snapping her attention away from the pool.

"You will keep silent, Camilla," he said, pulling her close enough that Hydra could taste the girl's delectable scent on her tongue. "And you will keep that name a secret, or I will feed you to Hydra one piece at a time!"

Hydra licked her lips, but knew the threat was empty. He prized the girl too much to sacrifice her for such a transgression, but he could not let the name of Flaxal become known to the rank and file of his pirate nation. No emperor's navy had sunk more corsairs than Orin Flaxal. Only a select few knew that the line of Flaxal had not been completely destroyed.

The girl averted her eyes, submissive and silent, but her gaze slid back to the wavering image of the woman on the ship as Bloodwind's attention was diverted.

"Which direction will they sail, Hydra?" he asked the sorceress.

"They will sail to the north, my captain. The hold is loaded with teak-wood and spices; these cargos hold no value south of the Shattered Isles."

"Why would she leave when the keels of her ships are just being laid?" Bloodwind stepped back from the pool, tugging absently at both his beard and the golden chain. "What does she seek from the north?"

"I know not, my captain." Hydra slumped against the edge of the scrying pool, her breath coming in a rattling hiss. "I can follow the progress of the *Winter Gale*, but I will require sustenance before I wield such power."

"Keep your eyes on that ship, Hydra. I'll bring you what you need." Golden chains rattled as he pulled his slave out of her domain. "But fail me, and I'll lock you down here to starve."

"I will not fail you," she said as the thick oaken door slammed closed. Her black nails raked furrows in the stone of the pool's pedestal as her rattling breath evolved into a wet-throated hiss. "My *captain*."

≈

Cynthia gripped the taffrail with bridled exhilaration as the rocks of Southaven's breakwater passed abeam of the *Winter Gale*. The heavily laden galleon rounded the point and began her rolling, roaring way, splitting the great swells of the Southern Ocean. This felt nothing like cutting through the tiny chop of the harbor in Koybur's little boat.

She looked up at the rig, at the men scrambling over the yards. The entire vessel heeled sharply as canvas cracked, filled and was sheeted home. Cynthia clenched the rail with renewed vigor, this time to keep herself from falling. She had watched ships at sea since she was old enough to hold up a spyglass, but never realized just how much everything *moved*.

Mouse wasn't helping matters by flitting and fluttering around her like a moth about a flame. He had not been to sea since the day of his tragic encounter with the business end of a broom. With his damaged wings he had to be careful not to get blown away, but he could not resist flitting around his mistress, doing tricks and hanging onto her hair.

"How are ya likin' it?"

She turned her attention to Koybur, and then back to her surroundings as a great swell grasped the ship like a toy, pushing it forward in a rolling, pitching, corkscrew motion.

"I don't know yet, Koybur." She stared at him in wonder, standing with his one good hand on the aft stay, puffing on his pipe. He looked so relaxed, as if part of the ship. She tried to emulate his easy stance, grateful that her skirts covered her shaking knees. "Trying to get my sea legs, I guess."

"Takes longer with some than others. Don't worry if you don't feel quite right. It'll pass."

"I hope it passes sooner rather than later." She tried to look beyond the rolling deck, away from the men scrambling up and down the rigging, piling on even *more* sail. "If it doesn't, I'm not going to be much of a—"

"Mistress Flaxal!"

Her eyes jerked from the horizon to the burly captain of the *Winter Gale* as he strode across the poop deck without even bracing himself. If Koybur looked to be *part* of the ship, then Captain Uben surely *was* the ship. He stood before her, hands on hips, swaying perfectly with the motion of the vessel.

"Yes, Captain Uben?" She concentrated on meeting his steely gaze, pushing down the rising discomfort in her stomach with a forceful swallow.

"I'll have a word with ye, if I may, regarding this little excursion."

"Of course." She turned to face him more fully, bracing her backside against the rail, her back to the rolling swells. "There's no problem, I hope."

"Meanin' no insult, Mistress, but you bein' here's already a problem. My officers have been displaced to crew's quarters, which are overcrowded; we left port early, which didn't give the crew time to spend their pay properly; and, well, I'm nary too comfortable in havin' the owner of the *Winter Gale* aboard."

"Let me assure you, Captain, I have no intention of—"

"What you intend is of little import, Mistress," he interrupted, his eyes narrowing at her. "And while I respect what you are tryin' to do, I've got to clear up a sore point. The *Winter Gale* is *my* ship, Mistress Flaxal. She may belong to you when she's inshore, and I appreciate the money you put into her this last fortnight, but when she's on the sea, she's my ship, hull and sticks. If you can't agree to that, then you better just fire me now and find yerself a new captain."

"As I was saying, Captain, I have no intention of telling you how to run your ship while she's at sea. I have no experience, and it would be ludicrous for me to advise you." She tried to smile disarmingly, but was worried that she only achieved a grimace. "In fact, I would appreciate very much if *you* would advise *me*. Our trip will take weeks, if not months. In that time I need to learn as much as I can about how my business is *really* run. I know we'll lose time by ducking into harbors where we will not be trading goods, but the loss on the cargo is mine. You and your crew will receive full sea pay for every day we are ashore trying to hire crew for my new ships."

"Well!" His stern mien suddenly split into a grin. "That'll keep the grumblin' down to a mumble. Thank'e fer yer time, Mistress." He tipped the brim of his cap and returned to the quarterdeck with an easy rolling gait.

"That was well done," Koybur said, his tone low as he joined her at the rail. "He'll give you no trouble from now on, but pickin' up the crew's tickets while we're ashore could cost you a pretty penny."

"No choice," she said, turning back to fix her gaze on the horizon. "If I didn't, we'd have a mutiny on our hands in a month."

"Oh, I don't think that'd happen, but you'll have a happier crew for it." He looked at her sidelong, squinting at her pale face and white-knuckled grip. "You feeling okay, lass?"

"No, Koybur. I'm feeling like— like I'm going to—"

The sea finally had its way, and Cynthia retched unceremoniously over the rail. Koybur kept a hand on her back, steadying her, and offered what encouragement he could while Mouse peeked over her shoulder and made a face. When she was finished, Koybur offered her a handkerchief.

"I think I should go below," she said, steadying herself on shaky knees.

"That'll only make it worse, lass. You'd best stay up on deck, maybe amidships where the motion's less, or take a turn at the wheel. That usually helps ship's sickness more than anything."

"And have the whole crew laughing at me? No, thank you. I'd rather be sick than have them all watch me try not to be sick." Mouse flitted to Koybur's shoulder, frowning at her condition. He clearly didn't want to go below, but he didn't want to leave her either. "Stay up on deck, Mouse, but have a care. Don't get blown away."

"Well, suit yourself. It should pass in a day or two, anyway." Koybur offered his good arm for support. "Here, let me help you down the steps."

She managed to get to her cabin without retching again, but it wasn't long before she sat heaving into a pail between her knees, wondering how fulfilling a dream could feel so awful.

≈

The sun had just passed its zenith when a small fishing smack rounded the last turn into Blood Bay and cut a line straight for the stone quay. The lookouts had done their job, and Bloodwind stood waiting, a scowl creasing his features. He had no idea why the Flaxal wench had left Southaven, which left him impotent to respond to the unexpected move. Everyone knew Bloodwind's foul moods, and avoided him like they would a hungry shark.

The slave girl Camilla would have been a convenient outlet for his temper, but she was the only person on his island at least partially immune to his rages. Bloodwind valued her in ways that had nothing to do with slavery, or even his unbridled lust. He had long practice in breaking the psyches of children he recruited into his pirate nation, but Camilla had never broken, had never been seduced by his promises of riches or comfort. He valued that strength above all else, so his temper found other targets.

Bloodwind watched the boat's approach, too preoccupied with his own fuming anger to appreciate the pilot's skill. The little craft rounded up into the wind, and drifted right up to the dock. The pilot threw a loose mooring line over the rusty iron bollard and stepped ashore.

"From Southaven, Captain," he said, extending a wax-sealed tube to Bloodwind with a flourish.

Bloodwind stood looking at the scroll case with trepidation and a tight smile. His desire to read the contents tempered by his usual caution, he told the messenger, "Open it."

The man's smile faded, but he cracked the seal with a thumbnail and handed it over. A single rolled parchment fell into Bloodwind's open hand as he up-ended the tube. The pirate captain ignored the messenger's discomfort as he unrolled the scroll to read.

Bloodwind:

The Flaxal girl leaves on the Winter Gale *by the time you receive this note. She is bound west and then north in search of crew and officers to man the two new vessels that are being constructed. Her first port of call will be Scarport, then Snake Harbor, before crossing the Shattered Isles and rounding the peninsula. Their final destination is Tsing, where they will sell their cargo and search for more crew, though they may stop at any of the smaller harbors on the way north. I know not when she will return to Southaven, but will contact you via messenger when she does.*

The note was not signed, but that was usual. What was not divulged on paper could not be used in retaliation. He reread the note once, and a slow smile spread across his thin lips.

"A hiring expedition," he said to no one, crumpling the scroll and stuffing it into a pocket of his doublet. "Excellent!"

He turned and strode back up the stone pier, shouting for one of the idle cabin boys to fetch a messenger, quill and scroll. It was too late to get anyone to Snake Harbor or Scarport, but he would have men waiting in every port from there to Tsing, posing as able seamen, officers and even captains, all ready to hire. Then a deliciously devious thought struck him, stopping him dead in his tracks.

"Yodrin..." he thought aloud, his thin smile turning to a feral grin. "He would make a fine captain for one of those new ships, I think."

He shouted again to have another messenger brought. With Yodrin and a few others aboard the two new ships, Bloodwind might very well be able to add them both to his fleet without risking a single vessel. With surprise on their side, taking the ships and delivering them to Blood Bay with half-crews should be easy. And what a delicious victory it would be over the last of the Flaxal line.

"And I get the two fastest, most maneuverable corsairs in the Southern Ocean!" he said with a laugh. He strode into his palace, his mood much-improved, itching to draft the messages that would set the trap.

≈

The stink of sickness hit Koybur like a wall as he edged through the door into Cynthia's cabin bearing a steaming pitcher and a mug in his one good hand. He frowned at the noisome odor, the thick air and the low moaning that emanated from the disheveled lump of skirts in the corner.

"Cyn?" Receiving no answer, he put the pitcher down on a recessed shelf made for charts and worked himself down to one knee; no mean task, since his maimed leg barely bent at all. "Are you all right?"

"No, I'm bloody not bloody all right," she croaked from beneath a head of matted hair. "I'm sick as a dog!"

She looked up at him and he knew immediately that this was not a simple case of sea sickness. She sat with a bucket propped between her knees, her head bent over it. He didn't have to look inside to know she'd emptied every last drop from her stomach and then some. Her skin shone pale, her cheeks and eyes were sunken, and utter exhaustion lay upon her like a blanket. He felt her forehead, and his hand came away coated with chill sweat. Even the small movement of looking up sent her into another bout of heaving.

"We gotta get somethin' in ya, lass. Even if it comes right back up, it'll soothe yer throat."

"I can't," she moaned, shaking her head without raising her face from the bucket.

"Come on now, you've got to try. The cook's made some nice beef broth. You lose a lot a salt when yer sick like that, and whatever ya may think now, it'll taste good."

He helped her to sit upright and placed the empty cup in her shaking hands. The pitcher held warm broth, and he poured half a measure into her cup. Her tremors set the liquid dancing.

"Sip slowly. If you get sick, use the broth to rinse and spit. It helps to get the taste out of your mouth. I'll see about getting you a clean bucket and a washcloth."

"How long, Koybur?" she asked weakly as she sipped from the cup.

"How long what?"

"How long until we reach Scarport? I can't remember if I slept or not."

"We've only been on the sea about twelve hours, Cyn. We've got another day and a half to Scarport. Now shut up and drink some of that broth. You need it."

He took a moment to open one of the ports in an attempt to freshen the fetid air before he left the cabin in search of a clean bucket and a wash rag. It was going to be a very long first voyage for Cynthia Flaxal.

CHAPTER TWELVE
Dashed Dreams and Appetites Unsated

CYNTHIA'S KNUCKLES SHONE WHITE as bleached whalebone on the companion-way railing as she forced herself up the steps. With nothing passing her lips for two days except water and a bit of broth, her strength equaled that of any stout cobweb on the ship. She climbed grimly, knees quaking with every step, grateful that there were only seven. The hatchway onto the deck stood at the top of those steps; a gateway to fresh air, sunshine and a flat sea.

"A flat sea," she mumbled. Those words had become her litany, wishful thinking until they rounded Scar Point early that morning. She had felt the change in the motion of the *Winter Gale*, and her nausea slowly subsided. Two cups of broth had finally stayed down, and she had begun to think she would survive, at least in body, until they reached Scarport.

The ornate bronze latch felt cool in her hand as she grasped it and stood for a moment, catching her breath and collecting her courage. She opened the hatch and stepped onto the deck without pitching flat onto her face, which was quite an accomplishment, all things considered.

Around the deck, the crew bustled about their tasks, cleaning and polishing, swabbing and oiling. A few glanced her way, smiled politely and nodded or tipped their caps. She knew what they were thinking. They all knew she'd been sick. Here stood the Mistress of House Flaxal, daughter of a seamage, and she couldn't manage a two-day sail in good weather without puking up her guts. Mistress in name only, they would say. Mistress, but no sailor.

No captain.

Not ever.

She walked carefully to the starboard railing and gripped it with all her strength. Mouse landed on her shoulder with a cry of glee, dancing a jig and pulling on her ear, all smiles and sunshine. She tried to smile back, but couldn't. At least some happiness had come from this trip; Mouse had gotten to go to sea again. She hoped he would stay aboard when she went ashore... and didn't return.

Cynthia gripped the rail and stared out at the coastline: green bluffs dotted with fig plantations, the swaying sentinels of coconut palms lining the shore. The water shone a sparkling azure, shallow compared to the depths of the open ocean. Scar Point sheltered the wide bay of Scarport from the prevailing easterlies, but it boasted only a small port, and had little protection in a southerly blow. She knew it all. She'd studied the charts and imagined it from the diatribes of a thousand sailors, but she'd never seen it until now.

And she never would again.

"You feelin' all right now, Cyn?" Koybur asked from the foot of the steps. She'd heard him descend, but didn't want to turn around to face him.

With naught but her misery to occupy her thoughts for the past two days, she had dwelled on her own misgivings, her weaknesses and her losses. Who was she to think she could do this thing she'd set out to do? A strip of a girl, barely a woman, and suddenly a mistress of ships. What had she ever done to earn the respect of these men and women who had spent their lives on the sea?

Who was she?

Nobody.

What was she?

Nothing.

"You still look a little pale, but we'll get some food in you soon enough. You got a lot of eatin' to make up for, and not but today and tomorrow to do it. We're sailin' fer Snake Harbor with the mornin' tide day after tomorrow."

"Without me," she said.

"What?" Koybur's voice was flat and hard. "Whaddya mean, without you? This whole expedition's fer you, lass. You can't leave it!"

"Sure I can, Koybur," she said with a shrug. "You know more about who and what we need than I do. You can do the hiring, and I'll take a caravan overland back to Southaven. You don't need me."

"Don't *need* you! What are you thinkin', lass?" He grabbed her arm and jerked her around to face him. Mouse flipped from her shoulder and flittered to a nearby ratline, staring at the two in shock. "You givin' up after two stinkin' days of pukin' yer guts into a bucket? You want to go back to your big house on the hill and rot away in your tight-laced finery like yer gram?"

"Koybur, I—" she started, but he would have none of her argument.

"I take that back! Your gram at least had the spunk to *fight* fer what she wanted. Why, I never thought I'd meet a Flaxal who was so bent on failure!"

"I'm not *bent* on failure!" she snapped, a little of the accustomed fire in her voice. "I still want to build ships. Hell, I want to build a whole *fleet* of ships! I just can't sail in them. That much is obvious."

"Obvious? After two days?" He laughed a bark of derision and spat into the water. "I've known sailors, *real* sailors, who spent four *years* so sick they couldn't get from their hammock to the rail without pukin'. Here you think you can give up after two days?" He glared at her openly, his one eye livid with challenge. Then his voice lowered to a hoarse whisper as he said, "Don't you *dare*, lass. Don't you dare quit now."

She stared at him in wonder as he wheeled away and limped up the steps to the quarterdeck, one leg doing all the work, the other a fused, maimed lump that gave him pain with every step. She felt a wash of guilt, but then a similar one of resolve. Koybur quit sailing after his injury. For her, whole and hale of body, and knowing what sailors thought of those who were chronically seasick, things were different. She couldn't stand that kind of behind-the-hand ridicule, not if she was going to be who she wanted to be. Not if she was to be a Flaxal, or a mistress of ships.

And she wanted to be a mistress of ships, even more than she wanted to sail in them.

≈

The sweet scent of blood tickled Hydra's senses as she approached the feasting hall in search of Captain Bloodwind. Having recently fed, she resembled an alluring young woman, but even sated, the smell of human blood kindled her hunger.

Not now, she admonished the ever-ravenous creature within her. *Later... Later we will feed.*

The hunger eased, receding into the depths of her tainted soul like a great coiled serpent laying in wait for its next meal. But it would not wait forever. The power she stole from it had kept her alive longer than any mortal human, but to keep that power, to keep the beast imprisoned, she had to feed it. She no longer remembered her former life, no longer recalled the reason she had enslaved the beast. They were one now, and they had to feed. But feeding had driven her out of the lands of civilized men. So began her association with Captain Bloodwind. It had not been difficult to seduce him with this body, and he had accepted her unusual...habits. He saw the value of her soul-purchased powers. In payment, he fed her well. Now, knowing something of what truly dwelt within her, he loathed and feared her, as any sane man would.

A perfect relationship.

The clash of weapons greeted her as she opened the door to the great hall. He was here, and so was the source of the scent that tickled her appetite. She swaggered forward, oozing sensuality, her clothing altered with a simple illusion to make her even more alluring.

The scent of blood became strong now.

The feasting table had been moved aside, and two young men barely beyond boyhood fought with blunted cutlasses in the middle of the room. Bloodwind sat upon his gilded chair, looking much the monarch upon a throne, calling out encouragement indiscriminately to each of the youths, his prize slave standing obediently at his elbow.

The young men fought for position; a pirate crew only took those who proved themselves capable. There was no room for dead weight aboard a corsair. Both young men coveted a single berth aboard the *Hellraker*, one of Bloodwind's leanest and fastest corsairs. They each bled from half a dozen shallow cuts and contusions where the blunted swords had struck. She walked past them, drinking in the scents of sweat and blood. Hydra forced her hunger down once again, focusing upon her captain.

"Captain Bloodwind," she said, her voice husky and sensual, "the *Winter Gale* has reached Scarport. The one you seek will be ashore shortly."

"Good," Bloodwind said, not even looking at her, his attention trained upon the two young fighters. He opened his mouth and took a peeled fig from the fingers of his gilded slave.

Hydra watched him chew and swallow, annoyed at his disinterest in her. Once it had taken only a twitch of her finger to get his attention, and he would satisfy her hunger eagerly. Now he only paid her attention when he needed information.

Bloodwind turned and cocked an eyebrow at her, as if realizing she still stood there. "Was there something else?"

"I wish to know where you want me to direct my efforts, Captain," she said, smiling with all the warmth of a serpent.

"Just watch for now, Hydra. Keep an eye on Southaven and another on the *Winter Gale*. I want to know when the framing timbers and planking arrive for those ships." He accepted another fig and shouted encouragement to one of the young men who'd just scored a touch. "Oh, and watch Rockport harbor. I want to make sure my message gets to Yodrin."

"You will send me something tonight to sate my hunger?" she asked, glancing over her shoulder at the two young men. "The loser of this match, perhaps?"

"You look well fed. I'll send you something tomorrow, but not one of these two. They're too valuable. I've got fodder aplenty for you."

"Then send me one tonight, my captain. My appetite grows, and I cannot watch without rest unless I feed."

"In the morning, Hydra," he countered, his voice hard. "Now leave us.

Your yammering is distracting me from more important matters." He sat up in his chair as the youth who had been winning the bout suddenly slipped in a puddle of sweat or blood and received a resounding crack to the skull for his inattention. The boy fell like a steer in a slaughterhouse, landing on the floor in a boneless heap.

"Enough!" he shouted, clapping his hands and striding forward past Hydra. "Well done, Judin! Well done! The berth on the *Hellraker* is yours!"

"Thank you, Captain!" The youth knelt and bowed his head to Bloodwind.

"Don't thank me, Judin. You earned it. Now, go fetch a couple of slaves to take Belek here to the healer. If he wakes up, you can tell him he'll have to wait for the next open berth. Now, off with you!"

The young man raced out of the room. Bloodwind turned to his slave girl; when he noticed Hydra still standing there, his eyes narrowed.

"Why are you still here, Hydra? I told you to leave us."

"The boy is beyond your healer, my captain," she said, her gaze slipping past him to the crumpled form on the floor. "Give him to me, while he still breathes."

"No. Now back to your hole, you bloodthirsty crone." He waved a hand in dismissal.

"You waste this," she hissed, moving to step around him to the young man's prone form. Blood flowed sluggishly from his nose and mouth to pool on the flagstones. She licked her lips. "He will die. Give him to me!"

"I said no!" Bloodwind growled, jerking the golden-hilted cutlass from his hip and bringing the tip to her throat in a flash of steel. "He fought well enough to deserve a better end than at your hands. Now, off with you!"

Hydra looked down at the razor-edged steel at her throat and smiled. Any other man would have trembled to see that smile directed at him, but Bloodwind's hand remained steady.

"As you wish, my captain." She bowed low and left the room, reining in her hunger and her temper. She knew his threat was an empty one; she was more valuable to him than any two of his captains, let alone this slip of a boy. But there was no profit in a confrontation now. Her hunger would have to remain unsated until morning.

But one day Bloodwind would push her too far, and she would slip the rein on the beast within her long enough for him to learn the true meaning of horror.

≈

Cynthia mopped up the last of the hearty stew with a heel of bread and popped the bite into her mouth. She chased the bite with a final swallow of ale and stifled a belch, her stomach stretched as taut as a drum. Mouse sat with his back to the breadbasket, snoozing happily, his stomach bulging visibly, too. One of the maids came by to take her empty bowl, and asked if she wanted another ale.

"No, thank you. Any more and I'll be asleep in half an hour. I'll have tea, if it's not too much trouble. That stew was delicious."

"Be just a moment." The woman hurried off.

Cynthia took the opportunity to examine her surroundings in detail for the first time since leaving *Winter Gale*. Beside herself with misery and set on leaving for Southaven by the first available caravan, she hadn't taken time to notice much. Granted, this was just Scarport, but she'd never been here, and probably never would be again.

The inn sat perched up on a hill overlooking the wharf, and was the cleanest of the four the town sported. She'd not wanted to walk so far, her hunger outweighing her taste, but Koybur had insisted. "Won't do fer a mistress of ships to spend the night in one of them fleabag dives," he'd said. He left her here with firm instructions to eat and drink as much as she could, and relax. He was going to "just do some pokin' 'round."

Her tea arrived, a porcelain pot snug in a quilted cozy with a small chilled pitcher of goat's milk, bowls of sugar and lemon wedges, a saucer and cup, and a tiny plate of dainty cookies. Mouse opened one eye at the cookies and licked his lips.

"Will there be anything else, Miss?"

"Nothing for now, thank you."

She was halfway through the pot—Mouse halfway through a cookie— when Koybur entered the room. He limped toward her and took in her condition with a sidelong glance.

"You look better." He snatched a cookie from the plate and popped it into his mouth. "Got some food in you, I see. Your color's back."

"Right as rain," she assured him, sipping her tea. "You could've walked this town end to end and visited every inn and shop in the time you were out. Find anything interesting?"

"Did visit every inn and shop, and talked myself hoarse!" He waved to the serving woman and asked for ale. "Aye, and there's a few men lazin' about who might do for crew. One woman who you'll want to talk to, name of Finthie Tar. She'd make a fine boatswain, without a doubt."

"Didn't figure you'd find that much. Did you tell them to come by? I know you picked good sailors, but I'd like to talk to them."

"Figured you would." He accepted his ale with a nod and his usual crooked smile. "They'll be comin' by later this afternoon. There's two fellers from up north, tall as trees and used to them northerly storms that put ice on the riggin', the Tar woman, and another fella who claims to have sailed with the Royal Navy, though I don't know about that. On top of that, Finthie said she'd heard that a mate of one of the ships moored in port might be interested in a new employer." His grin grew, and he squinted with mirth. "The feller's not happy with the deal his captain's makin' with some southern prince. Runnin' sword steel to some group in the desert that's stirrin' up trouble."

"Principles, from a merchant officer?" She laughed shortly. A merchant unwilling to run a cargo simply because it might be used in an unsavory endeavor would limit the ability to profit. Then another thought came to her, and she asked, "Or does he think his tender skin is being put to too great a risk?"

"Well, not the latter, I'm sure. The feller's name is Feldrin Brelak. You heard of him?"

"Not that I remember, but the name's enough to tell me he's a Morrgrey."

"Aye, that he is, and everything that bein' a Morrgrey implies." Koybur took a pull at his ale and sighed. What he meant by the comment, Cynthia knew, was that the man exemplified the typical Morrgrey mixture of quick temper, hardiness, a certain stubbornness, and as much salt-water as blood running through his veins. "Never met him, but he's got a reputation as an honest man, and never walked away from a fight."

"I'd like to talk to him," Cynthia decided aloud, liking the sound of the man already. "Can you arrange for him to join me for a drink after dinner?"

"Aye, yer name alone'll get his attention. And I ain't never known a Morrgrey to turn down a drink." He chuckled.

"I think you overestimate the weight my name carries, Koybur." She sipped her tea and gazed out the window to the swaying palms and turquoise waters beyond the streets of Scarport. "It's been fifteen years since a Flaxal's been to sea."

"And I think you underestimate yer old dad, lass," he said with a scowl. He finished his ale with a single swallow and pushed himself up, taking another cookie from the plate. "His name carries as much weight around the Southern Ocean as any sea god you can name."

Before she could comment, he whirled on his bad leg and limped out of the inn. She watched him go, wondering about his quick shift in mood.

He's probably still sore about my decision to take a caravan back to Southaven, she thought, sitting back and sipping her tea, thinking about events that had propelled her into this situation. It was almost as if they'd been orchestrated by some beneficent deity.

"Well, if some god is doing it," she mumbled, "whichever one it is should have thought to bless my queasy stomach instead of my fortune."

CHAPTER THIRTEEN

Tactics of Negotiation

CYNTHIA SAT BACK AND sighed, satisfied with the events of the afternoon and the wonderful plate of roast lamb and new potatoes she'd just finished.

Four interviews with prospective sailors had filled the afternoon. The two northerners had raised their eyebrows that a woman so young would be their employer, and flinched again when Mouse landed on her shoulder. She'd told them flatly that if they had a problem with her or the company she kept, the door and the street beyond were theirs to explore. They shrugged and agreed to her terms. Finthie Tar turned out to be a diamond in the rough. She'd been sailing the Southern Ocean since she was a girl, had been boatswain on half a dozen ships, and could speak as many languages. Cynthia offered her a boatswain's billet with the implication that she might be in the running for an officer slot if Koybur found nobody with more experience. The other southerner, a man from Rockport, arrived half drunk. She sent him packing without another word. To the three she found acceptable, she gave enough money for passage to Southaven, and told them they would be working as laborers for Master Keelson until the new hulls were in the water. They grumbled at this, but the prospect of earning a seaman's wage while ashore had its lure, and they agreed.

Koybur had shared the meal with her, but left to meet the Morrgrey mate and escort him back as soon as the last bite passed his lips. Cynthia was unused to such pretenses, but knew it was best to play along with Koybur's lead. It frightened her slightly, the degree to which she relied on him, on his judgment, his expertise and his razor wit. He alone would put her in her place when she made an ass of herself. She thought of him as her home, her one infallible reliance. Let the rest of it burn, sink, or blow away; as long as Koybur stayed with her, she would be fine.

When the two men finally came through the door, Cynthia thought for a moment that the wine she'd had with lunch had been stronger than she thought. Koybur looked to have shrunk, for the top of his head barely reached the Morrgrey's shoulder.

She blinked. It wasn't just Koybur—the entire room seemed to have gotten smaller the moment Feldrin Brelak ducked under the lintel. The man towered a head taller than Koybur, and sported a chest and arms fully twice as broad. He was not particularly muscular, and certainly not fat, but Cynthia thought he looked more solid than any man she'd ever seen.

Mouse let out an "Eep!" of alarm and dove down her collar, peeking out nervously. She stood as the two men approached, trying not to feel intimidated. Several people cast glances at Brelak as he passed, and a few even greeted him by name or raised a hand in welcome. He nodded and smiled in passing, his dark eyes glinting in the dim lamplight. He seemed friendly enough, and well known by the locals, which made Cynthia wonder why she had never met him. Both Southaven and Scarport were common stopovers for merchant ships; if he'd been sailing the Southern Ocean long, he would have passed through both. He exemplified the typical Morrgrey from head to toe: wavy hair the color of midnight, a close-trimmed beard, olive skin and an easy rolling gait that bespoke of countless hours aboard ship. Finally he loomed before her, still smiling, his eyes crinkled with deep lines of pleasure or mirth.

"Feldrin Brelak, first mate of the *Peerless*, this is Mistress Cynthia Flaxal," Koybur said.

"Pleased to meet you," Cynthia said, matching his smile as she held out a hand.

"Likewise, Mistress Flaxal." His voice did not shake the room, as she might have guessed, and his grip was only firm and friendly, not crushing as she'd expected. "Master Koybur here tells me yer buildin' new ships, and are lookin' fer crew and officers to man 'em."

"That is true enough." He released her hand and she gestured to a chair, wondering idly if it would take the strain. "Would you join me? We can discuss the matter over a drink, if you like."

"Oh, that would suit, that would suit," the big man said.

He sat carefully, Cynthia noticed, as Koybur joined them and gestured to the serving woman.

"Well, Master Brelak!" the woman said with a laugh as she approached the table. "It's been far too long since you passed our door. Where have you been, you great behemoth?"

"Away north, Beatrice, and far to the south. We've been takin' the long run with silks and steel, but not fer much longer. There's trouble brewin' down the desert."

"Aye, that explains a lot. Your usual?"

"Why, yes, now that you mention it, if you've still got a bit of yer private stock."

"Never run out as long as there's sailors plyin' the trades." The woman looked to Cynthia. "And you, Mistress?"

"A glass of port would suit nicely." She did not miss the raised eyebrow from Brelak as Koybur ordered a rum.

"I see you've got a little friend there," Brelak said with a smile, indicating Mouse, who was peering over her shoulder. "Good luck to have a seasprite along."

"Mouse has been with my family for years. He sailed with my father before going into hiding for a time. He just came back to me, saved my life, in fact." She chucked the little sprite under the chin and grinned at him. "If that's not lucky, I don't know what is."

"A little worse for wear, I see. A run in with pirates, no doubt."

"A run in with a broom," Cynthia said with a chuckle, ignoring Mouse's snort of indignation. "A long story." She took the last sip of her wine and changed the subject to business. "How much did Koybur tell you about my new ships, Master Brelak? Not everyone would be comfortable with a new design."

"He just said it was different; smaller than a galleon and faster than a corsair. Said you were planning on runnin' lighter, more valuable cargoes. Perishables, or the like."

"That's the gist of it. It's a two-mast, fore-and-aft rig with main and foresail gaff rigged. Tops'ls are fore-and-aft tris'ls, and there's one square rig tops'l forward when she's not close to the wind. Thrice forestays, adjustable sprit for variable wind and running backstays to tension the masts to windward. She won't haul a third what your *Peerless* will, but she'll get there in half the time, a third if the course is close to the wind."

"Sounds interestin'," he said with a raised eyebrow and a nod to the waitress as she arrived. The drinks were passed around; a very dark rum in a small glass for the Morrgrey, a lighter rum for Koybur and Cynthia's port in a thin-stemmed glass. "How close will she sail?"

"The keels are just being laid, so nothing's been tested, but with the feel I get from similar, smaller vessels, I'd say two points higher than any galleon. They'll hold a line as close as any dhow or lugger with less leeway."

"What crew?"

"Captain and mate, bosun and six more able seamen, and a cook. The rig is simple in comparison to a galleon, and the profit margin should be higher with the smaller crew."

"That *is* a tidy crew. What'll you be shippin'?"

"Well, after they shake down and we see what they can do, I'm thinking of running perishables to the far north—pineapple, mango and the like to Fengotherond, maybe. In winter, we'd bring ice back south; in summer, spar timber and copper."

"How many?"

"Two initially, but as they start to pay for themselves, as many as I can put to sea." She lifted her port and sipped daintily. "And I'll need experienced officers to captain them as they're built." The offer was implicit: Mate for a year or two, then a ship of his own. "Speaking of which, how long have you been mate of the *Peerless*?"

"Three years, and second on *Tommy's Pride* before that." He let that stand, and she immediately picked up on the implication.

Tommy's Pride had gone down with all hands, a victim of piracy. He could not have survived without stories of it reaching her. *Is he testing me to find out if I know the tale,* she thought, *or is he lying to puff up his reputation?* She didn't glance at Koybur, but phrased her next question very carefully.

"So you were aboard when she was lost?"

"No, Ma'am. I'd transferred to the *Peerless* a month before." He looked into his drink and took a sip. "I didn't find out fer almost four months. I lost a lot of friends to them bastards, and not just them aboard *Tommy's Pride*. Seems half the ships I've sailed in met with trouble one way or another, either while I was aboard or after. I been on the sea near twenty years, man and boy, and I've n'er met a captain who sailed the Shattered Isles and hasn't had at least one run-in with 'em."

"True enough," she agreed, still wondering about his veracity. The story of the Flaxal family's near destruction at the hands of Bloodwind had been told far and wide. Would a prospective officer try to sound sympathetic by telling of his similar loss? "And before *Tommy's Pride*?"

At her prompt he gave a business-like account of all the ships he'd sailed in, working backward to manning river barges up to Twailin as a boy. It seemed his uncle owned a barge, and recognized the value of a strong young man whom he wouldn't have to pay because he was young *and* a relative.

"Which was why I jumped ship at the first opportunity, and made crew on the *Bonnie Belle*. Then, at least I was getting' *paid* to work."

"Well, Master Brelak, from what you've told me, I think you'll do nicely as first mate in one of my ships. Would tomorrow evening suit for negotiating your pay and accommodations?"

"That would suit nicely, Mistress Flaxal, very nicely, indeed. I'll be here tomorrow evening." He drained his glass and stood, shaking hands all around and wishing them good health.

When he had gone, Koybur leaned in and asked her, "You think he's lyin' about the *Tommy*?"

"Not really, but you should check it. Should be simple enough, no?"

"Like fallin' out of a second story window with your pants half down."

She snickered at his wit, but then he became more serious. "You think yer up to bargainin' with that Morrgrey?"

"By tomorrow evening, I should be. I couldn't do it tonight, though. I'm already tired."

"You do know what Morrgrey bargainin' means, don't you, lass?"

"Sure," she said, standing and stretching her aching back. "It means I'm buying the rum."

"All right, then. But don't get cheap on it, or you'll have a hangover like a barrel of chatter vipers."

"Good advice." She collected Mouse, who had taken an interest in the dregs of Brelak's rum, and headed for the stairs. "Goodnight, Koybur. I'll see you for breakfast."

≈

By the time they finished lunch the following day, Cynthia knew a great deal about Feldrin Brelak. His account had been as accurate as Koybur's subtle questioning could verify. What had not been brought out by their short interview was Brelak's reputation among his fellow sailors. Three of the ships he'd crewed aboard before the fateful *Tommy's Pride* had been attacked in the Shattered Isles. Brelak had shown such determination, leadership and vicious fighting during two of those occasions that the corsairs had been beaten off. The third attacker, though the story may have grown with the telling, he had boarded with two other seamen. They had done such damage to her rigging and tiller that the corsair could not bear up into the wind and ran onto a reef. Brelak and the one other surviving sailor, both wounded, had escaped the wreck by diving overboard and swimming for their lives.

"I want him, Koybur, and not just because he's a damn fine mate. I want him because he hates pirates as much as I do." Sipping her chilled tea, Cynthia glared out to sea.

"You got a fire in your gut for that motherless bilge rat Bloodwind, Cyn, I understand that, but you gotta rethink just what you're tryin' to do." He sipped his ale and nodded at her questioning stare. "If it's vengeance you want, you should sell these plans to the Imperial Navy and let them clean up the scum. Yer not buildin' warships, lass, you're buildin' merchantmen. There's a vast difference."

"No, I'm not building warships," she agreed, "but these new ships *will* give me my revenge, Koybur." She forestalled his reply with a raised hand. "Not by fighting him, but by denying him prey. Do you think it coincidence that the *Tommy* wasn't touched for three years, then a month after Brelak steps off the ship, it's sunk?"

"Actually, I do think it was coincidence. Why would they care about one man aboard one ship?"

"Because there are so many without such men," she countered, shrugging. "If you're a wolf, do you attack a ewe or a ram? It's that simple. But my ships will be immune to the bastards."

"Unless Bloodwind copies the design."

Cynthia's ardor flagged at that, for the consequences of a pirate fleet of her design had not crossed her mind. That Bloodwind had eyes in every port was no secret; he could get as close a look at her ships as any competitor, closer if he managed to place someone in Master Keelson's yard during construction.

"Well, we'll just have to make sure that doesn't happen, won't we?"

"Aye, lass. Ghelfan and Keelson'll keep their mouths shut, and their crews are hand-picked. Problem is every crewman we hire and send back is a mystery."

"I hadn't thought of that," she admitted, biting her lip. "When I get back, I'll tell Ghelfan to keep an eye on things. He's a smart fellow."

"So is Captain Bloodwind, Cyn, or he wouldn't still be alive."

≈

An hour after sunset, with a small crowd filling the inn, Cynthia and Koybur sat at a table with a case of fine spiced rum at her feet and two small glasses on the table. A single bottle from the case sat between the two glasses.

The rules were simple: Cynthia would make an offer, and Brelak would make a counteroffer. If they did not agree, each would drink a measure of rum. They would continue until an offer was agreed upon. If one of them could not continue, the last offer made from the other party would stand.

It would be in Cynthia's interest to make an agreement as quickly as possible, since she was severely outweighed, but she also didn't want to give too much away in haste. If he thought she couldn't hold her liquor, she might surprise him.

Feldrin Brelak entered the inn with two of his mates. He smiled and waved amiably as they approached the table. Koybur stood with Cynthia and they smiled and offered greetings.

"This here's Balik Tonkland, second of the *Peerless*, and Shmeeka Sanarro, bosun's mate."

"Gentlemen, good to meet you. I believe you all know my man Koybur. It's good that you brought two, Master Brelak. I'd hate to see one man try to carry you home after this."

"Ha! Very good, very good!" He smiled genuinely, as did she. The laughter around the inn told her that her bluster had been just right: sincere enough to raise an eyebrow but laughable enough to diffuse any tension. "Shall we begin?"

Mouse whooped with glee and attacked the cork of the rum bottle, trying in vain to pull it free. That elicited another round of laughter. Cynthia coaxed Mouse to her shoulder and everyone save Koybur sat.

"Very well, then," Koybur said, nodding to Brelak and then to Cynthia. "It is the understanding of all present that Mistress Cynthia Flaxal has made an unspecified offer of employment to Master Feldrin Brelak, first mate of the *Peerless.* Have you, Master Brelak, been given leave by your captain to accept said employment?"

"I have," he said, licking his lips as he examined the bottle of aged rum. One dark eyebrow lifted in appreciation. "Bloody *fine!* I certainly have, indeed."

"Very well. Mistress Flaxal, would you please make your opening offer."

"The offer is for the position of first mate aboard a ship as yet to be built by the Keelson yard in Southaven. As mate you will receive one one-hundredth share of any profit from cargo sold, plus half a crown per month sea pay. You will supply your own clothing, food and water. You will be allotted one hammock in crew's quarters, and half a standard sea chest for personal effects. There will be no pay for time spent ashore, and half pay for time spent aboard, but in port."

Brelak smiled thinly; new able seamen earned about that rate, more if the crew was small and the craft speedy.

"Master Brelak, do you find these terms agreeable?"

"I do *not,* Master Koybur."

"Your offer?"

"As first mate aboard this *as-yet-to-be-built* ship, I'll earn one-twentieth of *gross* earnings fer cargo sold. I'll receive an additional ten crowns per month, with full sea pay fer every day I'm aboard, at sea or in port, and half pay fer days ashore. I'll have my own stateroom, with a bunk built to accommodate my height and girth, and I'll be provided food, clothing and one bottle of this fine rum fer every day I'm at sea. Money spent in negotiations with landsmen fer cargo will be fully reimbursed."

"Mistress Flaxal, do you find these terms agreeable?"

"I do *not,* Master Koybur," she stated flatly, trying not to smile at the big man.

"Very well, then!" Koybur snatched up the bottle with his one good hand, wrenched the cork from its neck with his teeth and spat it onto the floor.

He started to pour, but Mouse let out a whoop and dove right down the neck of the bottle. His shoulders wedged in the opening and he kicked his little feet, trying to reach the dark liquor. Laughter erupted around the table, with many suggestions how Koybur, with only one good hand, could extricate the little sprite from the bottle. He settled for slamming the butt end onto the table, sending the sprite and a geyser of rum skyward. Mouse managed to gobble up a good amount of it before he and the rum splashed onto the table. He kicked up his feet and rolled in the spilt liquor, giggling with mirth.

"Now, where was I? Oh, yes." He poured an equal measure in each of the two glasses and said, "Lady and gentleman, drink up."

And they did.

The rum was remarkably smooth and lightly spiced, leaving a lovely warm glow down to Cynthia's stomach. She placed her glass down and smiled at Brelak, who smiled back. This was going to be a tough negotiation.

"Mistress Flaxal, your counteroffer?"

And so it went.

The hardest part for Cynthia, after a few rounds of offer-counteroffer, was remembering what she'd offered the previous round. That and getting the glass to her chin without spilling rum all over herself.

In the end, she did remarkably well. One bottle lay empty by the board, and a second stood down by half. She lost the bout, of course, but Feldrin Brelak had indeed underestimated her capacity. When she finally slid down to the table top, face down in spilled rum, their offers had been quibbling over a few farthings a month, and how much of landside negotiating expenses would be reimbursed.

"Congratulations, Master Brelak, you are hired as first mate of one vessel, as yet to be named, or built, by Mistress Flaxal. You will answer to none but yer captain and Mistress Flaxal in all matters, save in the buying and selling of cargo, for which you will answer to me when I am available for advice. Is this agreeable?"

"This is agreeable, Master Koybur," the big man said, pushing himself up from the table with only a slight wobble. "Would you be needin' any 'elp in takin' the good Mishresh, er… Mistress Flaxal to bed?"

The amassed group of onlookers roared with laughter, though Brelak remained oblivious to his own witticism.

"I might ask your mates to lend a hand, Master Brelak, but only in taking Mistress Flaxal down to the *Winter Gale*. You may have your things brought aboard presently, for we sail with the morning tide."

"Aye, sir!" Brelak said, nodding and touching a knuckle to his forehead in the customary deference. "I'll be aboard by midnight and ready for duties at dawn."

"Very good!" Koybur paid the innkeeper for his service. He was taking Cynthia aboard *Winter Gale*, and fully intended to be well out to sea before she woke. She would be madder than a crocodile with a toothache, but that was something he would deal with later. Right now, he needed Cynthia Flaxal on this expedition, and on it she would go.

≈

Not everyone in the crowd found the exchange so amusing. One slim sailor who hung back near the door watched carefully as the men from the *Peerless* lifted the Flaxal girl, tucked her drunken seasprite in her cleavage as a joke, and carried her down to the *Winter Gale*. He seemed less interested in her than in the Morrgrey, however, and when the crowd thinned, he followed the big man down the street toward the docks.

He belabored the merits of putting a knife in the man's back. Surely Brelak was drunk enough to fall prey to a quick thrust before he started fighting back, and if placed well, there would be no fighting back. But would Captain Bloodwind praise him for his bold initiative, or would he find himself hanging from a yardarm, awaiting the jaws of the denizens of the deep? Or worse, would he find himself bound upon Hydra's altar?

His skin rose into gooseflesh despite the warm evening, and he decided that information would be more valuable to Captain Bloodwind, and himself, than any rash action.

CHAPTER FOURTEEN
Misery and Company

CYNTHIA'S FIRST THOUGHT AS sleep eased into wakefulness was that she'd been cheated on that case of spiced rum. Nausea welled up in her gut, her head pounding to the beat of her heart. Then she opened her eyes and recognized her cabin aboard the *Winter Gale*. The motion beneath her confirmed it: she was at sea.

"Koybur!" she yelled at the top of her lungs, forcing herself up from the bunk. A familiar bucket stood next to the head of her bunk, a towel and a cup of water in the little rack next to the wash basin. "Koybur, you son of a motherless pig! You're *fired*, you bastard! You hear me? *Fired!*"

She heard the pounding of running feet and a few shouts. One glance out of the port showed her the vast rolling swells of the deep Southern Ocean, and her stomach heaved in protest. Cynthia managed to reach the bucket before the little sustenance still in her stomach came up. A moan of misery escaped her lips as she worked her way out of the bunk to her customary position, bucket cradled between her knees.

"Koybur!" she yelled between retches, cursing him with great volume and imagination. Finally, the latch rattled and two men entered, Koybur and Feldrin Brelak with Mouse perched on the Morrgrey's shoulder, his quirky imp smile intact.

"Cynthia! You're awake!" Koybur limped forward and worked himself down onto his good knee. "How do you feel?"

"Sick as a bilge rat, you son of a pox-ridden whore!" she spat, glaring from under her disheveled hair. Mouse made a face and flew crookedly to her shoulder, patting her on the head before returning to the Morrgrey's broad shoulder. She ignored him, focusing all her ire upon Koybur.

"Well, look at it this way; you're not hung over." He grinned his lopsided grin. "And you're not on your way back to Southaven in a stinkin' old wagon."

"Bastard," she managed before retching again. When she finished, she glanced up at Brelak. "Koybur, get him out of here. I don't want anyone to see me like this."

"Oh, don't worry about Brelak, lass. He's seen ship's sickness before, and I told him you were still workin' on your sea legs." He handed her the cup of water that stood next to her basin. "Here you go. Just have a little bit now."

She rinsed her mouth and spat, then took a small swallow. She knew it would come up later, but it eased her throat. "You *know* you're fired," she said coldly, glaring at him in sincere hatred. "Kidnap your employer and take her to sea against her wishes? I could have you strung up for this."

Mouse flew up to Koybur's face and mimed being hung, fluttering there with his tongue lolling out until the salty old sailor pushed him gently out of the way. His humor unappreciated, the sprite retreated to Brelak's shoulder and sulked.

"Oh, I suppose you could, lass, but we both know you won't." He struggled to his feet, clenching his jaw against the pain, his constant companion. "Our next landfall is Rockport. Brelak and I decided to skip Snake Harbor; naught but dregs there from what he tells me. We'll be passin' through the north straits of the Shattered Isles in two days. After that, another four to Rockport. That ought to give you some time to get acquainted with the ocean." He took the towel from the rack and handed it to her. "Give a yell when the bucket's full or the glass is empty. I'll tend you night and day, Cyn, but I'm not gonna let you coddle yourself out of this."

"Thanks a lot," she growled as he turned away.

"One day, lassie, you *will* thank me for this. I promise you that." With that little quip to occupy her mind he closed the door, leaving her to her misery.

≈

"Are ya sure she's well enough to be left alone, Master Koybur?" Brelak asked as they ascended the companionway back to the deck.

"She was just comin' out of her doldrums two days out from Southaven. She'll come around."

"Has she never been to sea a-fore this, then?" the big man asked, concern edging his voice.

"Only once before," Koybur answered eying the new man skeptically. "She was but a strap of a lass then, though. Lost her mum and dad on that trip. That was when that bastard Bloodwind put a ballista bolt through 'em both. Right in front of her, mind ye."

"Bloody hell and Odea preserve us!" Brelak murmured as the two men moved to the midship rail. "And how old was she then?"

"About seven summers," Koybur said flatly, watching the Morrgrey.

Brelak turned back to the aft cabin door, his dark eyes soft with pity. "And she saw it? Bloody hell."

"Aye, and she was old enough to remember it, though I don't think she really does."

The big man closed his eyes and shook his head somberly. "A wonder she ever recovered."

"They tell me near a year passed before she did much but sleep, cry and wake up screamin'. By that time, old Master Garrison had been lost as well, swept off the deck of *Peggy's Pride* out lookin' for Bloodwind in a damned hurricane." He shook his head and sighed. "She had a right structured up-bringin' from her gram, which was probably best. She turned into a bit of a hell-raiser in her teens, and she's tougher than she looks. She never was allowed to go to sea, though, which had always been her only real want. Her gram died in a fire some weeks ago, and now the business is all hers; what's left of it that is."

"Which is why she's buildin' new ships," Brelak said, nodding sagely. "She's got some spunk in her fer one so young."

"Aye, and you don't know the half of it, my friend." Koybur tapped out his pipe and grinned lopsidedly. "You don't know the half of it."

≈

"Feldrin Brelak..." Bloodwind seethed, pronouncing the name like a curse as he crumpled the parchment in his hand. "Another thorn in my side come back to haunt me." His eyes focused on the cowering messenger before him. "Did my man in Scarport say exactly *why* the Morrgrey is still breathing?"

"He said there was never an opportunity to strike, Captain. Brelak was always in the company of others."

"I must be paying my spies too much when a hundred crown bounty isn't enough to induce them to take a little risk."

He walked to the edge of the balcony, a wide stone terrace that had been laboriously carved out of the living rock of the volcano. This, his favorite spot on the island, embodied both beauty and risk; the balcony had no railing, and the beach lay more than a hundred feet below. Everything he had achieved had been gained at an equally great risk.

He turned away from the view and returned to his chair, admiring how the morning sun glittered from Camilla's golden adornments. *Yes,* he thought, *beauty and risk.* He sat between Camilla and the balcony's edge. If she truly hated him as much as she professed, would she not have tried just once to push him over the edge? He knew he had not completely broken her spirit, so there must be some other reason.

Yes, there must be something more in her mind now than hatred.

"You may go," he told the messenger as he cut a sausage and popped a piece into his mouth. He chewed thoughtfully, trying to think of a way to rid himself of Feldrin Brelak. Rockport was out of the question. Yodrin lurked there, and a murder in such a small town would put the Flaxal girl on guard. But Tsing would be their next stop, and in that great city anything could happen. If a gutter thief put a knife in the big man's back, they would probably dismiss it as bad luck and hire another officer to take his place, presenting yet another opportunity to place one of his men among the crews.

Yes, that thought had merit. Tsing was a dangerous city, and one of the busiest ports on the continent. What better place to do business?

≈

"Land, dead ahead!" The lookout's call and a stampede of footfalls overhead roused Cynthia from a near-comatose slumber.

More calls put the ship into a brief state of action. Even in her addled state, it did not take her long to comprehend the reason for the commotion: the *Winter Gale* had raised the Shattered Isles. This would be her one and only chance to see the inland passages, for their return trip would be a close-hauled beat to windward, and would take them well south of these shallow, treacherous cuts.

Her knees quaked like leaves in the wind as she forced herself to her feet. She found her way onto the deck, though those seven steps seemed to have multiplied by a dozen. The steady trade winds and a bright blue sky greeted her with cheerful mockery, but this time they were accompanied by water of the deepest blue Cynthia had ever seen. The wind and midday sky she could ignore, but as her hands came to rest on the rail amidships, her eyes were drawn down into that fathomless blue, and she felt as if she were being torn limb from limb.

How could something so beautiful, something she loved so much and wanted more than anything else in the world, torture her so?

"'Tis a beautiful sight, is it not, Mistress Flaxal?"

She felt the huge presence of Feldrin Brelak just behind her, but did not turn to face him. She kept her eyes on that blue-blue water.

"It's so *blue*," she said, sniffing back the huskiness in her voice.

"Aye, this here's the Easting Deep." His voice resounded with intense emotion, which surprised her. How could a sailor be so moved by just another stretch of open sea?

"Nobody ever told me it was so blue." She wiped the tears from her eyes and sniffed.

"Aye, the water's deep an' clear here," he said, offering her a pocket handkerchief. She took it gratefully, muttering her thanks. "The current sets east to west with the trades, and the drop-off pulls cold water up from the deep. On a clear day like this, when the swell's down, it's the pertiest patch of water on the sea."

After a short while, Cynthia realized that she did not feel as bad as she had, though her stomach remained bone dry and her head still throbbed with her heartbeat. Suddenly, something broke the surface near the ship—a fin and a tail.

"Dolphin," she said, smiling. "Good luck."

"Have another look, Mistress." Brelak pointed to the roiling water where powerful flukes pushed close to the surface. "There!"

The creature broke the surface again, and for a bare instant Cynthia saw silvery scales, a ridge of spiny dorsal fin, arms with webbed hands and bright green eyes looking up at her from beneath the surface.

"A mer!"

"Aye, and good luck it is, but only because there's just one." Brelak's tone was jovial, but not joking. Large schools of merfolk had made war on shipping in the past for some unknown offense. For all she knew, they were trespassing right now. Conversing with the mer was impossible, but they were never dangerous except in large numbers. *En masse*, they were worse than a sea drake.

The mer rolled over, looked up at her, then dove deep, its tail flapping once before vanishing into the limitless blue. Cynthia lifted her eyes from that deep clear water to the strip of white on the horizon: the low, barren shoals of the northernmost of the Shattered Isles. This would be Cynthia's only chance to see them, but from her current position, the view would be poor. She needed to be higher.

"Master Brelak, I'd like to make my way to the poop deck, but I doubt I have the strength." She turned and tried to smile, though she realized she must look no better than a vaguely feminine shipwreck. "Might I ask your help up the steps?"

"O'course, Mistress Flaxal." He held out an arm roughly the diameter of the ship's mainsail yard and took her hand. "You just lean on me as needs be."

"Thank you." Cynthia took him at his word and leaned on him for support. His arm proved every bit as stable as the bulwark railing. Nine steps loomed up to the quarterdeck, and another dozen to the poop. She looked up grimly, determined to do this.

Four steps up, her knees buckled. With one hand on the rail and the other on Brelak's rock-steady arm, she did not fall, but she couldn't continue. She gritted her teeth against the weakness pervading her limbs, and the humiliation of failing in front of professional sailors.

"Here ye' are, Miss Cynthia. I gotcha." Brelak's huge arm encircled her waist, his other hand propped up her elbow. Her feet suddenly left the step. He picked her up as easy as a sack of sailcloth and put her down as steady as a summer breeze, her feet firmly upon the quarterdeck. Before she could even protest, he braced her, supporting more than half her weight, and they walked a perfect unwavering line to the poop deck steps. These stood higher, narrower, and much steeper than the steps to the quarterdeck.

"Brelak, I don't know if I can—"

"O'course ya can, Miss Cynthia. Easy as pie, and don't you think fer a second that any of these scupper monkeys'll give you a bit of grief fer it. Not while I'm on board." His voice barely rose over the wind and sea, for her ears alone. "Up we go now."

Her feet hardly touched a step, and the next thing she knew they stood on the poop, looking down at the helmsman. Clear, clean air greeted her, with no smell of the ship and none of the close mustiness that pervaded her cabin. She gratefully accepted his help to the starboard rail and looked forward at the white line of sandy shoals.

"Thank you, Master Brelak." She tried another smile, and this one came more easily. "For everything."

"Naught to thank me for, Mistress. Nothin' at all. 'Tis you I should be thankin'." He tipped his cap and grinned, his teeth unnaturally white against his olive skin and dark hair. "Koybur's been showin' me the plans you made. Ain't a thing I ever thought I'd see, but there's somethin' about that design that calls to the sea. They'll be fine ships, Mistress Flaxal, and none'll be sayin' a thing bad about you once they see 'em sailin'."

"That'll be months from now," she said, keeping her eyes on the low islands ahead. "I'm sure my reputation will be tarnished enough before they're launched."

He remained silent, but also kept his station close to her elbow. She felt as if she stood next to a tree, and had to resist the impulse to lean against that comforting solidity.

"Mistress Flaxal!" Captain Uben's booming voice caught her off guard, but her exhaustion left her unable to actually jump. "Good to see you on deck!" Mouse swooped in from nowhere and landed on the captain's shoulder, earning a chuckle from the man.

"It is good to be on deck, Captain. Thank you."

"Beautiful weather for it." He stood facing the following trade winds, one hand on his hip, the other shading his eyes from the midday sun. "Hardly a bit of swell, and the air's clear as a bell. This is the *only* way to pass the straits. I think your little sprite's good luck for us!"

Mouse flew crookedly from the captain's shoulder to Cynthia's and smiled, patting her head and tugging her ear, whispering his faerie nonsense at her. She smiled back at her little friend, thinking she might just survive.

Yes, if this were the worst of it, she could bear it.

They sailed on until she could hear the dull roar of surf on the reefs ahead. The water lightened to the color of burnished turquoise, and she could see the tide running past the hull. As a consequence of the tide, the ship's progress slowed. The swell mounted slightly; not much, due to the calm winds, but she could feel the uneasiness building in her gut. She willed it down, forcing herself to concentrate on the experience she would never live again. The wind, the waves and the... smell?

The thick stench of guano overtook the ship as the headland passed far enough astern that the shore birds' rookery lay upwind. She gasped, coughed and heaved over the rail while Mouse yelped and fluttered away. She felt Brelak's huge hand on her back, offering support and some measure of comfort, but deep down she wished he would just push her overboard.

When she finished, he handed her a water flask. She took a mouthful and spat it out, then swallowed a tiny bit to ease her throat.

"The smell," she said, handing the flask back.

"Aye, it's a bit strong, ain't it?" He rummaged at his belt and handed her a tiny vial. "Here. Put a drop o' that on yer upper lip. You'll ferget you ever smelt anything bad in yer life."

She looked at the tiny vessel skeptically. "What is it?"

"Mint extract. I keep it handy just in case I get a bunkmate who's, uh..."

"Who stinks?" she asked, pulling the tiny cork from the bottle and sniffing carefully. Her head swirled with the overpowering scent of mint.

"Right you are, right you are. Makes life aboard ship a mite more pleasant sometimes. Don't use much, now. It's strong."

She dabbed her little finger on the lip of the vial and wiped the tiny bit of moisture onto her upper lip. The stench of guano vanished in a wash of mint, settling her stomach a bit. She smiled at the mountainous Morrgrey and held out the vial.

"Thank you."

"Oh, keep it, keep it, Miss Cynthia. My gift to ya." He pressed the knuckles of his right hand to his forehead in a sailor's salute.

"Thank you," she said, tucking the vial into her belt. She looked out at the bleak islands creeping past and took a careful breath. "Not so bad, if my stomach would just—"

"Sail! Sail on the horizon!" The cry from the foremast drew every pair of eyes on the ship.

"What bearing?" the captain bellowed, raising his own eyes to search the distance.

"Three points, starboard bow!" came the call from above. "A single sail. Small. Mayhap a fisherman."

"And mayhap it's me Aunt Perdy's backside!" Koybur hoisted himself up the steps to the poop deck. "Gotta be one of Bloodwind's messengers, Capt'n."

"Or a lookout," Brelak said in a dark tone. It had long been suspected that the pirates of the Shattered Isles used small, quick craft to look out for prey. Smaller boats could spot the taller sails of a merchant before their own could be seen, then they would dart away to signal a lurking corsair.

"What course?" Uben yelled back to the lookout.

A pause ensued during which not a breath was drawn on the poop deck. They were committed to their course, could not turn back, but if they had to run, knowing sooner could be the difference between escape and watery tomb.

"Can't say her heading, Capt'n," the lookout's called. "She's hull down, on a steady bearing."

"Damn and blast!" Captain Uben glanced around the deck, obviously reviewing his options.

"That could be very good, or very bad," Koybur put in, his tone almost jovial compared to the captain's.

"If they're headed northwest, they're no threat. If they're headed southeast, there could be a corsair behind them, just over the horizon."

"Exactly, lass," Koybur said, his scar-ravaged face twisting into a hideous grin. "How lucky you feelin'?"

"Right now I'm not feeling anything but nauseous," she said, gripping the rail and swallowing hard.

Uben looked at her incredulously. "This ain't no time for jokes, Mistress Flaxal."

"I'm not joking, Captain." She nodded to the spy glass in his hand. "But I'll wager your glass is a finer instrument than the one the lookout is using. A pair of sharp eyes on the main-top with that glass could tell us more of the threat."

"Aye, and a good suggestion." He handed the bronze tube to Brelak. "Care to have a look, Master Brelak?"

"Quick as quick, Capt'n." Brelak snatched the glass from Uben's hand and trundled down the steps to the quarterdeck, then the main deck. He swarmed up the ratlines to the mainsail yard before Koybur could hobble across the deck to Cynthia's side.

"He moves well fer such a big feller," Uben said, squinting up at the Morrgrey. In moments, Brelak stood at the topsail yard, as high as he could go without sprouting wings. He braced himself, wrapping one huge leg around the topmast, and brought the telescope up to his eye. In a few moments, his voice boomed down to the deck.

"Headin' nor'west. Looks like a fishin' smack. She's leavin' us behind."

"Well, that settles it. She's no threat, at least not to us."

"Meaning exactly what, Captain?" Cynthia asked, concentrating on not succumbing to another bout of nausea after watching Brelak's breathtaking climb.

"Meaning she's either not a pirate or she's deliverin' what they've already taken from some poor merchant." He nodded up the coast. "Many's the small harbor where they won't ask questions if a small boat delivers a load of silks or teakwood. They just pay 'em about half the market value, then sell it again to another merchant captain."

"There's a story of a cask of Nort'amber whiskey that was pirated and resold and repirated so many times, that it started out a ten-year old, and was finally sold at market as an eighteen!"

"Not bloody likely, Koybur," Brelak said, his feet back firmly on the poop deck. He handed the glass back to the captain and grinned at the old joke. "Bloodwind would'a drunk it himself if it ever made it past a twelve-year-old."

"As much as I'd like to listen to tales, gentlemen, I think I need to get back to my cabin." Cynthia tried to smile, but her knees quaked so badly she could only manage a grimace. "I need to lie down."

"Oh, come on, Cyn. The air's doin' ya good! Let me get you a cuppa tea and a biscuit. It'll settle yer stomach."

"Koybur, I don't think I can stand—"

"Oh, the biscuits ain't that bad. I'll put a dollop o' honey on it and it'll go down like Marta's scones."

"No, Koybur. I mean... I really don't... think I can..." Cynthia tried to force her words out, tried to focus on Koybur's face, but the bright sunlight dimmed, and the blue water went gray. What little strength remained in her limbs melted away, and it felt as if the waves beneath the keel came up her legs and engulfed her. She felt herself falling, and heard a stream of curses before her senses finally fled.

CHAPTER FIFTEEN
The Jaws of the Trap

A SWARTHY MAN STOOD abaft of the main sheets of the small fishing smack, leaning against the creaking boom and chewing a piece of sun-dried fish. The little vessel heeled on a broad reach, making his perch quite comfortable, the boom resting firmly against the seat of his ragged trousers. He looked forward, then aft, eying the angle on the headland and the distant speck of white on the horizon, the topsails of the *Winter Gale*.

"Looks like we're leavin' 'em, sure enough." The short man at the tiller grinned up at him, showing the gaps in his broken and yellowed teeth.

The swarthy man made a noncommittal noise and took another bite of the salty fish.

"Wha'd you 'spect, Vash?" a third man said from his position within the boat's tiny cabin. "Nothin' but a man-o-war could catch this li'l smack." He patted the hatch combing affectionately. "Fastest li'l boats e'r made, like."

"Nix on the talk o' warships, Berl," the man on the boom said around his mouthful of fish. He spat a bone overboard and glared at both of them. "Your flappin' mouth brings one down on us and I'll have your liver on a stick for fish bait." He shook his head in disgust, thinking, *Why can't these two tongue-wagging old women be more like Wopek?*

Wopek just lay in his hammock snoring, swinging with the sharp motions of the smack. Granted, the man was a desert savage, but he didn't yammer on like a fishwife either, and he had some skill with those two funny-looking, backward-bent knives of his.

"Aye, *Capt'n* Karek," Berl said, his tone less than subordinate.

"I *am* captain, Berl, so don't forget it!" Karek held no true rank, but he *was* in command. That didn't mean they had to like it, only that they had to obey. "Now get some sleep. You're on the tiller for the next watch." Vash laughed at the other man's scowl, but cut it short as the toe of Karek's boot prodded him from behind. "Tend your sheets, Vash! I wanna pass close enough to Point Haze to wet it with a stream o' piss."

"Pissin' distance it is, Capt'n," Vash said cheerfully, hauling in a hand's breadth of the main sheet and steering half a point to windward without a fault. Karek grunted with satisfaction; *at least the scupper dog's good for somethin'.*

The rocks off Point Haze induced larger ships into giving the headland a wide berth, but a small boat could cut inside the reef and use the profound cape effect to dash up the coast at a reckless pace for five leagues. Not that they were really in a hurry, but time ashore beat time on a small boat with two men who wouldn't shut up.

Karek looked astern again, but the sails of *Winter Gale* had vanished over the horizon. "Wish we was huntin' instead of settin' a trap for that Gods-damned Morrgrey," he muttered, spitting the last few fish bones over the side.

"Aye, Capt'n. Huntin'. That's what I'd rather be doin'!" The helmsman chuckled to himself, but Karek just glared at the man's back.

Damned chattermouth, he thought. *Eight more days on this damned little smack before we're in Tsing, and I gotta listen to that mouth the whole way.*

But four men did seem overkill for one fat Morrgrey. He glared harder. Maybe Vash would get clumsy tending his jib sheets and fall overboard... by accident... at night... with a knife in his ribs.

≈

As evening faded into night, an unlit ship with her hull and sails painted the color of midnight sailed past Rockport harbor two hundred leagues north of Point Haze. The ship passed the harbor's mouth, rounded the great rock that earned the harbor its name and turned toward shore. The huge promontory sheltered the ship in its lee; a perfect anchorage for delivering a dangerous or illicit cargo.

Sails were furled as the anchor splashed into the inky depths, all without a shout or call. The anchor bit into the sand, but even before the ship settled on her rode, a launch swung outboard and lowered into the gently rolling swell. The creek and groan of wood against wood and the rattle of metal buckles and scabbards were the only sounds as the boat shoved off and the oarsmen pulled for the beach. The rhythmic hiss of the surf masked the rasp of the boat's keel grinding upon the sand and the splashes of a dozen sailors pulling the boat ashore.

A man strode forward flanked by several others; tall, dark and powerfully built, he had a self-assured bearing. This was Tyhoon, boatswain of the *Black Guard*. He stopped a few yards up the beach and listened for a moment, but nothing reached his ears except the hiss of the surf.

"Good," Tyhoon said, turning back to his crew. "Fala, Brudie and Jeb with me. The rest of you stay with the launch. Anyone comes down the beach without whistlin' a boarding pipe's ditty gets a bolt in 'im. A'right?"

A quiet course of aye's confirmed the orders.

"A'right. With me, then." He strode into the night, three shapes following closely.

He found the beach trail easily, and started up the sandy path over the hill. As the trail crested the hill and started down the other side, the thrill of a whippoorwill stopped them in their tracks. He whistled a boarding pipe's three note call into the night and waited.

A cloaked figure stepped from the shadows and moved toward the group, his steps as silent as the night breeze. He stopped two strides from Tyhoon.

"Well?"

"Bloodwind's got work for ya, Yodrin. Two, maybe three days, the *Winter Gale*'ll sail into Rockport. The owner, some rich girl, has got plans to build a couple-a new ships. A new *kind*-a ship. Bloodwind wants people here and in Tsing to get hired on as crew and officers so we can take these new ships for corsairs. He wants you to get picked as a captain or mate."

The man paused, but Yodrin didn't respond. The silence grew oppressive, and Tyhoon shifted uncomfortably.

"Is that all?" Yodrin finally asked.

"Aye, sir, that's all. We're to leave four men here to pose as crew for hire, and you're to pick up an officer's slot."

"Good." Yodrin took a step forward and plunged a knife into Tyhoon's stomach, just below the sternum. He silenced the gasp with his other hand, supporting the larger man's weight with the blade as his victim's knees buckled.

"This is the price for using my name outside Blood Bay," he said to the dying man, just loud enough for the others to hear.

As Tyhoon's last breath escaped between Yodrin's fingers, the assassin let the corpse drop to the sandy trail. The others backed away a step, shocked at the incident but not willing to confront Yodrin for the murder of their boatswain. After all, one of them might be promoted as a consequence. The assassin stooped to clean his blade on the dead man's tunic before addressing the others.

"Pick him up." It was not a request. When two of them had him by the arms and one held his legs, Yodrin said, "Good. Now back to the ship."

"You... you're comin' wi' us, sir?" one of the men asked as they started forward.

"I will go to Tsing. Four are enough to hire here. More will cause suspicion."

"Aye, sir!"

The grim procession followed him up over the crest of the hill and down to the beach where the others waited. Without being told to do so, Yodrin whistled a boarding call as they neared the men waiting beside the boat.

"How'd he know to do that?" Fala whispered to Jeb.

"Because your bosun was as subtle as he was secretive," Yodrin said without turning. "I was not twenty paces away when he barked out his orders. It's a wonder the entire Rockport militia didn't hear. Put his body in the launch."

He paused to survey the others.

"Which of you were told they would stay here to pose as crew to be hired?" Four sailors stepped forward, one of them a woman. "Fine. Now, Rockport is too small to have four sailors just walk in without an explanation, so here is your story. You were all crew on the timber hauler *Blakely Boy*. She was run aground near Bird Bay five days ago and lost on the rocks. The captain's name was Thorn, and he was drunk when the ship grounded. He'd put an inexperienced hand on watch and gone to his bunk. The Iron Point Timber Company sent a man who fired the captain on the spot, and gave you all your walking notices and your back pay. Now you're looking for work. Got it?"

"Where was the ship comin' from?" one of the men asked.

"Good." Yodrin nodded, obviously appreciating the man's willingness to take on the part. "She was outbound from Beriknor with spruce spars, bound for Fornice. Some prince down there's building warships. The cargo was lost, as were the ship's papers. No lives lost. Any more questions?"

"Who was the mate?"

"A woman named Kali Drin. She caught a caravan northward, and may be in Tsing when I get there."

"You mean she's a real person?" the same man asked. "This ain't a made-up story?"

"Of course it's real. What kind of idiot would believe it if it weren't?"

"What if one of the real crew shows up in Rockport?"

"That shouldn't happen, but if it does, cut his throat before he can smoke you out. There's a nice deep sinkhole just west of town. I've used it before. Make sure the body stays sunk if you have to use it. Anything else?"

There were no other questions.

"Good. Now, play yourselves as mates. You've sailed before and you know your business and each others' as well. That'll make you more likely to all get hired together. Got it?"

They all said yes, though some puzzled looks passed between them. Yodrin eyed them dubiously; if they failed to get hired there would be no big problem, but if they were smoked out as imposters, the Flaxal woman would be wary when she arrived in Tsing.

"You've got two days to blend in and get your stories straight. Make up some names of other crewmen, and talk a lot. Spend some money in the pubs, like a sailor would if he'd been set ashore with all his back pay. By the time the *Winter Gale* gets here, you'll be solid citizens. All right?"

They all agreed, a bit more confidently this time.

"Good. Now, off with you. Don't go into town until midmorning."

They all nodded and vanished into the darkness. Yodrin hissed orders at the skiff's crew, and the boat pushed through the gentle surf, its oars biting into the deep black water. The assassin crouched in the stern of the launch, eyes forward, his agile mind racing far ahead to his landfall in Tsing, the greatest city on the south coast, and the seat of the Empire. *Yes, a fertile hunting ground indeed...*

His thoughts were so focused that he did not notice the dull red glow emanating from the eye sockets of the magically animated water construct lurking beside the dark hull of the *Black Guard*. The translucent reptilian head turned lazily in the water, its gaze taking in the image of the approaching skiff and the tall man kneeling in the stern.

≈

"Miss Cynthia!" Brelak's broad knuckles rapped on the cabin door smartly. "Miss Cynthia, we're comin' into Rockport. We'll be passin' the outer mark any moment." He tried the handle again, but it would not yield. She had been locked in her cabin for more than three days now, allowing no one but Koybur inside.

"Miss Cynthia, you've gotta answer me! Everyone's a mite worried 'bout you. Lockin' yer door ain't doin' nobody no good." Still she would not answer. He gnawed his thumbnail nervously. Koybur said she was in no danger, that she was keeping some water down, but losing weight. Still, he worried. She did not have much weight to lose, and she'd been so weak at the Shattered Isles.

She had been mortified at her fainting spell, and though there were rumors, they were not the kind she feared. They were all concerned for her, from the captain to the lowest cabin boy.

"Miss Cynthia, if you don't open this door to me, I'll break it down. I swear, I will."

"No, you will not, Master Brelak," came a weak reply from within. "I told Koybur to bring me soap and water. Where is he?"

"Probably tryin' to talk that skinflint of a steward out of a whole bucket of fresh water." The ship's motion changed, and Brelak knew they had passed the breakwater. "There, Miss Cynthia, we're in the harbor. Can you feel the change? You'll be feelin' right as rain in no time."

"After Koybur returns, bring me something to eat, something mild, like porridge and tea. But not until *after* Koybur returns. Do you understand, Master Brelak? Not until after."

"Aye, Mistress. I understand."

He walked away, wondering why Cynthia wouldn't let him help her, and feeling about as useful as an anchor on a sinking ship. If he could just talk to her, maybe read to her, he could distract her from her misery...

He heard the bump-thud of someone coming down the corridor, then another thud, the splash of water hitting the deck and a stream of curses that could only have come from Koybur. His lopsided form lurched down the companionway and stopped, his one good eye fixing upon Brelak in surprise.

"What're you doin' down here?"

"I just figgered since we was near shore, she might be feelin' up to some comp'ny."

"Not with her pride, my friend." Koybur edged past the big man, slopping some water on Brelak's boots. "Until she's feelin' herself and set to rights with a judicious application of soap an' water, she'd not let the emperor himself come in that cabin."

"She said to bring some food once you'd seen her, so I'll roust the cook and see what he can make up quick-like. Her pride's gonna be the death of her if she ain't careful," he said, turning for the companionway steps.

"Just knock when you bring the food," Koybur said. "I'll wager it'll take longer to scrub five days of seasickness off her than it'll take to make breakfast."

Brelak nodded, wondering how anyone as young as Cynthia could have built up such a store of stubbornness.

≈

When evening found the *Winter Gale* swinging gently on her mooring, and Cynthia had scrubbed, eaten two meals, and dressed in clean clothes, she finally made an appearance on deck. It would be a brief appearance, for she'd already ordered Captain Uben to prepare the launch and a shore party to escort her into town. To her surprise, the entire ship's company had turned out for her departure. She would rather have taken a dozen lashes than face them after her disgraceful fainting episode; she knew what sailors thought of weakness, and what they thought of landsmen.

"Mistress Flaxal," Uben said with a tip of his cap, "the launch is at your disposal, and the crew wishes to pay their respects." Mouse chose that moment to flutter down from the rigging, tooting a shrill note on a pilfered boatswain's whistle. He landed on her shoulder and danced a jig, tooting his whistle again and again.

Laughter and comments rang out from the crew.

"That little rascal"

"That's where me whistle went!"

Cynthia shushed the little sprite and tried to snatch the whistle, but he ducked and wobbled away on his tattered wings, continuing his shrill tune. She took a breath and turned back to Captain Uben.

"Thank you, Captain, and please relay my regrets to the crew. I'm in a rush. Their respects are appreciated." She moved to the boarding ladder, oblivious to the crestfallen faces in her wake. A low murmur swept the deck, silenced immediately by the boatswain. The only sound she could hear as she stood looking down at the waiting launch was the incessant two-tone toot of Mouse with his whistle. Koybur and Brelak sat in the boat with half a dozen oarsmen and a boy to tend the lines.

"Please send a messenger around midmorning tomorrow, Captain. I should have an estimate of our departure time by then." She looked dubiously at the haphazard cluster of pale stone structures lining the waterfront of Rockport. "I don't suspect we'll have much to choose from, so my guess is that we may sail morning after tomorrow."

"We've made good time so far, Mistress. If you'd like to take an extra day to—"

"Morning after tomorrow will be fine, thank you, Captain." She swung out on the chains and made her way down without pausing or accepting a hand to aid her descent. She sat stone-faced and staring forward, knees shaking under her skirt, her cheeks glowing in the waning evening light.

"Cast off!" Brelak barked. "Smartly now. Not a drop comes inboard from them oars, or I'll personally stick 'em where the sun don't shine."

The shrill whistling stopped as Mouse realized that Cynthia had left the ship. He dropped the whistle and fluttered like a drunken butterfly down to the launch, landing on her shoulder. The launch pitched with the first thrust of the oars, forcing the seasprite to grab Cynthia's collar to keep from toppling over backward.

Minutes later, Cynthia, Brelak and Koybur stood on the small stone quay, two seamen armed and ready behind them. Cynthia wasn't armed, of course, not knowing the first thing about how to use a cutlass or even a dagger, and Koybur wore only his rigging knife. Brelak bore two heavy boarding axes tucked into his belt instead of the more traditional cutlass of a sea officer. Rockport didn't really have that bad a reputation, but they saw no point in taking chances. Unlike Scarport, which had a steady traffic of goods and services changing hands locally, Rockport did not support much more than a transition station for caravans and ships.

"Which inn, Koybur?" she asked, trying to ignore the tickle of Mouse as he cowered behind her collar, shy in the unfamiliar surroundings.

"No idea." She gaped at him, but he just grinned his horrible maimed grin. "I ain't been here in twenty years, Cyn. Might ask Master Brelak. He's probably been through these parts recently."

At her questioning stare the big Morrgrey said, "About a year ago. The Flying Monkey is right up the road, and about the best in town."

"The *Flying Monkey*?" Cynthia's features faded from questioning to skeptical.

"Aye. The feller who bought the place some years back said he'd seen one. He blamed a witch for conjuring the things and runnin' off the whole populace of his home town. Never said nothin' 'bout 'zactly *where* he was from, but he'll tell ya there's no place like it." He paused and scratched his chin. "He's a strange bird, sure enough, but he runs a tight ship."

"As long as the food's good and the bed's soft, I'm in."

An hour later, as she polished her plate with the last crust of bread, Cynthia began to feel more like herself. Mouse had eaten so much he could no longer fly, and lounged with his back propped against a gravy boat, eyes closed in bliss and his hands spread over his distended tummy.

"Passable. Right passable," Koybur announced as the maid took the dishes.

"Any more passable and you would have licked your plate," Cynthia said.

"I think our Mistress is feeling som'at better," said Brelak, waving for the barmaid to bring another round of ale.

"Better, but still not very good," she said, frowning with memory of her unforgivable display on the deck of the *Winter Gale*. "I don't know how I'm going to manage six or seven more days to Tsing."

"Mayhap we should take an extra day here to let you recover some. Captain Uben said there was—"

"Captain Uben is not in charge of the timetable. I am."

"Sorry, Mistress Cynthia. I didn't mean to imply—"

"Never mind, Master Brelak. I know you didn't mean anything, but with the whole crew laughing at me behind their hats, I don't want to delay the trip any longer than necessary."

"Laughin'?" Brelak barked incredulously, his dark features flushing. "Not a single sailor aboard the *Winter Gale* is laughin' at you, Mistress Cynthia. There ain't naught in 'em but concern for you."

"You don't have to lie to save my feelings, Feldrin."

"Now Cyn, don't—"

"I am *not* lyin', Mistress," Brelak said through clenched teeth, straining to hold his temper in check.

"Oh, come on. I know they're all chuckling about the mistress of ships who can't even sail in one without voiding her guts all the way across the Southern Ocean."

The big man stood abruptly as the second round of ale arrived. "You *might* know some o' the banter sailors pass around about lubbers, but not a word o' that applies to you, Mistress Flaxal. They were turned out this afternoon to pay you their respects and wish you well. You *might* have seen that if you'd've taken the time to hear 'em out."

The barmaid cringed and moved away, while several other patrons looked nervously at the big man. Mouse vanished behind the bread basket, peeking around the wicker frame in terror.

"Brelak, please. Sit down."

"My pardon, Mistress, but I feel the need for a breath of air." He snatched up one of the three tankards and turned on his heel, striding out of the common room without another word.

"He *does* have a temper," Cynthia said worriedly, thanking the barmaid and sipping her ale.

"He's a Morrgrey, Cyn, and that weren't nothin'." He drank deeply and struggled to his feet with a grimace of pain. "Callin' a Morrgrey a liar's usually worth a busted jaw. He was tellin' you the truth, by the way."

"So now you're angry with me, too."

"Na, I'm not angry. I just think you need to open yer eyes wide enough ta see past yer own pride." He took another deep draught of his tankard and put it down. "I gotta do some business tonight if yer gonna have anyone to talk to tomorrow. I'll be back late, so don't wait up."

She watched him leave, wondering whether either of them were telling her the truth. As she sat lost in her thoughts, Mouse emerged from hiding, waddled over to Koybur's abandoned tankard and peered over the rim, obviously wondering if he could get at the ale without drowning.

Cynthia watched the seasprite absently, thinking about the actions of her two companions. She couldn't imagine the crew of the *Winter Gale* harboring any measure of respect for her after her display on the poop deck, but Brelak didn't seem the type to lie about something like that. She sipped and thought, wondering about Koybur's comment concerning her pride. Was she being a spoiled brat, letting her pride blind her?

A tiny splash brought her out of her reverie as Mouse toppled headfirst into the tankard. The sprite's feet kicked frantically from the top of the cup before he managed to curl up and stand. Drenched in ale, his thistledown hair plastered flat and his pointed little ears drooping, he smacked his lips and grinned.

She fished him out and sat him on the table, offering her napkin. Mouse scoffed at the cloth, stripped out of his shirt and held it over his head, wringing the ale from it into his upturned mouth. He burped, the sound like the chirp of a tree frog, which drew a smile from Cynthia. She poured some of Koybur's ale into a saucer and watched the little sprite drink himself into a happily sodden slumber.

CHAPTER SIXTEEN
Baiting the Hook

"VERY WELL, THEN," CYNTHIA said, shaking the hands of the four sailors she'd just hired, three men and a woman who had worked together on a timber hauler. The negotiations had been simple enough. They were eager for work and intrigued by the new ships. Mouse lounged on her shoulder throughout and drew only curious mirth from them.

"Master Brelak will give you enough for passage to Southaven, and half of your first month's pay. I'll draft a letter to the shipwright there, Master Keelson. You'll be working under his supervision until the ships are afloat."

"Scuse me, Mistress Flaxal, but I ain't no carpenter. Ain't ne'r claimed to be one. We hauled timber, we never built nothin' out of it."

"Well, I daresay you'll learn a bit of carpentry before we're afloat. I'm sure there will be plenty of splicing, hauling and general labor to be done."

They thanked her, saluted in deference and turned to Brelak for their pay. They certainly looked like they'd been working on a timber hauler; two of the four were missing fingers, and all bore scars on hands, wrists and even faces. Working under an overzealous boatswain could earn a sailor a few scars, but they bore more than average.

After they'd gone, she asked him, "What do you think of them?"

"Seem capable enough, Mistress, though a bit rough." He'd not called her by name all morning. His temper from the previous evening still simmered, but he only acted aloof, not straining to hold his anger as he had before. "Don't know about them comin' down from the Northlands, though. They seem a bit tan fer this time of year."

"You think they're lying? Why didn't you say something?"

"Not my place, Mistress."

"Not your *place*?" Now it was Cynthia's turn to be angry. She placed one hand flat on the table, turning her full wrath on him as Mouse bolted for cover. "It is *exactly* your place, Master Brelak, and you very well know it! If you spy something odd about anyone I intend to hire, and do *not* say something, I'll have your contract in the fire faster than you can spit. Do you hear me?"

"Yes, Mistress. I hear you," he said, his tone flat and his dark eyes never leaving hers. She could see the temper smoldering in them.

"You're angry with me," she said, turning back to her papers, "and rightfully so. I had no right to question your word. I apologize for assuming that you would lie to save my feelings."

"I *would* lie to save your feelin's," he said with a hint of a smile as Mouse poked his head from around the water pitcher to see if it was safe. "No need to apologize. I just didn't lie about yesterday on the ship."

"Yes, there *is* a need for me to apologize, Feldrin. Aside from Koybur, there's not a soul on this expedition I can trust to tell me when I'm making a mistake. I need your help."

Cynthia stared intently into his dark eyes. Unlike their earlier exchange as they passed the Shattered Isles, when she had had no choice but to accept his help, now she was asking for it. He fidgeted, uncomfortable with that trust; and bowed his head in assent.

"Very well, then, Miss Cynthia. I'll be as honest as I can, and to the Nine Hells with yer feelin's." He stood. "I better go find Koybur. He said he had a prospect, but that it might turn out to be nothin'. It's past mid-mornin'. He should-a been here by now."

"And about these four we just signed on?" she asked as Mouse fluttered back to her shoulder.

"Do I think they're lyin'?" He shrugged his massive shoulders. "About somethin' maybe, but not about bein' stout sailors, and that's all what really matters. My guess is they might have had somethin' to do with the *Blakely Boy* goin' aground and are uncomfortable about it."

"And about their tans?"

"They could've had a bright and sunny fall up north for all I know. Rest easy, Miss Cynthia. They ain't saints, that's fer sure, but none of us are."

"That's all I needed to know. Send word to Captain Uben that we'll be hauling anchor in the morning." He turned to go, but she stopped him with a hand on his arm. "And thank you, Feldrin. I value your honesty very much."

He smiled uncomfortably, knuckling his forehead. "'Tain't nothin', Mistress Flaxal."

She watched him leave, and then said to herself, "You're wrong, Master Brelak. It's everything."

≈

"Haul away!" Karek shouted from the bow of the little fishing smack, bracing himself as the shore crew hauled the vessel up onto the beach atop a row of long planks. Karek gripped the forestay and braced his foot against the short bulwarks as she careened, riding her up the beach like a man guiding a madly rampaging elephant. When her transom cleared the high tide line he called, "Belay haul!" and leapt down to the sandy shore.

"Chock her up and scrape her clean, boys," he said, tossing a silver half-crown to the master of the beach crew.

The smack would be ready for sea by the time the Morrgrey was just another corpse lying in one of the gutters of the Dreggar's Quarter. Karek had three or four days until the *Winter Gale* made port; plenty of time to set up a nice thorough trap.

"Come along, boys. We got money to spend!"

Vash and Berl cheered, joking about the age-old fisherman's trade of fish for gold, gold for rum, rum for women, and then being driven back to sea by a woman's scorn. Wopek just followed along, his dark face impassive, his palms resting on the long knives at his sash. They climbed the steps from the beach to the quay and were immediately confronted by a city constable. Karek smiled; he had counted on this, knowing it would work to their advantage.

"Hold there a moment, gentlemen," the officer said, tipping the iron helm that earned the constables of Tsing their nickname of 'caps'. "You just landed, yes?"

"Aye, sir. That we did." Karek stuck his thumbs in his belt and grinned proudly. "Sold four hundred weight 'o fresh-caught grouper, we did, and we're aimin' to spend about half of it afore we put back out fer home."

"Not from here then?"

"No, sir. We be up from Moorington. Been here once or twice, but never had so much money in our pockets afore."

"Well, be careful what you flash about for people to see. There've been cutpurses workin' the inns around the wharves lately. If it's female companionship you're lookin' for, you might try one of the houses on Bright Street, just up five blocks. They cost a bit more, but the girls are clean and won't knife ya for your purse."

"I'll keep that in mind, but I thinks we're just in for a drink first." He started to lead his men past, but stopped at the constable's raised hand.

"Not but daggers in the city now, right? No swords or axes on you." This was the law Karek knew would help even the odds against the Morrgrey.

"What would a poor fisherman do with a sword, sir?" Karek asked, grinning and showing the poor-looking rigging knife at his belt. He had two long stilettos hidden under his tunic, but even those would not get him in trouble; but the cap was ignoring Karek and looking at the oddly shaped hilts of Wopek's knives.

"And what are those?" the cap asked, pointing at the other man's belt.

"These?" Wopek asked, drawing one slowly from his wide sash. "Surely you have seen the kukri before, good sir constable." He flipped the angled blade and handed it to the cap hilt first. "They are the knives of my desert folk people, the Shinthraha. They are made for fighting and for skinning the chohethra, the great desert cats."

"Damned heavy," the cap said, hefting the blade. It measured almost as long as a short sword, but still qualified as a knife. "You be careful with them things, mister."

"Oh, aye, sir," he agreed.

They left the cap at his post and worked their way into the city.

"Now, the first thing we need," Karek said when they were safely out of earshot, "is some proper bait."

"Bright Street?" Vash asked, grinning and rubbing the stubble on his chin.

"I don't think so." Karek glanced around carefully and said, "I think we need someone who'll work the game for us. A whore won't do for that."

"You want us to snatch some girl for the job, like?" Berl's kept his tone low, his grin sly. "Maybe follow someone home from the bazaar, find out where her family lives?"

"That sounds more to my likin'." Karek grinned and clapped Berl on the shoulder. "Good thinkin'. We'll split up into pairs and have a look 'round. Berl, you and Vash work the bazaar. Wopek and I'll check the inns along the waterfront. Meet back here round dusk. Right?"

They agreed and split up, Vash and Berl heading up the street to the wide city square that held the open-air market. Karek turned and headed back toward the waterfront, Wopek close at his heel. There had to be at least one poor barmaid with a vulnerable mother or child they could use as leverage. The best performances were well-motivated, after all.

≈

"And so the pieces move into place," Yodrin murmured, sipping a glass of spiced rum and gazing out the window of the waterfront inn. He'd recognized the tall, dark-skinned pirate with the strange-looking knives as one of Bloodwind's men. *A real killer, that one,* he thought, smiling thinly. If all went well, there would be more pirates than regular crew aboard the ships.

"Wha'd you say, dearie?" the woman asked, raising her tousled mop of red hair from the rumpled pillow.

"Nothing, my dear. You just rest your pretty head a moment and let me enjoy the view."

"All right, my captain," she said, lolling back on the bed, rolling over tantalizingly for him, "but don't forget I'm here."

"I won't forget," he told her, turning back to the view of the quay. He'd arrived only yesterday, the *Black Guard* easing into port under a North-lands flag and bright white sails, her transom covered by a cunningly fitted false one bearing another name. He'd started spreading stories of a lazy crew, a thieving paymaster and a ship full of rotten framing timbers; a captain looking for a ship.

The act came easily, as did the women, and the money he spent helped both. By the time *Winter Gale* made port, he'd be low on his funds and looking in earnest for a permanent billet.

Now more of Bloodwind's thugs were arriving, undoubtedly intent on taking crew berths. It would be quite a waiting game, playing the dutiful crew, the honorable captain, but it would be worth it.

≈

Exhaustion vied with vigilance in Marci's mind as she made her way home from the Hairy Parrot. The hour was late, but she'd earned a good number of tips, enough for a trip to the market tomorrow with some left over for rent. She didn't really like working on the waterfront, but the sailors had money. Most were nice enough, just hard working men and women spending their money on a little fun. Some even seemed to care about her plight—a mother without a husband, whose parents had refused to support her. Those who weren't so kind... Gringle, the bouncer, would talk to them.

She smiled at the thought of the big man suggesting that a sailor be nice to her, because she was a nice girl, and only nice men got to stay in the inn and talk to nice girls. The bouncer might be a little slow of wit, but Gringle was truly gentle and kind, and made sure nothing happened to the girls. The walk home was usually the most dangerous part of her job.

Two blocks into the Dreggar's Quarter she turned right, up Hill Street. She glanced back down Ferryway out of habit as she made the turn, and her breath caught in her throat. Silhouetted by the light of a street lamp, three tall figures approached. She hitched up her skirts and dashed up the hill, making another turn as soon as she could, not taking time to look back. Another half block and she could cut back to her tenement.

She came to the wider street and paused to listen, wondering if she had imagined things. After a moment she crossed the street, entered the alley and climbed the stair where four single-room apartments crowded above a row of shops. She sighed in relief as she topped the stair and tapped quietly on her neighbor Julia's door.

"Marci?" Julia's voice sounded muffled and slurred with sleep.

"Yes, it's me," she answered, knowing the woman had probably been sleeping with her back against the door again. She couldn't expect her to stay up half the night watching her daughter sleep, and was thankful enough that she only charged her a few coppers a day for the service.

The door cracked open and Julia's homely features filled the gap. She smiled and opened the door fully, letting Marci in.

"How was she?" Marci asked as the door clicked closed. Nan, her little girl, slept soundly alongside Julia's twin boys, Pip and Daniel. They were all about the same age, and got along famously.

"A little demon, as usual," Julia said with a tired smile. "I swear, when the three of them get going, they're just impossible."

"Well, at least you tired them out." She paid Julia and lifted little Nan from the bed. The girl barely stirred, a limp weight in her arms. "Thank you, Julia. I'll drop her off around midday tomorrow."

"G'night, Marci." Julia let her out, and she climbed the second flight to her flat, balancing the little girl on her hip and murmuring a quiet lullaby. She worked the latch and entered her tiny apartment, putting Nan on the bed and making her way to the kitchen nook for a cup of water.

The door creaked and she turned, the cup falling from numb fingers as three large men came through the door. As the cup shattered, she filled her lungs to scream, but stopped as the largest of the three lowered the tip of a long knife to the sleeping child's throat.

"Now, missy, you just be quiet and listen, like," one of the others said, his tone calm, almost conversational. "We got a li'l business proposition for ya, and if yer smart, you and your li'l daughter'll be just fine, and ye'll have a bit 'o coin in your pocket besides."

With that knife so near Nan's throat, Marci was too scared to even speak. She could only nod.

"Good girl. Now you just listen. We got a li'l job to do, and yer gonna help us."

CHAPTER SEVENTEEN

Shore Leave

THE BREAKWATERS OF TSING harbor passed abeam of *Winter Gale* as the sun ascended to her main yardarm, seven days after their departure from Rockport. By noon the ship rested at a mooring, her crew scrubbing every square inch of her decks and furling her sails as tightly as sausages. They would not get a spot at the quay for at least a day, so Captain Uben would let them go ashore by watches. The crew behaved accordingly, attending to their duties with all gusto, laughing and joking about how they would spend their pay ashore. Mouse became caught up in the fervor, swooping crookedly around the masts and yards, yanking on pigtails and shirt tails and occasionally tying one to the other. His antics were accepted with good grace, if not gentle language.

But of Mistress Cynthia there was no word.

"They say she hasn't had a bite or a drop past her lips fer seven days," one of the sailors said to his mate as the hands turned out for their midday meal.

"Aye, and her man Koybur ain't left her side, neither," the other agreed, taking his plate and cup to a comfortable nook.

"Never seen the likes," Boatswain Riley said, joining the men and passing out their ration of grog. "Don't know how she'll manage the trip back to Southaven."

"Mayhap she'll take a caravan back," one of the cabin boys speculated around a mouthful of stew.

"It'd take near two month ta get back that way, not to mention the danger of it."

"Aye. The mountain ogres are up in arms again. They et a whole caravan just last week!" The sailors laughed, though the inference was more accurate than not. The high mountain passes had become dangerous in the extreme.

"She'll have us duck into port to get her strength back, I'm thinkin'. That'll bite into her profits a bit, ay."

"It don't matter," Riley said, taking his seat. "When it boils down to it, she owns the *Winter Gale*, and she'll do as she likes with 'er. Even if she don't make a bent copper on this haul, she's done what she come to do, and that's hire crew for them new ships."

"Which 'ad be'er make a bloody profit," one of the topmen added, raising a chuckle from a few of his mates. "She's puttin' a lot o' eggs in that basket."

"Near all of 'em, from what I hear," the boatswain agreed.

"Will ya ask the capt'n if we might pay our respects again?" another sailor asked, raising a murmur of ascent from the rest of the crew.

"Aye, I'll ask 'im, but don't expect too much from 'er. The lady's been through a lot."

≈

When Cynthia finally came onto the deck of the *Winter Gale*, the sun stood low to the west, and the crew once again stood lined up precisely in their best clothes with their hats doffed. But this time, when Captain Uben asked if the crew might pay their respects, she surprised them.

"Of course, Captain. I would be honored." Her face shone pale in the light of the setting sun, but her jaw remained firmly set. Mouse whooped in glee and swooped to orbit her head before landing on her shoulder.

"Very good, Mistress." Uben turned to the boatswain and said, "Mister Riley, if you please."

The boatswain piped the traditional two note call, and turned to the crew. "All hands, cheers for Mistress Flaxal! Hip, hip—"

Three cheers rocked the ship from beak head to poop, and rolled across the anchorage so loudly, sailors from nearby ships called out as well. Mouse cheered along with them, doing back flips and kicking up his heels. As the echoes died, Cynthia stepped forward, her smile wide and her face showing a healthy glow.

"Thank you, Mister Riley, and thank you all." She curtsied to them, amazed, now that she really looked at their faces, at how many she recognized from her years of late nights at the Galloping Starfish. "You've all been very understanding about my... condition on this trip, and I'd like to show my appreciation. You deserve more, but when we get back to Southaven, I'll stand you all to a round of drinks at the Starfish."

Mouse did another back flip on her shoulder and let out a whoop as another cheer broke out, more ragged than the prior three, but every bit as genuine.

"The ship's launch is at your disposal, Mistress Flaxal." Captain Uben held out an arm to the boarding port. "If you need anything at all, just send a messenger."

"Thank you, Captain."

The launch's crew swarmed down the boarding ladder to take their places. As Koybur worked his way down, Cynthia looked around the anchorage and caught her breath in astonishment.

"Holy mother of... uh... I mean... my goodness."

She stood marveling at the number of ships filling the anchorage and lining the quay and docks. Upwards of thirty ships, she guessed. Though there were none of the low xebecs or galleys of the south, there were ships of every other type she had seen, and one that she had not. A massive man-of-war swung slowly on her cable, her towering triple masts and quadruple yards dwarfing every other ship in the harbor. Rows of catapults crowded the upper deck and two rows of ports for heavy ballistae studded her hull below.

"I'd like to sail *that* through the Shattered Isles," she commented with a chuckle.

"She's not likely ever to go that far, Mistress," Brelak said, his tone openly scornful. "That's his Majesty's flagship, *Clairissa*. She don't leave harbor much, but when she does, it's fer good reason."

"I'd love to see her under full sail," Cynthia said, letting her eyes drift beyond the ships and take in the rest of the vista.

The city sprawled between two tall bluffs, filling the space between them to overflowing. The Imperial Palace dominated the highest point to the north, its golden spires reaching to the sky as if to grasp the heavens themselves. A long beach lay at the base of that cliff, and served the local fishing fleet as a boatyard, the colorfully painted hulls lined up like parrot fish in a market bin. To the south of the beach a great stone quay lined the entire length of the city's waterfront, broken only at the river mouth where a high bridge spanned the gap. Two heavily built towers guarded that bridge, their crenulated peaks standing like a pair of titanic shoulders.

"I've read that the palace and the quay are dwarvish stonework," Cynthia said, staring in awe.

"Aye, and the towers as well, is what they say," he agreed.

South of the quay, beneath the other broad bluff, lay the legendary shipyards. A dozen ships could be hauled up on that broad expanse to have their hulls cleaned, painted, or rebuilt entirely. Huge gantries towered at either end to replace or refit masts, and a row of drab workshops lined the base of the cliff.

"You could put Southaven right in the middle of that and nobody would notice."

"Aye, true enough. You'll be seeing it up close soon, and if the wind were from the east, you'd be smellin' it already."

"Oh, sorry." Cynthia realized she'd been taking in the sights while everyone waited for her. "Here I stand like a statue! You should have kicked me or something, Feldrin." She stared dubiously down the boarding ladder, took a deep breath and started to climb carefully down.

≈

Cynthia was surprised by the armed constable who met them at the dock and insisted that no weapons other than knives be brought into the city. Brelak knew of the stringent ordinance, and carried only two long daggers, one in his belt and another in his boot. Koybur scoffed and showed the constable his short rigging knife. Mouse spurted a raspberry and made a rude gesture, but the constable ignored him and waved them into the city.

"Any ideas about where we should stay, or do we just find someplace close to the—"

Brelak's piercing whistle cut her off, and even before she could turn to chastise him for startling her meager lunch right out of her, a hackney pulled up.

"Where to, Mistress?" the driver asked, even as the vehicle pulled to a stop.

"I don't think we—"

"Midtown," Brelak answered, opening the carriage door for Cynthia.

"Brelak, I really don't think we need a carriage." Cynthia stared at him, a warning in her eyes as she hissed quietly, "I'm not an invalid!"

"You may want to walk two miles uphill on cobbles to reach a decent inn, Mistress, but I don't care to, and I don't think Master Koybur could make the trip in two hours."

"Damned right," Koybur said, mounting the carriage without pause. "You comin', Cyn?"

"Two *miles*, just to midtown?" Cynthia boarded, ignoring Mouse's giggle of amusement.

"Aye, and that's not even halfway across the city. Tsing's wider north to south than she is east to west, but it's near five mile from the wharves to Eastwall Street."

"Anywhere in particular, sir?" the driver asked Brelak, deciding the big man would be making the decisions and most likely paying the fare.

"A nice inn. Nothing too high-priced, but not the dregs. Someplace that serves good food. I'm makin' a point to remember yer face, my friend, so if we get stiffed, I'll be lookin' for ya."

"No need to insinuate, sir. I know just the place. The chef's my brother-in-law, and if you gauge the size o' my sister's backside as an indication of his culinary prowess, he's the best cook in the whole bloody city!"

They all laughed and agreed to the choice. Brelak hoisted his considerable bulk into the carriage, the coachman cracked his whip and the stout pair of bays trotted up the wide avenue.

The clatter of iron-shod hooves and wheels on cobbles prevented any kind of normal conversation, so Cynthia occupied herself by taking in the sights as they passed, while Mouse yammered and pointed from her shoulder. The air became close and more oppressive as they progressed into the city, and with each block the smell of tightly packed humanity became more overpowering.

Brelak noticed Cynthia's wrinkled nose, and shouted, "See what I meant about the smell?"

"I'm wishing I hadn't left your mint oil on the *Winter Gale*, but I'm sure I'll get used to it," she replied. "I don't think anything could interfere with my appetite right now."

"The Downwinds might," he said, making a face as more odors wafted through the open carriage windows. "Open sewers, and naught but a call of 'look out below' to warn ya when a chamber pot's bein' emptied from three floors up."

"Lovely," she said, as Mouse held his nose and emitted a squeal of disgust.

They rumbled along without trying to continue the conversation. When the carriage pulled aside and slowed to a stop, Cynthia looked dubiously out at the façade of the Red Gryphon Inn. It was a three-story structure with a shallow pitched roof of red tile, less than spitting distance from the adjoining buildings. The foyer could have used a coat of paint, and some of the gilt-work on the hanging board had flaked off.

"Here we are!" the driver announced, vaulting down and making a show of helping the passengers exit. "Just tell 'em Tobi sent ya, and I'm sure they'll do right by ya." He smiled up at Brelak and held out his hand discreetly. "A silver bit for the ride, sir."

Brelak helped Koybur and Cynthia down from the carriage and fished the appropriate coin from his pouch, adding a fair tip.

"I'll be rememberin' you, Tobi," he said, smiling down at the man. Mouse knew that tone and ducked under Cynthia's collar, but Tobi seemed oblivious, simply smiling back up at the huge sailor.

"Most excellent, sir! If you need my services during your stay, just ask my brother-in-law to send for me. I'm at your disposal." He tipped his cap and vaulted back to the driver's seat. "Cheers, now!"

The interior of the inn showed them exactly what the exterior suggested: comfortable and clean, but slightly worn, as if the owner were too lazy or uncaring to replace a cracked lamp chimney or paint a chipped door frame.

The low, wide desk occupying the entry could have used a good application of oil, and smoke had stained the ceiling above the hanging lamps. But wonderful aromas of well-cooked food and the sound of clattering dishes and animated conversation from the common room suggested that the place sported a loyal clientele. Brelak stepped forward and rang the hand bell.

"If yer here just for supper, go right in and ask Belela for a table," said a voice from behind the door beyond the desk. The voice had a surly tone, so Brelak answered in kind.

"We are *not* here just fer supper. We need rooms. Good rooms, *and* a table fer supper."

"Oh! Well, then." The door swung open and a rotund dwarf hobbled out. "Why didn't ye say so?" One of the fellow's legs ended at the mid thigh, and was fitted with a wooden post that thudded against the floor as he stepped to the desk and scowled up at the foursome.

"I just *did* say so, Master Dwarf."

"So ye did." He squinted up at the big man, then at the other two. "Two rooms, or three? I like to know a bit about my guests, ye understand. Ye don't look like a married couple."

"Married?" Brelak's dark skin flushed darker, and his fists clenched at his sides while he sputtered out a reply. "Of all the... Why I... O' *course* we're not married!"

Cynthia stepped forward to rescue the tongue-tied Morrgrey, smiling at the short innkeeper. "Maybe I can clear this up. I'm Cynthia Flaxal, Mistress of the Flaxal Shipping Line. We'll need two rooms, adjoining ones if you have them. One for myself and one for Master Brelak and my man Koybur to share. I'm in Tsing on a hiring expedition, so I'll be using your common room to interview prospective officers and crew. We were fortunate enough to meet Tobi, the brother-in-law of your chef, who said that you would do right by us."

"Yer pardon, Miss Cynthie Flaxal, but not everyone's who or what they claim to be, and ye don't look like no mistress of no shippin' line. Ye look like a girl what hasn't had a decent meal in a month." The innkeeper's tone held no animosity, but he was obviously not impressed by Cynthia's speech.

"Not quite a month, Master...?" She cocked an eyebrow questioningly.

"Me name's Knorr, and I'm the owner of the Red Gryphon."

"It hasn't been quite a month, Master Knorr, but I have been at sea for a week, which has left me quite famished. I assure you, I am who and what I say. If you require a deposit for the rooms, that will be fine, but if you insist on knowing more about your guests, you will have to wait until after dinner. If I am forced to stand much longer without sampling the fare that I am inhaling with every breath, I'm going to faint."

Whether the innkeeper believed her last claim or not, it brought a smile to his aged features, and he nodded his approval.

"I've got one suite that would suit yer purposes nicely, Mistress Flaxal. It's a bit more than two rooms, but considerin' you'll be bringin' in business with yer interviews and ye were recommended by Tobi, I'll give it to ye for the same price. It's got a small sittin' room that'll do for your interviewin'. Half a crown per night, breakfast included for all. Lunch's on yer own, and supper here is our busy time, as ye can see, and it's an extra silver bit for each guest."

"That will suit perfectly, Master Knorr. Please book us for three nights, and I may require an extra night or two depending on our success. Three for dinner tonight and we'll decide later if everyone wants to eat here or sample the variety of your fair city."

"It ain't my city, lass, and it ain't as fair as all that." He pulled a heavy ledger from under the desk and opened it. "Please sign, and if ye'd be so kind as to include the name o' the ship ye sailed on, I'd appreciate it."

Cynthia signed. "Can you accommodate us immediately for dinner, or must we wait?"

"And risk havin' you faint dead away right in my front hall?" He flipped the book closed and lurched around the desk. "This way!"

Tables full of diners crowded the huge common room, but the three were seated with no trouble. Cynthia listened patiently to the harried waitress, ordered the pheasant pie and asked if they could get a round of ale and a plate of fruit and cheeses while awaiting dinner. The others ordered, and their waitress came back with their drinks and the cheese plate before Cynthia's stomach could growl three times.

"Mmm, food," she said around a mouthful of creamy white cheese and papaya. "What a marvelous creation."

Mouse fluttered down to the table and broke off a corner of a crumbly red cheese as he eyed the crowd. He hefted the cheese knife experimentally, decided it was not balanced for throwing and settled down to munch. Cynthia sampled combinations of sharp, mild and spicy cheeses with the assorted fruits, delighted with each. The men nibbled at a less lupine pace and talked of the city and how things had changed in the two decades since Koybur had been here.

"O'course, it was the old emperor back then. Not the same city at all, by the feel of it. Wonder who finally put a dagger in the old bastard's back."

"It was poison, from what I heard," Brelak said, sipping his ale and letting his eyes drift to a comely serving girl. He jerked his gaze back to his ale and glanced sidelong at Cynthia.

"Whoever did the deed, I'd like to shake his hand. We're all the better for it." Koybur grinned and jogged his elbow, but their mistress didn't notice the exchange.

"Aye." Brelak drank deeply and sighed. "Emperor Tynean's twice as powerful and three times as rich, not to mention havin' the common folk on his side, and we have some poor sap with a vial of poison to thank for it."

"And nobody's done a thing about the piracy in the Shattered Isles, because it's not a kingdom or nation or empire doing the burning, killing and pillaging." Cynthia drank some ale and shook her head.

"It's a harder war to fight," Koybur said, spearing a slice of mango and biting off half. "Just like the roads through the mountain passes and the brigands and ogres. You can't fight what you can't find."

"Come on, Koybur, how hard would it be to sail that monstrosity of a warship up and down the Shattered Isles until you found the one Bloodwind is using for a stronghold?"

"Not that easy, Cyn. That ship can beat any corsair, or even half a dozen, in a stand up fight. But how do you find their stronghold without explorin' every cove and inlet? That means riskin' runnin' up on a reef, or comin' across one of them tribes of head-huntin' savages, or even a school of merfolk. On top of that, Bloodwind'd probably smoke out the plan a month before the *Clairissa* shipped anchor."

"He's got spies in every harbor, sure enough," Brelak agreed, the muscles of his jaw bunching and relaxing rhythmically.

"Well, there's not much we can do about it tonight," Cynthia relented with a sigh. "So, how do we get the attention of every out-of-work captain, bosun and sailor in Tsing? You going out tonight, Koybur?"

"I might if Master Brelak wants to come along, but only to have a drink and maybe a bit of fun. You'll want to draft a note for the poster boards to bring in sailors. We can draft one tonight, and have it up by mid-morning tomorrow."

"I'll go out with you tonight if you wish," the Morrgrey said with a grin. "Been a while since I had a night in Tsing with money in my pocket."

"You afraid to go out alone, Koybur?"

"Here? Damn right, I am. Any sane man would be, and any woman would be plain foolish to go out alone." He affixed his one good eye on her and scowled. "You remember that, Cyn. Tsing might have a truly benevolent and kind emperor, but the city is still about as safe as a chatter viper."

"Fine. I'll stay locked in my room every night," she said with a pout, only half joking; it would take her a couple of days to build her strength back to the point where she could enjoy an evening of drinking and carousing.

Conversation halted as their dinners arrived, three plates mounded with meats, vegetables, potatoes, yams, sauces, gravies, jellies and a pheasant pie the size of an entire dinner plate. The waitress almost placed one of the plates on top of Mouse, and was startled as badly as the sprite. She'd never seen a seasprite before and made a big fuss over him, earning a glare for calling him cute, but making up for it by promising to bring him a special treat from the kitchen.

≈

The door of the tiny flat opened without a knock and Vash stepped inside.

"They're here," he said, grinning at his companions. Wopek sat on a ragged divan, bouncing the little girl Nan on his knee, his huge hands encircling her tiny torso completely. The girl laughed at her " Unca Opek" and urged him to bounce faster. Berl just looked disgusted. "They're stayin' at the Red Gryphon. The Morrgrey hangs on the Flaxal wench like he's her damn bodyguard 'er somethin'."

"Well, our li'l helper will just have to distract him, won't she? The story we cooked up will pull him out in the open." Berl nodded toward the small kitchen where a pot of stew bubbled on the stove. "Eat. I'm goin' out to let Karek know what's hap'nin'."

"He still thinkin' to hire on?" Vash asked, moving to the pot and sniffing. He grabbed the large wooden spoon and shoveled a huge bite into his mouth, nodding approval.

"Yeah. If he gets a bosun's billet before we do the job, he might just make mate."

"Not likely," Wopek said, settling the little girl down for a moment. "They won't hire him for mate. He has no reputation. Bosun, maybe, but not mate."

"Tell him that. I'm here to kill a Morrgrey, not play sailor, nor play with little brats. I'll be back before midnight if I can find Karek."

"Shouldn't be hard," Vash said, showing a gap-toothed grin around a mouthful of stew. "Just sniff real hard. Even in Tsing, you should be able to find a pile o' crap that big."

They all laughed, including little Nan, for she had come to like the men who stayed with them. The big dark man she called Unca Opek played with her, so when he laughed, she laughed, which just made them all laugh harder.

CHAPTER EIGHTEEN

Consequences

THE POSTERS WORKED BETTER than Cynthia had hoped; the common room was packed with shore-bound sailors by mid-afternoon. The only problems were keeping them sober and keeping the peace, both of which Brelak managed simply by his presence. Since there were only six crew positions, only a few hours passed before the Morrgrey entered the common room to inform the rest that they were out of luck. He had four burly constables flanking him, each bearing a sword and a heavy cudgel. The crowd dispersed with some grumbling, but no threat of violence.

"Thank you, gentlemen," Brelak said with a smile, passing a few coins among the constables. "Always a pleasure workin' with His Majesty's armed representatives."

"Just keep the peace, Brelak," one of them said with a dour face.

"Such was my only intent, Constable." The caps left without a gesture of thanks or even acknowledgment. When the inn door closed behind them, Brelak said, "Bloody land pirates."

"Oh now, just because you've been their guest at your own expense, there ain't no need to hold a grudge." Koybur chucked him on the shoulder hard enough to stagger a lesser man.

"You have four of 'em pound on you with their sticks an' see if you don't hold a grudge," he growled.

"Only four?" Cynthia asked as she entered the room. Mouse lounged lazily on her shoulder, half asleep and obviously bored with the long day of nothing but talk. "What foul deed did you perpetrate to earn a night as their guest?" She joined the others at a table and motioned for the barmaid to bring a round of drinks.

"That was back when I was young and rowdy, Miss Cynthia. You can't judge a man by what he's done as a lad."

"The way I heard it, it wasn't so long ago," Koybur said, fishing his pipe from his pouch. "In fact, wasn't it just two years ago?"

"Three years. I'd just made first mate of the *Peerless*. And it weren't my fault. Someone set me up; tried to make me look bad by gettin' me drunk and payin' some lout to start a fight."

"Which you finished, I presume," Cynthia said, interested in the story.

"Well, I tried to, but a bunch of caps showed up right miraculous like and started poundin' on me. I woke up in the lockup the next mornin' with a head like a garbage scow on a reef. Called it disorderly conduct."

"The way I heard it, you put two caps in the infirmary before they put you down." Koybur puffed his pipe and blew a perfect smoke ring at the big man. Mouse giggled and swooped up and through the ring.

"Aye, and they called *that* resistin' arrest, when they was the ones who started beatin' on me." He shook his head ruefully, and the table lapsed into silence for a while.

"We did well today," Cynthia said finally, stretching her legs and twisting her neck to ease the tension. "I must have talked to three dozen people, and I hired six sailors and one cook. That leaves a bosun, a mate and two captains. I talked to three applying for boatswain, and two for mate. One of 'em, a woman named Kali Drin, worked the *Blakely Boy*, and probably knows the four we hired in Rockport. They'll all be back tomorrow. No takers for the captain's billets yet."

"We won't see no captains 'til tomorrow. They won't be so eager as the rest."

Cynthia looked at Koybur skeptically. "Why is that?"

"Lots of fish in the sea when it comes to able seamen, and even mates, and they know it'll be first come, first hired. A captain'll know you'll interview several and hire the best."

"Sounds reasonable, but I—"

"Feldrin?" a feminine voice said from behind Cynthia. "Feldrin Brelak?"

They all turned to the young woman standing a table-length away, wringing a kerchief in her hands and looking like she'd seen a ghost. She was pretty, or would have been if she weren't terrified. Her dress was that of a woman who worked in an inn, low in front with a tightly laced bodice of decent material, but hardly luxurious.

"Yes, I'm Feldrin Brelak. Can I help ya, Miss?"

"You... You don't remember." It was a statement, not a question; a matter of fact, expected, but obviously painful for her to say. "You don't remember me."

The table was as silent as a graveyard; only Mouse ventured a whistle and a little giggle at the Morrgrey's sudden discomfort.

"I... Uh..." Brelak stammered and squinted at her. "My pardon, Miss, but I don't. We've met?"

"We've more than just met," she said with a wry smile. "If you don't remember... Well, I can't say as I'm really surprised. It was several years ago, and there was quite a celebration going on at the time." She shrugged and shuffled her feet, obviously uncomfortable with everyone staring at her.

Koybur kicked Brelak under the table and said, "Please, have a seat, Miss—"

"Marci. Thank you, but I don't want to interrupt your dinners." The girl was well spoken, obviously the product of an upper-class family. "I just heard from some sailors that Feldrin Brelak was in town, and thought I would pay my respects and, uh..." She faltered, looking scared again, then forged ahead. "And ask if you would like to meet your daughter."

"Daughter?" Three of them said in unison. Mouse let out a high-pitched peep of query.

"Her name is Nan, short for Nanci. She's almost two and a half."

"Well, I... I..." Brelak sat dumbfounded by the claim.

Cynthia's eyes narrowed. Something didn't seem quite right. The woman's eyes avoided Feldrin's face when she spoke, staring alternately at the floor and some distant point above his head. That could have been simple discomfort with confronting the long-lost father of her child, but it didn't seem right; almost as if her manner verged upon flirtatious instead of confrontational.

Or, Cynthia thought, *I'm skeptical because I don't want to lose a good first mate.* She trusted Brelak, which made him more than just a valuable officer. Cynthia spoke up.

"Miss, surely you can't expect Master Brelak to assume any role as the child's father. Even if your claim could be verified, which is impossible, it's been more than two years."

"Almost three years," Marci agreed, her jaw clenched and her tone unapologetic. "And I don't *expect* anything. I'm not asking for anything, and I don't *want* anything except for my daughter to know the man who fathered her."

"Then why didn't you bring your daughter with you?" Cynthia asked, her doubt undiminished.

"Then it really *would* have looked like I was asking for a handout, wouldn't it?"

"I don't see the point to making the claim if you—"

"Please, Mistress Cynthia, let me handle this." Brelak stood, recovering some of his poise. "I'd sit with you and share a meal, if you'd join me, Marci. I'd like to hear more before I meet yer daughter."

"You... You'll see her?"

"Aye, I will. But I'd like to talk a bit before. And no disrespect, Mistress Cynthia, but I'd like to talk alone." He grinned lopsidedly, shrugging his massive shoulders. "I've got a good number of gaps in my memory, it seems, and I'd like to have 'em filled in proper. Excuse us."

He offered his arm to the woman and ushered her to a smaller table some distance away. Mouse took to the air to follow, but Cynthia snatched him by a leg and told him to stay put. He sat on the table and pouted. She and Koybur watched, trying not to look nosy as the couple sat and talked. After a short while, Brelak called a waitress and ordered a meal.

"He's making a mistake," Cynthia said as their meals arrived.

"How do you figger?" Koybur asked, spearing a wedge of stewed yam and popping it into his mouth.

"She's after something, even though she won't admit it."

"Maybe, but you have to let him take care of it." Koybur shrugged and tucked into his dinner, smiling between bites. "He's a grown man, and able to handle himself. If she's trying to get something out of him, he'll smoke her out."

"I guess I'm just trying to protect him. He just seems so—"

"You see him as a big strong man without much guile," Koybur suggested around another mouthful. "That's what he wants people to think. He's a good bit sharper than the average sailor, Cyn, or he wouldn't ever have made first mate."

"In matters of seamanship, I don't doubt it, but in, uh... social situations, I think he might be less sharp than you think." She glanced pointedly over her shoulder where Brelak listened avidly to the woman's story. "She's already gotten a meal out of him."

"Oh, come on, Cyn. The girl's not out for a free dinner. She's got more class than that!" Koybur speared another yam and shook it at her. "You're way too cynical fer one so young. Let the man dig himself out of this. If he really did get her with child, he should at least own up to it."

"And if she's setting him up?"

"Then he's got the job of smokin' out the scam and bustin' it up. She'd be a fool to try it, though. It's nothin' new, and the penalty for such scams is steep here."

They sat in silence as the couple ate and talked. Finally, when Marci got up to leave, Brelak offered her a few coins. She started to decline, but he remained insistent. When she had gone, he returned to the table.

"Well, that was interestin'," he said, sitting down and waving to the barmaid. "I think I need an ale, Mistress. I've had a trauma and it needs soothin'."

They all chuckled.

"Isn't that what got you into this in the first place?" Cynthia asked.

"Well, I don't rightly know, since I still have no proper recollection of the lass. It might have been the same night we were talkin' about earlier, or the night before. The drink might have to take second prize to the beatin' I took. I was celebratin' plenty, to be sure, and when I woke up in the lockup

I didn't remember half of the last two days."

"You remembered the fight well enough."

"Only because me mates told me all about it later." He took a deep draft of ale and sighed, shaking his head in regret. "None of 'em ever mentioned a girl to me."

"That's no surprise," Koybur said with a laugh.

"Why not?"

"Sailors were celebratin', Cyn. Would it be unusual if there were a few girls helpin' 'em with their merriment?" Koybur chuckled, obviously remembering his own youth. "It'd be like telling you there was sand at the beach."

"Or that we might have drunk a bit o' rum!" Feldrin agreed.

"Or that there may have been some singin'."

"All right, all right," Cynthia said, acceding to the fact that she might not be as wise in this area as she thought. "Just have a care, Master Brelak. I don't want to lose you to a claim of paternity."

"Aye, Mistress. Nor do I want to be a full-time daddy, though I am rather lookin' forward to meetin' the li'l lass."

"You're going to meet the girl? When?"

"Tomorrow night after her shift. She works as a barmaid down at the Hairy Parrot. I'm going to walk her home and meet Nan."

"Then walk back alone?"

"Well, I hadn't thought about that, but you're probably right. I'll take someone along fer company."

"Good," Cynthia said, waving the waitress over to order dessert. "I wouldn't want you to wake up with no memory again, and *married* this time." Mouse cackled in mirth and orbited Brelak's head, miming faces of love-struck bliss and swooning while whistling wedding marches.

They laughed and ordered sweets, tea and blackbrew, though Brelak ordered another ale instead.

"Strictly medicinal," he said, "to treat the shock."

Cynthia muttered something about giving him a shock of her own if he ended up tied down to a wife and daughter, and let it go.

CHAPTER NINETEEN

Captains Three

By MID-MORNING THE FOLLOWING day, Cynthia had six strong candidates for the remaining boatswain position, having decided that Finthie Tar, the woman she'd hired in Scarport, would take one of them. She had spoken to four captain applicants and received two notes by messenger requesting interviews that afternoon. She had also hired someone for the other mate billet, simply due to the fact that one interviewee failed to show up, and the other one, a woman named Vulta Kambeo, had such an impressive career that she saw no need to look further. She was a tall, dark-skinned woman from the Isle of Jombraka in the Southwestern Sea. She'd been sailing since she was thirteen on every kind of ship Cynthia could name, and knew the Southern Ocean like the back of her hand.

It had been a busy morning.

The six boatswain candidates, five men and a woman, sat in the common room chatting with Brelak and awaiting her decision while she discussed the matter with Koybur.

"They all seem capable," Cynthia said, sipping blackbrew and nibbling a glazed blueberry scone. "No sure way to tell which one has the most experience, though. I'm sure they're all painting pretty pictures for me."

"It's every sailor's sworn duty to boast, Cyn." Koybur smiled crookedly around his pipe. "But I think we can figure out how to separate the sailors from the scalawags."

Cynthia grinned. "What did you have in mind?"

"Well, we used to have splicin' contests when I was a lad. We could rig somethin' up in the stable out back easy enough. We'll have that new mate you hired officiate. The fastest wins the billet. That simple."

"That sounds good. It'll give me time to concentrate on the captain applicants." She sipped her blackbrew and bit her lip. "So, what do you think about our first four candidates?"

He pulled out his ledger and ticked off the names. "Let's see, you've got Mayers, Thorn, Ulbattaer and Ulaff."

"So far. And Troilen and Dankel this afternoon."

"Give me your impression of 'em first, Cyn."

"Well, Ulaff doesn't know the Southern Ocean as well the others, and something rubbed me the wrong way about Thorn, though I can't put my finger on it. He seemed nervous."

"He was nervous 'cause he thought you knew he was the captain of the *Blakely Boy*."

"Hey, that reminds me. What happened to that other woman, Kali something or other?"

"Don't know." He filled his pipe and lit it from the lamp on the table. "Mayhap she got a better offer. Anyway, word is Thorn's got a problem with the bottle and is too proud to admit it. Yer right about Ulaff. He's been runnin' the inner sea from Fengotherond to Beriknor, with only an occasional trip to Tsing, fer far too long to be of use south of the Shattered Isles." He made two check marks on his ledger. "That leaves Mayers and Ulbattaer."

She sipped her blackbrew and thought about it for a bit. "They both know the Southern Ocean. Rafen Ulbattaer has been in and out of every inlet south of the peninsula; he knew Southaven well enough, though I don't remember ever meeting him. He used to run spices and teak south to the desert, and tin and lead back north. He captained a shallow draft xebec for a few years, then a dhow. He knows smaller ships. Toren Mayers has more open ocean experience; he's run the silk trade, and copra, but always in a galleon. Nothing smaller than three masts, and nothing that would sail close to the wind like my ships."

"You think the experience with the closer hauled rigs'll do you a turn for the better?"

"I think so. Though Ulbattaer is a little, well, too friendly, maybe? I felt like he was trying to woo me."

"He's from the desert, Cyn. Women don't hold high positions in that culture unless they're royalty. He might find it hard to adjust to a female boss."

"Maybe." She nibbled her scone, thinking. "Well, it's either of the two, or both, depending on this afternoon's interviews. Do you know either Troilen or Dankel?"

"Heard of both of 'em. Troilen's a half-elf, and he's been sailin' longer than I've been alive." He puffed his pipe and made a face as if mulling over something distasteful. "Dankel's got a temper, or so the word goes. He was a navy man for the old emperor. Runs a tight ship, but he's a big fan of hard discipline. He goes through crew like wire through cheese, and he's been known to flog a man senseless for insubordination."

"Great. Well, I'll talk to him, but I don't think I want a tyrant as a brand new captain on a brand new ship."

"We'll see how the interviews go, then you can choose from the four." Koybur tapped out his pipe and started to stuff the bowl. "Not bad."

≈

Cynthia's afternoon consisted of two long interviews with the remaining captain candidates while Koybur, Brelak and Vulta tested the potential boatswains. She had given Koybur leave to make the final decision, but wanted a tally of their performance in the tests.

Her first interview went well. The half-elf Troilen boasted a vast amount of experience as well as a phenomenal memory. He could recite the cuts, coves and inlets, reefs, rocks and trenches of every coastline from the Southern Ocean to the Far West. He'd sailed in every type of ship from a smack to a four-masted galleon, and had battled pirates on three continents. He even told a harrowing tale of flight from a tribe of ruthless cannibals in the southern-most Shattered Isles—a night of light winds and a ship suddenly surrounded by dugout canoes full of savages thirsting for blood. He spoke eloquently and intelligently, and she knew instantly that he would make a fine captain for one of her ships.

The second interview went less satisfactorily. Cynthia confirmed that Captain Dankel had been a naval officer and asked him about his experiences in the Southern Ocean. His answers were stiff and brief. He told her flatly that he considered the piracy in the Shattered Isles to be a bunch of foolishness, overblown in its impact on shipping.

In the end, she thanked Captain Dankel and sent him packing, with assurances that she did plan on building more ships, and that she would keep him in mind. Troilen she asked to please meet her downstairs for dinner, as she already had Ulbattaer and Mayers. The count was down to three.

≈

The company for the evening meal consisted of eight: Cynthia and her two companions; the newly hired mate, Vulta Kambeo; the new boatswain, a dark-skinned man named Karek Darkwater; and the three captain candidates. Stories flowed like water over a mill wheel amid the platters and tankards of food and drink, tales from every coast and harbor around the great western sea. Yarns of the merfolk, great sea drakes, and deep-sea nymphs who lured sailors on night watch into a watery embrace, all vied with one another. Mouse sat upon Cynthia's shoulder, still as a stone, rapt with the sea stories. He got on well with all three of the potential captains and the new boatswain, but favored Vulta second only to Cynthia; a lady's sprite, to be sure.

Finally, she brought out the sketches of the new ship, to the admiration of all. When Cynthia mentioned that she'd hired Master Ghelfan as her shipwright, eyebrows arched in unison and Ulbattaer let out a low whistle.

"That must have set you back a small fortune, Mistress Flaxal," the dark man said, twisting the ends of his long moustache.

"More'n a fortune, I'd say," Karek agreed, alternately puffing on his pipe and sipping ale. "A bloody king's ransom, more like."

"Actually, it wasn't as much as you might expect," she said, shooting a warning glance to Koybur. She did not want the rumor to spread that Ghelfan had agreed to do the job for free. "He was intrigued with the project."

"With the project, or with the mistress of ships?" Rafen Ulbattaer asked with a wolfish grin, his teeth flashing like pearls on brown silk.

"By the project, I assure you, Master Ulbattaer," she said, smiling at his inference. "Master Ghelfan is a perfect gentleman."

"Nobody's perfect, Mistress Flaxal," Troilen warned, arching one slim eyebrow and sipping his wine.

"Though some might like to think they are." Mayers cracked his tankard against the half-elf's delicate goblet, laughing at the fellow's indignant glare.

The subject drifted to the particulars of the new ships, from rigging to framing to the types of wood to be used. Hours had passed when Brelak finally stood and made his excuses.

"I'd best make my way down to the wharves. I'll be seein' ya all in the mornin', bright and early."

"Someone *is* going with you, right?"

"Well, Mistress, I actually—"

"I'll tag along, if ye need a chaperone, Master Brelak," Karek said with a gap-toothed grin.

"Thanks, but I—"

"I'll go, too, if you think you might want some privacy," Vulta offered, grinning at Karek. "I wouldn't want Mister Karek to be waylaid while standing on a street corner tapping his foot."

"I really don't think—"

"And I think you'll be taking your own advice, Master Brelak. *Someone* will accompany you tonight. You choose." Cynthia put just enough authority in her voice to make it understood that this was not a request.

"With all due respect, Mistress, I am takin' my own advice. I sent for Tobi, the carriage driver. I thought it'd be nicer, anyways."

"You are a true romantic, Master Brelak," Troilen said, raising his goblet in toast.

"Romance ain't no part in it," the Morrgrey said, his face flushing darker than its usual olive hue. "I just thought it'd be nice is all. The girl's been on her feet all night. A carriage ride'd let 'er relax a bit."

"I think it's a fine idea, Feldrin. Just make sure you're back by morning, unmarried and unmarred."

"Aye, Mistress. That I'll promise ya."

"I hear the carriage drivers will do a slow circuit of Riverwalk Park for a few coppers extra." Cynthia grinned and chucked him on the shoulder while the others laughed. He opened his mouth to protest, but she cut him off with, "Just have a good time, Feldrin."

"Bloody jokesters," he grumbled, downing the last of his ale and nodding to the table. "In the mornin' then."

They all called out their goodnights and well-wishes, some more colorful than others. When the door to the Red Gryphon banged closed, Cynthia took a deep breath and tried to relax. She never thought of herself as the suspicious type, but something still bothered her about the woman Marci and her claim of Feldrin's paternity.

≈

The *Black Guard* glided into Blood Bay under unusually light winds, one of her launches pulling from her bow to aid in steerage. Though the oar crew swam in their own sweat with the heat of the still air and their exertion, when the anchor crew snagged the mooring line the captain ordered them to take him immediately ashore to convene with Captain Bloodwind.

An eager young lass named Sam met him at the dock. She was barely old enough to heft the cutlass that hung proudly at her skinny hip, but she had that vacant-eyed, do-anything look that told him she had been well initiated. She guided him all the way to the top of the keep, to Bloodwind's private chamber, and he knew before entering that his master was involved in a matter of discipline. The screams told him that much. The girl knocked and worked the latch at Bloodwind's command to enter.

"Captain Corrien, good to see you." Bloodwind waved a hand at a slave girl adorned with golden chains and said, "Camilla, be so good as to pour the good captain a glass of wine."

"Thank you, Captain Bloodwind." The crack of a whip against flesh and the ensuing cry punctuated the atmosphere of the room. Corrien took the glass, not due to thirst, but because refusing Bloodwind's hospitality was madness. "Yodrin and the rest are in place, sir. I know at least four of our people have already been hired on. Yodrin insisted on traveling to Tsing. The bastard killed my boatswain for having a loud mouth in Rockport. I dropped off another dozen of our people with him. With any luck we'll have four or five on each of the Flaxal woman's ships when they set sail."

"Excellent!" The whip cracked again, and the woman who hung by her wrists, her tattered dress torn away from her bleeding back, whimpered miserably. "That's enough for now, Tim. I see your sister Sam is here. Why don't you hand the lash over to her and escort the good captain back to his ship."

"Yes Captain Bloodwind!" The boy handed the lash over to the girl, and grinned. "Hey-ya, Sam."

"Tim," she said, taking the lash and limbering it up in her hand. "See ya down in town later, 'ey?"

"Aye," he answered, moving to the door and opening it for Captain Corrien. "This way, if you please, Captain."

Captain Corrien followed the youth, but could not help but overhear Bloodwind instructing the girl in the application of the lash.

"I'm sure you recognize your old nursemaid, Miss Straff, eh, Sam? Well, she tried to steal a boat and row out to sea. She broke the only law I put her under, and this is her punishment. I think another two dozen ought to do, but your brother's already done a good job on her back. Let's find some un-plowed ground, eh?"

Corrian looked back to watch the girl cut away the rest of the woman's dress. Too bad he'd been sent away. The coming spectacle would be worth watching.

"Good, Sam. Now remember, the force comes from the shoulder. Keep your wrist straight to guide your aim." The crack of the lash and another scream of pain split the air as the boy closed the door.

CHAPTER TWENTY

Knives in the Dark

THE CARRIAGE SQUEALED TO a halt in front of the Hairy Parrot as Tobi hauled back on the reins and the brake. Feldrin stepped out of the door before they were fully stopped and flipped a gold crown to the driver.

"That's fer the whole night."

"Bloody *right*, er, I mean yes sir, Master Brelak, it'll do nicely. Quiet as a mouse and discreet as a ghost. No tales comin' from this hackney, I guarantee!"

"Good. Now go home and meet me here at first light."

"But sir," Tobi looked at him questioningly, "why pay me for the whole night, then send me home?"

"Because if anyone asks you where you were *all night* yer gonna tell 'em you drove me around, took me to a lady's home, then waited like you was told. This just saves you all the drivin' around and waitin'."

He entered the Hairy Parrot without another thought about Tobi. The last thing he wanted right now was to give Marci the wrong impression. A carriage ride would insinuate extravagance, which might suggest an interest in a romantic or paternal role he definitely did not want.

The Hairy Parrot could have been any one of the thousand waterfront pubs: the air was thick with smoke and the scent of rancid ale, the noise required a raised voice just to be heard, the barmaids showed far too much cleavage and the waterfront whores showed even more. Twenty years of places like this had almost soured Feldrin's appetite for such distractions.

He took a deep breath, smiled at a wench whose eyes lingered on him in passing, and shouted at the barman for an ale. *Almost.*

A tarnished pewter tankard thumped down in front of him, and he sampled it. His nose wrinkled and he swallowed forcefully, wondering what was in the ale besides ale before realizing it was probably best he didn't know. Either his tastes had changed with his rank, or it was the ale that was rank. He pushed the tankard away and sighed.

"Tell Bort to draw one from the red keg. The other's spiked with wood alcohol." He turned and smiled at Marci as she placed a tray of empty mugs on the bar and dusted her hands on her apron. "Another round here, Bort! I'm glad you came. I won't be long. Please, have a drink."

"Thanks, I will." He accepted the new tankard and sat back down, sipping ale and watching the crowd while Marci tended her customers. It wasn't long before she came back, removed her apron and bid the barkeep goodnight. She also called a goodnight to the hulking bouncer, a man even larger than Feldrin, and not by a small margin.

"Not too many fights with that feller hangin' about, I'll wager." He stepped into the sultry night and breathed the relatively clear air.

"No fights at all." She walked past him, starting up the street before turning back to ask, "You coming?"

"Oh, aye, I'm comin'. Just didn't know we was in a hurry." He caught up easily and matched her quick pace.

"I like to get off the wharves quickly. Some rough types hang about down here."

"No worse than across the river, I'll wager."

"Quite a bit worse, actually. It's not bad until you get into the Downwinds." Her tone sounded humorless, almost bitter, and Brelak wondered how much the poor girl had gone through raising a child alone.

They walked in silence for a while, finally making the turn that would take them over the river and into the Dreggar's Quarter. The neighborhood along the river wasn't bad, shops and three story tenant houses with balconies lining the broad avenue. Two blocks further on the streets narrowed and the houses devolved into ramshackle tenements, some so disheveled that braces had been hammered from balcony to balcony to keep them from falling down.

"How far?" he asked, checking behind them by force of habit.

"Not much farther. Just around the corner and up the hill." Her voice sounded strange, quiet but trembling, as if afraid of something. It was not difficult to guess why.

"Don't worry, Marci. I won't tell Nan who I am. If you want to, you can tell her. If not, that's fine." He put out his arm for her to take. "I'm pretty good with kids, actually. Might just surprise you how she takes to—"

Fire exploded in Brelak's back as they rounded the corner.

He stumbled, his breath leaving his lungs in a guttural roar of shock. He reached back by reflex, snatching his attacker's wrist, slick with his own blood. The knife had been driven deeply into his back, just below the ribs. Even through the pain, he knew if his attacker twisted or pulled it free, he would bleed to death before he could stumble a block. The wrist jerked in his grasp, sending bolts of pain lancing through him, but he dug his fingers in and squeezed hard, exerting all his strength.

The grip on the knife went slack and Feldrin twisted around. He got one glimpse of the man's thin, astonished face before his roundhouse left laid the would-be assassin out flat. He staggered into the light of the street lamp, turning to see where Marci had gone.

"Marci, I—"

Steel glittered in the shadow and he dodged just before it plunged hilt deep into his flesh. He grunted, staring down in shock. It had been aimed at his heart, but his movement put the point too high and to the left, piercing the hollow of his shoulder instead. His left arm blazed with fire, but his right gripped the attacker's wrist and he drove a kick into the man's stomach. The attacker crumpled, leaving his knife where it stuck.

Then he saw her.

She just stood there, not running, not screaming, just stood there with her hand pressed to her mouth, eyes streaming with tears as another man strode from the shadows. This one was taller and hefted two curved knives ready to slash Feldrin to pieces.

"Run, Marci!" he shouted, jerking the dagger from his shoulder and flinging it at the advancing assassin. The throw would never have struck true, but it did serve to distract the man long enough for Feldrin to draw his own dagger. Unfortunately, the man he'd kicked was regaining his feet and the other did not look daunted by the show of a naked blade.

"Give it up, Morrgrey," the bigger man said with a chuckle. "You'll only die harder if you fight us."

Feldrin took a step back and felt blood squish in his boot—his blood. It ran from his back, down his leg in a warm torrent. He had to end this quickly or he wouldn't have the strength to fight. He stood straight and grinned at the advancing man.

"Come on, you son of a pig-humping whore. You should know better than to stick a Morrgrey with a knife. You just make him mad." He sidestepped toward the wall, knowing they would want to flank him. Feldrin tried to draw his spare dagger from his boot, but his left hand hung limp. He could move his arm, but his hand would not grip.

The man laughed and moved in, weaving the two kukri in deadly arcs.

Feldrin saved his breath, parrying one cut with his knife and the other with his useless left arm. The blade cut to the bone, but didn't reach his throat as intended. His own thrust met only steel, the countering slashes lightning-quick. He turned one blade aside; the other cut a furrow from his collar halfway to his belt, skittering down ribs like a stick on a picket fence.

The pain of the cut sent him to his knees, but his knife turned the next killing slash and lashed out low to score a hit on the man's thigh.

"He's still got some fight in 'im, Wopek. Finish it quick." The second attacker stood aside, interjecting his own brand of encouragement.

"Don't tell me how to—" the other began, but shouts and the sound of pounding boots cut him off.

Brelak risked a glance and saw three men running toward them, weapons raised. Then he recognized them—the three captains Cynthia had interviewed.

"Kill the bastard!" the other man shouted, moving to the groaning man Feldrin had knocked flat.

The larger man—the one called Wopek—moved in, slashing his kukri at Feldrin's throat, but Feldrin was not yet ready to die, not with friends so close. He jerked back, twisted and kicked out as he fell to his side, sweeping the other's feet out from under him. As the big man crashed to the street, Feldrin rolled, thinking only to get out of reach until help arrived. He forgot the dagger still in his back. The hilt hit the unyielding cobbles, the blade tearing through the sinews in his back before it broke off. He screamed in pain, dropping his knife and pressing his good hand to the wound.

As Wopek regained his feet, Ulbattaer, Troilen and Mayers arrived, knives flashing in the street light, curses filling the air.

Brelak's eyes squeezed closed against the horrific pain. He rolled onto his stomach, gasping and pressing the wound hard with his hand. Blood oozed from beneath his fingers, but he felt no hard spray that would indicate a severed artery. He knew he was in trouble, real trouble, and cursed himself for his own stupid, arrogant confidence.

A horrible gurgling scream snapped his eyes open just as Mayers fell beside him, both hands clutching at his throat to staunch a crimson flood. The captain's eyes widened, then went slack as the blood flow slowed and stopped. Then the big assassin fell right beside them, his left eye a ruined, bloody socket, his face frozen in shock and death.

A hand pressed at his back and he heard Troilen's calm voice. "Hold still, you great lummox. You're bleeding badly. Any other wounds?"

"Shoulder," he managed between clenched teeth. The half-elf's hand pushed hard on the wound, trying to staunch the flow. "And my chest. Blade's still in my back. Broke off when I fell."

"Probably saved your worthless hide!" Ulbattaer cursed as he knelt beside Mayers. "Don't pull it out. We need to—Gods! What the hell happened to Mayers?"

"He stepped in too close to that one," Troilen said. "The man was very good. He cut Mayers open like a fish before I could get a dagger in his eye. Damned shame."

"We've got to get him to a healer. Now." Ulbattaer stood and started shouting for a constable while Troilen rummaged through a pouch at his belt.

"Here," he said, holding a cloth-wrapped bundle the size of his thumbnail before Feldrin's eyes. "Tuck it in your cheek and chew. Swallow your spit. It tastes horrid, but it will help with the pain. I'm going to put something on your back that will help stop the bleeding, but it will sting. Bite down on the pouch, not your teeth. We don't want you to break them."

"You a healer?" Ulbattaer asked between shouts.

"Just some herb-skill. Comes with the pointed ears, if you know what I mean."

Ulbattaer chuckled. "Aye, like playin' the lute and singin' like a songbird, I suppose."

"Right." He dipped two bloody fingers into a small jar from his pouch and applied a white paste to the wound in Feldrin's back, smearing it deep into the gory mess of torn meat.

"Mother of—" the Morrgrey said with a gasp as the searing heat of the unguent lanced through him. He bit down hard on the packet in his mouth and swallowed the bitter fluid.

"Aye, that slowed it some. Let's have a look at your chest." The half-elf rolled him gently onto his side and parted the sodden tatters of his shirt. "That's a nasty cut, but it's not bleeding so badly. You can breathe all right, I see."

"I—can breathe, but..." Feldrin's vision narrowed from the edges, darkness closing in. "Dark," he said, fighting to stay conscious. "Wha'sat noise?"

"Stay awake, you lummox! The constables are coming. That's their whistles you hear, but you've got to stay awake!" Two sharp slaps opened his eyes. "Stay awake!"

"Where's the girl?" he asked Troilen, blinking and spitting out the wad of cloth-wrapped herbs. "Where's Marci?"

"She ran away. What did you expect her to do?" Boots clattered, amid more shouts, questions and raised voices.

Brelak managed to remain conscious until they rolled him onto a pallet, then the world exploded into a haze of pain. The darkness at the edge of his vision closed in to overwhelm his senses.

CHAPTER TWENTY-ONE

Homeward

"You awake, Feldrin?"

"No." His voice came out as barely a croak. He cleared his throat and squinted into the morning sun. The feather pillow beneath his head felt like a brick. Or maybe it was his head that felt like a brick. "I'm dead."

"Good! Now I don't have to kill you." Cynthia stepped in front of the window, blocking the sunlight, her arms folded and her face clouded with anger and concern. "You lied to me, Feldrin! I ought to let you rot on the beach."

"Lied?" He worked his tongue around in his dry mouth and tried to sit up. Clean sheets covered him, and save for bandages they were the *only* thing covering him. He took a quick inventory: arm, chest, shoulder and back, though his back hurt the least of all, which seemed strange. "How do you figger?"

"You said you'd take Tobi with you. You sent him home and chose to walk around the Dreggar's Quarter alone."

"I didn't lie to you, I just changed me mind is all. And I weren't alone. Marci was with me." He tried to clear his throat again, but coughed and grimaced against the pain.

"Hell of a lot of good that did you." Cynthia handed him a glass of water from the nightstand. He winced at the pain in his shoulder, surprised at his lack of strength, but drained the glass greedily. She glared at him, leaning down close. "You also broke your promise; unmarried and unmarred, remember? You go and get yourself mugged, stabbed and nearly killed!"

"Aye, stabbed. Near killed? Well, I dunno about—"

"They pulled this outta yer back, Master Brelak." He turned to where Koybur held a six-inch knife blade. He handed it over for the Morrgrey to inspect. "Would'a killed any man with much less blood to spill."

"The healer tended the worst of it." Cynthia continued, still glaring. "The rest will heal with time. Time we don't have, Master Brelak. I want to ship anchor tomorrow morning. If you're not able, what am I supposed to do for a first mate?"

"Healer? You paid a healer to fix me up?"

"You'd be dead if I hadn't," she stated flatly. "Your back was the worst. He said you might piss blood for a few days, but that you're out of danger. He stitched up your chest and arm, and closed the hole in your shoulder with some kind of potion, but said to call him back if you couldn't move your hand. Can you?"

"I... Yes, I can." He raised the hand and flexed it, looking from Cynthia to Koybur. The miracle of his survival suddenly hit him; he lived solely due to the generosity of Cynthia Flaxal. "Thank you, Mistress. I'll be ready to sail in the mornin' and I'll pay you back every copper for the healer's fee. I promise."

"Damn right you will, but don't think for a minute that I give a good God's damn about the money. I care more that you might have gotten yourself killed being foolish than the few crowns it cost to heal your carcass up." Muscles writhed in her jaw, giving him a hint at just how deeply her anger ran. "What were you thinking, Feldrin, falling prey to a mugger?"

"They wasn't after money."

"What?" She stiffened, the anger vanishing. "What do you mean?"

"Three of 'em, and they ne'r took my pouch. If it was money they wanted, they'd've taken it and run."

"Makes sense," Koybur agreed, chewing on the stem of his pipe. "The girl got away clean, and nobody's seen hide nor hair of her. Chances are she was workin' for 'em."

"Well, if they weren't after money..."

"They wanted him dead, Cyn. It's the only explanation."

"Aye, that seemed clear at the time, but who would want *me* dead?" Feldrin finally managed to sit up, barely wincing. "I don't have that many enemies. Least ways, none that would pay to see me dead."

"Unless someone wanted your billet. Everyone in the city knows I'm hiring officers and crew. The other woman, Kali Drin, never showed up. I wonder if she met with a similar accident. Someone could have thought to kill you and take your spot."

Koybur chewed his pipe and frowned. "Well, if someone did, he's one of the ones we didn't hire. None of 'em seemed the murderin' type. I'd like ta think we been lookin' at these fellers closer'n that."

"So would I."

"I didn't recognize any of the three that jumped me. They didn't look like professional killers, but—"

A knock at the door ushered three people into the room, four if you counted the painfully cheerful seasprite. Vulta carried a tray piled high with bacon, sausage, half a dozen poached eggs, as many freshly baked muffins and a whole pot of blackbrew on top of which Mouse rode as if it were his own private pachyderm. He fluttered into the air and over to the recumbent Morrgrey's shoulder. Behind Vulta walked two of the men who had saved his life.

"Well, the Morrgrey proves he is indeed harder to kill than he looks!" Troilen smiled and shook the big man's hand.

"Aye, it's good to see you breathing, you thick-skinned lout!" Ulbattaer pumped his arm strongly, grinning beneath his long mustaches.

"What can I say but thank you, sirs." He looked past them hopefully, but without expectation. "Mayers?"

"Dead." Ulbattaer plucked a muffin from the mounded tray and bit off a corner. "Stepped in too close, and took a bad cut. But the half-elf here evened the score nicely."

"You'll be happy to know that Captain Ulbattaer and I managed to dispatch all three of your assailants." The tall fellow smiled and nodded to Ulbattaer. "The exchange of a few coins even managed to enlist the aid of the constabulary in hauling your heavy carcass down the hill to the nearest healer."

"I'll leave you all to talk it over, but don't stay long." Cynthia nodded to them, her face still set in a stern mask as she headed for the door. "He needs rest if he's going to be worth more than camel spit tomorrow, and the rest of you need to prepare for departure. Captain Uben has secured cargo and we're loading today. We haul anchor at first light."

When the door closed, Feldrin asked, "*Captain* Ulbattaer? So you two..."

"Aye, she made it official this morning. With Mayers dead, there weren't any other candidates worth their salt." Rafen Ulbattaer smiled sardonically.

"And who sent you after me, as if I didn't know?" Feldrin asked, eying the door through which Cynthia had just departed.

"Aye, she suggested we might all go out and have a drink together," Ulbattaer admitted, twisting his long mustaches. "She even mentioned a good inn down the wharf district."

"The Hairy Parrot." Feldrin scowled at the door.

"Which turned out lucky for all of us, except Mayers, of course." Troilen shrugged. "If we had arrived half a minute later, you'd be dead and Rafen and I would be looking for work!"

"Oh, bilgewater," Feldrin grumbled, furrowing his brow in consternation. "But that means..."

"Aye, it means one of them will be your lord and master, and the other mine." Vulta grinned at the two captains. "Though no decision has been made yet as to who will serve under whom."

Troilen smiled and patted the Morrgrey's broad shoulder. "But don't worry. We'll make it fair. We were thinking of drawing straws, and the loser gets you." The room erupted in laughter as Feldrin grumbled and tore into his breakfast.

≈

Cynthia left explicit instructions to be roused two hours before first light, which would give them time to get Brelak from the inn to the *Winter Gale*. When the tap came at her door, she surged out of bed, turned up the lamp and stripped out of her nightgown, reaching for her clothing as Mouse groaned a cricket-chirp of misery and hid under her pillow.

"Fantastic," Cynthia said to herself, finishing the last of her buttons as Mouse burrowed deep under the covers. She cast about the room, but the rest of her personal effects had long since been returned to her cabin in the *Winter Gale*, the cabin that would be her prison for the next sixteen days if the winds were favorable. She steeled her nerves, tightened her belt a notch, plucked her seasprite from the bed, strode out of the sleeping chamber and stopped in surprise.

There in the middle of the common room of their small suite stood Feldrin Brelak, fully dressed, his thick arms folded across his barrel chest. He straightened as she entered and sketched a half bow, showing only slight stiffness.

"Ready to sail, Mistress Flaxal."

Mouse chirped with surprise and flew a wobbly orbit of the first mate's head before landing on his shoulder.

"Bloody right he's bloody ready to bloody sail!" Koybur stumbled into the room and glared at the Morrgrey. "Woke me up a full hour ago with his bangin' and bumpin' and mumblin'. I would'a put another dagger in 'im if we didn't need a decent first mate."

"Well, I thought we would need extra time for Master Brelak, but since he is obviously right as rain and strong as a summer squall, we'll head down and you can both get a bite if there's anything available."

They found the common room empty, but the smell of baking bread wafted from the kitchen doors.

"Blackbrew?" Koybur asked, heading for the kitchen.

"Well, we'll be aboard in plenty of time, I think. Perhaps one cup won't kill me." Cynthia called for Koybur to bring enough for everyone.

Koybur emerged from the kitchen with a blackbrew service for three in one hand and a platter of cold leftovers, a fresh loaf of bread and a crock of butter balanced on his mangled one. Brelak relieved him of the blackbrew and poured for them. Cynthia savored this last bit of luxury as the others ate. While she considered a second cup, a bell from the street announced the arrival of their carriage. All accounts had been settled the previous evening, so they piled aboard without delay and clattered down to the wharves. She did not realize until they stopped at the broad stone avenue along the quay that the carriage and driver were the very same that had conveyed her to the Red Gryphon four days ago.

"Tobi! Thank you for your service and your friendship. If I'm ever able to make the trip back to Tsing, I promise to look you up." Cynthia shook his hand warmly.

"All part of the service, m'lady." He shook hands with Koybur, then stepped aside as Brelak draped one huge arm over the driver's shoulders and ushered him several steps away from the group.

"What's that about?" she asked Koybur.

"Damned if I know." Koybur started working himself down into the launch.

Cynthia saw a small package pass from Feldrin to Tobi, and noticed the smaller man nodding and smiling. Finally, they shook hands and went their separate ways, Feldrin joining her at the quay ladder.

"Everything all right?"

"Oh, aye, Miss. Just askin' 'im a favor." High tide made a short climb down to the launch. Brelak managed it without help, moving very carefully.

"What sort of favor?" she asked, taking a seat next to him. The coxswain barked orders and Mouse mimicked his every motion and order.

Brelak sighed deeply, trepidation furrowing his brow. Just as she opened her mouth to tell him to forget it, he said, "Had a long talk with the chief constable yesterde'. Nice woman name of Voya. Seems they don't like such big bunches of dead people litterin' their streets all at once. Especially when they don't have all the answers, like who and why and such."

"The girl?" she asked, making the intuitive leap. Marci remained the only unaccounted-for element of the incident.

"Aye. They can't find her. Her flat's empty, she didn't show up fer work, and her neighbor says three strange men were stayin' with her fer a few days before the attack." They rounded the stern of the *Winter Gale*, her decks bustling with activity. "They plan to arrest her and charge her with murder."

"Maybe they should." Cynthia met his flashing eyes steadily. "She set you up, Feldrin. Don't you think she should pay for that?"

"She's exactly who she said she was. She really worked at the Hairy Parrot, she really had a daughter named Nan and she really bore the girl out of wedlock." He stood and accepted a line from the deck of the ship, pulling the launch in firmly before helping her to her feet. His motions were easier with the launch under his feet, as if the sea had taken away his pain.

"That doesn't make her innocent, Feldrin." She took his hand and stepped from the gunwale of the launch up to the entry port. Feldrin climbed aboard behind her.

"It don't make her guilty, either. I asked Tobi to look into things. Just poke around, ask questions, maybe visit the girl's neighbors. He said he'd find out what he could and send a post. I think they were holdin' Nan to make her do what they wanted."

"That could be." Cynthia wondered how she would respond to that kind of pressure—watching a loved one in danger, unable to act. "Well, I hope she's okay then."

"Aye." He took a deep breath and winced, ushering her aside as Riley ordered the launch hauled aboard and secured. Vulta approached and clapped the big man on the shoulder, which elicited another wince.

"Ready for sea, Mistress," the dark woman said, looking up at the predawn sky. Mouse flitted around them and settled back onto Cynthia's shoulder. "Going to be a beautiful day for it."

Although there were twice as many officers aboard as usual, Uben had assigned them all specific tasks. He was adamant that there would be no laggards in the employ of Mistress Cynthia Flaxal. Even the two new captains were given duties. Each would stand alternate night watches, giving the captain and his mate the day watches only, a luxury for any seaman.

"Well, I'd best get to my cabin before the anchor's hauled." She sighed. "Damn it, but blackbrew tastes so much better going down than coming up."

"Ha! That's a good sign, Cyn." Koybur shuffled up and chucked her shoulder, knocking the sprite flat and earning a chirp and a glare. "When you can joke about it, you've took the first step to gettin' the problem licked!"

"Problem? What problem would that be?"

They turned to Troilen and Ulbattaer as the two superfluous captains descended from the quarterdeck.

"Nothing serious, I hope."

"Aye, it's serious, but nothin' we can't deal with." Koybur was being evasive, but she knew everyone would find out the truth eventually. It would be best to hear it from her rather than from the rumor mill.

"I suffer from ship's sickness." She watched their faces closely. Ulbattaer's mustache twitched and one of Troilen's slim eyebrows arched.

"Aye, to the point it near killed her on the run up from Rockport," Brelak added.

"That *is* a problem," Ulbattaer agreed, keeping his face neutral. "I've heard of such serious cases before. Time seems to be the only cure."

"The only cure, yes, but I have something that might help you endure the journey with fewer ill effects." Troilen hefted the pouch at his hip and shook it.

"Not another cure, please," Cynthia said, raising a hand and smiling. "I appreciate the effort, but—"

"He's got quite a skill with herbs, Miss Cynthia," Brelak said. "He saved my life with that stuff he smeared into the hole in my back. Hurt like a hot poker, mind ya, but stopped the bleedin'."

"There is an extract of the bittersweet plant that—"

"Bittersweet? Ain't that Black Nightshade?"

"Why yes, Master Koybur, it is."

"And isn't that poisonous?" Ulbattaer looked at the half-elf as if he were mad.

The clatter of the capstan winding in the anchor rode set butterflies fluttering around Cynthia's stomach.

"There are many varieties of nightshade, Master Ulbattaer. Not all are deadly. The extract of the bittersweet can be administered safely with some knowledge and care." He retrieved a vial from his pouch. "A few drops in a cup of tea and you'll sleep for a day, wake rested, though probably a little groggy, and you'll be able to eat. You must, however, take another dose within a short time of waking, or you will succumb to your sickness once again."

"So it will cure the sickness, but I'll sleep the whole way?" The prospect was not entirely distasteful.

"Not cure, Mistress. It will only make you sleep and not feel the sickness. You will not become acclimated to the sea as long as you take it, but it will allow you to travel by sea without risking your life."

Mouse flew over and peered into the murky glass vial.

"I'd be careful, Mistress. You'll never get over the sickness if you rely on a drug." Ulbattaer pulled on his mustaches with a frown. "Time and patience will cure it."

"Could I take it later, after a few days?"

"It is best if you do not. Weakness from sickness can make the drug's effect unpredictable."

"So," she said, listening to the clank and clatter of the anchor being hoisted and secured, "it's now or never."

Winter Gale bore off the wind, her foresails clapping and filling. Riley shouted to the topmen and the great mainsail dropped and billowed, snapping taut as the sheets were drawn home. Mouse left Cynthia's shoulder to flutter aloft, wobbling like a drunken butterfly around the yards and braces for the sheer joy of it.

"It would be best to take it now if you choose to take it at all, yes." The half-elf shrugged and smiled disarmingly. "I have made it for others, passengers usually. I *do* know what I am doing, Mistress."

"I never doubted it for a moment, Troilen." She sighed and smiled.

"Why don't you brew me a cup of tea, then. I'll be in my cabin, starboard of the captain's cabin."

"Very well, Mistress."

The small group went their separate ways, Koybur accompanying her to her cabin and making sure a bucket and a pitcher of water were handy. The cabin shone like a newly minted coin, scrubbed clean after her previous occupancy.

"Now, I'd have a care with this stuff he's brewin', lass," Koybur warned in a low voice. "Take only as much as you need. Some of these things can leave a man quakin' like a drunk off the bottle when you stop takin' it."

"I'm sure I'll be fine. Just check on me every once in a while. Don't let me do anything stupid."

"That's me job, lass," he said, grinning his horrible lop-sided grin.

She felt the ship move under her, the first easy swells as they rounded the breakwater. Her stomach knotted. *Where is that pointed-eared apothecary?*

A knock on the door and the tall half-elf ducked inside, bearing a mug of steaming liquid. "Here you are, Mistress. It's not very hot and it may taste a little bitter, but it is best if you drink it quickly."

"It's not going to knock me flat, is it?" she asked, accepting the cup in a shaky hand. "Should I sit?"

"That shouldn't be necessary. The effect will take a few minutes."

She nodded and took an experimental sip, her nose wrinkling in distaste. "Tastes like rigging tar." She took a deep swallow, then another until the cup ran dry. "Well, if I'm going to sleep the whole voyage, I'd best make myself comfortable. If you gentlemen would give me some privacy?"

"Yes, Mistress." Troilen bowed, obviously pleased at her trust in him. "Please remember to eat as soon as you wake, then call me and I'll mix another draught. You will be a little groggy and may have some vivid dreams, even waking ones, but you will not be sick."

"Just give a yell, Cyn. I'll be close."

"Thank you both."

The door closed and she began changing into her nightgown. By the time she slipped between the sheets the room around her seemed to move with more than the motion of the ship. The morning sun playing on the water cast wavering bands of light and shadow onto the cabin's ceiling. Her mind played with the patterns, making pictures and then stories from the pictures until the stories became dreams.

In her dream she sailed, but *under* the sea. The water played with her hair and clothing, making them flutter like flags on a breeze. Fish swam alongside. The webbed hands of a merman reached out of the gloom; not to grasp, but to caress her smooth skin, so different from their own scales. Its face materialized before her, flat but expressive, broad blue-green lips parting in a smile that showed rows of needle teeth.

The water in her dream buoyed her up as the soft hands of an entire school of mer, now all cradling her, all caressing, bore her along with the waves. It felt wonderful, and she let herself be borne along by a thousand loving hands, as comforted as a babe in her mother's arms.

CHAPTER TWENTY-TWO

Bittersweet Dreams

"KOYBUR?"

Cynthia rolled over, struggling against her bedclothes. Light streamed in through the port, but she had no idea the time of day, or even how many days they'd been at sea. She looked around the little cabin, squinting into the shadows, but Koybur wasn't there.

"Troilen?"

No one materialized from the gloom. She was alone. That was good. She had to use the chamber pot, and didn't want to offend anyone.

She rolled out of the bunk, wobbling slightly with the roll of the ship. She hoisted her nightgown and saw to necessities, then stood and remembered that she was supposed to do something when she woke up. She *was* awake—a quick pinch confirmed this—and they'd told her to call them when she woke because she was supposed to do something, but she couldn't remember what.

"Maybe the captain knows," she said, starting for the door to the cabin. "Captains know everything. 'S why they're captains."

There were two latches to the door. She grabbed the one that wasn't looking at her and turned it. She knew the other one wanted to bite her hand, and felt a rush of satisfaction that she'd outsmarted it.

"Maybe next time," she told the false latch, stepping through and closing the door behind. "Now, where are my seven lucky steps?"

She found the companionway up to the main deck with little difficulty and ascended the steps with remarkable ease. Only one latch on this door, and it didn't look like it would bite, so she turned it and stepped onto the deck.

"Mistress Flaxal?"

A crewman stood before her. She recognized him, but couldn't recall his name. He didn't look like he would bite her either, but the snake coming out of his ear might, so she mumbled a greeting and turned away to climb to the quarterdeck. She heard the crewman call out her name, then call out some other names, names she knew, although she couldn't really remember who they belonged to. She needed to find the captain and find out what she was supposed to do.

Another crewman met her on the quarterdeck and she remembered his name. She'd hired him in Tsing. He didn't have any snakes coming out of his ears.

"Mistress Flaxal, are you a'right?"

"I'm looking for the captain, Mister Karek." She looked past him to the helmsman and wondered how he could steer the ship when the spokes of the wheel had turned into pickles. They had to be slippery. She looked back to Karek. "I need to speak to Captain Uben."

"The Captain's off watch, Mistress. Master Smythe the mate's on watch, but he's below."

"There is something I have to ask the captain. Something I have to do."

"Aye Mistress. You're supposed to eat a meal when you wake, and call for Capt'n Troilen." He looked at her nervously. "I don't think you was supposed to come up on deck, leastways not with nothin' but your night dress on, Mistress."

"I wasn't?" She looked down and realized she was indeed wearing nothing but her nightgown. "I like the fresh air, Mister Karek. Please bring a robe from my cabin and have the cook prepare a meal for me."

"Aye, Mistress." He looked at her worriedly again, but as he turned someone else approached, a tall dark-skinned woman with a curious little winged man on her shoulder. That seemed very strange. She wondered if it was a hallucination. Troilen had said the tea could make her have waking dreams.

"Mistress? Are you all right?" the woman asked.

"Yes, I'm fine. I just forgot my robe. I wanted to find the captain, but he's off watch, so Mister Karek is going to get my robe."

Then the little winged man fluttered from the woman's shoulder and landed on her own, chattering high pitched nonsense in her ear. She started, but then suddenly remembered: this was Mouse, and the dark woman was Vulta. She looked around the quarterdeck, shaking her head.

"Sorry, I'm a little confused. I think it's the tea."

"I think so, too, Mistress. Let's just go back down to the cabin, okay?"

"I like the fresh air," she said, stepping to the rail. Vulta was instantly at her side, one hand on her shoulder, but Cynthia's steps were sure and steady. She liked the motion of the ship, the easy roll as the big swells lifted her bow and let her rise over them. "Can I have my lunch up here?"

"I don't see why not, really. The weather's fine. We could set up a table."

Cynthia looked down and into the depths, past the dancing shafts of sunlight into the blue... into the undulating colors... into the heart of the sea. There were shapes down there, shapes moving in the darkness. They had long graceful tails and webbed hands. She remembered them from her dreams, their fluid motions and their caressing touch.

"Can I sail with them?"

"With who, Mistress?" Vulta looked down into the water, squinting and shading her eyes. "There's nothing down there. Just water."

"They're down there. They're always down there. Their hands are so soft. I'd really like to—"

"I don't think that's a good idea, Mistress. We're well offshore. The nearest land is the Shattered Isles there, so it wouldn't be a good place for a swim."

"The Shattered Isles?"

Cynthia's gaze rose from the mesmerizing depths to the distant row of islands abeam of the ship. She could see four of them clearly, towering and green, each with a cap of clouds, and one sporting a plume of smoke from its center.

"These must be the southern ones. They're nothing like the northern ones, all flat and sandy." She squinted, trying to remember her charts.

"Aye, Mistress. Those are Minos, Ataros, Plume and Tar islands. We've a half dozen more to pass before we make our tack."

"Of course." It all made sense coming from Vulta's mouth, but she couldn't dredge up the details from her own mind. The confusion frustrated her, but she couldn't seem to make herself care a great deal. "Is lunch ready yet? I'm hungry."

"It'll be a bit yet, Mistress, but Karek's here with your robe, so you should be more comfortable."

They draped a robe over her shoulders, and several more men appeared from the lower deck. One she didn't recognize immediately, but he just gave her a cursory glance before going to the helmsman and giving orders about steering the ship. He didn't mention the pickles. The other two, she knew.

"Good to see you on your feet, Mistress Cynthia. How do you feel?"

"Good. A little confused, but good. Thank you, Troilen. Are you going to make me some more tea?"

"Yes, but not quite as strong as the last, I think." The tall fellow bowed to her and turned to go. She decided not to tell him his ears were on fire. If he didn't know, he would find out soon enough.

"Hi, Feldrin. How are you?"

"Very good, Mistress." The huge man grinned at her, moving to the railing beside her.

"All your cuts healed up? I'd hate it if you started leaking blood."

"Not yet healed, but better, thank you. I won't be leakin' blood. I promise."

"Don't make promises you can't keep, Feldrin. Hey, why is that island smoking? Is it on fire?"

"That's Plume Island, Mistress; it's one of the islands that has an active volcano. Nobody goes there."

"Oh, right. Camels."

"Camels?"

"The southern islands have camels, so nobody wants to go there and be eaten."

"Oh, ya mean cannibals. That's right. We give 'em a wide berth."

"Cannibals. Right." She looked at the islands to windward. They were far enough that their bases were lost in the mists cast up by the surf. All the islands were volcanic, but only a few put up plumes of smoke like Plume Island. Only one was active enough to be dangerous: Fire Island lay near the end of the chain, and it erupted frequently, sending huge clouds of smoke and ash skyward.

She wondered if all of the smoking islands belched up clouds with faces in them like this one. She started to ask Feldrin when a portly man she knew only as "Cook" came on deck with a large wooden tray. Another man staggered up the steps carrying a small folding table. She immediately recognized Koybur.

"Lunch! Koybur! Wow, everyone's here!" She whirled in a circle, letting her robe flap in the wind, oblivious to the fact that the breeze pressed her thin nightgown to her skin, cutting a very fine outline of what lay beneath. She stopped when Feldrin's huge hands clapped her shoulders tightly so that her robe blew back around her body. "What? Oh, nobody else is having lunch?"

"You're feeling fine, I see," Koybur said, flipping the little table open and bracing the legs. Cook put the tray down and she could see there were thick slabs of mutton, spiced potatoes, greens and sliced apple all vying for space with two thick biscuits and a cup of the fruity concoction they drank to stave off scurvy.

"Yeah. Hungry though. Wow, food! My favorite dish!" She sat right down on the deck in front of the low table, crossing her legs in a most unladylike fashion. Luckily, her long nightgown and robe covered her adequately. She speared a thick slab of mutton and bit off a corner. It was wonderfully tender, which either meant it was well-cooked or rotten. She hoped it was the former, but it tasted so good that she really didn't care. Mouse fluttered down to the edge of her plate and tucked right in, scooping handfuls of potatoes into his face. She laughed at his antics, cutting a small piece of meat for him.

"She's really loopy, ain't she?" Koybur asked Vulta.

"Well, she asked me if she could go swimming, so I think that's a yes. I think she's okay, but she's seeing things that aren't there. She said there were things under the ship and wanted to go swimming with them."

"They *are* under there. They're always under there, Koybur. Really." Cynthia glared at Vulta's skepticism and stuffed a forkful of potatoes into her mouth. They were spiced with garlic and swimming with butter. "They're really fun to sail with. Their hands are so soft." She gave a little full-body shiver and hugged herself with the remembered sensation of a thousand hands buoying her along under the water.

"See what I mean?" Vulta shook her head and grinned. "Like she's three sheets to the wind."

"Well, someone should watch over her until she's back in bed." The crippled man shrugged and looked at others. "I don't think I could stop her if she decided to take a dip, and I wouldn't put money on you right now, Master Brelak, so who gets the duty?"

"I'll stay with her, but I'd welcome an extra hand," Brelak said, leaning casually against the bulwark. "Karek? You're not on duty, are you?"

"No, sir. Not 'til third watch. I was jist workin' a new monkey's fist into the bell rope. Be happy ta watch over her."

"Good! I'm overdue for a date with my hammock." Vulta waved and descended the steps to the main deck.

The others paid their respects and went below as well, leaving Karek and Feldrin to watch over Cynthia while she finished her meal.

"You been here before, Feldrin?" she asked, spearing an apple slice and taking a bite.

"Many times, Miss Cynthia. It's the trade route from the north to the Southern Ocean, unless yer in a ship that'll sail better than six points to the wind."

"That island. The one with the smoke." She indicated the one she meant by pointing a forkful of potatoes. "Does it always smoke?"

"Lots of the islands smoke, Mistress," Karek put in before the big man could answer. "Some smoke more, some less. That'n's lousy with cannibals. I been close on the windward side and with a glass you can see the skulls of their meals on sticks all up and down the beach. You won't e'er catch me on *that* island, not fer all the gold in Odea's private vaults."

"And does the smoke always have a face?" she asked, looking up at her two experts as she sliced and sampled another bite of mutton.

"A face?" Karek and Feldrin exchanged skeptical glances then looked to the towering column of smoke trailing up from the caldera of Plume Island.

"I don't see it, Mistress," Karek answered, keeping his face neutral. He cast a glance at Brelak. "Jist looks like smoke to me."

"What about you, Feldrin? Do you see anything in the smoke, or is the tea making me see things that aren't there?"

He looked to her, not expecting such lucidity.

"There!" Her fork clattered to the plate as she lurched to her feet and then to the railing. Her finger pointed like a wind vane to the looming cloud. "There. Tell me you see it, Feldrin."

The two men were at her side in an instant, far more concerned with keeping her aboard than scrutinizing some sulfurous cloud. Once they each had a hand on her, however, they both let their eyes drift up to the billowing cloud.

"No. No, I don't see it, Miss Cynthia." Brelak squinted hard, straining eyes that could spot a sail from the foretop at three leagues, but he saw no mysterious face in the smoke of the volcano.

"There you are!" she said, snapping his attention. But now she stretched one hand down over the bulwark, down toward the water.

Something large splashed, a broad tail flipping once before vanishing.

"What the hell?" He pulled her back from the rail. "That's enough, Mistress. Time fer yer next cup 'o tea, I think."

"But they want me to sail with them," she argued, trying futilely to break his restraining grip.

"I'm sorry, Mistress, but we'll have ta keep our sailin' aboard the ship. If they want to come up here and sail with us, I'll make 'em a right nice splash pool to keep 'em comfortable, but you can't go down there with the fishes unless you can grow some gills right quick." He shouted for a crewman to take the platter and table back to the galley, then enlisted Karek's aid in ushering Cynthia to her cabin.

"Gills?" She felt along her ribcage for the long slits that the mer breathed through. "No. No gills. Damn, I knew there was something."

She stopped struggling and went with them to her cabin where Troilen waited with a cup of tepid tea. He handed it to her and left the cabin, nodding to the glowering Morrgrey in passing. Only after he watched her drink it down did Brelak relax and exit the room.

"No gills," Cynthia said to no one in particular, shrugging out of her robe and returning to her bunk. She lay back and watched the light on the cabin ceiling, then held up her hand. It was still wet where the mer had touched her. It had leapt high out of the water to reach her. She smiled. There were two tiny scales stuck to her palm. She touched her fingertips to her lips and tasted the salt.

"So soft," she said with a sigh as the drug took hold, spiraling her down into the realm of sleeping dreams. She thought it a shame; she rather enjoyed the waking ones.

CHAPTER TWENTY-THREE

Southaven

THE *WINTER GALE* SAILED into Southaven harbor without incident and without Cynthia seeing much of anything but the inside of her cabin for the remainder of the voyage. One day from their destination, Troilen gave her a much smaller dose of the bittersweet extract. As a result, she managed to be on deck as they sailed through the gap in the breakwater. She stood on the poop deck of the *Winter Gale* with Koybur and Captain Uben, watching the familiar buildings grow closer.

Not such a bad little town, she thought, smiling at the children waving from the eastern jetty.

"Looks like yer spars are here," Koybur said, pointing at the long rough-cut spruce boles lying on the quay near the shipyard.

"I'm dying to see how far the construction has gone."

"Don't expect too much. It's only been about six weeks we've been gone. They won't have worked the kinks out of the plans for a month, so..." He squinted and chewed on the stem of his pipe. "I'll bet a night's bar tab they don't have the keels finished yet."

She thought about it for a bit, calculating how long it would take to lay out the long mosaic of hardwood and lead, all dovetailed together, doweled and laminated with resin. She ran some numbers through her head and smiled.

"I'll take that bet, Koybur, and I'll even go a step further. A bottle of Brulo's best rum says they've got four frames up on each hull when we walk through the door."

"Done!" He laughed heartily. "You've got a lot of faith in Master Ghelfan."

"Yes, I do." She gripped the railing hard as Uben shouted the order to ware ship and shorten sail; they were making their turn into the anchorage.

≈

A reasonably short eternity later, she stepped from the launch onto the Southaven quay and turned to address her recently hired crew of two captains, two mates and one boatswain, as well as six stout seamen and Borell the cook.

"Ladies and gentlemen, you have two days shore leave starting right now." The seamen grinned and clapped their hands in anticipation, whereas the officers shrugged or cocked eyebrows in surprise. "Please find a place to stay; there are several good boarding houses in town. Two days hence, report sober and whole to Master Keelson at Keelson's Shipyard. I'd like to have the officers and boatswains up to the hill for dinner tomorrow evening. Tonight, I'm going to eat at the Starfish, and if good captain Uben will allow his crew ashore, I think I'm going to be buying some drinks."

"Ha! That's right! You owe the crew a round, don'cha?" Koybur patted her shoulder and laughed as Mouse cheered and orbited her head. "I'd forgotten about that."

"Well, I'm sure *they* haven't," she said, dismissing the officers with a nod. "Koybur, shall we see about our little wager?"

"O'course!"

She walked at his pace toward the shipyard, though she wanted desperately to break into a run. A fat galleon sat up on the lift having her bottom scraped and caulked, a team of carpenters chiseling away a bit of rot around the rudder post.

"They don't look short of laborers," she commented as they approached.

"I imagine Keelson hired a few extra hands for the work. Carpenters aren't hard to find. Besides, didn't Ghelfan say he was bringin' in his own crew?"

"Yes, but only a few. He mentioned a foreman and a few specialists for the metalwork and the wire-rope rigging." She had wondered about the wire-rope many times; would it be too heavy? Would it rust and crumble in a few months? So many questions rattled around in her head that she felt she might scream before they reached the shipyard building.

Then the side door to the looming structure stood before them. Suddenly, she didn't know what to do. Would she be disappointed? Would she find something wrong with the construction and not know how to confront the shipwrights?

"Go ahead, lass," Koybur said, and she realized that she'd been standing stock still, staring at the door handle. "You've earned it."

"Yes. By all the Gods, yes, I have earned it." She reached for the bronze handle and turned it, pushing the door aside and stepping into a realm where the very air was tinged with the craft of the shipwright.

Wood shavings crunched underfoot as she stepped over the lintel, the scents of fresh-cut timber and resin washing over her in a wave, sharp in her nostrils yet as familiar and welcoming as those of vinegar and yeast to a baker. The cacophony of dozens of hammers and saws all working at individual rhythms struck her ears, and the noise reminded her of waves crashing on a beach. But the sight she beheld—the stark lines of the looming frames, the graceful sweep of the keel timber as it arced up into the bows, the sensual curves of the bilges as they swept up from keel to chine—stopped her in her tracks and left her gaping like a gaffed grouper.

"Oh, my..." She fell speechless. Even Mouse sat in stunned silence on her shoulder, his little mouth hanging open in awe.

She had underestimated Master Ghelfan and his crew of specialists.

The keels were long finished, and half a dozen frames stood in place on each of the two hulls. They stood bow to bow, each set off the centerline of the huge floor to best share the space and leave as much open area as possible. Less than skeletons of what they would be, she could still see their lines starting to take form.

As she stood gaping, a cry of "Haul away!" rang out, and a newly finished frame lifted from the floor The crew heaved on the tackle and the heavy oak frame tilted to vertical and took flight. Chains rattled, turning the wheels that would move the overhead trolley down to the waiting keel timber of the nearest hull. Another team held guide ropes to keep the frame steady while a short and incredibly broad figure stood upon the keel just where the frame would be fitted. The figure raised its stubby arms to make hand signals to the crews, bringing the huge frame into line and down into the precut slot in the keel.

Mallets pounded braces into place and several large copper bolts were threaded through pre-cut holes in the frame and keel, fitted with wide nuts and tightened down with wrenches as long as a man's arm.

"Mistress Flaxal!" a voice crowed above the din, and dozens of faces turned her direction. A ragged cheer went up, and Cynthia realized why. She was *paying* for all this. Her money, virtually all of her remaining family fortune, lay right here before her, transformed from numbers into gold and then into wood and nails and resin and labor. When these hulls finally touched water, she would have precious little real money left to her name.

"This had better bloody work," she said as Ghelfan and Keelson hurried up to her, both grinning broadly. This was all too much for Mouse; he hid behind her neck, peeking around from under her collar at the two men.

Covered in sawdust and obviously pleased beyond measure to see her safe and sound, they pumped her hand, a dozen questions burbling out of their mouths before she had a chance to answer one. Finally she raised her hands in surrender.

"Please, gentlemen! Please! One question from one of you at a time, and I daresay this is hardly the venue for meaningful discussion." She pushed between them and advanced on the skeletal structure of the nearest ship. One hand rose to touch one broad oak frame as if drawn by some force within the primordial vessel. Unfinished and rough under her fingers, she still felt as if she could sense a heart barely beating within.

"She's beautiful," she whispered, caressing the wood. Mouse came out from behind her collar and gazed up at the great wooden frame, then at the adoration on her features. He shook his head and shrugged, plopping down to sit with his chin in his hands as if convinced Cynthia's hallucinations had returned.

"So, as you can see, Mistress Flaxal, we're a bit ahead of schedule." Keelson grinned and clapped the slender half-elven shipwright on the shoulder. "I gotta say it's all Master Ghelfan's fault on that. His crew is right near amazin', they are."

"Not at all, Mistress. Master Keelson's people supply the skill with wood and the hearts of lions that have made our progress nothing but miraculous. My people but supply the organizational impetus to make sure everything is done in its proper sequence and in a timely fashion."

Cynthia started to turn to tell them both to shut up and let her enjoy this moment, when another, far rougher and slightly feminine voice entered the conversation.

"The *timely fashion* part, that's my responsibili'y."

She turned to find herself looking right over the head of the broad figure that had recently stood upon the keel and guided the new frame down into place. The woman, or more precisely, *dwarvish* woman, held out her broad hand for Cynthia to take. Mouse yelped and ducked behind her shoulder.

"Y'u must be Cynthie Flaxal." The hand engulfed Cynthia's, and she could feel the strength in it. She grinned as wide as her broad shoulders, her round face and jutting brow framed by perfectly trimmed mutton chops which, oddly, made her features no less feminine. "Dura ShunTaren, and 'appy te make yur 'quaintance."

"Dura is my foreman, Mistr—"

"Fore-*what*, Ghelfan?" The woman glared up at her employer with murder in her eyes, her eyebrows knitting together onto one broad brown brush of obstinacy.

"My apologies, Dura; fore-*dwarf*. But call her what you will, she is the most—"

"Y'u there, boyo!" the dwarf bellowed, loud enough to leave Cynthia's ears ringing. "Yes, y'u. Y'u hammer that shim outta there afore that frame's go' a proper cross brace and I'll be usin' yer scro'um ta hold me pocket money!" She nodded to the others and advanced on the hapless worker, railing in even more colorful language as she approached.

"She keeps everyone in line." Keelson's tone suggested that the list of those she kept in line included the two shipwrights.

"So I see." Cynthia tried to hide a smile at the demeanor of the man currently having the seat of his trousers soundly chewed. "She certainly is... uh..."

"Abrasive," the two men said in perfect unison.

Cynthia stifled a laugh, but Koybur had less success.

"Right useful with so many hands to watch at once, I'll wager," he said, nodding toward the unfortunate carpenter whom she had just finished chastising.

"Indispensable," Ghelfan said, his tone regrettable. "I learned long ago that laborers respond to a firm hand, one which my temperament does not accommodate. I hired Dura more than fifty years ago, and I have never missed a deadline since."

"Aye, she rides 'em hard, but she's fair about it. Those hands you hired in Scarport and Rockport arrived well enough, by the way. That Finthie Tar is right talented with riggin'. She had every block in the shop runnin' as smooth as a barmaid's... uh... well, plenty smooth, by the time the keel planks were cut."

"Good." She scanned the work crews, but couldn't see the woman at the moment. "And laying the keels went well, I guess?"

"Aye, well enough. O'course they've still got to be sheathed with red cedar, but that'll wait for the hull plankin'." Keelson pointed out a few challenges they'd had with the design, but nothing insurmountable. By the end of his explanation, Cynthia could see both men itching to get back to work.

"Well, gentlemen, I see that I'm impeding progress, so I'll say good afternoon. Please plan to come to dinner at my home tomorrow around sunset and relay the invitation to Finthie and Dura. I'm having all the officers up for a meal and some discussion."

They both agreed, relieved that she had noticed their discomfort and taken the hint. She could have watched the workers all day, mesmerized by the sights, sounds and smells, but she knew her presence would slow the work. She and Koybur left the building and ambled up the street.

"Come to the Starfish with me, Koybur. I'll buy you lunch." Mouse cheered in her ear at the mention of food.

"But you won the bet."

"I did, and you're going to pay up, but not just yet. I need to eat something and I hate to eat alone. Then I'm going to walk up the hill and see how Marta and Brolen are doing. I need the exercise."

Lunch evolved into an afternoon of tale telling with Brulo, Rowland and a good number of locals. She escaped before the ale started flowing, much to Mouse's disapproval, but vowed to return for dinner. She had to pause several times on the way up the hill, the toll of her drug-induced inactivity. She felt well enough, but the profound weakness in her limbs and her lack of endurance were alarming.

The old estate had not changed, aside from some additional repairs on the unburned portion of the house and the construction of a new foyer. The oleander was blooming, but the frangipani and honeysuckle had passed.

She had sent word of her return, not wanting to surprise Marta and Brolan. Marta made a big fuss, just as she had expected, while Brolan hovered nearby, wringing his broad hands as if wanting something to do while his face remained fixed in a broad smile.

It truly felt good to be home.

CHAPTER TWENTY-FOUR
Dinner Among Friends

TRUE TO CYNTHIA'S EXPECTATIONS, a meal at the Galloping Starfish and an evening among friends put her to rights. The entire crew of the *Winter Gale* came ashore for her promised round of drinks, and many stayed well into the night. Cynthia enjoyed herself thoroughly but, unlike Mouse, took care not to over-indulge. The following morning she woke early for a brisk walk around the grounds, but the sprite remained snugly huddled in her sock drawer, oblivious and unrousable.

Marta rushed her through breakfast, claiming she had to make a trip to town to purchase stores for dinner. She couldn't remember the last time guests had been invited, let alone such a number. Consequently, the woman verged on panic. Cynthia inspected the shopping list, started to say something about the expense, but then decided against intervening. One night's revelry for her new officers would be worth the cost. She had things to tell them that were best said after a good meal and a few drinks. The thought of money did prompt another idea, however: aside from one essential visit on the other side of town, she would visit her banker, Master Fergus, to evaluate her financial status.

After eggs, sausage, two of Marta's scones and three cups of blackbrew, Cynthia felt ready to face the day. That was when Mouse finally fluttered into the room. He peeped miserably at Marta and received a scowl, half a sausage and the corner of a leftover scone.

Cynthia refused a ride and thoroughly enjoyed the walk down the hill. Mouse wobbled alongside, investigating every blossom and leaf beside the road and terrorizing half a dozen squirrels along the way. Her financial concerns were minor, but being absent for six weeks during such a demanding project could have put a pinch in her funds. The last person she expected to bump into upon entering Fergus' office was Koybur, but chance and inattention brought them together in a tangle of skirts, twisted limbs and screeching seasprite.

"Koybur! I'm sorry. What are you doing here of all places?"

"Where should I be, lass?" He extricated himself from her skirts, propped a slightly squashed Mouse onto her shoulder and explained. "*Sunrise* and *Seven Sisters* made landfall while we was out gallivantin', both with tidy sums in their strongboxes."

"Oh? How much?" Perhaps her finances weren't as depleted as she'd thought.

"Well, as I said, tidy sums, but after Master Keelson dipped into the pot there weren't much left to pay the piper."

"Keelson? Why would— Oh, I forgot." She'd left orders for her other three ships to have whatever repairs were deemed necessary by their masters when they next made landfall in Southaven. Evidently both had needed extensive repairs. "Well, at least they're both ship-shape. They'll earn more in good condition than they would leaking like sieves and caked with growth."

"Aye, and as I said there was a bit left over. *Seven Sisters* made a good run on silks and spice."

"Good! That means I can pay you this month." She clapped him on the shoulder and grinned. "See you up the hill tonight. You don't want to miss it; Marta's all a twitter."

"Wouldn't miss it fer all the ladies in Southaven, Cyn, though you might regret tellin' Ghelfan to bring that acid-tongued little brick of a dwarf along. She'll eat you out of hearth and home."

"No worries, Koybur. From the shopping list I read this morning, there'll be enough to feed *Winter Gale's* entire crew and still have leftovers."

"My kinda party." He nodded and lurched out the door and down the steps, whistling and tapping the ashes out of his pipe as he made his way across the cobbled street.

She watched him for a moment and shook her head in wonder; Koybur always managed a smile. Considering what he had to live with every day of his life, her trials seemed minuscule.

With that thought she turned to Master Fergus to find out just how much money she had left. The result surprised her. She should have enough to outfit both ships nicely and have coin left to buy their first cargos.

She exited the office and took a deep breath. One more errand awaited her, and it would require a considerable walk. Weary but steady legs carried her through town. At the far end, she looked up at the distant lighthouse and wondered if the old lightkeeper would indulge her strange request.

≈

Dinner turned into an affair to be remembered.

Part of Marta's shopping expedition included hiring one of the serving girls from the Galloping Starfish for the evening. Kara was not the most comely of the girls Brulo employed, but her skills at seeing to the needs of her customers outshone the others' by far.

The guests arrived in pairs and small groups, Captains Ulbattaer and

Troilen first, then Brelak and the boatswain Karek. Vulta had struck up an instant friendship with Finthie Tar. *Two kindred spirits*, Cynthia thought, as they arrived arm-in-arm, already singing sea chanties. The last were Ghelfan, Keelson, Koybur and the stout dwarven woman Dura ShunTaren, all piled into one of the shipyard's wagons.

Kara met the guests and ushered them to the sitting room, where Cynthia had been instructed by Marta to keep them all company and, at all costs, out of the kitchen. The estate's extensive cellar had been broached, and all manner of rare liqueurs, whiskies, ports, rums, wines and ales lay arrayed for the guests.

"Drinks, lady and gentlemen?" Kara asked the last four to arrive as Cynthia shook their hands and welcomed them to her home.

"Bloody right, drinks!" Dura said, nodding to Cynthia and raising one bushy eyebrow at the expansive array of bottles. "Damned buckboard pu' a permanent dent in me arse! Somethin' ta kill the pain'd be much appreciated. The Nort'umberland single malt, neat."

When all had received drinks, Cynthia took them on a short tour of the house: from the cellar, which left Dura gaping in appreciation, to the top of the tower, where the night air refreshed their senses. Moonlight on a calm sea and an expansive view of the flickering lights of Southaven lay before them like a child's glittering toy.

"This, ladies and gentlemen," Cynthia said with a wave of one hand, "is where I fell in love."

Several eyes cocked at her curiously, but more than a few looked on knowingly. Mouse simply sighed, fluttered to her shoulder and planted a resounding kiss on her cheek. Finally Brelak voiced what many of them knew.

"With the sea. Aye, I can see it in yer eyes. But have a care, Miss Cynthia. She's a harsh mistress. Don't let her get her claws too deep in yer heart. She'll break it sure."

"Too late for that, Master Brelak," she said, her voice cracking. She sipped her wine and pointed to the harbor. "But not too late to have at least some of my dreams come true. This is also where I got the idea for the ships you're all working on so diligently. When I was ten years old, I watched a dhow cut a line for the channel that no galleon could match, but she was slipping downwind so badly that it did her no good. I thought, why not put a decent keel on her, or put her rig on a small galleon? The rest happened on paper."

"On paper?" Ghelfan asked, interest arching his brow.

"Well, mostly. I took some measurements from Koybur's little smack and there were some sketches in the library, things my father did when he was young. The rest I just drew because it felt right."

"Amazing."

"Aye, amazin' that my drink's empty again! Where's that girl?"

"Dura! We're guests here!" Ghelfan swatted her shoulder, but only succeeded in injuring his hand.

"Aye, an' thirsty ones! Shall we retire to the parlor?" Mouse cheered, fluttering from Cynthia's shoulder to Dura's, drawing a raucous laugh as she led the way back down the stairs. "Now there be a bug after me own heart!"

Kara awaited their arrival with a platter of tiny loaves of bread, each no larger than Brelak's thumb and stuffed with spicy sausage and garlic. Kara replenished their drinks, then opened the two mahogany-paneled pocket doors that joined the sitting room with the main dining room.

"Ladies and gentlemen, please be seated."

Light flooded from two crystal chandeliers and eighteen polished bronze wall sconces. The silk embroidered tablecloth glittered in the light, along with a mismatched set of crystal, porcelain and silver. None of the guests noticed, for the rest of the décor captured their attention fully.

A portrait of Benjamin Garrison dominated the far wall. This painting alone had hung there for as long as Cynthia could remember. Other portraits had been salvaged from closets and cellars after the fire and now hung on display.

Orin Flaxal stood upon the south wall, his slim form clad in a white linen shirt and a vest of azure blue, his deep green eyes squinting and his mouth turned up in a mirthful quirk. On the opposite wall, Peggy Flaxal stood in a light green gown, her auburn hair drawn up into a complicated coiffure, tendrils curling down the graceful curve of her neck. The two looked across the ornately arranged table at one another as if oblivious to the rest of the room.

Between the portraits hung paintings of every ship Ben Garrison had owned, from the greatest galleon to the lowliest barge.

"I must apologize for the mismatched place settings," Cynthia began, waving a hand for the others to follow her into the dining room, "but along with the entire north wing of the house, the dinnerware seems to have taken the greatest damage by the fire." She took her seat at the head of the table beneath her grandfather's portrait.

"Not used ta such fin'ry," Dura said, placing her glass of single malt whiskey beside the plate of alabaster porcelain edged in royal blue and gold. She tapped a crystal water goblet with a thick fingernail, smiling at the tone. "Somebody gimme a kick if I grab the wrong fork, ay?"

"I don't stand on ceremony, Dura. I was raised to all of this, but my parents and grandfather were sailors." She raised her glass in a toast. "All I ask is that you enjoy my hospitality."

"To Mistress Cynthia Flaxal!" Troilen offered, raising his glass. "May her hospitality never run short."

"And her cellar never run dry!" Dura agreed as the others burst into laughter and raised their own glasses in toast.

And enjoy they did.

Through courses of soup, to fruit and cheeses, to fish, to fowl and culminating in a fabulous rack of lamb, each course accompanied by a carefully selected wine, they ate and toasted and laughed, complimenting Marta at every turn. Hours passed with the meal, and wine flowed like water until all, including the seemingly bottomless Dura, declared themselves sated.

"I never knew food could taste like that," Karek said, holding his outstretched hands over his stomach.

"It usually doesn't, unless it is created by the hands of a true master in the culinary art." Ghelfan raised his glass to Marta as she helped Kara take away the plates. "My dear, if our ages were not separated by seventy years, I would ask you to wed."

"Why, Master Ghelfan!" Marta blushed and giggled like a girl. "If I were twenty years younger, I might accept!"

Cynthia stood and raised her glass. "Ladies and gentlemen, may I offer a toast to this evening's benefactor. To my lady Marta. May her skills never wane and her eye never wander."

They all cheered and raised their glasses amid the laughter of friends well-plied with good food and drink.

"Ah! But wait!" Marta raised a hand and favored them all with a sly smile. "You've forgotten... dessert!"

A series of delighted groans circulated the table.

"With the sweet I can offer you blackbrew, tea, brandy or port."

They all made their choices, some more than one, and Marta departed.

"Well, I hope the repast has not so befuddled your senses that we can't have a little conversation." Cynthia gauged her guests and saw the quirk of amusement only in Koybur. The others, it seemed, remained oblivious to her intent. *Just as well,* she thought, bracing herself. "Tonight I would like to divulge to you my true intentions behind building these new ships."

"Intentions?" Ghelfan asked, his ears perking up visibly. "I was under the impression that your intentions were to rebuild your grandfather's empire, to build a fleet of ships."

"That is only part of my intent, Master Ghelfan. But rest assured that is an integral part of my overall plan."

Marta and Kara entered bearing beverages and platters of tiny dishes. Each diner received a bowl containing a baked custard. On the surface of each an intricate silhouette of a ship lay rendered in spun sugar, the perfect profile of Cynthia's new design under full sail.

"As you may or may not know, my parents were murdered by the pirate who calls himself Bloodwind."

The table fell silent as Marta and Kara finished serving, all eyes on Cynthia. She took her spoon and sampled her dessert, signifying that they should all eat. Several sipped their beverages, and a few sampled the sweet custard.

"I am no warrior, and no seamage like my father, much to my chagrin, but I will have my revenge against the man who murdered my parents." A few eyes strayed to the portrait to Cynthia's left, that of Orin Flaxal, and she saw some trepidation in those glances. "By building these new ships, ships that can sail faster and closer to the wind than any corsair on the sea, I intend to starve Bloodwind to death."

They stared at her, some in understanding, some in utter shock. Finally, one of them voiced his concerns.

"Pardon me, Mistress, but with two ships, you can't be serious."

Cynthia met Rafen Ulbattaer's eyes squarely, and smiled. "No, not with just two ships. These two will be the first of many, and despite my own and Master Ghelfan's best efforts, the design will be copied and other ship builders will soon be launching similar hulls. Additionally, I have started plans for larger versions of the same design, three and even four-masted versions that can haul as much as any galleon on the sea, and reach their destinations in half the time."

She paused and fixed them all with an even, steady stare.

"I have patience, ladies and gentlemen. I've been waiting fifteen years for this, and I can wait that many more if need be."

"Why not just hunt the bastard down and kill him?" Brelak asked with all the direct honesty of his Morrgrey heritage.

"Two reasons, Master Brelak, the first of which I already stated: I'm not a warrior. The second is that war is very expensive, not only in money but in lives. I'm not prepared to spend anyone else's lives on this."

"Why tell us?" Karek asked casually, sampling his custard and sipping his brandy. "It's not like you're askin' us to go to war."

"Actually, that is exactly what I'm asking, Mister Karek." This brought everyone up short, even Koybur.

"But you said—"

"I said that I wasn't going to ask anyone to hunt Bloodwind down and kill him. I'm not so naïve that I think he won't be hunting me."

"What?" Troilen sat up like he'd been slapped.

"Think for a moment, please," she insisted. "These ships are faster, more maneuverable and sail closer to the wind than any ship on the sea. What would be their most profitable application?"

"Piracy." Rafen Ulbattaer's flat tone hung in the air like the blade of a guillotine.

"Exactly. These ships would make the perfect corsairs, and so, can *never* be allowed to be used for piracy."

They waited for her to finish that thought, knowing there had to be more. They could see it on her face. There were few ways to prevent a ship from being taken. Surprisingly, Brelak had the answer first.

"So, if we're boarded by pirates, the ships are to be scuttled," he said in a matter-of-fact tone far too casual for his words.

"No. Burned," Cynthia countered, raising her cup and draining the last of her blackbrew. "Scuttling a ship is too slow and unsure. I've spoken to the lighthouse keeper here in Southaven, and he assures me he can prepare a device that will ignite an entire ship in any weather or conditions. He is an expert in the area."

"What about the crew?" Finthie's voice sounded thin and somewhat strained.

"Pirates don't take prisoners," Cynthia answered, her eyes flint hard as she met the boatswain's gaze. "Abandoning ship and taking your chances in an open boat or even adrift is no worse a fate than the one Captain Bloodwind would offer, I think."

"True enough," Brelak confirmed, his voice steady as stone.

"But to try to eliminate piracy... It is impossible." Rafen Ulbattaer sipped his port and smoothed his black mustaches. "There will always be piracy, Mistress Cynthia. It is a fact of life, just as there will always be trollops awaiting sailors in every harbor. You cannot have one without the other."

"You sound very sure of that, Captain Ulbattaer," Troilen said, his eyes hard, his tone flat.

"Yes, I *am* sure. It is a simple fact: where there is wealth, there will be someone who wishes to take it. It is the same with the caravans. It is the same in every large city. It will remain so forever."

"And I agree with Captain Ulbattaer," she admitted, catching them all off guard. "But I'm not trying to eliminate piracy. I'm only trying to eliminate one pirate; the one who murdered my parents." Cynthia stood and inclined her head to her guests.

"I'm sorry if I've ruined the mood. We can move into the sitting room and relax if you wish. I just felt like you all should know the truth of my intentions."

"Yes," Koybur said, pressing himself painfully to his feet. "We've eaten well and drunk enough to float a skiff tonight."

"True enough," Cynthia agreed, calling for Kara. "And there's a whole cellar full of bottles yet to be breeched! Enough of *my* intentions. I want to learn more of all of your intentions, if they don't include getting as far away from that crazy Flaxal wench as possible!"

They all laughed and rose, moving into the sitting room to continue the evening's festivities, but the light mood had been snuffed out like a candle with Cynthia's talk of piracy, and the flame of camaraderie was slow to reignite.

CHAPTER TWENTY-FIVE

Labors of Loyalty and Love

WOOD AND COPPER, IRON and steel, cordage and resin, paint and lacquer; those are what dreams are made of...

This had become Cynthia's mantra throughout the dry season as she watched her ships take shape. She would sit for half an hour at the shipyard every day, precisely at noon, with the shipwrights, captains or some of the workers, discussing their progress, problems, needs, wants and wishes. Then, promptly at one half hour past noon, she would leave, for she knew her presence would only impede progress.

As the work continued, other ships came and went, some of them hers. With them came gold, news of civil war in the southern desert and the reminder of the ever-present threat of piracy among the Shattered Isles. Two galleons were lost in those months, their crews never heard from, their cargoes pillaged and sold in a dozen ports. But trade continued as it always would, for trade is the lifeblood of nations.

And in the Shattered Isles, safely ensconced within his slumbering volcano fortress, Captain Bloodwind waited. Through his spies and agents he knew every plank, nail and dowel driven home in Cynthia's new ships. He knew to the day when they would be launched, and how many people he would have aboard them. He even knew of Cynthia's preparations to prevent her ships from falling into his hands, which caused him many sleepless nights.

As to Bloodwind's plans, only one other person knew anything at all of them. Not a single message, not one of his plots, not a word that passed his lips—even when he spoke only to himself—went unnoticed by the sharp eyes and ears that rarely left his side. Camilla knew more of his plots than any of his captains, more than any of his spies and more than his foul sorceress Hydra. And still, she did not know it all.

All this knowledge was, of course, quite useless. She had no way to warn anyone, no means of communication, and had long given up trying to bribe anyone into helping her. This did not stop her from analyzing his plans in her mind. She saw many points at which they could be foiled and many opportunities where people could die. After all this thought, after reviewing all this information, one question rose in her mind that she simply could not answer.

"Why?"

"What?" Bloodwind's eyes shot up from the worn parchment in his hands, his brow furrowed in surprise. "What did you say?"

"Nothing." Camilla fixed her eyes on the floor, the tremor of her shoulders setting her jewelry jingling. Her mouth had given voice to her curiosity without her intent, an unthinkable mistake.

"No, my dear, not nothing." He rolled from atop the silk coverlet and stood, his eyes never leaving her. What exactly did you say?"

"I..." Her mind raced like a rat trapped in the bilges of a sinking ship, searching for an exit. "I only wondered."

"Wondered what, my dear?" His voice held a hint of his most dangerous tone.

"Why..." Only one thought surfaced in her mind, and she knew it could enrage him. She would have knelt, had the chain that linked her wrists not been looped over a peg high on the corner post of his canopied bed. This had become one of his favored torments, chaining her there to watch him sleep, read, or be entertained by one of the other slaves. She often wished he would just ravish her and be done with it, but she also knew that the years of degradation had been a far longer-lasting punishment than any physical violation could have been.

"I wondered why you study those drawings so much."

"And I wonder why you persist in thinking you can lie to me." His hand curled around the chain bound to her collar and pulled until his breath warmed her cheek. "Do you desire even more jewelry, dear Camilla? I can think of no small number of fleshy bits about your person that could be pierced for gold rings."

"No, Captain, I..." Her mind reeled at the thought of the glowing red sailcloth needles the pirates used to pierce their ears, noses and eyebrows, and just where Bloodwind's demented imagination might lend them to be applied. "I thought that you are rich. You have more money than you could possibly ever spend. You could live like a king in any city in the world."

An eyebrow lifted, and his tone mellowed a trifle. "Yes, that is true." He drew her even closer, the brush of his moustache tickling her cheek. "And?"

"I wondered why..." she whispered miserably, knowing her honesty would bring her punishment. "I wondered why you continue. Why plot and plan and raid and... and..."

"Pirate?"

She stared at him for a moment, wondering if she'd really heard him finish her question. His eyes told her she had, and though they frightened her to her innermost core, she said, "Yes."

"Money is nothing," he said, his voice as smooth as aged rum. "Wealth is only the illusion of power, my dear." His gaze traveled from her face down to her feet and back up.

"Power, real power, comes from something else. It comes from people, people willing to do *anything* for you, not only out of fear but out of loyalty."

"Loyalty?" She was risking all now and knew it. But she also knew he would not kill her outright. She would suffer, but she just might also have her answer. Pain, it seemed, had become her only currency. "Pirates have no loyalty."

"That, my dear, is where you are *wrong*." He whirled away from her and shouted, "Guards!"

Two men burst into the room, naked cutlasses glittering in the lamplight, their eyes scanning the expansive bedchamber for something to kill. Bloodwind approached them and held out his hands, palms up.

"Give me your swords." Two bronze hilts clapped into his palms before the echo of his words stilled in Camilla's ears. "Now, follow me."

He turned and approached her with the blades, but murder did not lurk in his eyes, only a calculated determination more terrifying than the naked steel. He brought the tip of one of the blades to her chin and applied careful pressure until her eyes met his. Behind him curiosity vied with amusement upon the faces of the two pirates. *If they weren't as insane as he*, she thought, *they would be terrified.*

"You both know my favorite slave, Camilla, don't you?" The two men nodded and answered in the affirmative, eying her briefly while Bloodwind ran the flat of the cutlass' blade along her jaw. "Camilla, I believe you know Billy and Tommy here. They're brothers, you know, and they've been with me for... well, from the beginning, ay lads?"

"Aye sir," they both responded, grinning.

"You see, we served together on a ship once, back before I even found this place. Before I called myself Bloodwind." He turned his head to the two and smiled. "You remember what I used to be called, lads?"

"Er, uh, no, sir," one of them said, his brow furrowing, while the other just scratched his chin, shook his head and said, "I only e'r called 'e 'sir'. They was too many officers ta keep 'em straight."

"Aye, there were quite a lot of us, weren't there? I was just one young lieutenant, and I daresay not even the captain or his bloody-handed mate knew my name. But there were quite a few more crew. Some of them like Billy and Tommy here are still with me, and some are gone. The Navy promised to take care of us, but once we were at sea that changed. They made us swear our loyalty, but never showed any in return. We watched a goodly number of our mates flayed alive by the cat, or dance at the end of a yardarm before we finally decided we'd had enough of that murderin' bastard's brand of discipline. Ay, lads?"

"Aye, sir!" they both agreed.

"When we took that ship from him, and fed him and his tight-laced officers to the drakes of the Fathomless Reaches, I made a pledge to those who survived, and they made the same pledge to me. Do ya remember that, lads?"

"Aye, sir!" Their voices rang like hammers on stone, cold and sharp.

"And what was that pledge?"

"By blood, by wind, by water and wave, loyal as one, or a watery grave," they answered.

"And that means loyalty to who, lads?"

"To you, Captain Bloodwind."

"And why me? Why do I deserve your loyalty?"

This brought them up short, as if every answer up to this one had been by rote. Now they had to think, which seemed to Camilla a formidable task.

"Why, 'cause you saved us, sir," one of them said haltingly, as if explaining to a dimwitted child an obvious fact of life. "We was fodder for them lordlings. You gave us our own home. We's our own *nation* now!"

"Aye, that's right Billy, and what is my one and only law?"

"Your word is law, and that goes for everyone."

"And betrayal means?"

"Death!"

"And failure means?"

"Death!"

"Good! Now," he flipped one sword in his hand, caught it deftly by the blade and held the hilt out to one of the brothers, "take your sword, Billy."

The man took the cutlass.

"And I have something for you, Tommy. Here." He fished a bronze key from his pocket and handed it over. "Open that chest."

Camilla knew the chest's contents. By their gaping mouths and bulging eyes, the two pirates did not. Jewels and heavy golden coins stamped with the mints of a dozen nations filled the large chest; a fortune, enough to live like a king, or even *become* a king.

"Good. Now come here, Tommy. Right there. Good."

When the man stood within easy reach, the cutlass in Bloodwind's hand flashed from Camilla's throat to Tommy's in an instant, the razor edge resting on his bobbing Adam's apple. Both brothers gasped in surprise.

"Now Tommy, I must ask you to stay silent. And Billy, I'll ask you to place the tip of your cutlass against my chest, just over my heart."

Both men gaped at him in shock, but complied. The tip of Billy's sword rose until it rested against Bloodwind's chest, and Tommy remained utterly silent.

"Now, let me explain this little game." Bloodwind stood as steady as stone, his voice smooth and relaxed. "My dear slave Camilla confessed to me that she and Tommy here have had a, shall we say, liaison. She has coerced him into a plot to kill me in my sleep, and then take this chest and flee in the messenger boat tied at the quay. Your duty, Billy, is to carry out my order to execute your brother for his betrayal."

Silence hung in the air. The tip of the blade against Bloodwind's chest quivered enough to prick the skin, but the pirate captain stood without flinching.

"Your other alternative, of course, is to drive that blade through my heart and join them in their escape. I have given you this opportunity, Billy, because I know how you love your brother. Also, I know that if he were to die at my hand, you would never truly forgive me. You see, this way, his death is by your hand, not mine. Or, you can simply kill me and join your brother in his betrayal."

"But, sir, I—"

"Ah, ah, no conversation. Just decide and act." Bloodwind's tone became commanding. "Strike now! Him or me. I do not wish to do it myself, but I will if you force me." He pressed the edge of the cutlass against the terrified Tommy's throat until a line of blood welled onto the blade.

Kill him! Camilla thought viciously, a lifetime of torment rising in her like a vengeful tide. "Kill him," she whispered, realizing only as the words left her lips that they leant veracity to Bloodwind's clever lie.

Billy's sword left Bloodwind's chest and lanced at Tommy's with such speed that the pirate captain was hard pressed to knock it away in time. The parry came as a shock to everyone, even Camilla, who thought he would allow one brother to kill the other just to make his point. But as the lethal stroke rang off his blade, Bloodwind surprised her again. He flung his cutlass aside and embraced Billy in a crushing hug, laughing at the top of his lungs and pounding him on the back.

"Well done! Oh, well done indeed! Ha haaa!" He released the stunned pirate and clapped Tommy on the arm. "And you, Tommy. I must apologize for the ruse, but I was trying to make a point to my dear Camilla. Here!" He strode to the open chest, filled his hands with enough gold to choke a horse and brought it to them.

"Take it, lads. Enjoy yourselves. I'm sorry to have abused you so, but you did not disappoint me. Oh, you did not disappoint me at all!" They fumbled to pocket the coins, mumbling thanks and looking at each other sheepishly. Camilla could imagine the awkward conversation they would have after leaving Bloodwind's company. "Now, off with you. Send up a couple more guards, if you please. And enjoy that! You both earned it ten times over!"

When the door boomed closed, Bloodwind turned back to Camilla, his smile triumphant as he pulled her close.

"Now *that*, my dear, is loyalty, and loyalty is power." He pulled her face toward him until she could look nowhere but into those disturbing blue eyes. "All the gold in the world won't buy that. That is what makes me more than any king, duke, merchant or mage, and that is why I am what I am."

And as he kissed her roughly she trembled in fear, for she knew he was absolutely right.

≈

As Cynthia's ships neared completion and the hulls were moved out of the lofting shed onto the broad stone quay—much to the torment of her nerves—she decided that the time had come for another meeting with those who had helped her to bring her dreams to reality.

The evening proved to be a much more sedate affair than the previous dinner, with only seven diners and four courses: conch chowder, lightly grilled mahi-mahi with a mango glaze, pineapple-rum marinated pork roast, and a tart lime pie. Light conversation made dinner a relaxed affair, which suited Cynthia perfectly.

Business, she decided, *should never interfere with a really good meal.*

Afterward, however, with all her guests comfortably ensconced in the sitting room with their drinks of choice, and Mouse safely comatose on her shoulder, Cynthia wasted no time in getting down to business. She began by standing and raising her glass in toast.

"Lady and gentlemen, I would like to propose a toast to Master Ghelfan."

A round of cheers and raised glasses answered her call, as well as an embarrassed smile and nod of gratitude from the shipwright.

"To the artist who helped bring my dreams to life, may he build a thousand more like these." Another round of cheers followed, along with some exclamations.

"Dunno if the sea is big enough for a *thousand* such ships, Mistress," Rafen Ulbattaer commented, sipping his rum and fingering the points of his mustaches.

"You are just afraid of the competition, Desert Rat?" Troilen asked, earning a round of laughter.

"Not from you, Poet," the dark-skinned captain countered with a grin.

Cynthia had listened to the two captains' good-natured jibes for almost half a year now, and expected similar banter from Brelak and Vulta, but they had been uncharacteristically quiet all evening. She suspected they knew why they were here, and were slightly nervous. *Well, it's time to end the suspense*, she thought, tapping her glass with a fingernail.

"Master Keelson has informed me that the time has come to put names and faces to our ships." That got their attention, for they knew what would follow.

"I've decided to assign officers to ships first." That earned a few pointed glances between her guests. "As far as I can tell, the two hulls are identical, but if either captain has a preference between the two, please tell me now."

"I have no preference," Troilen said with a shrug.

"If it's all the same to you, then, Master Poet, I would prefer the ship that was brought out of the shop second." Everyone turned to Rafen in surprise.

"You have discerned some superiority to that one?" Ghelfan asked, arching an eyebrow. It was virtually impossible to construct two truly identical hulls. With dozens of frames, hundreds of planks and thousands of joints between them, some inconsistencies were bound to occur.

"Not at all, Master Ghelfan, but you might remember when I got this." He held up his left hand to show a broad scar across the back, still very light against his dark skin but well healed. "I left a good bit of blood between her keel and her fourth frame. Part of me is in her already."

"Appropriate, Captain Ulbattaer, and unless there are any objections, she'll be yours."

There were none.

"And so, the other is yours, Captain Troilen." At his nod of assent she continued. "In the last months, I've seen how you both interact with the other officers, and I've made assignments of mates and bosuns based on that. Unless there are valid reasons to the contrary, Captain Troilen will have Vulta as his first mate, and Finthie as bosun. This, of course, means that Captain Ulbattaer will take Feldrin and Karek."

She took careful note of the faces of the four as they exchanged glances, nods and smiles. She wondered for a moment if Troilen would object to the assignment of both women as his officers, but saw little concern on his smooth features. Rafen Ulbattaer, she knew, would have been less satisfied with such an assignment, and so, seemed pleased. The fact of the matter was that Vulta and Finthe had become fast friends and worked well together. This was a rarity, and many would see difficulty with such a fast friendship between superior and subordinate, but Cynthia had watched them closely. Splitting them up would be a mistake.

"Any objections?"

There were none.

"Good. Now, you have your ships. They will hit the water in about three weeks. You will be expected to name your vessels before that time." They all stared at her wide-eyed before Koybur finally broke the shocked silence.

"The ships belong to you, Cyn. You should name 'em."

"Aye!" Brelak stood, his heavy brow furrowed. "They're yer dream, Mistress Cynthia. You should give 'em their names."

"No," she said without a hint of the pain that had brought this decision about. "The timber of their hulls and the labor of putting them together were paid for by me, and I'll be the owner of record, but the ships shall be yours. I'll not voyage in them. You will. Give Master Ghelfan at least a week before they're launched with instructions for the script and the figureheads."

"But Mistress, I—"

She stood and held up a hand, forestalling Ghelfan's objection.

"My decision on this is final. I'll endure their maiden jaunt if you promise a fair sea, but that'll be my last voyage." She lifted her glass and said, "Name them well." She downed her port in a gulp and turned to the liquor cabinet.

The room remained silent as she filled her glass. Pleased that her hands didn't shake as she poured, she turned back to them and surprised herself with a genuine smile.

"You now have the task of assigning crews to your vessels. Please feel free to avail yourself of my hospitality as late as need be, though the final decisions need not be made tonight. Goodnight."

Leaving the study, she climbed the long stair to the tower, and let her pent-up emotions finally surface. Her hand quaked as she placed her glass onto the embrasure and gazed out over the sea. Tears welled up and overflowed at the beauty before her, the sea she loved so dearly but would never sail on except in her dreams. The ships she had wrought, her dreams incarnate, had become her torment, a golden ring she could never reach.

Her knuckles whitened with her grip on the stone as she gazed out over that limitless expanse of moonlit water. She looked up at that moon, her namesake, now showing half its waxing face. She wondered why her parents had chosen that name for her, but then remembered the amulet at her breast. She withdrew the silver crescent and held it up in the moonlight, its tiny gems glittering in the hilt of the stylized sword. The Scimitar Moon would have been her true namesake, but fate had robbed her of that and her parents in one wrenching jolt.

"No. Not fate." Her husky voice smoldered with long-nurtured hatred. "A pirate named Bloodwind."

She raised her glass and made a silent toast to his demise, even if it took her a lifetime.

CHAPTER TWENTY-SIX

Revelations

THE PACE OF WORK escalated to a fever pitch following the announcements of the permanent assignments of officers and crews. A new camaraderie and competition sprouted up instantly, but the frantic pace could also have been attributed to the sizable wager between the two captains. The first ship to touch water would win the wager and its crew would earn the winnings as their first bonus.

A fortnight before the scheduled launch date, Cynthia made her daily trek down the hill to the shipyard for lunch, and found canvas barriers erected over the transoms and bows of each vessel. She knew their purpose instantly, which brought a thin smile. This competition had gone far indeed. She waited patiently until the lunch bell sounded and approached Master Keelson.

"So, they're even keeping the names from one another, are they?" Mouse promptly flew from her shoulder to one of the draped bows and vanished behind the canvas. He fluttered out immediately, grinning widely, and bolted behind the other.

"Aye, and not just from one another, Mistress Flaxal." He held up a forestalling hand as she ventured nearer. "They figured that you put the task of naming the ships on their shoulders, so they're keepin' the names secret from you until they're ready to launch."

"Well, I..." She groped for words. Mouse fluttered from behind the second ship's draped bow, his face ashen and eyes wide. He landed on her shoulder, hopping up and down and tugging on her collar, pointing toward the further of the two ships, his fervor only intensifying her curiosity. "I guess I don't know what to say."

"Good." The shipwright grinned and dusted his hands. "Rest assured, Mistress Flaxal, they're coming along nicely. We're almost a full week ahead of schedule. Only a bit of deck hardware, some joinery and the chain plates yet to finish. We'll be in the water by the end of the week!"

She left the shipyard in a daze, her curiosity heightened and her heart hammering with anticipation.

During that week, Cynthia paced the rugs of the estate to tatters, finding it hard to concentrate and impossible to sleep. When word arrived that one of the ships had been deemed by Master Keelson as "fit to be wetted," Cynthia raced to town and cheered along with the shipwrights and crews as Ulbattaer handed over the wager to Troilen. She even tossed in a few crowns to ensure that all the winnings weren't spent on the ensuing celebration.

When news arrived at the estate that the launch date had been set for two days hence, Marta let out a shout. "Thank Odea! Now maybe that woman'll calm down for half a tick!"

Cynthia arrived for the occasion in a rented carriage, dressed in her finest sea-blue gown, and saw that she had not been the only one to go all-out for the occasion. Her heart fluttered with excitement at the ribbons and garlands that draped the entire shipyard. Save for their masts and rigging, the ships were finished... and they were hers.

The cacophony of cheering crews, workers, and most of the population of Southaven cascaded over her as she descended the carriage steps. The noise sent Mouse diving for cover, but her gown had no collar. After one failed attempt to crawl down her plunging neckline, he found a hiding place amid the complicated coif of her hair.

The cheering subsided as she climbed the platform erected beneath the bowsprits of the vessels, but rose again as she embraced Master Keelson and Master Ghelfan, kissing each on the cheek. As Keelson's ruddy features flushed an even deeper crimson than normal, she turned to the two captains. They stood as stiff as a pair of masts, dressed in traditional block-shouldered blue coats and flanked by their first mates. Troilen's vessel would, by virtue of being the first finished, be the first in the water. Even as Cynthia shook their hands and thanked them, she felt a curious rush of jealousy at the thought of handing over her dreams-made-real into their care.

Cynthia turned to face the crowd, raising her hands to quiet the hundreds of voices all cheering, laughing and talking at once. When they refused to be readily silenced, a high-pitched, two-tone whistle cut through the air. Cynthia nodded her thanks to Finthie as the noise abated. The boatswain flashed a grin and a quick salute.

"Thank you all for coming," Cynthia began, looking out over the familiar faces, people she'd known all her life. These were her only remaining family, the only souls who really knew what this day meant to her. She looked down at the rolled parchment in her basket, the carefully prepared speech she'd taken so long to write.

"I wrote a speech for this occasion," she said, holding up the parchment and shaking her head. "I don't know what possessed me to do such a thing, but here it is. Maybe someone can put it in the archives or something, because I can't make myself read it right now." That brought out a few solitary cheers, and she laughed.

"It wasn't *that* long."

This brought a few more laughs and some applause, but it faded quickly and she found herself staring out at those faces, not knowing what else to say.

"You all know me." The words came out before they formed in her mind, as if part of her subconscious spoke of its own volition. "Many of you knew my family. You all know what my grandfather Benjamin Garrison built here, what my father Orin Flaxal hoped to carry on. Well, here I am, the last of the Flaxal line, and here behind me is the rebirth of my grandfather's dream, and my father's legacy."

Applause rose from the crowd, a few cheers, but she silenced them with one raised hand.

"Unlike my grandfather, I am not a sailor, and unlike my father, I am no seamage. Nor will I ever be." This brought out a few surprised mumbles, but most already knew the story.

"But I do have one family trait left: I am a builder of ships. And with these ships I am going to rebuild my grandfather's empire and more. I'm going to make Southaven the center of production for a new kind of ship, a new breed of sailor and a new way of shipping that will end the plague of piracy that has been our scourge since before I was born. These ships will out-sail any corsair on the sea, and deliver cargo anywhere in the world in half the time of any galleon."

She turned and raised an arm toward the two shipwrights. "I owe more than can possibly be repaid to Master Ghelfan for help with the design, and to Master Keelson for his skill in bringing these fine vessels to life." She turned to the crowd. "Please join me in showing them my appreciation."

Applause rose from the crowd, and Cynthia joined in. Ghelfan bowed to her gracefully, but Keelson just nodded stiffly and clenched his jaw, embarrassed at the attention.

"Now, I think it's time to reveal the secrets that have been plaguing me for the last week. Captain Troilen, if you would do the honors, please."

"My pleasure, Mistress." The half-elf nodded to Vulta, who pulled the line that held the concealing canvas in place. It dropped away, and the crowd's gasp of surprise echoed Cynthia's own. On the bow of the ship, in exquisitely rendered detail, loomed the shape of a great steed, its equine head extended, mane flowing back as if blown by the wind. But below the massive forelegs, the steed's form transformed into that of a great fish; a body vaguely equine in shape, but covered in scales of sea green. The tail split and curved around to each side of the bow with broad flukes spread wide as if to propel the ship forward. On the wide placard above and behind the tousled mane, the name "*Hippotrin*" glowed in gold script.

"The Hippotrin are Odea's steeds," Troilen explained loudly enough for the crowd to hear. "They draw her chariot through the sea, and are the fastest swimmers in all the oceans."

Cynthia nodded, having heard the legend as a child. She noticed Kurian beaming with pride, and wondered if he might have had a hand in choosing the name.

"Well done, Captain Troilen. Master Kurian, if you would perform the benediction."

"With pleasure, Miss Cynthia."

While the old priest performed the rite, raising his hands and splashing the figurehead with blessed seawater, Cynthia let her eyes wander over the carved figure. It bespoke of power, to be sure, and of the speed this ship would boast; a good omen and a fine choice.

"Thank you, Master Kurian." One of the priest's assistants moved a stout wooden step up to the fore, and nodded to Cynthia. She withdrew a bottle from her bundle and stepped carefully up. Everyone edged out of the way, the two captains taking station to either side of her in case she lost her balance.

"I name you *Hippotrin*!" she called out, raising the sacrificial bottle of wine in readiness. "May you sail swift and true, and protect all who serve in you." The bottle met the heavy cranse iron that capped the bowsprit and shattered into a spray of wine and shards of glass.

The crowd erupted in cheers and applause, and Cynthia accepted a hand from Troilen as she stepped down. Keelson shouted the order, and the ship rolled upon its mobile platform down the inclined flagstones into the water. Long tending lines trailed from her bow and stern, easing her around as she floated free for the first time. She rode high in the water, of course, bereft of her masts and the stabilizing weight of ballast that would line her bilges, but she rode well, her lovely lines even more evident.

"Well done, Master Keelson," she said as the cheering diminished, moving to the next ship's prow. "Shall we continue? Captain Ulbattaer, if you will do the honors."

"Of course, Mistress!" He nodded to Brelak, who jerked the restraining line smartly. The canvas fell away, and Cynthia found herself looking at strangely familiar feminine features. The woman was comely enough, hair flowing back not unlike the mane of *Hippotrin*, her gown showing a marginally decent amount of impressive bosom that was not unusual in a figurehead. But Cynthia couldn't quite place the face.

The roar of the crowd snapped her reverie, and she looked past the figurehead to the name emblazoned in flowing gold script: "*Orin's Pride*." Then she realized where she'd seen those features before—every morning in the mirror, but in reverse. The face was hers, though the artist had taken a bit of creative license with the figure's prominent bust.

"Captain Ulbattaer, I... I really don't know what to say."

"Don't say a thing, Mistress, at least not to me. It was my first mate's idea, and he was quite insistent."

She looked past the captain to Feldrin Brelak, who stood stock still, his face a mask of stiff control. At first she'd been embarrassed, but now, knowing that Feldrin had requested it, she felt deeply touched. She stepped past the captain and smiled up at the big Morrgrey.

"Thank you, Feldrin." She stretched up on tiptoe to give him a peck on the cheek, but came up a hand short. He stood ramrod straight, jaw clenched, eyes staring past her. Cynthia tried tugging on his shirt, but he didn't budge. *Well*, she thought, *two can play at this game*. She looked to Ulbattaer.

"Captain, would you please order your first mate to bend down so I can kiss him? Otherwise, I'm going to have to use the step."

"Master Brelak?" he said sternly, twisting his moustaches in mock disapproval. "Do as the lady asks."

"Aye, sir." Feldrin bent stiffly at the waist, turning his face slightly away from her to proffer one cheek.

Cynthia thought it only fair that he share her embarrassment, so she grabbed him firmly around the neck and planted a kiss right on his mouth, much to the delight of the crowd. But looking into his eyes, wide with shock and only an inch from hers, she felt something tense within her, a rush of excitement she had not expected. She released him and patted him warmly on the arm, smiling and trying to dismiss the surge of adrenalin.

"If I'd have known *that* was the thank you, I'd have suggested it myself!" Ulbattaer exclaimed, provoking an eruption of laughter from everyone, and a blush from Cynthia. The first mate of *Orin's Pride* simply stood there flushing darker than his usual olive hue, his stiff demeanor somewhat strained.

"Master Kurian, the blessing if you please." Cynthia took a step back as the old priest dutifully performed the benediction. She looked around, avoiding Feldrin's eyes, though he appeared to be doing the same. Her gaze fell upon the figurehead, and she examined it more closely. She would have to speak to Dura about the proportions.

When Kurian bowed and withdrew, and the step thumped into place under the bowsprit, she climbed up and addressed the crowd.

"Thank you, Master Kurian, and thank you again, Master Brelak. I do appreciate the thought behind the name of this vessel. Though I feel I might never be able to live up to the uh... *stature* of my likeness here." She looked down at her chest skeptically, drawing a laugh from the crowd. "I think Dura must have used a mirror to get those proportions, 'cause they sure aren't *mine!*"

When the roar of the crowd died away, she raised her voice and called out, "I name you *Orin's Pride*. May you sail swift and true, and protect all who serve in you." The bottle met the cranse iron perfectly and shattered into a thousand pieces, heralding another cheer from the people of Southaven.

Orin's Pride made her stately descent into the harbor and floated free, riding high just like her sister ship, ready for her rig and her first trial at sea.

≈

Camilla stirred from a fitful half-sleep to confusion, pain and hunger. Something had roused her, but she could not focus her addled mind.

"The ships are afloat, Captain Bloodwind!" Hydra flowed into the room like an oil slick, smooth, beautiful and poisonous.

Camilla tried to stand, realizing that the sorceress' entry must have woken her, but her legs would barely support her. Her arms hung suspended over her head by the golden chains, high enough that she could not sit fully to rest, but could only prop herself against the footboard of the bed.

"I don't remember giving you permission to barge in here unannounced, Hydra." Bloodwind shooed a young girl out of his bed and propped himself up against the elaborately carved headboard. The girl padded out, her clothing draped over her arm. She paused briefly at the foot of the bed to furtively pat Camilla's shoulder and whisper, "Sorry," as Bloodwind's attention centered upon his sorceress. The witch's eyes followed the girl's slim curves as she passed.

"You told me, Captain, to inform you the moment the ships were launched. That event has just transpired. The masts are to be stepped tomorrow."

"And where are my guards?" Bloodwind asked as if he hadn't heard a word Hydra had said. He rolled out of bed and strode to a small table laden with food and drink left over from the previous night's revelry. Camilla let her eyes sag closed as he poured rum and several different fruit juices into a mug and speared a slice of roast pork. "If you harmed them, Hydra, I'll have you skinned."

"They are not... damaged permanently." The witch approached Camilla and ran a finger down the girl's forearm where a slim trickle of blood oozed from beneath the golden shackle. "They will awaken wondering why their heads hurt. That is all." She brought the wetted finger to her mouth and licked it clean.

Camilla edged away, too exhausted to put up any real resistance. She'd spent the entire night chained to the foot of Bloodwind's bed, forced to endure the spectacle of the pirate and two of his recently successful captains being entertained by a few of the local whores. She'd been unable to sleep, barely able to relieve the strain on her legs by propping herself onto the footboard of the bed. Even facing Hydra, Camilla's only thoughts were of sleep... sleep and food.

"I did not give you leave to touch her, Hydra!" Bloodwind barked, snapping Camilla out of a half-dream, a fleeting vision of the creature feeding on her, sucking her life away gulp after gory gulp. The blade of a cutlass flashed between her face and Hydra's, the edge coming to rest against the witch's throat.

"Her blood is sweet, my captain," the monster in woman form said, her languid tongue dabbing at a bit of blood from her lip. "You have used her to her end. Let me have what is left, and I will bring you the Flaxal girl without a fight."

"Don't spew your lies to me, witch. I'll have the Flaxal girl and her ships with or without your help. You've told me what you came here for, now be gone before I decide I need you less than a good night's sleep!"

"Very well, my captain." Hydra smiled sweetly and withdrew, flowing out of the room as smoothly as she had entered.

Camilla's eyes fluttered closed and she sagged against the chains, wishing only for sleep, but a strong arm encircled her, and the chains rattled above her head. Her arms dropped in a searing jolt, shocking her awake. As her eyes flew open, she saw Bloodwind's face a finger's breadth before hers. She could not even make herself recoil from him; she was simply too tired... tired from the agony, tired of her subsistence as his slave... more tired than she had ever been in her life. She sagged against his chest, weeping openly.

"Please. Please just let me sleep." She experienced a flash of déjà vu: torment, then kindness, a pattern she'd experienced many times. But never before had she felt this utter exhaustion, this complete hopelessness.

"Here, my dear. Drink this."

He pressed a mug to her lips, and she drank. The sweet juice burned with rum, but her thirst overwhelmed her distaste. She drained the mug in one long draught. Next, he held a slice of roast pork for her to eat from his hand, and she did, bite by luscious bite.

"More?" she asked in a whisper, barely hoping for a real meal, not knowing how far to stretch his kindness. The feeling began to return to her arms and hands in waves of fiery tingles, but it meant nothing next to the prospect of food.

"Yes, Camilla, but you must rest, so you mustn't overeat. Here, let me help you." He lifted her in his arms like a bit of fluff and placed her on his bed. The silky sheets smelled musky, but the featherbed was wonderfully soft. She drifted for a moment on that cloud of comfort as the tingling in her hands eased. Then he lifted her again, but only to sit up. Another mug of juice and rum pressed against her lips: a swallow, then another bit of meat. She ate more slowly, less ravenous.

"There you are, my Camilla. You'll be as good as new on the morrow, won't you?"

"Please," she whispered. Never before had she pleaded to him. She had always found a core of strength that allowed her to keep her tongue quiet and her pride intact. She knew her mind wasn't working properly, but could not make herself care. Her defenses had finally been exhausted, and she only wanted an answer to the question that had burned in her mind for more years than she could remember.

"Please, tell me why?"

"Why what, my dear?" Bloodwind moved back from her, his eyes questioning. He offered another bite of meat and she took it, despite her stomach's complaints at the sudden overfilling. She'd eaten more than she usually had for two days' fare.

"Why not take me? Why even keep me alive?" She chewed another bite and swallowed forcefully. "You could lie and still keep your spy in Southaven. Why do you keep me?"

The pirate's answering smile flashed a warning into her mind. A sudden triumph lurked there. She'd seen the like only when he'd won a contest or a large wager. But what did he think he had won with her?

"Why, my dear Camilla, I thought you knew."

Bloodwind offered another bite, which she again took, chewing slowly to savor the spicy taste and tender texture of the meat.

"I love you."

"You... what?" The food Camilla had eaten clenched in her stomach and almost came up, but she swallowed and forced it down while those words burned her mind like a branding iron.

"I intend to make you my wife, Camilla. All you need do is say yes, truly say yes to me, and all the chains, all the punishments, will go away. I will dress you in the finest silks and satins, and you will feast on all the food and wine you desire."

Camilla stared at him in shock, her sleep-deprived mind whirling in a morass of questions and lies. Could he really mean it? Could he honestly be offering what he said? Could he be trusted? Did she *want* to be his wife, even if it meant an end to his torments?

"How can I trust you?" she asked finally, unsure if the question might provoke him. Meeting that icy blue stare, she saw in his eyes... for just a moment... a flash of hope.

"Loyalty, my dear. What you give, you will receive." He took her tingling fingers in his hand and kissed them. "All you have to say is 'yes'."

She fought against pulling away, wondering if this would be her only chance at salvation after so many years. If he wanted loyalty, even if that was *all* he wanted, could she give it?

Her mind rushed with the possibilities of a free life; an existence without torment. All she had to say was yes. One little word and the chains would come off, the torments would stop; the pain would end.

All she had to say was...

"Yes."

CHAPTER TWENTY-SEVEN

Shakedown

"I SHOULD BE BACK by nightfall, Marta, but don't wait dinner." Cynthia accepted Brolan's hand and climbed into the carriage, settling onto the hard seat. "You should be able to see from the tower well enough." She waved as Brolan lashed the reins, barely able to keep a foolish grin from her face.

Today's the day! she thought for perhaps the hundredth time since waking some two hours before dawn. She had not slept well, anticipation of this event overpowering her fatigue. In fact, she had not slept well for days with this event looming on the horizon. *Plenty of time for sleep after. Today, my ships sail!*

The ride down to Southaven town seemed to take an eternity. She fidgeted in the seat, looked at the scenery, twiddled her thumbs and tried not to tell Brolan to use the whip.

The two weeks since *Orin's Pride* and *Hippotrin* first touched water had been nerve wracking, to be sure, but they had also been some of the most fulfilling and satisfying days Cynthia could remember. The stepping of the masts had nearly undone her. After one glimpse of the one-ton spear of milled timber poised over *Hippotrin*, held aloft only by a few stout lines and a flimsy looking derrick, she left the shipyard and went home.

The rest of the rigging had gone well, each vessel taking on an individuality that reflected the unique skills and tastes of the boatswains who were in charge of tuning every block, line, stay and shroud. During this process, stores, cordage and sails were taken aboard, stowed and rigged.

The last item to be loaded arrived in a small wagon driven by the crotchety old lightkeeper. Cynthia met him on the quay with Captains Ulbattaer and Troilen at her sides, their first mates flanking them, all as serious as stone. The lightkeeper laughed at their dour faces and rattled off a long assurance of how his "gifts" were perfectly safe. None of the sailors liked this idea, but Cynthia would not be swayed. Two crates were loaded onto the ships, unpacked, and their contents installed securely in the captains' cabins. Only the captains, mates and boatswains knew exactly what the contents were and how to use them if the unthinkable should happen.

Just a precaution, Cynthia told herself, shaking off the recurrent dread of her ships being taken by pirates. More than one nightmare had plagued her infrequent sleep—dreams of fire sweeping through her ships, exploding up through the hatches, and men and women screaming as they burned. *Just a precaution...*

All her worries fled like leaves on the wind as Brolen pulled the carriage to a stop on the Southaven quay. Resting beside the pier stood the ships— her ships. On deck, the crews stood in precision lines, awaiting her arrival.

Cynthia stepped down from the carriage, Mouse hopping up and down on her shoulder in unbridled glee. Today, her dreams would *sail*.

≈

First *Hippotrin*, then *Orin's Pride*, eased away from the dock, each with a dancer's grace. Cynthia, Koybur and Ghelfan were aboard *Hippotrin*, while Keelson stood on the deck of *Orin's Pride*. This division made sense, but had met with some resistance from Feldrin Brelak. Cynthia wanted Ghelfan's opinion of the vessels' performance, and Ghelfan felt that Troilen's broader experience with varied hull and sail designs would give him the best assessment.

Hippotrin's mainsail jibed with a crack of canvas, and Mouse squealed half an inch from Cynthia's ear. She poked him, which earned her another squeal as he fluttered crookedly aloft. Even in the harbor, the ship heeled under the wind and picked up speed.

"Set the forestays'l!" Troilen ordered, his words immediately echoed by Vulta at her station amidships. Canvas exploded up from the forestaysail boom and filled, pulling the bow downwind. The helmsman corrected, and the ship accelerated toward the harbor mouth, cutting through the water at an easy six knots.

"She's moving well," Ghelfan commented, gauging the set of the sails and nodding. "Your boatswain knows her business."

"We'll see once we get outside," Cynthia said, biting back the first twinges of nausea as the ship slid down the swells at the breakwater. Although the trade winds were mercifully moderate today, no more than twenty knots, the swells peaked at eight to ten feet. Though Troilen had offered her a weak brew of his medicinal tea, she had refused; she was not going to sleep through this experience.

Cynthia looked back to *Orin's Pride*, only half a dozen lengths behind and already setting her jib. Brelak's booming voice rose over the rush of wind and water, bringing a smile to her lips. This sea trial would very likely turn into an all-out race, and everyone knew it.

They cleared the breakwater, and the first full swell of the Southern Ocean lifted *Hippotrin* high, and then dropped her to plunge deeply into a trough. Cynthia's stomach dropped with the ship and settled somewhere around her ankles as they rose up the next swell. The game was up; the sea had them and there was no letting go.

"We're in it now, lassie!" Koybur brayed in her ear, grasping a shroud with his good hand and grinning horribly as the first splash of spray wetted the foredeck.

"Aye!" Cynthia agreed, gripping the lee rail with white knuckles. Wind and sea grasped the ship and *Hippotrin* responded like a thoroughbred, leaping forward to strain at her reins.

"Can you feel it, Ghelfan?" She watched the foam flying past and couldn't help but grin, her nausea easing with the rush of adrenalin. "She's flying!"

"Log!" Troilen yelled. A sailor tossed the log line overboard and let it run out through his fingers until his mate called the time.

"Ten and a half knots!"

"She is moving very well, Miss Cynthia," Ghelfan said, "but I think she is a little light in the bilges. She's heeling more than I would have expected with this press of canvas."

"Cargo will help," she said, stifling a yelp of alarm and glee as spray dashed the deck from a white-capped swell. The ship's low profile would mean wet decks and wet sailors, but the increase in speed would be worth the price. Mouse fluttered madly against the wind and landed back on her shoulder, panting and laughing shrilly.

They sailed south for some time, the wind directly abeam. They would not put the ships through their paces until they were in deeper water and out of the land's intensifying effect on wind and wave. The time was not spent idly, however, for Troilen ordered many changes in sail configuration and Vulta paced from the foredeck to the wheel, then forward again, ceaselessly relaying the captain's orders and throwing in a few of her own. Finthie raced around the deck, tuning and tweaking every block, sheet and halyard. They were gaining a feel for the ship with every mile they logged.

As land sank below the horizon behind them, Borell the cook came on deck bearing a tray laden with several tin cups. He moved easily despite his precariously balanced tray and the ship's pronounced heel, his bare feet slapping the planks as he advanced on the group and smiled at Cynthia's excitement.

"Great idea gimbaling the stove, Mistress Flaxal. With this heel, it'd be near impossible to keep a kettle in place otherwise." He lifted a cup for her. "Some ginger tea, just to settle things a bit."

She took the tea with one hand, her other firmly grasping the railing, amazed that he could stand without support and balance the tray. He offered a cup to Ghelfan, another to Koybur and finally one to his captain. She sipped the tea, surprised at the strong ginger flavor. Her stomach eased even more, despite the brisk action of the ship. This was more like sailing Koybur's little smack than the slow rolling motion of a galleon. The excitement, the unusual motion and the tea all had her feeling relatively well, and set a flicker of hope in her heart.

"It would appear, Captain, that *Orin's Pride* is gaining on us." Borell nodded aft with a smile.

They looked back to see that the other ship had closed the gap by half, her jibs smartly set, drawing her bowsprit through the swells and sending spray flying with every wave.

"We will see about that, Borell." Troilen finished his tea and handed back his cup, then turned to Ghelfan and Cynthia. "With your permission, I'd like to see what she'll do, Mistress Cynthia."

"By all means, Captain, but I'd suggest having a look at her mast step before you push her much harder. The wedges are dry and if one should slip under this strain, well, I wouldn't want to break a spar today."

"Point taken, Mistress. Vulta! Please have a look at her mast steps and report back. Finthie, put the tops'ls on her. Helmsman, two points to windward!"

Cynthia opened her mouth to protest the change in course, but reconsidered. This was, after all, Troilen's ship now.

≈

"She's making more sail!" Feldrin lowered his glass and took another breath to suggest a course change, just as his captain's voice filled his ears.

"Tops'l please, Master Brelak, and send a man below to check the mast steps. Helmsman, put our bowsprit one point upwind of her transom and don't deviate."

"Aye, sir!" Feldrin grinned as he turned and barked orders. Karek leapt to, adding orders of his own and diving below to check the steps himself. Feldrin stood tall, barely suppressing a broad grin. The ship and crew responded like veterans, her topsails cracking in the fresh breeze. A sidelong glance confirmed that Rafen Ulbattaer echoed his thoughts; proud of his crew, and his ship. They would both shape up nicely with a little seasoning.

When the sails were set and all the seamen back on station, he ordered, "The log please, Mister Karek."

"Fifteen and a half!" A whoop of triumph rose from the deck. This was faster than most of them had sailed in a lifetime of plying the seas.

"How many points to the wind, Brelak?"

Feldrin took a quick sighting, estimating the true wind angle, and placed a small protractor on the compass card. He blinked at the indicator, took another sighting and got the same number.

"Fifty degrees, Captain." That was ten degrees closer than any galleon could manage.

"She's griping a bit," the helmsman said, leaning hard on the wheel to keep the ship's bow in line. "Wants to come about."

"Too much heads'l?" Brelak offered, squinting up at the bar-taut jib sheets.

They topped a large swell and plunged into the trough, the leeward rail awash as they heeled over.

"Not enough ballast," Keelson suggested. "She's runnin' light."

"Aye, indeed," the captain agreed, looking to the telltales on the mainsail. "She's not working her mains'l like she should, but the jibs are drawing. Shifts the balance forward." He looked around the deck. "Shift some weight. Make sure all the water casks are low and amidships. Helmsman, let her have half a point, but watch your main luff."

"Mister Karek!" Brelak bellowed, relaying the captain's orders. The boatswain vanished below with another stout crewman, yelling for Rowland to lend a hand. "You plannin' on stealin' her wind, Capt'n?"

Rafen Ulbattaer grinned beneath his dark mustaches, white teeth gleaming. "Would I do such a thing, Master Brelak?"

"Aye sir, I think you would." Brelak grinned back.

"Well, you'd be mistaken. I'm simply seeing how close she'll sail to windward."

"O' course, Capt'n. I didn't mean to suggest any other thing."

"Good. Now keep an eye on *Hippotrin's* masthead pennant and tell me when it starts to flutter. We'll bear off and take the wind from her sails like a cutpurse nippin' a money pouch."

"O' course, Capt'n." Brelak grinned again, shouting for all idle seamen to move to the windward rail.

"Half a point, Capt'n!" the helmsman announced, drawing everyone's eyes aloft. The sails were still drawing well with no signs of luffing. "The helm's eased a bit."

"She's found her tack, Capt'n!"

"Aye, Master Brelak, and we're gaining on *Hippotrin*."

≈

"They're moving to steal our wind," Vulta told her captain, pausing in her relentless prowl of the deck.

"Sheet in and take her a point to windward. If she luffs, bear off, but I want every man on the sheets."

"Aye, Captain. Finthie! Snatch-block the jib sheets inboard and take in the mainsheets! Borell, shift what cargo we have to the windward side. That should level her out."

"Captain, I—" Cynthia paused to swallow hard; her knees quaked and her head swam with the drastic heel and movement of the ship, but her main concern lie in the pressure being put on the rig. "Have a care for her, Troilen. She's just getting her sea legs."

"She's fine, Mistress. No better way to break in a ship than a little trouncing."

"Breaking in is fine, just make sure it doesn't become breaking *down*." The shrouds creaked and groaned as they eased upwind. "If we part a shroud..." She looked to Ghelfan for support, but his eyes were focused aloft as if mesmerized by the play of canvas and sky. She looked up, but her head swam with dizziness.

"Part *these* shrouds?" Troilen's voice sounded strange, as if amused at her naïve notion. "Not likely in this weather, Mistress."

"We're a point to windward, Capt'n," the helmsman announced, bracing himself at the wheel. "She's not luffin' but she wants to round up somethin' fierce."

"Something's not right," Ghelfan said, his voice barely audible above the rush of wind and water.

"What?" Cynthia tried to look aloft again, and stumbled with dizziness. She forced it down, grasped one of the leeward shrouds, and looked up. All seemed well. The mainsail luff was backfilling slightly with the rhythm of the ship's pitch, nothing to cause alarm, and certainly nothing she would consider unusual. "I don't see..."

Troilen's gaze shot aloft. "Vulta, tighten the main halyard and tend the mainsheet! She's pulling from her bow."

"Aye, sir. We're cutting a tighter line to the wind, but we've lost a bit of speed. She's coming up on our port stern."

"We'll cross her bow and steal her wind."

Cynthia looked over her shoulder at *Orin's Pride* and tried to make sense of Troilen's tactic. She knew what he was trying to do, but the words somehow would not make the proper picture in her mind. She looked to Ghelfan for help, but he was still staring straight up.

"Koybur, what's going on? I don't understand what..." She looked at her old mentor's face, and the scars marring his features flowed and writhed into a flesh-hued chart of the Shattered Isles. His one good eye squinted, and the coastline of his face collapsed into a whirlpool of swirling skin and bone as he spoke.

"Cyn? What's wrong? Ya don't look good."

"Your face..." She knew something wasn't right, knew what she was seeing could not be real, but her mind refused to tell her what she should be seeing, or what *should* be real. A tiny little man fluttered before her face, his shrill little voice ringing in her ears before he flew away. She raised a hand and looked at it, and her fingers lengthened into writhing tentacles before her eyes. "Koybur, I think there was something..."

She looked to her friend, her mentor, and saw despair darken his ruined features.

"The tea." Ghelfan's voice sounded strange, and when she turned, he was falling to the deck. She stared in astonishment as he splashed into the wood and floated there, but then she was falling, too, and nothing she saw, heard or felt made any sense at all.

≈

Yodrin watched the two crumple to the deck and smiled. For a moment, all eyes were focused on Cynthia and Ghelfan. He stepped behind the helmsman, drew his dagger and buried it in the man's back. One sideways jerk cut the man's heart in half. With a gurgling cry of shock, blood fountained from the helmsman's mouth. The wheel spun free, and the ship rounded up into the wind alarmingly. Yodrin blew a single long note on a boatswain's whistle—the agreed-upon signal—then turned to take care of Vulta as everyone aboard grabbed something and hung on for their lives.

"Captain! The wheel!" Vulta reached for the spinning wheel just as his knife slashed for her neck. Whether she saw the blade or just dodged instinctively, the edge skittered along her jaw instead of slitting her throat. Yodrin swore and lunged again, but she had already rolled away.

"Koybur! Finthie!" Vulta's shrill cry alerted the entire crew, but Yodrin knew his men were already carrying out their deadly duties. Forward and belowdecks, he heard shouts and cries. Nearby, a sailor groaned and fell to the deck with a knife wound to his back. Here by the wheel, only his first mate and the boatswain remained.

Yodrin grinned and drew a second dagger, letting the ship round up through the wind and across the path of *Orin's Pride*. He glanced at the onrushing ship, her bowsprit dead centered on *Hippotrin's* mainmast. It would be close.

"Koybur, mind the helm. Steer her downwind while I see to our unwanted guests." He didn't even bother to spare a glance at the cripple, knowing he would follow the order. He'd been following Bloodwind's orders for more than a dozen years. Why should he falter now?

≈

"Koybur!" Vulta could not believe her eyes. How could Koybur be part of this insanity? Troilen advanced on her with two bared daggers, one bloodied to the hilt. Staying alive suddenly required more of her attention than gaping at Koybur as he calmly took the wheel.

"Finthie!" she shouted, rolling to her feet and out of reach of the traitorous captain's blades. The cut on her jaw stung and blood ran freely into her shirt. All she had was a rigging knife—sharp enough, but not a fighting weapon. She spared a glance and saw Finthie using a boat hook to fend off two crewmen with daggers. The helmsman and another crewman were dead, and Mistress Flaxal and Ghelfan lay on the deck, either dead or unconscious; Vulta had no way to tell, and could do nothing to help them. Was this some kind of crazy mutiny?

"Troilen! You'll die for this, you traitorous pig!" She sidestepped his advance and leapt to the leeward shrouds.

"The name's Yodrin," he replied, advancing and following her up the lines. The grace of his movements caught her eye as he sheathed one dagger and climbed after her; this man was a trained fighter. "And I'm no traitor. I've served the same master for more than a decade, and that master is Captain Bloodwind."

Realization of exactly what was happening hit her; the crew had been infiltrated by pirates. Two of her crewmates lay bloody on the deck while others she'd known for months advanced on Finthie. Then, out of the corner of her eye, she saw something that made her hang on for her life and cry out. *Orin's Pride* had turned upwind and now bore down on them. Mayhem had broken out on the other ship, too. As her cry rang out, the other ship's bowsprit passed over *Hippotrin's* stern, snapping the mainsail sheet with a crack like a coach whip. *Orin's Pride's* bobstay struck the taffrail, shaving off two inches of teak in passing.

With the sheet parted, *Hippotrin's* mainsail swung wide, the force of the wind pushing the boom forward into the very shroud to which Vulta and Yodrin clung. She had to move or be killed.

Vulta leapt to grab the main gaff sheet and swung wildly as *Orin's Pride* thundered past, missing by no more than five feet. She almost wished the two ships had struck, for the impact would have torn the stern out of *Hippotrin* and sent her to the bottom, denying the pirates their prize. But she also had a way to deny them their trophy.

The lightkeeper's gift! she thought, realizing what she had to do.

A glance as she scrambled up the line confirmed that Troilen—Yodrin, as she now knew him—had not been crushed by the swinging mainsail boom as she'd hoped, but had fallen to the deck. Finthie still held her attackers at bay, but even as Vulta opened her mouth to shout out her revelation, the cook Borell lunged up from the companionway behind the harried boatswain, cutlass in hand.

"Finthie!" she cried, swinging crazily on her halyard.

The boatswain turned too late. The blade took her in the armpit. She cried out, slamming her boat hook against Borell's shoulder, but the force of the blow only tore the blade from her, and her scream turned into a torrent of blood.

"No! Gods damn you all to the Nine Hells!" Vulta climbed for her life. It was all she could do. She blinked back tears, swallowed her sobs of anguish and loss, and climbed. Three other sailors were still after her. Koybur—the unbelievable traitor, Koybur—stayed at the wheel, steering them downwind while another crewman tended the sheets to set their sails for the new point of wind.

She reached the foregaff and stopped. She had nowhere to go. The question now was what to do before the traitorous crew of *Hippotrin* killed her. She drew her knife and set the blade against the topsail sheet. The line parted with little coaxing, and the sail flapped free. Next was the main gaff sheet, the line controlling the very boom on which she perched. The boom swung wildly, sweeping forward of the foremast yards. The men climbing after her shouted in alarm as the flapping sail threatened to knock them from the rigging.

Vulta shouted curses down at them, knowing instantly what she would do next.

She shimmied along the gaff boom until she reached the foresail halyard and stood up, using the taut line for support as she made her way to the topmast hounds. Her pursuers were still ten feet below her when her knife parted the foresail halyard and sent the boom crashing down to the deck. The ship slowed markedly with the lost sail, and she grinned.

"Now for one more," she said, reaching down to the forestay where the jib halyard ran through its block. The taut line exploded with a slash of her knife, sending the sail flapping to the deck.

"Ha! Having trouble keeping her helm, Koybur, you bastard?" she screamed, even as she looked for something else she could damage. The shrouds were wire and would not yield to her knife, and she couldn't climb down to cut the forestaysail halyard without fighting her way through her pursuers.

Someone on deck eased the main gaff sheet, and the great sail billowed out fully, pulling *Hippotrin* forward. Vulta looked down at her pursuers, only feet below, and made up her mind. She grasped the block that ran to the mainmast from the foremast for tensioning the rake, and cut the tarred hemp binding it into place. The mast shuddered under her feet as they left the fore topmast hounds. She swung free, clutching the block with one hand and her knife with the other, right into the tightly drawn mainsail.

She slashed the canvas, and it split beneath her from gaff to boom in an explosion of tearing cloth. She cut one of the lines running through the block, jammed her knife in the sheave to slow her descent and rode it to the deck.

"You'll pay for that, you black bitch!" Yodrin spat, advancing on her with a cutlass in one hand and a dagger in the other. Borell advanced from the side, his sword red to the hilt with Finthie's blood.

"I'll see you all in the Nine Hells, first, *Captain*," she said, feinting toward the rail, then lunging past Borell in a roll.

His blade whistled past her head, but the companionway belowdecks lay open before her. She dove and rolled down the steps, bruising her back but managing to land on her feet. She dashed toward the captain's cabin, not even bothering to close the hatch behind. What she had to do would only take a second, then they would all burn.

The cabinet looked like a storage bin for charts, but she knew better. She slipped the pin free of the lid and wrenched it open. Inside, a two-foot sphere of fired clay lay lashed into a teak frame, its only feature a wide, red-painted handle dangling from a stout hemp cord. Pulling it would release the fire. She gripped the handle and pulled smartly, muttering a quick prayer to Odea that her traitorous captain would burn for his treason.

The cord broke.

"What the...?"

Something struck her in the back, and she stiffened with the shock. Her numb fingers released the red handle, and slowly wrapped around the crimson-stained blade of a cutlass protruding from her chest. Vulta felt herself falling, the numbing shock of hitting the deck, then searing pain as the blade pulled free, cutting her fingers to the bone.

"You didn't really think we was that stupid, did ya?"

Borell's sarcasm was the last thing she heard before despair and darkness overwhelmed her.

CHAPTER TWENTY-EIGHT
Blood in the Water

"SHE'S ROUNDIN' UP!"

All eyes shot forward at Brelak's bellowed warning, just as *Hippotrin* turned hard into the wind directly across their path. Curses rang out across the deck, and the helmsman was already turning the wheel when Ulbattaer cried out, "Hard a-lee!"

"What the hell's Troilen thinkin'?" Brelak asked rhetorically, lending his weight to the wheel to avoid crashing into the other ship. Then the high-pitched note of a boatswain's whistle cut the air. He looked toward the sound, toward *Hippotrin*, and on the down-roll saw no-one at the wheel and several figures lying on the deck. One wore skirts, and another bore a broad red stain.

"Capt'n! Somethin' ain't right!" But his warning came too late, for when he turned to his captain, he met only the vacant stare of a dying man.

Rafen Ulbattaer's mouth gaped silently, his hands clutching at the horrible wound in his throat. Blood flooded from between his fingers as he fell to the deck. Karek, a bloodied dagger in each hand, lunged—one blade was aimed at him, the other at the helmsman's back. Brelak stared in shock, but reacted without thinking. He released his grip on the wheel and shoved the helmsman aside while trying to block the thrust aimed at his gut.

The helmsman cried out and fell as the blade cut him along the ribs. The wheel spun freely for a moment, and the ship turned upwind toward *Hippotrin*. Brelak felt the stinging slash of the second dagger across his forearm even as he knocked it aside and brought his left fist around to smash Karek in the face. The force of the blow knocked the boatswain back, giving Brelak a moment to grab the wheel and heave it over to point *Orin's Pride* downwind.

"Hold the helm over!" he shouted to the helmsman, never taking his eyes from Karek.

"Aye, sir," came the shocked reply. The man held the gash in his side with one bloody hand, but reached up with his other to grasp one spoke of the wheel, his eyes wide with terror.

Brelak let go of the wheel and dodged Karek's next attack, a sweeping slash that would have opened his belly. A scream from the deck told him that Karek was not the only traitor, but looking away from the daggers now would mean his death. He sidestepped to the rail and grabbed a bolt pin; a poor weapon, but better than nothing. More shouts rang out from the deck behind him, shouts of alarm and fighting.

"To arms!" he bellowed, slipping the reins on his rage. "We've got traitors among us! Fight fer the ship! Fight fer *Orin's Pride!*"

More cries rang out from the crew, punctuated by the dull thump of a body falling to the deck. A crewman yelled out, "We're gonna hit!" and Brelak spared a half-second to glance, just as *Orin's Pride's* bowsprit lanced across *Hippotrin's* stern. He braced himself, but the ship only jerked as their bobstay raked *Hippotrin's* taffrail, sending a shower of splinters flying. A glance as the two ships passed showed more than he needed to know. Finthie Tar fought off two men on deck, while Vulta scampered up the rigging and Troilen leapt to evade the mainsail boom as it swung free, a bloodied dagger in his hand. All hell was breaking loose on both ships.

Karek lunged at him again, trying to take advantage of Brelak's inattention. "Yer not gonna survive this one, Morrgrey! Not like in Tsing!"

"Come on, then!" Brelak brandished his bolt pin and reached for another, his mind reeling as he realized how deep this plot must be. "I took three of yer friends down that night. You think you can do what they couldn't?"

"I *know* I can," Karek said with an evil grin. He feinted low, but shifted, sweeping his other knife toward Brelak's face. The tip of the blade cut a line from the Morrgrey's cheekbone to his nose, but did little real damage. Brelak jammed the end of one of his bolt pins into the boatswain's gut as he dodged.

He circled carefully, putting his back to the open stern of the ship. The maneuver brought the deck into view, and he risked a quick assessment. One of the tall northerners hired in Scarport lay sprawled flat, his head split open by the heavy blow. Next to him lay Keelson, rivulets of blood flowing from his body to the leeward scuppers. The helmsman, Horace, lay on the deck, but held grimly to the wheel. The other tall northerner fought against three more seamen, while another sailor struggled to control the sails.

"Yer outnumbered, Karek," he said, grinning and backing away, hoping to draw the man away from the injured helmsman. "Give it up and I'll spare yer life."

"Brave words from a man holdin' a couple o' sticks." Karek lunged as quickly as a striking snake.

Brelak knocked one dagger aside and easily sidestepped the other, but the thrust had not been as ill-aimed as he thought. The blade cut the mainsail sheet, letting the huge boom swing free to crash into the leeward shroud with an unhealthy crack. It snapped in the middle, and the mainsail tore from gaff to boom, sending the ship slewing into the wind, the delicate balance of her sails destroyed. If they crossed the wind and then jibed, the foresail boom could also be damaged.

"Get the sheets off the jib and forestays'l! Don't let her round up!" Brelak called out. Karek's tactic was simple, draw the defenders away by putting the ship in peril, and then finish them off. Brelak suppressed a grim smile, seeing one element Karek had not figured. He sidestepped and backed up to the taffrail to draw the traitorous boatswain toward the stern.

"Where you runnin' to, you Morrgrey coward? There's nowhere to go but... but..."

Karek collapsed to his knees and fell forward, face down onto the deck, one of Rowland's heavy cleavers buried in the back of his head.

"Well done, Rowland!" Brelak clapped the cook on the shoulder. The old cook held another cleaver and had two long butcher knives tucked into his belt. "Now let's see to that last one and—"

But there was no need. The last mutineer lay backed against the midships rail, one arm badly broken, the tip of a boat hook pressed to his throat.

"Secure that man," Brelak ordered, pushing the cook over to the wheel. "Take the wheel, Rowland. Someone see to Horace here, and check on Keelson."

As he moved to check his fallen men, another sailor cried out, "Captain! Look!"

He started to look for the captain then realized the seaman was talking to him. He looked aft just in time to see a dark shape swing from *Hippotrin's* foremast and cut the mainsail, which tore from top to bottom.

"Vulta!" A cheer rang out from the crew of *Orin's Pride.*

"Secure the mains'l! Get that broken boom housed." Brelak moved to the crewman who was checking the fallen shipwright. "How is he?"

"I don't think he's got much blood left in 'im, Capt'n," the sailor said, cutting Brelak to the quick with his choice of words. Calling him captain only reminded him of Rafen Ulbattaer's vacant stare.

"Keelson!" He grasped the man's hand and squeezed, but the flesh was cold and the grip feeble. "Hold on, man!" The shipwright's eyes fluttered open and fixed upon Brelak.

"Don't..." He coughed wetly, blood flecking his lips. "Don't let 'em take her."

"She's safe, Keelson. The ship's ours." Brelak squeezed the man's hand harder, willing him to live.

"No!" Keelson shook his head weakly and coughed again, his eyes wandering over the sails overhead. "*Hippotrin!* You've got to save her!" And with that final plea, the shipwright's last breath left his body.

"Bloody hell!" Feldrin Brelak surged to his feet, his temper flaring. "Ware ship! Bring her about!"

Cries of assent rang out, and Rowland thrust the helm downwind even as the shattered mainsail boom thumped to the deck amid a mountain of torn canvas. They jibed smartly, just as another seaman cried out.

"Capt'n! They're gonna…"

But Brelak had been watching *Hippotrin* as they made their turn and saw someone heave the limp form over the rail. "Man overboard! Keep an eye on him! Rig a harness! Rowland, take direction from the man in the bow."

"Another!" Rowland cried, pointing forward.

Two men heaved another body over *Hippotrin's* transom. Vulta's distinctive dark skin and hair were unmistakable.

"Gods, no!" He raced to the foredeck and squinted. Yet another body splashed into the sea. He shaded his eyes and prayed that none of the corpses being heaved over wore blue skirts. "Keep an eye on yer mark!"

He could see something floating, but the shape was not swimming. Finthie's body bobbed past, face down.

"Holy Gods of Light," one of the sailors muttered.

"Watch yer mark! Keep your eyes peeled. Any signs of life, and we'll bring 'em aboard. Ready with that boat hook!"

Four corpses floated past, each easily identifiable. Cynthia, Ghelfan and Koybur were not among the dead.

"What about the Mistress?" a sailor asked. The crew looked to Feldrin for direction, for hope.

"Get a man aloft with a glass! Get yer sails trimmed. Rowland, put yer helm on her transom, and don't deviate."

"Aye, Captain. I was watchin' 'em close. Only four went over the side."

"Captain!" came a call from the foremast top. "Looks like Mistress Flaxal and that elf shipwright are on the deck. They're lashin' 'em to the mainmast. They look knocked out."

"What about Koybur?"

"Uh, yes sir. You ain't gonna believe it, but he's at the helm."

"The helm?" Brelak's heart skipped a beat. "You sure?"

"Aye, sir!"

"We're gonna bloody find out what the bloody hell's goin' on here." He whirled and surveyed the gory deck, his eyes fixing on the one person who might be able to enlighten him.

"Well, Brin," he said, glaring down at the northerner with the broken arm, "looks like you're in a hard spot here. Yer mates are shark bait, and you're trussed up like a chicken ready fer the pot."

The man spat a curse, and looked away.

"You there," Brelak shouted to a sailor. "Bring me that harness and start clearin' the deck."

"The bodies, sir?" the fellow asked, handing over the rope harness.

"Overboard, except fer Captain Ulbattaer and Keelson. Wrap them in canvas and secure 'em below." He bent and started affixing the harness to the bound man.

"Whadaya think yer doin', Morrgrey?" The man's voice was steady, but his eyes were wide with fear.

"I'm goin' fishin', unless you want to tell me what the hell's gone on here." He cinched the harness and lifted the man, propping him up against the leeward shrouds, the roaring sea at his back. "We're leavin' a trail of blood that ought to draw some attention soon. I'm just gonna trail you behind and see if I can't get a bite."

The sailors pitched Karek's body over the side and sluiced the deck with seawater. Blood ran through the scuppers. Something large broke the water with a splash. A mer surfaced, its scaly visage grinning at them before it plunged back into the depths.

"Bloodwind," the man said through clenched teeth.

"What?" The name left Brelak cold.

"Bloodwind planned this from the start. Set us up as crew to take these ships."

"And Mistress Flaxal?"

"Yodrin was to take her and the shipwright if he could, kill 'em if he couldn't."

"Yodrin? Who's Yodrin?"

"Captain Troilen. He's Bloodwind's assassin."

Brelak's eyes widened, his stomach clenching in knots. "And Koybur?"

"He's been spyin' fer Bloodwind fer longer than I can remember."

"I don't believe it!" He lifted the man, leaning him backward over the rail. The sailors pitched the other northerner's body over the side, and the water roiled with the thrashing tails of mer as they dragged it down to the depths.

"Believe it or no, it's truth! Bloodwind's got somethin' on him. Pulls his strings like a puppet. Koybur picked us out in Scarport to be hired even before Bloodwind gave the orders."

"Bloody hell." Brelak dropped the man back to the deck with little care for his broken arm. "Secure him below!"

"Capt'n!" Rowland altered course slightly and said, "She's makin' more sail."

He looked after *Hippotrin*. The mangled canvas was being replaced and repaired.

"How's Horace," he asked, moving back to his place beside the helm.

"He's cut pretty bad, but—"

"I'm fine, sir! Just get this stitched up and I'm back on duty."

"Good man. Rowland, how are you with a needle and thread?"

"Better'n with this ruddy wallowing ship, Capt'n." He was fighting the helm, trying to keep her in line with not enough sail. "You're goin' after 'em?"

"Bloody right I am. I'll take her and you see to our wounded. If Horace can stand a watch when you're finished, I'll make him bosun."

"I can stand one now, Capt'n," the man said, trying to stand up.

"Not before you're stitched up. Now hold still." He took the wheel while Rowland dashed below for a sail needle and some twine.

"But Captain," one sailor interrupted, "they're armed to the teeth and ready for us."

"Then we'd best find some weapons."

"What's yer plan, Capt'n?" Rowland asked, coming back up through the companionway with needles, twine and a bottle of rum.

"First, we catch up, then we ram and grapple, then we cut them to pieces." He surveyed the rig, barking orders to get more canvas aloft. "Any questions?"

"Not a one, sir," Rowland replied, kneeling beside Horace and wrenching the cork from the bottle with his teeth. He tore the man's shirt open and doused the deep gash with rum.

"Odea's scaly arse, that burns! I thought you'd let me drink it."

"Just shut up and bite this." He thrust a piece of leather between the man's teeth and threaded his sail needle, dousing the twine with more rum. "You think she's alive, Feldrin?" he asked as he applied the needle.

"I don't know, Row." He wiped the blood from the gash on his forearm and inspected the shallow cut, dismissing it as insignificant. "But if she is, I'll get her back. Count on it."

≈

"Get that halyard spliced, damn you! Koybur, keep yer helm downwind or I'll pluck out your other eye!" Yodrin paced the deck, glaring up at the mangled rig and then back at *Orin's Pride*. He briefly considered turning to attack, but with so few hands, he could not ensure victory. Karek had obviously failed. The boatswain's boasts that he could kill off the officers and Keelson by surprise had never been very realistic. Attacking now would only risk his most precious cargo: the shipwright Ghelfan and Cynthia Flaxal.

"Get the foretops'l on her and rig the spare mains'l. I want every scrap of canvas we've got aloft."

"What about these two, Capt'n?" one crewman asked, toeing Ghelfan and Cynthia's slumbering forms, lashed to the mainmast. "Should we take 'em below?"

"No. I want them where I can see them. Bloodwind wants them both alive."

"That wasn't part of the bargain."

Yodrin turned a malicious grin toward Koybur. "Oh, I'm sorry. Would you rather I threw them overboard? Those are the only options. You choose."

Koybur didn't answer, his ruined face twisted into a mask of tortured despair. Yodrin laughed and turned back to the task at hand, ignoring the traitor. What Koybur didn't understand was that his value to Bloodwind had just expired; he could no longer act as their spy in Southaven, could no longer pass information about ships, cargoes and the secrets of the Flaxal family. He was nothing now but an old crippled sailor, and as soon as his value as a passable helmsman expired, he would be following the bloody seawater that sluiced out the scuppers.

CHAPTER TWENTY-NINE

The Chase

"THE WIND'S BACKIN' TO the south, sir," Horace said, putting more weight onto the wheel to keep them pointed southeast. With only a trysail in place of the destroyed main, the ship's balance shifted forward, her bow pulling constantly upwind.

Yodrin had changed course not long after the chase began, heading on an unwavering southeasterly course straight for the Fathomless Reaches. This would have meant a broad reach and a comfortable run had the trades remained constant, but the wind was turning more southerly with every hour, bringing their course close to the wind once again.

"Good! Man the foretops'l braces. If she won't hold, house the yards and hoist a tris'l. She'll be faster without the weight aloft, and that lower yard'll make a fine mains'l boom."

"You think it'll take the strain, Captain?" Rowland watched the crew haul on the braces until the yards lay flat against the shrouds. The rising wind sang in the rigging and the foredeck ran with white water with every crashing swell. The wind was not only changing direction, but was intensifying as well, and the sky had turned an iron gray. "That spar's a bit thin for this wind."

Brelak scowled at the cook. "So are you, Row, but yer stronger than ya look."

"But strappin' a sail to my arse and haulin' me aloft don't make me a spar."

"Don't tempt me, Row. If it'd make the *Pride* a half knot faster, you'd be up that mast in a heartbeat." He watched the fore-topsail as it began to luff. "Give her half a point, Horace."

"Aye, Capt'n."

The Pride's bow slid to the west five degrees, and the fore-topsail firmed. *Hippotrin*, however, continued to pound upwind, her fore-topsail furled long ago, her full rig pulling her ahead of them steadily. With their courses diverging slightly, the gap between them began to lengthen.

"This won't do. Topmen aloft! Furl that foretops'l and get those yards on deck. Rowland! Fetch me some line from the fo'c'sle locker. We'll whip that yard to add strength. Is that mains'l ready?"

"Aye, as ready as she'll ever be. Not my best stitchery, but I was in a rush."

"Good."

Rowland vanished down the companionway, but reappeared a moment later.

"Captain! Lookie here what I found in the fo'c'sle under a bail of sail cloth!" Rowland stumbled up the companionway steps with a canvas-wrapped bundle that rattled suspiciously. When he drew back the oiled cloth, several shiny cutlasses, daggers and boarding axes shone in the afternoon light.

"Bloody fine!" Brelak chose two heavy boarding axes and tucked them into his belt. "Spread the rest 'round the crew, Row, and get me that whippin' line double quick!"

"Aye, Capt'n!" The cook handed out the weapons, and vanished down the hatch.

"Why don't you give 'em a hand with that mains'l, Horace." He took the wheel and motioned the helmsman forward, then looked to his quarry. *Hippotrin's* canted rig could be seen easily about two miles ahead. He fixed his bowsprit half a point upwind of her masts and gripped the wheel with a feverish intensity.

"Faster!" he muttered under his breath, his palms warming against the spokes. "Faster, *Orin*. Faster!"

≈

"She's housed her yards, Capt'n!"

Cynthia's head throbbed in time to her heartbeat, waves of nausea intensifying with every rise and plunge of the deck. Pain scored her wrists when she tried to bring her hands to her face.

"She's coming upwind, but looks like she's fallin' back."

She opened her eyes cautiously. She faced the ship's port side, just aft of amidships, which meant she was bound to the mainmast.

"She's got no proper mains'l."

Troilen sounded strange. She watched a seaman pass aft, surprised by the cutlass hanging from his belt. She followed him with her eyes and saw Troilen and another crewman looking aft, trading a telescope back and forth. Koybur stood at the wheel, his one good hand guiding the ship, but his features looked different, too. Anguish or pain had twisted the unscarred half of his face into something resembling the scarred portion. For a moment she wondered if another hallucination skewed her perception, but then Troilen turned and gestured to the rigging.

"House her fore-top yards and furl the main tops'l. We're pulling away. No sense in stressing the rig. And see to your leeward deadeyes. The windward shrouds have stretched a bit."

"Aye, sir."

She coughed involuntarily as nausea rose once again. She retched, but her stomach was gratefully empty. A hand grasped the fabric of her blouse at the small of her back and she realized that someone must be bound behind her.

"Easy, Mistress Cynthia. We're in trouble." Ghelfan's husky whisper surprised her, but her attention immediately diverted to Troilen as he swaggered forward.

"Mistress Flaxal," he said in greeting, looking down at the two captives. "And Master Ghelfan. Good to see you both recovering from your slumber."

"What in the names of all Nine Hells is going on here, Troilen?" Ghelfan asked. Cynthia felt him straining at his bonds, but the knots weren't likely to loosen.

"Ah, you see? You've made another mistake. Your first was to join forces with someone named Flaxal. The second was coming aboard this ship. And now you're still calling me by my pseudonym. My real name is Yodrin. I only go by Troilen when I need to establish an alibi or impress a mark with my captain's credentials."

"Yodrin? What the..." Cynthia's question trailed off into confusion as she looked around the deck, then aloft. "Where are Vulta and Finthie? What's going on?"

"What's going on, dear Cynthia, is that I have taken this ship. My former boatswain and mate are dead. *Hippotrin* is mine, or rather *will* be mine, when Captain Bloodwind formally presents her to me. We are headed for Blood Bay by a necessarily circuitous route, since your friend Feldrin Brelak is still doggedly pursuing us. Regardless, we should be there in about two days."

"Bloodwind?" Cynthia Flaxal's rage swelled until she felt she would explode. "You... you..."

"Yes, me, Mistress Flaxal. Me. In more ways than you know." Cynthia yearned to slap the condescending smile from his lips. "You really have a lot to thank me for, you know. If not for me, you'd still be kowtowing to your grandmother's every whim. I made you what you are, a mistress of ships, and now I've made you my captive."

"What do you mean, *you* made me what I am?" Cynthia seethed with rage, straining at the line around her wrists. She felt trapped in a nightmare; anger, nausea and fear whirled in her mind like a cloying fog, making it hard to think.

"Has the tea muddled your brain, little girl?" he asked, smiling sweetly as he knelt before her. "Let me clear your thoughts, then."

Yodrin drew a gleaming dagger and held the point an inch from her eye.

Fear quickly superseded anger and nausea as Cynthia imagined that blade darting forward.

"Ah. Now I see you start to understand. I have visited you before, dear Cynthia. I visited your grandmother the night that horrible fire broke out. It was a shame about the overturned lamp, wasn't it? And the mosquito netting caught fire so quickly. Why, it was like it was doused with rum."

He flicked the tip of the dagger across her cheek, leaving a tiny scratch, but drawing a gasp of shock from her. He grinned and stood, sheathing the dagger as her fear coalesced into a seething ball of hate. The extent of his treachery stoked that hate like a furnace.

"I'd love to entertain you further, but—"

Her spittle only reached the leg of his trousers, but the shock and anger on his slim features told her that she had scored a serious insult.

"You're nothing but a bloody murdering pirate! Does killing old ladies in their sleep make you feel like a man, you filthy—"

The toe of Yodrin's boot struck her an inch beneath her sternum, driving the breath from her lungs and leaving her retching. The blow was not as hard as it could have been, but it felt like an eternity before she could draw a breath. As air filled her aching lungs, he gripped her by the hair and wrenched her head back. Once again, the dagger gleamed before her face.

"The only reason I don't open your throat with this is that I was ordered not to kill you. I was unfortunately also ordered not to cause permanent damage, but Bloodwind said nothing about a few cuts just to make sure you don't cause trouble. How would you like it, eh? The face? The fingers? Maybe you'd like me to cut your tongue down the middle, you little viper!"

"Rot... in... hell," she croaked, gasping for each breath. Deep down, she knew they would kill her. It would be better sooner and quicker, rather than later and slower.

"I'd give you over to the crew for some entertainment, but we're a bit busy right now. I think I'll just make sure you don't run away."

He slashed the laces of her shoes and tore them free, ripping off her stockings as she kicked at him; visions of severed toes flooded her mind's eye as curses worthy of a seasoned sailor flew from her lips.

"Hold still now, little girl." He grasped one ankle and brought the blade to the sole of her foot, but stopped as Koybur's raspy voice called out from the helm.

"No permanent damage, Yodrin!"

"Shut your mouth, Koybur, or I'll sew it shut!"

Cynthia's scream shivered the air as Yodrin's knife sliced the bottom of her foot from heel to toe. Another scream wrenched at her lungs as he cut her other foot. The cuts were not deep, but deep enough. Blood pooled at her feet as her screams devolved into sobs.

"No permanent damage," Yodrin said, cleaning his blade on her skirt and sheathing it. "Somebody wash this blood off the deck!"

One of the sailors dashed a bucket of seawater over her feet. She bit back another scream as the salt water struck the cuts. She clenched her eyes tightly against the nightmare. Ghelfan was right—they were in very deep trouble indeed.

≈

"Haul away!"

Three seamen hauled, and the recut trysail soared aloft. Rigged with its tack and clew hoisted to the mainmast, and the head drawn forward to the foremast cap head, it made a passable staysail and moved some of the effort aft. The helm eased somewhat, and Horace sighed in relief.

"She's not gripin' so much now, sir. Right nice!"

"Log!" Feldrin shouted, and the log line was pitched over the side.

In less than a minute the crewman shouted back, "Eighteen!" A cheer rang out from the deck, but Feldrin's features remained set in stone.

"Sighting on *Hippotrin*!" His tone was curt, his manner as sharp as the axes at his belt. They had lost another half mile on the other ship as they worked, and the wind wasn't cooperating. It would pick up, rising to near-gale strength, but then ease off to a mere stiff breeze.

"She's not pulled away any more, sir," the lookout called from the bow. "We may have gained a bit."

"About bloody damned time!" Brelak turned and scanned the deck for anything else they could throw over the side, but aside from the longboat, every spare bit of equipment had already been jettisoned to lighten their load.

"This ain't no ordinary blow, Capt'n." Horace's eyes scanned the horizon, the leaden sky, and the dark streaks of cloud. "Got the feel of a cyclone."

"Too early for it," he said, clenching his jaw. He knew the feel of a hurricane, and had seen and felt the telltale cloud patterns and the constant shifting of the wind, but such storms were generally not seen for another month. "Just a blow. It'll peter out by mornin'."

"Hope you're right, sir. This new rigging's not up fer a real storm."

"Capt'n!" Rowland trundled up onto the deck, grinning like a maniac. "I've got it! The stove! We can set it on chocks, manhandle it into the main hold and use it as a counterweight. It's gotta tip the scales at eight hundred-weight. We rig blocks and shift it to the windward side and block it in place. That'll bring her upright!"

Feldrin thought for a moment. There was a great deal of danger in having that much weight loose belowdecks. If a line parted, the heavy cast iron stove could smash through a frame, or even through the hull.

"Do it." He bit his lip and glared up at the darkening sky as Rowland barked orders to the crew and dashed below.

"Don't you worry, sir. We'll catch up."

"Aye, but it's gotta be a'fore dark." He looked at Horace, then at the distance between the two ships. "Two hours, at best."

They looked at one another, knowing that the gap was not closing quickly enough to meet that deadline. Neither said it, but they both knew *Hippotrin* would still be well ahead when darkness fell.

CHAPTER THIRTY

Old Friends and New Enemies

DARKNESS AND DESPAIR DESCENDED on Cynthia like a cold damp blanket. Spray from the bow left her wet and chilled, adding misery upon misery.

Whispered discussion with Ghelfan yielded little hope; their only value to Bloodwind was their ability to render working drawings of the new ship design. A fleet of the new ships outfitted as corsairs would decimate shipping in the Southern Ocean.

"And I gave it to him," she muttered, clenching and re-clenching her hands. "I gave him the one thing he couldn't get for himself, and I gave it to him without a fight."

"Hush, Cynthia." Ghelfan's voice was calm and matter-of-fact, as always. "You gave him nothing. You followed your heart, and he stole your dream from you. That is nothing to be ashamed of."

"But think, Ghelfan! Think of what he'll do with a fleet of ships like this!"

Hippotrin capped a swell and plunged into a trough, then soared up the next wave, flying like her namesake in the climbing wind.

"How fast do you think we're going? Fifteen knots? Twenty? I've never heard of a ship that'd do twenty knots, and here we are doing it. Wet decks and a bit of a stiff ride, but we're sailing twice the pace any other ship on the sea could manage, and she's not even straining. What will Bloodwind do with this?"

"He'll take the whole Southern Ocean, and the Emperor of Tsing will be forced to send a naval force against him, which will fail. Bloodwind will demand tithe from every ship that passes the Shattered Isles, and will eventually build a nation of his own." The shipwright paused, and Cynthia could hear the logic of his words whirling in her mind. "That is how nations are born, Mistress Flaxal."

"Under the yoke of someone like Bloodwind? Impossible!"

"Not at all. He is probably no worse than the first Emperor of Tsing, or some of the northern warlords or the princes of the southern deserts. Authority, whether good or ill in nature, builds stability, which builds a nation."

"Which makes me feel that much worse. I've made him a bloody king! What next?"

"You two should keep quiet."

Neither had noticed Koybur approaching from the stern cabin. He bore a steaming tin cup in one hand and a cloth-wrapped packet under his maimed arm. "I can hear you from well aft. Yodrin's called fer silent runnin', so unless you want a gag in yer mouth…"

"And you should take a flying leap over the rail!" Cynthia said between clenched teeth, turning away from the cup he held before her. Her stomach clenched again, but this time it wasn't nausea. Koybur's betrayal hurt worse than all of her other injuries combined. He had been her friend, her mentor, her confidant and more. And he had betrayed her, uniting with the very man who had killed her parents. Until now she had only been able to glare at him as he stood at the wheel. Now, here he was offering her a cup of tea. "I don't want anything from you!"

"Be that way, then." He offered the cup to Ghelfan, who drank deeply, though he offered no thanks. Koybur put the empty cup down and offered jerky and bread, which the shipwright ate.

"I'm the only friend you've got on this ship, Cyn. You'll not get a scrap from this lot, and like as not more stripes from Yodrin's dagger, if you don't learn yer manners."

"*Friend?*" She could barely pronounce the word in his presence. "You were *more* than a friend to me, Koybur. You were the only father I've had for the past fifteen years, and this is how you treat me? You sell out to *that?*" She choked back tears, but felt that she had to continue. "How much did it cost to buy you, Koybur? How much gold did Bloodwind pay you for your soul?"

"You think I did this for *money?*" The utter disgust in his voice brought her eyes up to his tortured face. She saw the pain there, and wondered. "I din't *sell out*, Cynthia Flaxal. Some things in this world're worth more'n gold. Some're worth more'n friendship. Some're even worth more'n a man's soul!"

He spun on his maimed leg and limped aft, leaving her dumbstruck.

Ghelfan nudged her with his bound wrists and whispered, "He may be a traitor, Cynthia, but he is also the only one aboard likely to bring us anything to eat or drink. It may be a long time before we get a real meal."

"I don't want anything from him," she said, keeping her voice as low as possible.

"You might change your mind in a day or two."

"No, I won't! You don't understand, Ghelfan. I've known Koybur twice as long as I knew my parents. He taught me everything I know about sailing and shipping. How could he *do* something like this?"

"Who knows what motivates a man to betray his friends? But from his tone, I believe that it was not money."

A hissed curse and a kick from a passing seaman forced them into silence as the clouds faded from gray to black. As *Hippotrin* climbed a swell, Cynthia looked aft into the confused seas of their wake. About a mile distant, she could barely make out the straining jibs of *Orin's Pride* fading into the gloom.

≈

"Lookout!" Brelak called up to the man stationed at the top of the foremast. "Where away?" He could no longer make out *Hippotrin's* sails in the darkness, but there was more than one way to track a ship at night.

"Dead ahead, Capt'n!" The lookout called, waving a hand forward. "I can still make out her trail clear as day!"

Every sailor who plied the Southern Ocean knew that a ship sailing at night threw up a considerable wake of luminous foam. On a clear night, that trail could be seen for some distance. To aid in the lookout's task, all shipboard lights were doused, but the rough seas were a problem, for every white-capped swell also shone with the green-white radiance. It would be very easy to lose the trail.

"Keep a sharp eye. Call out if the bearing changes."

"Aye, sir."

"You think we got a chance of followin' 'em all night?" Rowland asked.

"If we keep up and the weather don't go to hell, yeah. If it rains, or if the seas start breakin' more..." He didn't need to finish that thought. They both knew their chances.

≈

"They follow, my captain," Hydra hissed, fresh blood dripping from her fingertips into the tepid pool of swirling seawater. "*Hippotrin* leaves a trail in the water. The Morrgrey follows it like a hound on the scent."

"Obscure the trail, Hydra." Bloodwind didn't even bother looking to the witch; instead, he ran a rough finger down the flawless curve of Camilla's arm. She leaned into the caress instead of pulling away as she had so many thousands of times before. It was such a simple action, but it brought him more pleasure than any of the whores in Blood Bay could have. He smiled, and his thoughts wandered to the other sweet curves of Camilla's body before Hydra's voice brought him back to the present.

"There is a storm building, my captain. It will require much to bend the will of such a storm. I shall require more... nourishment."

"Very well, Hydra. One more." He called to the guard, and the man brought a struggling slave down the steps. "Give him to her."

The slave pleaded and strained at his bonds as the guard handed the lead over to the crone's bony grip. Bloodwind turned and drew Camilla away from the grisly spectacle. "Just see that they lose the trail, Hydra."

"Of course, my captain," she agreed only moments before a bloodcurdling scream rent the torrid air of the cavern. By the time the screams died, Bloodwind and Camilla were at the thick oaken door that sealed the cavern. The door closed, muffling the sultry, gurgling laughter of Hydra taking her meal. He'd watched her feed once; he would never make that mistake again. He caressed Camilla's shoulder again, but her smooth flesh shivered and she pulled away.

"Something wrong, my dear?" He trailed his hand trail down to her wrist, so conspicuously absent of her golden chains and manacles.

"Just the sound of it," she said, turning to him with a weak smile. She took his hand, and squeezed it reassuringly. "She makes my skin crawl."

"Her claws will never touch your flesh again, my dear." He guided her through the rough-hewn caverns until they exited onto the main foyer of the palace. The sky above bore no stars and no moon, nothing but foreboding clouds, and the wind-whipped tops of the palms. Yes, a storm was brewing.

≈

A fog blew in on the heels of gale-force winds, adding a chill to the air. Cynthia began to shiver. Despite the nausea that hung over her like a shroud, she longed for a mouthful of water to wash the vile taste from her mouth.

"This fog's not natural," Ghelfan whispered. The shipwright's words startled her; what he said made no sense. How could fog be anything but natural?

"What do you mean?"

"Winds and seas this high are not naturally conducive to fog. Someone is wielding power here, helping Yodrin obscure this ship."

"Power. You mean magic?" Cynthia's mind whirled in a morass of misery, leaving her unable to think.

"Yes. A seamage, or a priest of Odea, or even a common wizard might conjure such a mist."

"You think Yodrin's a wizard?"

"If he is, he has not previously shown any talent. Then again, he has been hiding his true identity for months."

Faint laughter reached them from aft, though Cynthia could not identify the voice. The mists were now so thick that both the bow and stern were obscured. Several crewmen ran past, going forward. The large wooden wheel creaked, and the yards thumped against the mainmast as the sails shifted—they were turning.

The ship heaved over as the course change set them beam-on to the great seas for a moment, then stabilized as the waves shifted to her aft quarter. Now, instead of beating against the weather, the ship's stern lifted to allow the waves to flow beneath her. *Hippotrin's* pace increased until she raced along the wave fronts, surfing with the enormous swells.

"They've made their turn," Ghelfan said unnecessarily. "There'll be no finding them in this soup now."

"I don't think—" Cynthia's comment came up short when something small grabbed her hand and crawled up her wrist. She almost screamed, her mind conjuring up images of hungry rats making their way up from the bilges to feast on her fingers. But no teeth or claws dug into her flesh; she felt only a faint tugging at the knots binding her wrists.

"Mouse?" she hissed quietly with realization. She hadn't seen the little seasprite since she passed out, but there could be no other explanation. A tiny flame of hope ignited in her breast. "Mouse, come here!"

"Cynthia, what is it?" Ghelfan sounded worried; she could feel him flexing against the mast.

"Don't worry, it's Mouse. Maybe he can..." The tugging at her wrist ceased and she felt the sprite crawl up her arm, clinging to her clothing to keep from being blown away by the ripping wind. Finally he reached her shoulder, his high-pitched twittering loud in her ear.

"Keep out of sight, Mouse." She turned to take stock of her little friend. He looked like he'd been run through a ringer, dripping wet and wind-blown. "You poor thing. You must have been hiding under a coil of line or something."

He twittered and shrugged, obviously unconcerned with his disheveled appearance.

"Mouse, I need you to do something for me, okay?"

He nodded vigorously, grinning and chirping.

"I need you to find Feldrin. I need you to fly to *Orin's Pride* and bring them here. Can you do that?"

Mouse looked up at the screaming wind, then over his shoulder at his patchwork wings. The storm had already torn some of the stitched-together bits of gossamer, and he had been missing a good bit from his lower left wing since his fateful encounter with Julia Garrison's broom. He flexed his wings, fluttered them, and tried to fly up against the wind. In a blink he was torn off her shoulder and flung to the deck in a tumbling heap. He crawled back to Cynthia and scaled her damp blouse, laboriously regaining his perch on her shoulder. She already knew the answer when he hung his head in shame and shook it. He just couldn't fly well enough to stay aloft in this wind.

"Its okay, Mouse. Don't feel bad. Maybe we can think of some other way to get these ropes off, though I don't know what I could—"

The seasprite's face lit up, and his head bobbed enthusiastically. He leapt off her shoulder and scampered across the wet deck, dashing from one hiding place to another until he vanished into the gloom.

"What was that all about?" Ghelfan asked, shifting his weight to a more comfortable position.

"I think he's going to try to help us," she said, worry for her little friend mixing with her other miseries. "I hope he doesn't get squashed in the process."

≈

"Where the hell did this come from?" Brelak cracked his knuckles and glared around the mist-shrouded deck. The bowsprit shone only as a dim outline, and the lookout had completely vanished in the veil of mists that shrouded the ship. "Lookout! Can you see anything?"

"Nothin' but fog, Capt'n."

"Damn! I never seen the likes of it! Not with this wind."

"Don't seem natural, Capt'n." He stared at Rowland as he emerged from belowdecks bearing two steaming mugs. "Do ya remember the tale of Orin Flaxal's fall, with the mists comin' up from nowhere when they was far out to sea?" He passed the hot blackbrew to captain and helmsman, nodding aloft. "Bloodwind's got a mage on his side, or so the stories go."

"We'll hold this course," Brelak said, making a decision. "He can't go too far west without running the risk of hitting a reef. He'll either turn north, or stay on course. This'll clear by mornin'; then we'll see what's what."

"Aye, sir," Rowland said, but they both knew that in these conditions, if their prey changed course they could be a hundred miles apart by morning.

CHAPTER THIRTY-ONE

Defeat

"BLOODY HELL!" BRELAK SWORE, gripping the wheel with white-knuckled fury as he glared at the mountainous seas, the screaming sky and his battered crew. Morning brought clearer air, but even higher winds and seas. Hurricane-force gusts and torrential rain cut visibility to less than a mile.

Hippotrin was nowhere in sight.

All hands had been on deck throughout the night, and everyone bore signs of exhaustion. They had held their course, or tried to, under reefed sails and greatly diminished speed, no-one knew how far downwind the storm had pushed them.

"We gotta make a run fer it, Capt'n!" Rowland made his way aft from the foredeck where he'd been handing out rations. "*Hippotrin* could be anywhere. We're slidin' downwind and the Shattered Isles are somewhere to leeward. We need to head back to Southaven."

"Bloody, bloody hell!" Brelak squinted to leeward. The southeasterly weather bore into them, pushing them toward the deadly leeward shore. "I'm not givin' up, Row," he said, wiping the spray from his face. Another crashing wave buried the foredeck, knocking men to the lengths of their lifelines. "The ship can take it. She's not even shippin' much water. She's tight as a drum."

"The ship can take it, but the crew can't. Even if we find *Hippotrin*, there's nothing we can do. We'd smash each other to splinters if we tried to board in these seas."

"We could follow them to Bloodwind's lair," he countered, turning into a crashing sea that buried the foredeck once again.

"They'd let you chase 'em to the southern ice before they'd lead you to Bloodwind," Rowland said, ducking his shoulder into the driving spray.

"I'm not givin' up! I *can't* give up!"

"I ain't sayin' give up. We need help, is all. More men, more weapons, and more ships. We'll find her, Feldrin, but we can't do it alone!"

He glared at the cook, clenching his teeth against the truth. Rowland was right. He knew it in his head, but his heart raged at him to continue the hunt, to find *Hippotrin* and gut that traitorous pirate Yodrin. He squinted out over the deck, taking stock of his exhausted crew. The night had taken its toll, and everyone sported minor injuries from hour after hour of batter-ing seas. Their eyes looked up to him—their captain, their sole link to life or death. There were no accusations there, no judgments; they would follow him whatever decision he made.

"Bloody hell," he muttered as the facts won out over his emotions. His heart ached as it never had before, but he had no choice.

"Prepare to tack! Man the foresheets! Backfill the jib as we come about! Rowland, take a man below and center that monstrosity of a stove. We're gonna be on a starboard broad reach. I want the flying jib on her as soon as we're downwind. We should rig the fore-top, but we've got no spare yard. These damned swells are so high we're losin' our wind in the troughs. Gotta keep her pointed or we'll broach."

"Aye, sir!" Rowland began shouting orders.

In only a few minutes they were ready, but timing would be crucial. Tacking a ship in seas like this was a dangerous maneuver. If they failed to come about, if the bow remained pointed into the wind and the sails flapped uselessly, the swell could push them backward down a wave, which could snap the rudder and leave them at the mercy of the sea and the rocks of the Shattered Isles.

"All hands, we're comin' about!" Brelak brought the wheel over as they mounted a swell, swinging her bow around into the wind.

The exhausted crew toiled with surprising speed. The bow came around smartly, smashing through a plunging swell. In moments, the sails were set and *Orin's Pride* raced ahead on her new course, surfing the monstrous swells with the wind now on her starboard stern quarter. With the seas no longer breaking over the foredeck, the entire crew heaved a collective sigh of relief. The helmsman bore the brunt of the duty on this tack, fighting every swell to keep her bow pointed downwind.

"Get the off-watch below, Row," Brelak ordered, "and see if you can manage a hot meal. Four hours and it's your watch. Get some sleep."

"Aye, sir." He shouted orders and the crew responded, struggling out of their harnesses and going below.

As the ship quieted down, Feldrin Brelak spared a glance over his shoulder to the southwest. Somewhere between them and the Shattered Isles sailed *Hippotrin*, but how far and on what tack, he had no way to know.

≈

"Furl the fores'l! Get another reef in that main, damn you!" Yodrin cracked a length of knotted line across the back of a slow sailor, urging him on. "Faster, damn you! I'll have your balls on a spit if you don't shape up!"

Cynthia smirked at the venomous glare the crewman cast at his captain's back.

Hippotrin clawed upwind, straining to maintain a southerly course. They'd spent the night pounding into the mounting seas in an attempt to keep the ship east of the Shattered Isles. With no moon or stars to fix a position, the distance to the lee shore was only a dangerous guess.

Neither of the captives had slept much. Cynthia's exhaustion, combined with her seasickness and lack of food and water, left her weak and shaking. Hope that Mouse would find some way to help them dwindled as the night wore on. The decks were often awash; the little sprite could have easily been swept overboard.

Dawn brought little comfort, but it did bring Koybur with another cup of hot tea and a sandwich of bread, cheese and beef jerky. Cynthia choked back her rage long enough to take a mouthful of tea. She swallowed forcefully, washing the salt and bile from her mouth, willing the warming liquid to stay put. She turned away from the proffered food, knowing she would be lucky if the tea stayed down. Koybur stumbled as the deck lurched, fighting to stay on his one good leg and hold the food.

"He's going to run this ship onto a reef if he doesn't change course," Ghelfan told Koybur while chewing the tough beef into submission. "He could make more sea-room if he beat northeast."

"Aye, he's less of a sailor than a killer." Koybur held the cup to Ghelfan's lips until it ran empty.

"Did you help him with that, too?" Cynthia's anger boiled away her nausea and calmed her ceaseless shivering for a moment. "Did you help him kill my grandmother?"

"What do you think?"

She looked into Koybur's tortured features for a moment; there was more pain in his one good eye than a lifetime as a cripple had dealt him. A surge of sympathy welled up in her, but the anguish of his betrayal promptly drowned it out.

"I don't know what to think anymore, Koybur."

"Think whatever you like, Cyn, but I never—"

"Enough talk there!" Yodrin strode forward, his voice ragged from yelling orders all night. "Back to your station! One more word out of your mouth to those two and I'll cut out your lying tongue."

Koybur turned his back to the bound pair and made his way aft without a word. Yodrin bristled at the lack of respect and raised the knotted line to strike, but a breaking wave buried *Hippotrin's* bow, tossing the ship like a child's toy in a bathtub. She watched Koybur disappear down the hatch, her thoughts straying to the same burning question: *Why? Why did you do it, Koybur? Why did you betray me?*

≈

"The storm grows, my captain," Hydra said, entering the room without preamble. She wore the familiar guise of a sensuous young woman, but Camilla ignored it, knowing what lurked beneath. She kept her eyes on her plate, concentrating on her breakfast. She had eaten well since her transition from slavery. The cost seemed trifling when compared to the years of hunger and degradation.

"I don't need a sorceress to tell me that," Bloodwind said around a mouthful of kippered flying fish. "I can hear the wind through the shutters and see it bending the palms. What I can't see is *Hippotrin*. Tell me if my new ship is in peril."

"The storm will pass through the Fathomless Reaches tonight. The winds will bear southeasterly, shifting south and then southwest as it passes." She shrugged, strolling slowly around the table while tracing one long, slender finger along the back of Camilla's chair. "*Hippotrin* sails west of Carbuncle Shoal, holding a southerly course. Yodrin does not know the force of this storm, nor its track. His speed is diminished, but even beating against the wind, he is making ten knots."

"So he's sailing right into it." Bloodwind considered the delicate fish arrayed on his plate, put his fork down and shifted his eyes to Hydra's pitiless orbs. "Can you protect them? Shift the storm, or divert some of the winds?"

"Such a storm is beyond my power, my captain. I can calm the seas around the ship, but doing so will require a great amount of energy. I will need..." her fingertips brushed Camilla's bare shoulder, "sustenance."

Camilla pulled away, shuddering at the chill caress.

Both women jumped as Bloodwind buried the point of his dagger into the tabletop. The violence of his thrust had upset a pot of preserves, and the sticky sweet stain, red as blood, spread slowly across the white linen tablecloth. Bloodwind's voice, low and as smooth as the freshly pressed tablecloth, bore an edge as sharp as the dagger in his hand.

"I told you once, Hydra. Touch her again, and I'll put this in your eye. Of the two of you, I value her company much more than yours."

"Ah, but my captain," Hydra said easily, slithering around the table in a caricature of feminine seduction, "she brings you only pleasure of the flesh, while I bring you gold. And at what price?"

The sorceress wrapped one slim hand around the blade of the dagger embedded in the table and slid her palm up the edge. Camilla cringed as black ichor oozed from between her fingers to hiss and smoke upon the table.

"Only a little blood."

"You'll have your price, Hydra, but not her." The pirate stood and wrenched the dagger from the table. The black liquid smoldered upon the blade, pitting the fine steel. He cast it aside and fixed her with an equally smoldering glare. "I will send as many slaves as you require. Protect *Hippotrin*."

"I will try, my captain." She inspected the cut on her palm and smiled. Her sensuous curves swayed like the undulations of a serpent as she left the room.

"She is dangerous," Camilla said, pushing away her plate, her appetite destroyed. "She will kill us all if she doesn't get what she wants."

"Rest easy, my dear." Bloodwind rounded the table and took her hand, escorting her from the breakfast area to the shuttered doors that led out to the balcony. The doors shuddered with the rising storm. "There is no shortage of slaves for her to devour. Unfortunately, her services are indispensable to my plan, and she knows it."

"And your plan? Your real plan?" She knew now that he coveted more than gold, that power was his true seduction. But how much power?

"My plan, dear Camilla," he said, reaching for the latch, "is to have everything." He turned the latch and flung the shutter aside.

Storm winds and tepid rain drenched them both to the skin in an instant as he pulled her onto the balcony. He encircled her with one strong arm, drawing her close, as he swept his other in an arc to indicate the entirety of Blood Bay.

Wind and rain thrashed through the palms and mangroves. The power of the storm gripped Camilla, even as she shivered with the drenching rain. Its strength and violence reminded her of Bloodwind, as if he were a personification of nature's most horrific force.

"I want it all, Camilla. This is just the beginning. I will have everything." He pulled her close, his palm cupping her cheek to bring her face up to his. "And you will have everything with me."

She moved with him as he guided her into the lee of one of the massive pillars that supported the stone over their heads. The rock pressed against her back, rough through the silk of her gown, in contrast to the softness of his lips as they pressed against hers. Slowly, gently, he drew down the shoulders of her dress. This was the cost of her freedom from torment. No small price, but she relinquished it, drawing him to her as his hands rent the fabric of her sodden gown.

"Everything," he said in her ear, his hushed voice barely audible above the driving rain and the roaring in her ears as he and the storm surged against her bared flesh.

"Yes," she whispered back. "Everything..."

CHAPTER THIRTY-TWO

Storm Child

ORIN'S PRIDE RACED BEFORE the storm, surfing the swells with gale-force winds filling every stitch of canvas the crew could hoist aloft. Brelak could not measure their precise speed in the following sea, but he knew they were sailing faster than any ship had ever sailed. If he had accurately estimated their position, they would be in Southaven by morning.

"My watch, Captain." Rowland's bony hand clapped him on the shoulder, and he handed over the wheel. "Anything I need to know?"

"Nothin' new. Just keep her bow pointed about forty degrees. Wind's clockin' west."

"Aye. Damn big storm. Thought we'd be out of it by now."

"As did I. As did I." Brelak glared up at the overcast, willing it to dissipate. "Bloody early fer a hurricane, but there ain't no doubt of it."

"Aye, we'd have been in the thick of it if we'd stayed on course. I imagine the Shattered Isles are getting the brunt of it."

"And *Hippotrin*." Brelak's voice rumbled like distant thunder. He looked over his shoulder at the seas, imagining *Hippotrin* pounding into a hurricane, and aboard her Cynthia Flaxal in the hands of the pirate Yodrin. "Bloody hell..."

He went below and sat down to a bowl of stew and biscuits in the captain's cabin, his cabin. Food calmed him, but his eyes fixed on the heavy teak cabinet that held the lightkeeper's fire and he began to wonder. Curiosity won out over caution, and he opened the cabinet. A moment's inspection showed him where all but a few strands of the pull cord had been cut through, the damage hidden with a bit of wax.

"Sabotage," he said, fingering the cut hemp. Karek or Yodrin must have done it prior to their departure. His temper flared, wishing he could jam the ceramic vessel of dormant fire down Bloodwind's throat and pull the cord. One of his dark brows arched speculatively with the thought that he might be able to do that very thing.

"Maybe..."

≈

Blood and water... life and death... power and the beast within all vied for a place in Hydra's over-taxed mind. The storm slammed relentlessly against her, pounding on the shield of her tattered sanity like a hammer against an eggshell. The shell was cracked, but it held; blood held it intact, and she needed more.

"Bring her!"

A scream shivered the air, but it went unheeded. The guard was either deaf or inured to the suffering and fear of those in his charge, and Hydra simply didn't care.

Blood was the only thing that mattered.

Keeping her mind focused on the task of calming the seas around *Hippotrin*, Hydra reached out and drew the struggling girl near. Briefly, she glanced at her prey, young and strong, one of Bloodwind's whores, no doubt. The horror and disbelief on the pretty face whet Hydra's appetite as her nails pierced the delicate flesh. The girl's screams devolved into gurgles as a torrent of sweet crimson flowed down Hydra's throat in gulp after luscious gulp. She fed until she felt her stomach would explode, then cast the lifeless husk aside and bent all her will back to her task.

Power flowed through her, slamming against the brunt of the storm, flattening the towering swells, preventing the plunging breakers from burying the ship. How much power, how many times she fed, all blurred in the morass of fatigue and concentration. One thought, however, did finally surface through the haze of magic, blood and madness: the expenditure of this much magical energy had drawn attention.

"Odea's minions..." she hissed, gazing into the swirling pool of bloody seawater. "They come."

≈

"Something's wrong!" Cynthia shouted, her words barely reaching Ghelfan's ears before being torn away by the howling wind. "The seas have calmed, but the winds are higher."

"Magic," he yelled into the wind, his face turned away from the sting of rain. "Someone is holding back the worst of the seas."

"Right now, I think I'd like to thank them." She squinted into the distance. They had seen flashes of lightning all night, but aside from that sporadic illumination, darkness enveloped them like a burial shroud. She could barely see the surface of the sea, a blur of foam-streaked water flowing past at an astonishing rate. "We're making better headway."

"Yes, but think, Cynthia. This is a cyclone, and we are on a port tack beating into the wind."

"We're sailing right into it," she said. "Yodrin's crazy! Unless our heading has changed, he'll run us ashore before he makes the Fathomless Reaches."

"That might be a kinder fate than arriving safely at our destination."

The shipwright's tone had gone grim. "Bloodwind *will* get what he wants from us."

Lightning split the sky in a sheet of white, revealing the sea around them in horrifying detail. They sailed in the center of a circle of ocean hammered flat by an unseen hand. Mountains of water encircled them, towering seas streaked white with foam that peaked at half the height of the mast. Only a circle of water perhaps two lengths of the ship lay in a relative state of calm, and that calm hardly resembled a quiescent sea.

"Holy mother of storms!" she heard Ghelfan gasp as shouts of surprise and alarm rang out around the deck.

"Bloodwind's witch protects us!" Yodrin bellowed from the aft deck. More lightning split the sky, once again revealing the surreal seas surrounding them. "Her eye is on us! Her magic is holding back the storm!" The exhausted crew cheered madly, laughing and shaking their fists at the storm, defying Odea's fury.

"Whoever is doing this is wielding an unbelievable amount of power," Ghelfan said, his voice holding a tone of awe. "Not even a seamage can challenge a hurricane."

"But if she can do this, why doesn't she—"

Cynthia's question died on her lips when something small, wet and vaguely sprite-shaped splattered against her sodden skirt with an audible squeal of alarm.

"Mouse!" She shifted and squinted into the stinging rain. Another squeak from beneath her sopping skirts told her the little sprite had not been lost. His tiny form struggled under the heavy cloth as he tried to crawl free, but every move he made, another fold of fabric pinned him against Cynthia's leg.

"Mouse, I can't—" She fell silent as three inches of steel stabbed up through her skirt beside her knee. The little blade, probably a paring knife stolen from the galley, sawed a hole through the cloth. Through that hole, a bedraggled seasprite emerged, dragging his stolen blade behind him.

"Oh, Mouse! You poor thing!"

He struggled to free himself, but his bent and broken wings were caught in the fabric. He grinned up at her, indicating his stolen blade with pride, and tried to free himself again. A portion of one wing parted with a crack, the broken end fluttering away on the howling wind. His smile broke as he looked after the departed wing, then he shrugged and crawled free, working his way carefully up Cynthia's leg and behind her back.

"What the—? Ouch!" Ghelfan's bound hands struggled against the small of her back. "Tell him to be more careful with that!"

"Keep your voice down!" she admonished in a hissed whisper. "He's cutting us free."

"If he doesn't sever an artery in the process!" The half-elf's tone was sharp, but his voice was hushed. "The question is: what do we do once we're free?"

That was a very good question, but before she could even think of an answer, Ghelfan's hands jerked free of their bonds. Mouse had done it! Cynthia felt the cold blade press briefly against her wrist, and cringed. The knife began sawing back and forth in a feverish cadence, the edge miraculously avoiding her flesh.

What can we do? she thought, running through the possibilities in her mind. They might be able to sabotage the ship, but that would leave them at the mercy of the wind and seas, and the unforgiving leeward shore. Then she remembered Ghelfan's comment about their future under Bloodwind's hand, and she realized he was right. She'd rather sink the ship and die in the process than live as a slave to the man who had killed her parents.

"The lightkeeper's gift," she said over her shoulder. She felt him go rigid at her suggestion. "We've got to, Ghelfan. There's nothing else we can do."

Only the howl of the raging wind passed between them as Mouse sawed at the line binding Cynthia's wrist. When it finally parted, Ghelfan's voice startled her in its determination.

"I'll do it, Mistress Flaxal. You draw them forward. Try to cut the windward shrouds free at the deadeyes. That should get their attention."

"All right." She swallowed, wondering if her nerves would hold. "I don't know if I can walk, but…"

"Oh, I forgot your feet. Perhaps you could crawl."

"I'll try to stand; they're pretty numb. Just wait until they're after me. The helmsman will see you, but nobody will be able to hear him, and he won't be able to leave the wheel. When the fire starts, run forward to the fo'c'sle hatch. The hatch cover should float if you cut it loose."

"And you try to cut the launch free. Once the ship's ablaze, it will be every man for himself." Both of them knew their chances of surviving a hurricane clinging to flotsam, but hope, however slim, would make their tasks easier.

Mouse pressed the handle of his little knife into her palm, tugged on her sleeve, and then started climbing, clutching at the sodden linen of her blouse. When he finally reached his customary place at her collar, she worked her feet under her, wincing at the pain, then reached up and took Mouse from her shoulder. "Well, my little friend, it's time to raise some hell!"

He squealed in glee as she stuffed him into her shirt and dashed for the windward rail. The wounds on Cynthia's feet sent shocks of pain up her legs, but she managed to grip the rail and start working her way forward before anyone called out in alarm.

"Oy! The Flaxal wench is loose!"

"She's got a knife! How the hell?"

"Never mind! Get forward! After her!"

Yodrin's bellow was unmistakable, and a glance showed three sailors working their way carefully forward while their captain remained at the helm. Cynthia grinned and threw them a curse, lurching ahead against the wind and rain to the foremast shrouds. Here, she put her knife to work. The shrouds themselves could not be cut, but the line through the deadeyes was tarred hemp, and fair game for a blade. The little knife was not as sharp as it could have been, but the line was under tremendous strain. She sawed only halfway through the first before it parted, cracking like a stone-mason's hammer. The rope burned through the hardwood of the deadeye, slackening the shroud.

Mouse screeched in delight at the mayhem and urged her to cut another, flailing his little arms from the relative security of the neck of her blouse. Somehow he'd worked his way into the "V" of her breasts, which seemed the most secure spot, though it would have been laughable under any other circumstance.

A shout of alarm from aft and the bang of the forward hatch warned Cynthia that she didn't have much time. They'd be on her before she could finish. A quick glance told her that Ghelfan had made his move. The ship would be in flames in moments, but she wasn't quite through yet.

She laughed and launched herself across the deck as a swell tossed the ship. Wind-driven spray aided her progress, and the leeward shrouds slapped into her outstretched palms.

The sailors pursued, and she realized with a surge of excitement that there was indeed one more place she could go. She clenched the tiny knife between her teeth, gripped the ratlines and hoisted herself up onto the railing.

The wind caught her skirt like a sail, trying to tear her away, but she managed to hang on by wrapping one leg around a shroud. She stepped onto the lower rung of the ratlines, and pain shot up her leg like a hot knife as the rough hemp tore into her wounded foot.

"Grab her!"

Hands grasped at her legs, pulling at her skirts, but the cut Mouse had made tore open around her knees and her assailants toppled to the deck holding only a wad of sodden fabric. The pins and needles of hurricane-force rain cut into Cynthia's bare legs, but the force of the wind against her diminished without the voluminous skirt. She could climb, though every step felt like daggers stabbing into the soles of her feet.

And climb she did.

When only five rungs separated her from the masthead, the ship lurched alarmingly, forcing her to hang on for her life. She looked down at the deck as lightning shattered the darkness, thunder hammering her ears a half-second after. She would have cowered in fear had she not been numbed by what the illumination revealed: No one stood at the helm. Yodrin had left the ship to fend for herself in the battering sea. Then she saw that the water around the ship swarmed with glittering shapes, the light of the storm's discharge reflecting from thousands of glistening scales. Merfolk, hundreds of them, schooled around the ship like sharks around a bleeding whale.

≈

Ghelfan tumbled down the hatch, his weak legs wobbling under him. He reached the corner of the passage leading aft when he heard the hatch bang; someone was after him. He passed the opposing doors to the galley and crew's mess, surprised to see the cook, Borell, slumped over the mess table, snoring loudly.

He dashed aft, bursting into the great cabin and whirling to slam the stout oak door. As it closed he saw Yodrin charging the door and cringed at the rage darkening the pirate's face. He threw the latch a second before the captain smashed against the door, and the heavy bronze bolt held.

A lantern swung on a hook from an overhead beam, creating patches of golden light and deep shadow that danced crazily around the cabin. Ghelfan stumbled to the heavy chest set into the forward bulkhead and knelt upon the dark stain where Vulta Kambeo had met her end. He flung open the lid, only to find the handle of the device missing.

"What the hell?"

Shouts and a heavy weight slamming against the door snapped his shocked immobility. He lurched to his feet, casting about the cabin for a heavy object to smash the thing and release the fire within. This would not give him any time to flee, but the stern windows of the great cabin would at least allow him to drown rather than burn.

He clutched the chart table and rifled through the contents, but rolls of parchment and fine navigation instruments were not likely to help him breech the thick ceramic of the lightkeeper's gift. He peered under the table and opened the compartments below, but the light from the swinging lamp did not reach their dim interiors.

Then he realized his own foolishness; there, over his head, hung the answer.

"There's more than one way to burn a ship," he said, steadying himself as he reached up to lift the oil lantern from its hook. As he lifted it free, a tremendous weight hit the door, sending oak splinters flying as both the bolt and its hinges ripped from the frame. Yodrin and Borell burst into the cabin brandishing cutlasses.

Ghelfan dashed the lantern down at their feet. Glass shattered, but the stout bronze vessel did not rupture, and the small trickle of oil that caught fire was less impressive than he'd hoped. Yodrin stepped over the small blaze and advanced on him, cutlass raised.

"Put out the fire, Borell," he said calmly, grinning like a wolf.

"You'll have to kill me, Yodrin," the shipwright said, side-stepping and casting about for something he could use as a weapon.

"Oh, you won't be that lucky, my friend," the pirate captain said, stepping in with a quick jab.

Ghelfan twisted away, but realized instantly that the attack had been a feint. Yodrin lashed out with the bronze bell guard of the cutlass, his stroke as quick as lightning. The heavy guard smashed into the shipwright's cheekbone. Light exploded behind his eyes, and he felt himself falling as the pirate's throaty laughter rang in his ears.

≈

Hippotrin yawed wildly, but Cynthia held on, working her way higher. Her pursuers had abandoned the chase, more concerned with the ship than her. As she reached the last rung of the ratlines, a gust tore her feet from their precarious position, leaving her dangling from hands alone. Terror gripped her for an instant, and the tiny knife tumbled from her mouth as she screamed.

Mouse, on the other hand, was having the time of his life.

The little sprite cackled with glee as they flapped in the hurricane-force wind until Cynthia finally wrapped a leg around a shroud and hugged the tarred hemp for her life. Mouse tugged at her collar, chirping and yipping in encouragement, but she couldn't share his enthusiasm. She gasped for breath and worked for a better perch.

Abruptly, the ship came about and stabilized, her bow pushing upwind, her sails filling and steadying. Cynthia squinted down and saw that someone had taken the helm. Another flash of distant lightning revealed that it was Koybur, his one good hand guiding the ship while he gawked up at her in astonishment.

Laughter bubbled up unbidden from her throat, not only at her former mentor's surprise, but at the entire situation. She laughed at the men on the ratlines below; she laughed at the school of merfolk surrounding the ship; she even laughed at the storm itself, at the rain stinging her face and the swirling clouds overhead backlit by flickering lightning. And with that mirth, that heady, crazy laughter, she realized that she no longer felt the weakness, the nausea or the dizziness of ship's sickness. In this lashing storm, in these mountainous seas, she felt fine. In fact, she felt better than she had in days, which brought even more laughter rushing up like water from a spring.

She climbed higher, up to the top of the foremast, and even up onto the trestletrees that held the topmast in place. She clutched the slick spar and whipped the line that still trailed from one wrist around it, tying a quick bowline to keep herself in place. She was now literally lashed to the mast. Let them come up here and try to cut her down; she would kick them to their deaths one at a time.

Then a sheet of white lit the sky, and her mirth transformed to awe. A great gap in the cloud cover loomed ahead. The eyewall of the storm curved away to the left and right, lightning crackling at its edge. They were sailing right into it, into the very center of the tempest.

Clear sky shone ahead, the wind-torn sea aglow with moonlight. She stared open mouthed at the sight of it, the eye of a hurricane. The cyclonic winds raged around it, hell surrounding a sea of calm, and through that cloudless expanse, she could see stars.

She felt the ship change course, and knew Koybur had also seen it. He intended to take the ship directly into the eye, seeking the calm within.

Through a haze of rain and spray, the pure, white glow of the crescent moon shone through. Cynthia stared awestruck by the insane beauty—the wall of clouds looming ahead and the electricity arcing within it, contrasted by the stars and moon shining in the clear sky beyond.

Something tugged sharply at her neck, jerking and pulling first from one side, then the other, then both together. She looked down to see Mouse wrenching upon the chain of her medallion to get her attention. The little seasprite pointed up at the crescent moon ecstatically, screeching unintelligibly, and pulled on the chain again and again.

"Yes, I see it!" she shouted into the wind. She could also see the deck and the entire crew clustered around the wheel. With that, she knew Ghelfan had failed.

Mouse tugged and pointed relentlessly, ignoring her response.

"Yes, yes, I see it! It's beautiful!" she shouted again. But he didn't heed this new response any more than her last. Finally Cynthia freed one hand to pat him, but he promptly seized her thumb and wrapped the chain of her pendant around it in a series of lightning-fast half hitches.

"Mouse! What the hell are you doing? Stop that!" She pulled her hand away and the chain snapped, drawing Mouse, the chain and the pendant out of her blouse. He clung to the pendant, flapping in the howling wind, yipping, screeching and grinning at her like a little fiend. She clutched him to her, worried that he would blow away, but he just clambered onto her hand, dragging the pendant with him, and pointed to the sky ahead.

She glanced up into the moonlight as he held her crescent medallion up before her, and the similarity struck her dumb. The crescent moon shone down in a perfect likeness to the silver amulet, right down to the cluster of blue, red and yellow stars aligned with the moon's lower horn to form the hilt of the jeweled scimitar. The stars shone in identical colors and configuration to those in the medallion.

"The Scimitar Moon!" she cried, holding the amulet high to view it side by side with the astronomical bodies. "It's real!" She had always thought the pendant just a pretty trinket, an abstract piece of art, not a rendering of an actual astronomical event. But now she knew: the stars and moon of her pendant signified a specific time, a time when the real stars and moon were aligned in an exact pattern.

And that time was now!

Her joyous epiphany took on a life of its own as Cynthia felt the mast come alive with static electricity under her hands. Her hair flew out in all directions as her damp skin crackled with energy. A ball of electricity raced from the mainmast forward along the stay toward her feet. She shouted in alarm, nearly losing her grip on the mast as the pendant, chain and Mouse all began to sputter and glow with sparks of static.

Unintelligible shouts from below drifted up on the howling wind, but she could not spare a glance. She was too busy hanging on to a mast lit with static and trying to save her little friend. But Mouse appeared to be remarkably unaffected by the tingling, snapping discharges racing up and down his little body. He whooped with glee, grasping Cynthia's pendant and fluttering his mangled wings in the howling wind.

Then she felt it, and her eyes were drawn up to the approaching eyewall. "Uh-oh."

Lightning arced along the clouds from both directions, crawling toward them like luminous spiders racing along the wall of clouds. She snatched Mouse with her free hand and flung him aft toward the mainmast, hoping he might somehow land safely. As he left her outstretched fingers, screeching in alarm, the pendant tied to her thumb flared with light. The static around her exploded up through the mast, and the sky above erupted in light and sound.

For one suspended instant, her mind perceived it all. The sea, the stars, the clouds and the thousands of merfolk surrounding *Hippotrin*, all one and the same, one great living thing of which she had just become a part. Her mind opened as lightning arced down to strike the medallion in her hand. The immense pulse of energy passed through her, into the wood she touched, and down the mast to blast the trestletrees beneath her feet to bits. Every thought of Odea, Goddess of Sea and Storms, entered her mind, and it all seemed as simple as a child's whirling top.

Without the braces, the topmast toppled free like the felled crown of a pine, with Cynthia still lashed on. With the link between sky and sea broken, her mind's link to Odea closed like the snap of a twig. The knowledge of the universe fled, leaving her empty and numb. Cynthia watched the glittering surface of the water approach with mild curiosity. The sea swam with lovely shapes, thousands of them outlined in luminescence against the dark of the depths.

Beautiful... she thought at the moment before impact. *How lovely it will be to swim with those luminous shapes at last...*

Then the warmth of Odea's embrace enveloped her, and she knew no more.

≈

A soul-searing cry of anguish tore from Koybur's throat as he watched the topmast pierce the sea like a spear. For a moment, he could only stare into the inky waters where Cynthia had vanished amid the roiling throng of merfolk. A simultaneous flip of tails thrashed the surface as the creatures dove, breaking his dreadful reverie. Decades of training took hold.

"Man overboard!" he bellowed, pulling the wheel hard over to bring the ship around. "Rig a harness! You there, get a line over the side. We've got to—"

The wheel wrenched out of his grasp as something heavy smashed into the blind side of his face. Koybur hit the deck and skidded until he lay in the scuppers, his senses returning as the ship rolled and seawater dashed his face. He sputtered blood and brine and glared back at Yodrin, who had taken the wheel and returned the ship to her former course. The pirate ignored him, shouting orders to secure the broken cordage and check the hull for leaks. Ships struck by lightning might survive untouched or be blown to bits. Miraculously, *Hippotrin* seemed to have taken the brunt of the bolt in her rigging.

Koybur levered himself to his feet as *Hippotrin* sailed into the eye of the storm. The winds eased, and he looked around as Yodrin ordered more sail aloft. To the east, at the edge of the eyewall, loomed the dark silhouette of an island. The unmistakable double peak told him exactly where they were: Vulture Isle, the southern-most in the chain. The Fathomless Reaches and calmer, deeper water lay to the south. If they could clear the island's reef while still in the storm's eye, they would be safe.

His gaze swept aft at their frothing wake, but there was nothing to see. No trace of the fallen mast, no trace of the merfolk, and no trace of Cynthia Flaxal. She had been swallowed by the sea. A wave of exhaustion unlike anything he had felt rose within him; he limped toward the hatchway, thinking only of a warm bunk and dry clothes.

"Get your arse back on this wheel, you old gimp," Yodrin shouted, breaking through his thoughts.

Koybur looked back at the pirate, his gaze as dead as Cynthia Flaxal.

"No."

"No? What the hell do you mean, no? Get over here or I'll have a knife in your gut!"

"You've just cut yer own throat, Yodrin." Koybur grinned his horrible lop-sided grin at the pirate's blank stare. "Bloodwind wanted her alive. No permanent damage, remember? Yer a dead man. You just ain't stopped breathin' yet."

He turned and headed below, ignoring the curses and threats flung at his back. If Yodrin came to kill him, so be it. He'd already killed the only real friend he had. He had only one thing left in this world that he cared about, and he wondered if it was too late for him to save even that.

CHAPTER THIRTY-THREE

Flotsam

THE ENTIRE POPULACE OF Southaven crowded the quay wall as *Orin's Pride* sailed between the breakwaters in a full gale. The storm had hastened the *Pride's* passage home; to Feldrin, it hardly felt like only two full days since they'd left on what was supposed to have been a simple day sail. They'd covered more sea miles than a galleon could have managed in a week.

"Bring her upwind next to the shipyard. We'll kedge off and tie stern-to."

"Aye, Captain." Horace altered heading and shouted orders to the men on the foredeck. "Looks like every man, woman and child in Southaven's here to meet us."

"Good. We need 'em."

Rowland stepped up beside the wheel and stared at the crowded quay. "They were prob'ly worried to start with when we didn't come back, and now seein' only one ship instead of two..."

"More the better," Feldrin said. His stomach clenched at the news he brought.

The ship rounded up in a perfect arc, her bow into the wind to curb their speed as the crew furled the sails. As they began to drift backward, the anchor splashed into the harbor, and the men in the bow paid out rode until her stern bobbed only a dozen feet from the pier. When lines were tied to the bollards and a gangplank secured to the stern he took his crew ashore, leaving a man on watch with strict orders to stand at the boarding plank with a naked cutlass in his hand. As Feldrin stepped onto the pier, questions broke over him like a wave.

"Where's *Hippotrin*?"

"What happened?"

"Where's the Flaxal girl?"

Feldrin pushed through the crowd, eyes straight forward. Finally, a figure of lesser stature but greater momentum than the rest pushed forward and stopped Feldrin's progress with a glare that would have hulled a warship.

"That's far enough!" Dura stood with her broad hands on her broader hips, squinting grimly up at Feldrin. "I aim tu know what's 'appened, and I aim tu know where Master Ghelfan is. Yu're not takin' ano'er step 'til I get me answer."

"*Hippotrin* was taken by pirates," he said without preamble. "The man you know as Troilen was a bloody traitor fer Bloodwind. We don't know about Master Ghelfan or Cyn—or Mistress Flaxal—but Rafen Ulbattaer, Master Keelson and several others were killed."

Shouts rose from the tight cluster of dockyard workers, among them Keelson's two sons, but Feldrin bellowed, "Quiet!" and even Dura fell silent at the rage that flashed onto his usually calm features.

"We've no time fer this! I aim to refit *Orin's Pride* with enough men and weapons to take *Hippotrin* back, but we've gotta move fast if we hope to find her. We'll be takin' volunteers, but only those who'll fight. We sail fer the Shattered Isles on tomorrow mornin's tide. Any merchant captains here who want a piece of the bastards who did this, talk to me tonight at the Starfish. We got a lot to do, and only a day to do it, so don't pester my people with questions. Dura, I need you."

"Damn straight ya need me, laddie," she said, her voice grating like a file on slate. "Yer no' leavin' this 'arbor wi'out me."

"Bloody fine!" He clapped a hand onto her massive shoulder; its strength and her determination filled him with hope that he hadn't felt in two days. With that hope, his fatigue and despair ebbed away. He lifted his head and strode through the crowd, calling out, "Somebody send fer the lightkeeper. We'll be in Keelson's lofting shed."

"What if he won't come?" someone shouted.

"Then tell him I'll come and get him myself, and I *won't* be gentle." He strode toward Keelson's shed, the crowd parting before him like the sea before the prow of a ship.

≈

Cynthia woke coughing and spitting sand and seawater.

She lay in six inches of surf with white sand stretching out before her. The topmast to which she was still bound had floated ashore, and she with it. A warm wave washed over her from foot to head, driving her further ashore and filling her clothes with sand.

She forced herself onto her elbows and coughed, spitting more bits of shell. Crawling forward proved impossible with several hundred pounds of timber hampering her efforts, so she rolled onto her side and sat up in the lap-deep surf, trying to collect her thoughts.

Her mind flooded with insubstantial memories and half-dreams, all jumbled into a morass of images. She remembered climbing the mast, but had no clear recollection of it breaking away or falling into the sea, though it obviously had.

Did the whole ship break up? she wondered.

An image of thousands of webbed hands touching her, caressing her and carrying her filled her mind's eye. She dismissed that as a simple dream, and shook her head to clear it. She remembered Mouse then, and recalled flinging him into the darkness as sparks glittered from her hand and the medallion.

"My medallion!"

She raised her hand; the token still dangled from her thumb where the little sprite had tied it.

"What the...?" She stared at the silver crescent—something she should remember about it. Another shallow breaker broke her reverie, flooding her skirts with grit and rolling her over the buoyant topmast.

Working herself upright as she spit more sand, she untied the knot that secured her to the spar then set to work on the one around her wrist. She fumbled with her left hand and her teeth, the amulet dangling in the way from her left thumb.

First things first, she thought. She applied her fingernails and teeth to the medallion's knotted chain, but was thwarted by wave after warm wave washing over her.

"Bloody hell!" she swore, struggling to her feet. Sand had invaded every bit of her clothing, and the buttons of her blouse had gone missing. The chemise and corset were sodden and full of grit. A memory flashed: sailors clutching at her legs, tearing her skirts off below the knee as she climbed the mast. The storm... thunder and lightening and wild laughter filled her head as she clung to the top of the mast and looked down at... Koybur. With a physical wrench of pain, her mind opened like a hatch giving way to a rogue wave, and the dreadful memories flooded in: Koybur's betrayal, the pirate Yodrin slicing open the soles of her feet, Ghelfan agreeing to set *Hippotrin* ablaze...

She almost fell back into the water.

She stumbled ashore and pitched forward onto her hands and knees, wondering blankly why her feet did not stab her with every step. She rolled onto her backside and pulled her knees tight into her chest, staring out across the sapphire-blue lagoon to the roaring surf beyond the reef. The remnants of the storm raged on, house-high waves crashing onto the barrier of coral, a razor-sharp wall ready to tear apart anything—ship or sailor—that tried to cross it.

"So why am I in one piece?" she asked. Although her clothing hung in tatters, her arms and legs weren't even scratched. She brushed bits of sand and shell from the soles of her feet, but the skin beneath shone unmarred.

"What in the Nine Hells?"

She sat and stared into space, trying to remember what had happened at the top of the mast, but she could recall nothing beyond pitching Mouse into the night.

Why would I do that? she thought, absently picking at the knots in the thin chain of her amulet. Finally, it lay free in her palm. She whipped the broken ends into a quick knot and hung it back around her neck. The topmast still rolled in the surf, and her eyes were drawn to the jagged line of charred wood that ran from its tip to the blasted remnants of the trestletrees.

"Lightning?"

All right, she thought, *lightning struck the mast.* But that conclusion only posed another question: *So how come I'm not dead?* She stood and started forward to inspect the charred spar, when a voice, low pitched and melodious, rose above the roaring surf in a sing-song call.

She whirled to scan the line of jungle beyond the flotsam-strewn beach, sudden hope rising in her chest. Someone lived here! Someone had found her! Someone...

"Uh-oh." Hope withered with her first sight of the two men emerging from the jungle.

They strode onto the beach, the sun glinting on skin darker than well-oiled teak stretched over long, well-muscled frames. Their wide, high-cheekboned faces were adorned with bone and shell ornaments, and their straight black hair was decorated with colorful feathers. They wore barely enough to cover their loins, but carried an assortment of items. One held a fishing spear, and the other a bow, one slim arrow nocked and ready. Each also bore a curved club set with sharp stones. They smiled as they approached, but the smiles seemed more the bared fangs of wolves than signs of welcome.

Cannibals, she thought, recalling all the grim tales of the savages of the Shattered Isles. *And dinner just washed up on the beach!*

She looked right and left; nothing but sand strewn with downed palm trees curved away from her on both sides, open and seemingly endless. She had nowhere to run, which didn't really matter considering their long legs and her sodden, encumbering clothing. She backed up, but her heels met with the fallen topmast and she pitched backward into the surf, yelping in alarm.

Laughter, it seemed, was the same in any language. Their mirth rolled forth in a throaty roar as they advanced, wading into the surf without pause. She scrabbled up and backed into the water, thinking only to put something, anything, between her and the two savages. The water deepened, slowing her retreat.

"Stop!" she shouted, throwing out her hands as if to hold them back, fear surging through her. "Just stop or I'll—"

Their reaction caught her off guard. She hoped they might slow their approach or even stop, but when they suddenly stared wide eyed, turned and ran for the shore, she stood dumbfounded. Then she heard the roar of surf, and looked over her shoulder.

She screeched in shock as a huge breaker reared up from the lagoon and swept forward, towering over her in a curl of azure and white. She braced herself for it, knowing it would bowl her over and tumble her down onto the hard sand. When it passed her without even ruffling her matted hair, she cautiously opened her eyes and stood in shock.

She watched the wave roar up the beach, chasing the fleeing men and rolling the fallen spar up onto dry sand before crashing flat. Even the backwash, which should have swept her off her feet, passed her by with no more than a brush at her legs. She stood in thigh-deep water, looking around for the source of the phenomenon. The shocked cries of the men turned to menacing mutters as they stared at her suspiciously, brandishing their weapons.

"What the hell?"

They approached again, this time more cautiously, their smiles absent. She watched them come, her mind whirling with too many questions. Where had the wave come from? Why hadn't it smashed her down like it should have?

She put her hands down into the water and swirled them about, but felt nothing unusual. The two men stood at the edge of the surf, staring at her cautiously and conversing in a melodious and alien language. Finally, they strode slowly forward, watching her every move.

"I said, stop!" she shouted again. This time, as she uttered the words she felt a rush of warmth. Once again, the sea surged past her, forming into a wave right in front of her, which, like its predecessor, chased the two men up onto the beach, then receded harmlessly.

"I did that," she muttered, realizing that both waves had come at her bidding, rising up to shield her from the approaching men. "But how?" She put her hands into the water and willed it to do something, anything.

Up! she thought.

The sea rose up around her, a mound of water flooding in from all directions until it covered her hips, then her stomach, and finally stopped when she overcame her surprise and thought, *Stop!*

The level of water held at her chest, a perfect dome perhaps ten strides across, centered on her. She looked around, but the rest of the lagoon glittered calm and unruffled. Cynthia could feel it now, the warmth of the sea surrounding her, permeating her as if it did not stop at her skin, but flowed through her every pore. She could also feel a slight effort, as if she held her arms out straight and her shoulders were beginning to tire.

Cries of alarm and fear snapped her attention, and the mound of water collapsed into concentric waves that broke on the shore in gentle curves.

The two men shouted at one another, pointing at her and gesticulating. They obviously did not know what to make of her, and were not about to try to capture her if it meant walking through a wall of angry water.

"But how?" she asked in bewilderment, struggling to remember what had passed, where she might have encountered this kind of power. Had the lightning affected her? Had Mouse imbued her with some faerie magic?

"Magic..." And with that word, that thought, her hand caressed the medallion at her breast. "Sea magic."

Cynthia lifted the scimitar moon medallion and held it up, stirring the memory of the previous night, when the sky held that very image. The alignment of the moon with the distinctive cluster of stars combined with the storm... *her* storm.

"Odea's requirements..." she said softly, remembering the words she'd read in her father's journal.

She tried her new trick again, holding out a hand and forming a simple request in her mind. *Up to my hand.*

To her surprise and delight, a column of water geysered up to splash her palm.

Laughter bubbled up from her throat in response. She tried it again, and again, swirling the water around her in patterns and wavelets at the sweep of her hand, sending it up into spouts and spurts with flicks of her fingers, laughing with each new display. Her father's gift had been awakened in her; she could feel the power, and more than the power, she felt a surge of satisfaction that she finally had a link to her parents that could never be broken.

More cries from the confused men drew her attention, but now instead of brandishing weapons, they had cast them aside and knelt on the sand, arms outstretched, palms up in supplication. They glanced up at her furtively, but cast their eyes down when she met their gazes. She laughed again, this time in satisfaction.

"Well, who's scared now?"

She risked a few steps forward, pulling a standing wave with her. The men remained still, mumbling in their own language, oblivious to her approach. She couldn't trust them, she knew, but if she could maintain a sufficient level of fear, she might get out of this in one piece. She would need food at the very least, and a boat, if they had one. She had no doubt that

Feldrin would scour the archipelago for her, so even a signal fire might be sufficient.

She wrapped a column of seawater around herself from her hips down and strode into the ankle-deep portion of the surf. *This,* she thought, *should be adequately impressive.* One of them glanced up, and immediately cowered again at the sight of her watery dress.

"You have boats?" she asked, not really expecting them to understand, but hoping they might, and not knowing what else to try. If they did understand, and thought her some sort of wizard or deity, they just might comply. "You bring me boat. You have food. You bring me food." The last, she realized with a start, might yield something she would not want to eat if they were indeed cannibals.

They remained silent and impassive, quivering in fear.

"Bloody hell," she muttered, stepping forward. "Come on, boys. Go get your headman for me. Maybe he can understand me. I need you to bring me food and a boat. Food and a boat, understand? Food and a—"

As she spoke and took one more step forward, the gentle waves swept back down the beach into the lagoon, leaving her standing on the damp sand. As she lost contact with the surf, the cocoon of water enveloping her collapsed with a splash. Cynthia stood in her dripping, torn skirt and ripped blouse, staring at the two dark faces that gazed up at her in surprise.

Their smiles slowly returned.

"Damn." She whirled and fled for the security of the water, but the length of rope tied to her wrist flung out in an arc and slapped into the outstretched palm of one of her erstwhile admirers.

The line came taut and jerked her right off her feet. She let out an involuntary squeal of alarm and landed like a sack of wet meal falling from the back of a wagon. Before she could even think, she was being dragged up the beach, the rough hemp once again digging painfully into her wrist. Halfway up the beach she thought to call on the sea for aid, and a great breaker roared ashore, but it failed to even wet her feet.

She felt the transition from sand to the soft mat of detritus beneath the canopy of jungle, but the pace of her captors didn't slow. She bumped and bounced along, cursing and crying out in pain and alarm every time they dragged her over a root or branch.

How ironic, she thought, *to finally receive the blessings of my father, only to be eaten by cannibals.*

≈

Mouse hunkered in the crook of the main topmast trestletrees, wedged into the tiny gap between plank and spar as tightly as a cork in a rum bottle.

The storm had finally subsided with the dawn, and though he had en-joyed the ride, he missed Cynny and wanted to find her as soon as he could. But things weren't looking good. First, she had thrown him away just when things were getting fun. That nearly sent him flying loose in the middle of a hurricane, but he'd managed to grasp a flapping halyard and hoist himself to the top of the mainmast. Now, however, he was pretty much stuck. He had no wings to speak of and couldn't fly more than a few feet. If he climbed down, someone would likely see him.

Odea's favored or no, he doubted if Yodrin would quail at squishing a seasprite, so shinnying down the mast wasn't a good idea. There was so much Mouse didn't understand. He thought Koybur and Cynny were friends. And he thought Troilen was also a friend, but now they called him Yodrin, and he wasn't a friend. It was all very confusing, so Mouse did what he usually did when things scared and confused him.

He hid.

He was good at hiding, having done so for more than a decade while the broom-wielder ruled the big house. He had thought his hiding days were over, but now it looked like he would have to go into hiding again.

He hunkered down out of the wind, sighing, and wished Cynny were here. Cynny was fun. Cynny climbed masts in storms and called the light-ning down to play. He wished she hadn't gone swimming with the fish people. The one place he couldn't follow her was underwater.

He sighed again; he missed her already.

CHAPTER THIRTY-FOUR

Unexpected Guests

BEING DRAGGED THROUGH THE jungle is usually not conducive to a good mood on the part of the one being dragged, even if that person is not expecting to be eaten at the end of the ordeal. Consequently, Cynthia was mad enough to chew iron and spit nails when her two escorts deposited her into a large clearing beneath a ring of towering banyan trees. Exhausted, sore and filthy from head to foot, she struggled to her feet and let out a stream of profanity that would have made her grandfather blush.

Musical language and laughter brought her up short; she stood in the center of an entire village of natives, none wearing much more than a bit of grass or leather around their loins, numerous necklaces and body jewelry of bone and mother of pearl. Cynthia stood and stared, watching the unfamiliar faces examining at her, listening to the whispers and trying to gauge their moods... or their appetites.

Her two captors yammered on to the audience, gesticulating wildly. From the pantomime, she guessed they were describing her tricks with the waters of the lagoon. The dark-skinned faces grew wide-eyed and slack-jawed at the tale, and some even averted their eyes from hers. She thought about trying to make a run for it, but knew they would catch her in an instant. While weighing her options, Cynthia finally managed to get the rough hemp line untied from around her wrist. She winced and blew on the ravaged flesh to soothe the bloody abrasion, but a shout from the midst of the crowd startled her, and silenced the throng.

A man with the girth of a small whale strode forward, a huge gnarled stick set with all manner of stones in one meaty hand. Bones rattled from half a dozen necklaces, and the feathers of an entire flock of tropical birds adorned his hair, neck, arms and loins. Around both wrists he wore spiral tusks, and from his ears hung two gleaming white shark's teeth, each as large as the palm of Cynthia's hand.

The headman, or shaman? she wondered, eyeing him cautiously as he inspected her. His eyes were sharp and shrewd, and did not shy away from meeting her gaze. He barked a short command at the two who had captured her and they stepped forward. He was not smiling, and they shuffled their feet nervously. A few sharp questions yielded hesitant answers, then he took a step toward her, his stride confident but cautious.

Cynthia backed away. He bore no weapon, but she felt like he was sizing her up for the cook pot.

He said a few words to her, smiling and holding out one pudgy palm, all the sharp edges of his tone suddenly gone. He took one more cautious step, but she again backed away.

The exasperation on his face would have been humorous if Cynthia weren't so utterly terrified. He turned away, scanning the crowd before shouting a single word. Everyone mumbled and repeated the word, and several cried out what sounded like answers. A bent old man hobbled out from under one of the huge banyans, leaning heavily on the shoulder of a strong young boy as he worked his way through the crowd. Cynthia saw immediately his need for support: his left leg ended at the ankle. He walked gingerly on the stump, using the boy as a crutch.

Aside from missing a foot, the man also appeared only slightly younger than the island itself, and the years had not treated him with a kind touch. His eyes were hazy, and his back bent. Hands like fists full of walnuts gripped the boy's shoulder, and when he grimaced at the obvious pain of every step, she could see that he had few good teeth remaining in his mouth.

When he finally stood nearby, the headman barked that one word again and added a string of other words. Then, to Cynthia's astonishment, the old man spoke to her in her own language, though broken and heavily accented.

"You some kine-a wizaad, eh? He say you move wata. Make wave big as a baobab tree." He squinted at her. "What he say true?"

"I, uh..." She thought about claiming to be a mighty sorceress, but for all she knew they burned mages for sport. The truth seemed the safest option. "I don't know. I have some... some way to make the water do what I ask, but I don't think I'm a wizard. I mean, I don't know any spells or anything."

"Hmph." He looked back to the headman and said a few things, then received additional instructions, which he translated. "He say you Odea's child. You swim wit da fish folk? You make da storm come? Or do da storm bring you from Odea? You Odea's gift to us, dey say."

"I am not a gift from Odea. My father was a seamage, and I think that I received some of his powers from the storm." Cynthia's curiosity began to overcome her fear. "Who are you, anyway? What island is this?"

"You fada? Who be you fada, girl?"

"Tell me your name first," she shot back obstinately.

"Ha!" He turned and rattled off a few unintelligible words to the headman, who laughed and grinned. "I be Whuafa," he said, making the name

264 ≈ Scimitar Moon

three distinct syllables. "Now what be you name, and who be you fada?"

"I'm Cynthia Flaxal. My father was Orin Flaxal."

The ancient eyes widened. "Flaxal? Na. You no be Flaxal." He shook his head sharply, his hazy eyes squinting at her. "You don' look notin' like 'im."

"You knew him? You knew my father?" She stepped forward, eager to learn more, even if he had only met her father in passing.

"Knew 'im, aye. Lost me foot to a shark de day we met. Saved me life, 'e did. Sent dat shark away wi' a wave of 'is 'and." He hobbled forward, his rheumy eyes narrowing. "Knew 'im well enough ta know what 'e wore 'round 'is neck! You got dat? You got dat same token?"

Cynthia realized that he had seen the chain around her neck, though the medallion lay hidden beneath her chemise. She drew it over her head and showed it to him. "Yes, I've got his medallion."

His ancient hand shot out, quick as a snake, bony fingers grasping her sore wrist with hysterical strength. He thrust her hand high and shouted at the top of his withering voice, "Shambata daroo!"

The entire population of the village charged forward, all of them shouting the strange words. Two hundred hands reached for her, a hundred voices crying out their glee. Laughter and shouts rang out all around, the headman bellowing commands that drew more shouts of assent. Hands grasped Cynthia, lifting her up and bearing her along. She screeched in protest, her fears of becoming their next meal instantly renewed. Then she heard Whuafa's reedy voice rise above the din.

"Relax, Cynthie Flaxal! You is da seamage! You is oua save-ya!"

Savior? She thought, trying not to fight the hundreds of hands bearing her along to who knew where. *You've got to be kidding me!*

≈

"Can you build it?" Feldrin asked, stepping back from his rough plans.

"Oh, aye. Easy enough. Though it might could use a bit'o beefin' up around the windings. How many you need?" She drew out a pair of calipers and started taking measurements from the rough drawings.

"Four at least. Depends on what the lightkeeper can come up with by mornin'. What about *Orin's Pride?*"

"Don't presume tu teach me ma own business, laddie. I c'n turn out the parts for half a dozen o' these contraptions by mornin' and they c'n assemble 'em aboard. The *Pride*'ll be fit fer sea a'fore sunset. Keelson's boys're all over it like ants on an apple core."

"Bloody fine. Now I've got to see about that old—"

"Feldrin!" Rowland's shout brought him around with a snap.

"Row, tell me you've got good news." He'd sent the cook into town to rally support from the locals. Without any ready cash, he doubted just how willing they would be to donate or loan their goods and services to the cause.

"Easier just to show ya." He waved him to the door, his ancient face splitting into a grin.

"Holy mother of..." Feldrin's voice drifted off as he took in the maelstrom of activity outside.

Six wagons sat upon the quay, an army of workers unloading provisions, weapons, tools and a hundred other items that he hadn't even thought to ask for. Beside *Orin's Pride*, two fat galleons were kedged off and tied stern to, their cargoes being off-loaded onto low river barges. He knew both ships; *Winter Gale* and *Southern Star*. The captains of both ships strode through the crowd toward him, their eyes as hard as diamonds.

"A nasty business, this," Dorren Clearwater, captain of *Southern Star* said grimly, extending his long-fingered hand to Feldrin. "Knew Benjamin Garrison all my life. Now his granddaughter's been taken by that bastard Bloodwind? Nasty business, indeed."

"I can't believe what Rowland told us about Koybur. I've known him near twenty years!" Uben shook his hand as well, and matched the Morrgrey's powerful grip. "So what's yer plan, Brelak?"

"You offerin' to help?" Feldrin didn't have time for banter, they would either say yes, or he had no use for them.

"More'n offerin', I think." Dorren nodded over his shoulder. "Already off-loadin' cargo and takin' on supplies. *Southern Star* ain't so speedy as your new schooner there, but she'll haul twice the men and four times the provisions."

"Schooner? You mean the *Pride*?"

"Oh, aye, you weren't here fer that. When you sailed out of the harbor every sea captain and mate in Southaven was up on the hill watchin'. Lorri Fender of the *Provender* said 'Don't they just schoon right along, now,' and the name stuck."

"Well, that's as good as any name, I guess."

"Damn near every captain in port has offered to help, though some can't commit their ships." Uben pointed out the ships still on their moorings or along the main city quay. "The *Independent*, *Southwind*, *Star Chaser*, and *Syren Song* are all comin' along, though we'll have to near empty Southaven to man 'em all." He grinned and clapped Feldrin's broad shoulder. "You've got a whole fleet, lad! Now we've got to sit down and decide how to put it to best use."

"Fine! Bloody fine!" Feldrin sighed like the weight of the world had just been lifted from his shoulders. "Tonight, then, at the Starfish. Bring every captain who'll come, and we'll lay out a plan."

"And we sail on the mornin' tide," Uben added.

"Aye," Brelak agreed, setting his jaw firmly. "We sail fer the Shattered Isles at dawn."

≈

Hippotrin limped into Blood Bay under reduced sail. As her anchor splashed into the water half a dozen longboats rowed from shore, Bloodwind in the foremost, his personal guard, his sorceress and his bride-to-be in company. As his launch pulled alongside, the pirate captain leapt aboard, his broad hand grasping that of the ship's captain in camaraderie.

"Well done, Yodrin!" He pumped the slim half-elf's hand, his eyes taking in the salt-crusted decks and the storm-worn rigging and crew. "She's a bit worse for wear, but she's ours, and that's what really matters. Well done, indeed!"

"I only regret that we could not take both ships, Captain," Yodrin said as Bloodwind turned to help Camilla aboard.

"Bah! A fish in the basket's worth two in the bay." He pulled Camilla close and began a slow circuit of the deck. "Smaller than I'd thought, but I imagine she's a speedy craft."

"We logged near twenty knots in the storm, sir. She'll make better than five points to the wind."

"And the prisoners? They fared well, I trust."

Yodrin stopped short, his calm features stiffening with apprehension.

"Only one prisoner survived the trip, sir. The Flaxal girl went mad during the storm. She climbed the ratlines and lashed herself to the topmast. We were struck by lightning, and as you can see, the fore-top went by the board. There was no way to recover her in the storm."

"That is..." Bloodwind paused, his elation slackening somewhat as his eyes took on a far-off look. "...disappointing. I assume she was restrained."

"Of course, sir. Bound securely."

"And yet she escaped." He fingered his ruddy beard, his broad smile thinning. "How might that have happened?"

"We don't know, sir. They got a knife somehow. They must have had help. I have my suspicions, but no proof."

"*They* had help?" One eyebrow raised in question, a danger signal for everyone who knew the pirate captain. "*Both* of them escaped?"

"Briefly, sir. They tried to sabotage the ship. Ghelfan was subdued and secured in my cabin. The Flaxal girl was lost."

"And your suspicions?" His eyes raked the small crew like a loaded ballista.

"That'd be me." Koybur emerged from belowdecks, hobbling forward, his one good eye focused on Bloodwind. "Which is just plain stupid."

"That's the last time you use that mouth, gimp!" Yodrin snarled, a dagger flashing into his hand too fast for anyone to see. He started forward, but a broad hand on his shoulder stopped him.

"Why, Mister Koybur! We finally meet in the flesh." Bloodwind smiled, dismissing Yodrin's rage as he stepped between the two. Camilla gasped, but Bloodwind's grip on her arm silenced her outburst.

"Your services have been indispensable over the years, my good man." Bloodwind extended a hand, but Koybur just looked at it, then up at the pirate's face, his one eye narrowing.

"I didn't do it fer yer thanks, Bloodwind. I did it fer my daughter. On yer word; I've done yer dirty work fer more'n a dozen years. We stand on the deck of the last part of our deal. You promised me if I got you one of Cynthia Flaxal's ships, you'd give me Camilla. Let me see my Cammy."

Bloodwind's hand dropped slowly, but his smile remained intact. Such an insult from any other man would have earned a knife in the belly, but Bloodwind knew that if he killed Koybur, he would lose Camilla. But that didn't mean he couldn't *hurt* the man.

"See her? Why she's right here. Don't you recognize your own daughter?" He nudged Camilla forward as if displaying her, arrayed as she was in sensuous silks and glittering jewelry.

"What?" Koybur's face fell. The pent-up rage of fifteen years seeped away like water poured into sand. He looked her up and down, and in his slack features Bloodwind could see that he knew she was no slave. "Cammy?"

"Daddy, I—"

"And your arrival could not have come at a better time," Bloodwind continued, cutting her off before she could ruin his surprise. "You'll be able to give away the bride."

"The *what?*"

He had not thought the old cripple's face could register more shock, but he was wrong. The man's good hand quaked at his side, his stance wavering unsteadily, until Bloodwind thought he might collapse. Koybur's good eye roamed over his daughter, her immaculate clothes, the intricate braids of her hair, the exquisite jewelry. He noted how closely Bloodwind held her, and how she accepted that embrace.

"You... you can't." Koybur's maimed features hardened, disbelief evolving into anguish. "Cammy, you can't *want* this!"

"I..."

Camilla trembled against him, and though Bloodwind showed nothing, he felt some of that tension in himself. Her answer would shape not only her future, but that of her father and countless others. If she denied him now, Koybur served no purpose. But this moment also defined her commitment to him. Bloodwind had devoted much to cultivating her as his perfect bride; if she had lied to him, if her love proved false, his wrath would sweep the southern continent in a tidal wave of blood.

"He's more than just a pirate, Daddy. He's building a whole empire here. He wants me to share it with him, *really* share it." Camilla paused, and Bloodwind felt the tension melt away from her. She had accepted it; she had accepted *him*. "I... I do want it."

As Koybur stared at her, disbelief plain on his scarred features, Bloodwind allowed himself a smile and a sigh of relief. With her simple commitment all their futures congealed into one: *his* future, his vision. It all unfolded in his mind, an immutable truth of what would be.

"So, you see," he said, dispelling the gravity of the moment with a wry wit, "we are about to become in-laws. Rather ironic, considering I've always been known as an *outlaw*." Everyone laughed dutifully—everyone except Koybur and Camilla.

"Then it was all fer nothin'," Koybur said as the laughter died, his stare boring into her like an auger. "All the blood on my hands, all the lives, and when I finally come to take you away from him, you want to *stay*. Do you know...do you have any *idea*...what I've done to get you back?"

His raspy old voice cracked at the last, his shoulders slumping as all the fortitude that held the pain at bay melted away, leaving nothing but a husk of agony and scars. He turned away, all confidence, all strength gone from his ungainly gait as he limped back to the hatchway and descended the companionway steps into *Hippotrin*.

Bloodwind turned to Yodrin. "I want no foolishness with him, Yodrin. No one harms him. Understood?" Camilla would love him all the more for keeping her father from harm.

"Aye, sir." He didn't sound happy about the order, but Bloodwind didn't particularly care.

"Good. When everyone's ashore, tell Koybur I want to see him. Bring the ship over to the yard dock and have them fit her with a new topmast and clean her up. We'll gut her and fit her for crew instead of cargo. I've had two ballistae built for her. I want her ready to hunt in a week."

"Aye, sir!" Yodrin's mood improved instantly with the orders. "She'll be ready!"

"See that she is. And have Master Ghelfan brought to the great hall. I'd like to talk with him." Bloodwind took one more look around the deck of his newest prize. With a smile of satisfaction, he gathered up his entourage and disembarked, his spirits soaring. That confidence might have been shaken had he known the malice burning behind the tiny pair of eyes that followed his departure from high atop the mainmast.

CHAPTER THIRTY-FIVE

Unexpected Feasts

LITTLE MOANS OF PLEASURE escaped Cynthia's lips as strong fingers kneaded her soapy scalp, massaged her shoulders and rubbed the soles of her feet. Water just short of scalding and smelling faintly of sulfur lapped at her chin. She smiled as bowl after bowl cascaded over her head, rinsing her hair free of the lather.

She leaned back and half floated, utterly relaxed.

Apprehension had given way to embarrassment when the throng of natives brought her to the hot springs and started stripping away her filthy clothing. At first she wondered if they intended to make soup, but when she saw one of them readying soaproot and sponges she stopped fighting. A bath was just what she needed.

Their amusement with her undergarments, especially the corset, broke some of the tension, but with half of the crowd men, she couldn't quite relax. When she was down to only her scanties and chemise, she opted to simply climb into the spring. This brought even more laughter from the crowd, but that was not the end of Cynthia's discomfort, for two men and two women waded in after her and began bathing her head to foot. That took some getting used to.

The crowd drifted away, taking her clothes. They returned bearing only a mat of plaited grasses woven with flowers, and a few wreaths of blossoms. The mat fit around her hips, but exposed a wide swath of thigh, while the wreaths covered the front of her torso, but left her back and midriff completely bare.

"If Grandma could see me now, she'd faint," she muttered, securing the wreaths with a strand of plaited grass tied behind her back.

As they escorted her back to the village, the aromas of wood smoke and cooking meat reminded her that she had not eaten in two days. Woven mats lay around a huge fire pit, over which slabs of meat, fish and even a few skewered fowl roasted on spits. Her escorts seated her as others brought bowls of fruit, dates and figs, as well as wooden cups filled with some type of fruit juice that bit her tongue as if spiked.

Whuafa hobbled over, grinning widely. "You see, Cynthie Flaxal? You in no danja. You is oua guest. Dis feast fa you!" He waved one skinny arm and would have toppled over if not for his stout helper.

"Please! Sit with me. I would like to talk, and if you could translate it would be much easier."

"My plesha!" He eased himself down onto the mat with considerable help.

"You must forgive me for the way I acted earlier. I was scared."

"I undastan," he said, accepting a cup from a passing girl and drinking deeply.

"There are stories about cannibals that live on these islands."

"Oh, aye, dere be many stories. Some true. Some not so true." He popped a fig in his mouth and gummed it into submission. "We do no eat da long pig, da man meat, but de oddas do. We say why, when dere is fish an pig an bird to eat what don fight back so much. Sometimes de oddas come an' try to take some of oua people, but we fight dem and kill dem. Make head on stick to tell dem not come back. You lucky we fine you fust." He reached out and pinched her arm, laughing. "You be tasty!"

Even a day before, such an inference would have revolted her, but now she somehow saw the humor, though the thought of cannibals did still elicit concern. "They're here? On this island?"

"Oh, shua, but you don' worry. Dey come, we kill dem and put head on stick. Dey know dat."

"You seem confident," she said, accepting a piece of cooked meat from a passerby. She sniffed it hesitantly to ensure it was really pork, not something else.

"Oh, aye. Between de oddas an dem pirates, we get good at fightin'. We no let 'em take nobody!"

"Pirates? You know about Bloodwind?"

"Dunno no Bloodwin', but we know about dem pirates. Hard not to. Dey come an' try to take da young 'uns. Dunno why. Maybe day eats 'em. Ha! We chase 'em back all da way to dere islan' once, but dey got lotta ship dere. Lotta men wit' steel sward. We can't fight 'em dere."

"You know which island they use as a base?" Excitement gripped her. "Where? Which one?"

"Oh, it de one wit de big smoke all de time. Not de one on fire, but de one what smoke."

"Plume Island." Cynthia mulled over the revelation. Bloodwind would be in for one big surprise when she managed to get home, raise an armada, return and ram the whole thing right down his throat. She lost herself in that fantasy for a moment, but realized that her plan might fail before it started if she did not get home. For that matter, she didn't even know where she was. "And how far is the pirate's island?"

"Why? You planning on goin' dere? Ha!" Whuafa downed his cup of juice and took two more, handing her one. "It be seven islan's up de chain.

We be most sout'. De merchant men call dis Vulture Isle cause o' de big birds what make dere nests on de mountain."

"Seven islands," she muttered, sipping the juice and nibbling at the roast pork while trying to remember her charts. "About sixty sea miles. Now all I need is a boat." She reached for a passing bowl of fruit, but almost pitched over. Her wreaths slipped, and she had to tuck herself back into place to avoid indecency. She shook her head and laughed, finding it utterly hilarious. "What the hell's wrong with me?"

"Wrong? Ha! Notin' wrong, Cynthie Flaxal. It's da drink! It got you!"

She looked at her cup and sniffed it. "So that's it. It *is* spiked! Where did you get the alcohol?"

"Oh, we make it. Put de juice in de cocoanut an' let it bake in de sun two day, you gotta *good* drink!" He drank again and laughed long and hard. "Oh, here come de chief man. He got big presen' for you! *Big* presen'!"

"A present? What..." One glance at the presents and Cynthia knew this would be a very long day indeed.

≈

"Gentlemen, thanks for comin'. Please have a seat." Six captains took seats around a table laden with food and pitchers of ale surrounding a large-scale chart of the Shattered Isles. "Brulo's put out some food fer us, not ta mention crackin' open his larder to help us provision." He raised his tankard to the innkeeper, but the rotund fellow waved the gratitude away.

"Least I could do for little Cynthia," Brulo said as they all began filling their plates.

The company nodded and murmured agreement around mouthfuls of welcome food. They had been working all day, and would be throughout the night. They all knew Cynthia one way or another, most having sailed under the Garrison flag at one point in their careers.

Feldrin broke the uncomfortable silence by smacking his palm down on the chart. "So here we got our problem. More'n a hundred isles, many wi' reefs and coves not well charted, and any one of 'em could hide a fleet of corsairs."

"More'n one's my bet," Dulky Tak of the *Syren Song* said, stuffing half of a gravy-soaked potato into his mouth.

"I spoke to Master Kurian, and he said the storm swept right over Vulture Isle on a west-nor'west course. Our course when we parted ways with *Hippotrin* was sou'-sou'west, and headin' right fer the Fathomless Reaches. When we turned back, the wind had clocked to sou'-sou'east. We might've made our course, but we'd've been sailin' right into the teeth of it."

"And you think that's what Troilen, er, I mean Yodrin, did?" asked Henri Farr, captain of the *Independent*. "You turned north; why wouldn't he?"

"No port'd take 'im if the storm turned north, and he'd have nowhere ta go but through the shallows."

"That'd be suicide in a hurricane," Dorrin Clearwater added, agreeing with Feldrin. "He'd've made for deep water."

"Which would've put him right in the middle of it. The ship must have been lost."

Feldrin shook his head at Brulo's comment. "Not if he's much of a sailor. The schooners handle weather well, though they're wet. If he made deep water, he could run before it, or turn back north on the other side o' the islands."

"Which could've put him several hundred miles out to sea."

"Exactly!" Feldrin agreed, nodding his thanks to Uben. "So here's what we do to catch him when he limps home." He drew seven diverging lines from Southaven toward the southern third of the island chain. "Each ship takes a different course, the slower on the more northerly shorter courses, and the faster on the longer southerly courses. Once we're there, we take up station on the leeward side and run patrol patterns, meetin' at scheduled times to keep a line of communication."

He drew seven zig-zag lines back and forth along the west side of the island chain, their ends almost touching. "We communicate by flag signal."

"How long do we patrol?"

"Until we find the bastard." Feldrin nodded to Brulo. "Each of us is layin' in more'n a month's stores. If we miss him, we search as long as it takes."

"And what about Bloodwind?" Julian Ventis of the *Southwind* asked. "He could pounce on us like a cat on a mouse."

"The galleons should keep a safe distance from the islands. Stay close enough to see sails on the horizon, but far enough out to make a run up or down the chain for help if you come under attack." Brelak leaned onto the table, his broad fists pressing down until the stout oak creaked in complaint. "But make no mistake, gentlemen, I mean to fight him. We'll all be loaded to the gun'als with men and weapons. If it's a lone corsair, make to flee, lure him in, grapple, board and cut 'em to pieces. If it's two or three of 'em, run toward yer nearest ally and we'll crush 'em together."

"And what do we do about them damn ballista they use?" Ventis asked pointedly.

"We've got somethin' better." Brelak pushed his chair back, reached under the table and pulled up a small rum cask. It was labeled with a single character, nothing any of them could read.

"What're we gonna do, get 'em drunk and take advantage of 'em?" Several dry laughs broke out at Ventis' comment, but Feldrin was not deterred.

"This here's a present from the lightkeeper." The laughter died as their eyes widened; the old mage had earned their respect, and more than a little fear.

Brelak placed the small keg on the table, rotating it until they could see the waxed cord sticking out from one side, a bronze hook spliced into its end. "Dura's buildin' six small catapults to throw these. We should be able to pitch 'em about a hundred yards."

"What's in 'em?" Captain Farr asked, eying the thing dubiously.

"Hell." Feldrin fingered the clip at the end of the pull cord. "Pull this hard, an' the barrel erupts like a volcano. Clip it to a length of line long enough to get the thing away from yer ship 'afore it goes off. Just one of these is a corsair killer."

"Bloody hell," Farr said in a hoarse whisper.

"How many do we have?" Uben asked.

"Right now only six, but he's workin' through the night; tells me he should have more'n a dozen by mornin'."

"Two per ship? That's not much."

"Should be enough. Remember, just one is enough to catch a whole ship afire. If there's one thing I'd trust him with, it's how to set things burnin'."

"And what about *Hippotrin*? Do we burn her, too?" Uben's question brought everyone's eyes back to Feldrin.

"You won't be able to catch her," he said with a wry smile. "But no; if Cynthia or Ghelfan might be aboard, I don't want to risk it. If she's sighted, we'll chase her down, board her and get 'em back."

≈

"May I be excused, my captain?" Camilla asked, suppressing a wave of nausea at the display of cruelty she'd been forced to witness. The shipwright Ghelfan sat tied to a chair at the other end of the feasting table, near starvation and unable to take a single bite. The taunts of Bloodwind's men were not gentle. She knew first hand what Ghelfan was going through, and it disgusted her. "I've lost my appetite."

"Oh, I'm sorry, my dear. Of course." He made a dismissive gesture. "You need not be here while Master Ghelfan learns his place."

"I'm sure he will learn quickly, my captain." She rose, bowed to him graciously and left the room.

Guards and servants bowed as Camilla hurried along the corridor in a swirl of multihued silks. Bloodwind had given her freedom to roam the palace and even the town, and she found the autonomy enjoyable.

Not such a bad bargain, she thought, justifying to herself once again that her decision had been the right one.

The shock of meeting her father after so long, seeing for the first time the twisted remnant of the man she'd known, had worn off. That shock had evolved into a sharp annoyance. He assumed she knew nothing of what he had gone through, not taking into account what the past fifteen years had been for her. After so much torment, when she had finally been given a means to end the torture, how could she not take the opportunity?

But he's still my father, she reminded herself. She had to confront him, but she had to do it alone, without Bloodwind looming over them.

Reaching her rooms, she quickly changed into a simpler dress and comfortable shoes, added a cloak with a hood, and hurried out. At the entrance to the keep the night guards barred the doors. Although she had her freedom, she was still subject to Bloodwind's curfew.

"Let me through," Camilla ordered them. "I am going to fetch my father. Captain Bloodwind wishes to speak with him." Both statements were technically true, although their implied meaning might not be.

"He sent you without a guard?" one of them asked skeptically.

"Of course not." Once again, her statement was true, her haughty demeanor adding just the right air of command. She knew if she were caught, there would be questions. Questions were always attended by Bloodwind's sorceress, and Hydra could tell if she had lied. "So which of you is going to accompany me?"

"We can't leave our post, Miss Camilla. You know that."

"Then summon someone to go with me, but be quick about it. I don't want to keep the captain waiting."

"Very well." One of them stepped into the guardhouse only a few strides from the keep's looming entrance and emerged a moment later with a rumpled and slightly drunk member of the day watch.

"I'm sorry, Miss Camilla, but I can't—"

"You can't protect your captain's fiancé? Is that what you were about to say?"

He stared at her, surprised at her tone. Until very recently she had been nothing but a slave, albeit a most vaunted slave; now she snapped orders like a boatswain.

"Oh, come now! It won't take long. You'll be back in an hour, and you can return to your rum and your trollop. I'm sure she'll forgive you your absence more than Captain Bloodwind would forgive you for letting me leave the keep unguarded. Let's go!"

"Very well, Miss. Just hang on while I get a... Hey, slow down!"

Camilla didn't slow and didn't look back as the guard scrambled to the guardhouse, retrieved a cutlass and rushed down the steps behind her. She had very little time before Bloodwind tired of Ghelfan and came looking for her.

In the third pub she visited, if the ramshackle shack could even be called a pub, she found Koybur in a corner, a bottle clutched in his one good hand, his chin resting on his chest.

"Damn," she swore, hoping he hadn't been knocked on the head and robbed. She knelt and lifted his chin, whispering, "Daddy? Daddy, wake up. It's me, Cammy. Come on. Wake up!"

He mumbled incoherently and tried to lift the bottle to his lips. She blocked it and shook him gently.

"No. Come on, Daddy. Wake up!" When he still didn't respond, she cracked him smartly on the cheek with her open hand. His one eye snapped open, and he raised the bottle to fend her off. Then his vision cleared and he stared at her in shock.

"Wha' the... What're you doin' here? Why don' you go back to yer fancy captain an' be his fancy whore, an' leave me alone."

The words stung her more deeply than she thought any could, but her anger also flared. She gripped the front of his grimy shirt and pulled him close, whispering harshly into his face.

"Listen to me! I don't have much time! I need to talk to you, or you're as good as dead. Do you understand me?"

"You want to be his *wife*? After what he's done?"

"You have no *idea* what he's done." Her tone became sharp, her grip on his arm quivering with the memories of his torments. "You don't know what I've gone through here. So many years; I couldn't take it any more. Being his wife is better than being his slave, or dead. Those were my *only* choices. Do you understand?"

His good eye focused on her, blinking repeatedly, tears of either drunkenness or sorrow wetting his cheek. Camilla looked over the mass of shiny tight scar tissue and remembered the man she had known as a child. She saw the pain there, both physical and emotional, and her anger seeped away. He had been through a hell of his own, perhaps not as a slave, but living every day as Bloodwind's spy, betraying his friends to their deaths... all for her.

"I'm sorry, Daddy, I..."

"No, Cammy, I'm sorry. I thought... I thought you... needed me." Koybur lowered his gaze and tried to turn away.

"No!" She cupped his ravaged face gently in her hands and said the one thing she hoped would bring him back to her. "I love you, Daddy. I know what you did for me. I can take care of you, but you have to come with me now."

"No, Cammy. He won't let me up there in that palace of his."

"He will. He knows I want you here. You don't need to take anything from him, and he won't hurt you. I'll make sure of that."

"I... I don't..." He sagged and shook his head, and let the bottle fall from his hand. "Okay, Cammy, but you'll have to help me up."

She smiled and pulled at his arms, but could not pull him to his feet. With the guard's help, she managed to lift the sodden sailor and help him from the pub. Outside, he managed with only her help, which was fine with her. She was with her daddy again, for the first time since the day she'd watched a burning sail fall upon him while an unknown pirate dragged her kicking and screaming aboard the *Guillotine*. Now that they were back together, they'd never be separated again.

CHAPTER THIRTY-SIX
Plans for Vengeance

DAPPLED SUNLIGHT PLAYED ACROSS Cynthia's face, warm and comforting until a sunbeam drifted slowly across her eyelids. The dull ache that had haunted her dreams exploded into a roaring hangover, wrenching her from the depths of sleep.

"Bloody hell," she mumbled, stretching carefully. Stiff muscles protested as she rolled over, opened her eyes—and stopped short.

A dark-skinned man slept next to her, his features relaxed and remote. Across his chest rested the slim arm of an equally dark-skinned girl, her hand clutched in his, their fingers intertwined. Cynthia sat up and saw that they wore nothing at all, lying like two dark wooden spoons in a drawer. She remembered that this was how they had been presented to her, mother-naked. Whuafa's words echoed in her hazy memory.

"Dey be yoas, Cynthie Flaxal. Dey belong to you now."

"Holy Gods of Light, what did I do last night?" Memories of feasting, and dancing, then *more* than dancing flashed through her mind. She hadn't participated in the latter, though in her state of inebriation being a spectator had seemed perfectly all right. And she had no recollection of retiring to this hut and whatever had happened after that.

"With any luck, I passed out."

Cynthia felt fine, aside from a raging hangover. Her flower skirt and halter were intact, minus a few blossoms, and she felt no soreness that would have hinted that she partook in their lovemaking. She stretched her aching back and looked around the dim hut. The trunk of a single banyan tree formed two walls, while the remaining two were woven from the same type of mat she had slept on. An overhead framework of driftwood hung with what looked like the flotsam of a hundred shipwrecks, including some familiar personal items.

"My clothes!"

She wasted no time getting dressed. A few items were missing, including her corset, but she didn't care. She looked at the discarded flower-garments, smiled, picked one garland out of the improvised halter and put it over her head. From the others she plucked all the remaining blossoms and cast them over the sleeping couple before padding out of the little hut into the daylight.

"Shambata daroo!"

The roar from the massed throng of natives ripped through her hangover like a shower of broken glass. Cynthia pressed her hands to her exploding head and tried to hush them, but they surged forward and escorted her to the center of the clearing where breakfast lie waiting.

"Whuafa!" she shouted, hoping her translator was within hearing. She sat and accepted a coconut cup from someone, astounded when it scorched her palm. Then she caught a familiar aroma and thought she just might survive.

"How did they get blackbrew?" she asked rhetorically, sipping the strong beverage and sighing blissfully. Of course there was no milk to go with it, but just the aroma cleared some of the cobwebs from her mind.

"Cynthie Flaxal!" a reedy voice called over the murmur of the crowd. Whuafa had a hard time making his way through the crowd. Cynthia's two "gifts" followed, now thankfully clad in the customary scraps of matted reeds and animal hides that at least covered their loins. For the first time, she realized she didn't even know their names.

"Whuafa. Please tell me what this is all about. These," she gestured toward the couple as they sat, "uh, these two. Why give me *people*? Who are they? Can I say 'no thank you' and not insult the chief?"

"Please, one question only fer me achin' 'ead, Cynthie Flaxal." He accepted a cup of blackbrew from someone and sipped, sighing expansively. "Dey are Chula and Paska," he gestured toward the man and woman in turn. "Dey are gifts to you. Dey will protec ya an' help ya." He sipped his brew and wrinkled his already wrinkly brow. "I dona t'ink you can say 'no tanke' to da chief. His pride is vera big but get hurt easy, an' you no wanna see dat!"

"Great," she said, sipping her blackbrew. Someone put a platter of sizzling meats and roasted plantain before her and she sampled it, chewing and thinking with equal energy.

"Well, I guess I could use some guides if I'm going to make my way to Snake Harbor. It'll probably take a couple weeks to get there, if you have a boat I can take."

"Oh, we got plenty boat. Why you wanna boat, anyway? You stay hea', make baby wit' Chula! Make baby wi' anybody you like!"

"Babies!" She just about lost her grip on her coconut cup. "Oh, no. No babies. Not for a while yet. I just need to get to the mainland."

"Why de rush, Cynthie Flaxal? You stay wit' us. We treat you nice. Eat plenty meat, swim in de sea wi' de fishy folk, make babies wi' *all* de men!"

"I'm sorry, Whuafa. I've really got to go. People are out risking their lives looking for me. I've got to get back and tell them what I've learned about Bloodwind. When that's taken care of, I promise I'll come back here and visit you for a month!"

"Only a month? Ah, dat be no good. You come, you stay as long as you like. Month, year, whole life. We get you boat and you an' Chula an' Paska go to mainlan'. Dey show you de way. Dey help you and protec'. Okay?"

"Yes! Oh, that would be wonderful, Whuafa! Thank you!"

After a hangover-quenching breakfast, the whole village followed them down to a small cove where a dozen outrigger canoes rested on the sand. The craft looked sturdy enough, but Cynthia had her doubts about their seaworthiness the open ocean.

"You take these from island to island?"

"Oh, no' me, Cynthie Flaxal. Me too old for dat. But Chula here, he good wi' de paddle, and you a seamage!"

"Oh. Uh, right." With all that had happened, Cynthia had almost forgotten her newly acquired talent. "Say, Whuafa, have you ever put a sail on one of these?"

"Oh, no, Cynthe Flaxal. We got no sails, and de wind, she is wrong for sailin' to de nort' or sout' from islan' to islan'. We only paddle."

"Well, I think I'd like to try it. I'll just ask the wind to blow the right direction, and we'll give it a go, okay?"

"Okay! Where you gonna get de sail?"

"Uh, yeah. Hmmm." She looked around at the crowd, spied two men with long fishing spears, and had an idea.

≈

With the first light of dawn, three ships emerged from Southaven harbor: *Orin's Pride*, followed by *Syren Song* and *Winter Gale*. The others were finishing their provisioning, crewing and last-minute modifications. They promised to be ready the following morning, but Brelak could not wait. These three ships would lead the way, meeting the rest at predetermined times and places to the west of the Shattered Isles.

A thin smile of satisfaction creased Feldrin's lips at the sound of hammering and Dura's coarse brogue. Thanks largely to the dwarf's ceaseless efforts, they were on their way right on time. Fifty new sailors struggled to stow their gear while Horace, his new first mate, barked out orders. Most of the new people knew less about sailing than Brelak knew about baking a cake, but they were all willing to learn, and they were all willing to fight.

"She's handlin' well!" he said to no one in particular as he felt the trade winds take hold of *Orin's Pride*. "The extra weight's keepin' her keel down. Set yer course three points west of south, Mister Rowland. Horace, get the tops'ls on her."

"We're already leaving the others behind, Captain," Horace said, cocking an eyebrow at him that made the statement a question.

"Aye, and they know we will. We'll patrol alone until the rest of 'em catch up. Tops'ls, Horace."

"Aye, sir. Rig tops'ls! Topmen to the foremast! Man the braces!" As new canvas billowed and filled, *Orin's Pride* surged forward, heeling with the added thrust.

"Now we're crackin' on!" Rowland shouted, eliciting a cheer from the deck. Spray rose from the bow as the ship clove a swell and raced down the backside, the bow wake roaring in a wave of white.

With the necessary shuffle of crew positions, Brelak had appointed Rowland helmsman of the watch—a position he had earned by sailing the ship through a hurricane short handed. He would also be cooking for sixty, having retained his position through popular assent, but he now had help in that department, since Cynthia's housemaid Marta had insisted on accompanying them. Even her man Brolan, aged though he was, had presented himself as ship's steward, a serviceable cutlass riding on his hip.

"We'll be holdin' this tack for more'n a day, Horace. Have the off-watch shift cargo to the windward side. That'll stiffen her up."

"Aye, sir!"

More orders rang out, but Brelak didn't hear them as his mind swept into his calculations of course, speed, current and wind. He glanced aft, noting *Winter Gale* and *Syren Song* making more sail. They were making good headway, but *Orin's Pride* was leaving them quickly behind. He shifted his gaze forward, squinting into the distance. In his mind's eye he saw *Hippotrin* clawing back upwind from her long run with the storm. He gritted his teeth as he considered what might be happening to Cynthia among a crew of pirates.

"I'm comin', lass," he mumbled beneath his breath. "Just hold fast, I'm comin'."

≈

Koybur's head pounded as he limped down the steps to the great hall of Bloodwind's palace, ignoring the churlish glares that followed him. His memories of the previous evening were hazy at best, but one element stood out in stark relief: Cammy still loved him and needed him. All the blood on his hands, Cynthia's death, the ships and sailors he'd betrayed had not been for nothing. He might not be free to take her away, but they could at least be together.

Entering the feasting hall, Koybur thought the room looked as if it had been under siege. Men, women, servants and slaves lay sprawled on chairs, rugs and even along the length of the great oaken table. Only one person in the entire room looked as if he had not eaten and drank himself into a stupor, but Ghelfan looked even worse than the revelers. Bloodwind was absent, so Koybur went to the half-elf's side, bending to inspect the damage.

"Hell and high tide, man, what'd they do to ya?" Koybur lifted the half-elf's head carefully where it sagged onto his food-spattered chest. Ghelfan's face had been smeared with gravy and his ears stuffed with bits of potato. His eyes fluttered open and his mouth gaped, trying to form words through parched lips.

"Wa— water," he managed, his voice a bare whisper.

"Hang on, lad. Le'me find somethin' here for ya." He cast about the mayhem of the leftover feast, but every ewer and pitcher held rum, wine or ale. He settled for a fruity concoction that didn't smell too polluted with alcohol, tried a sip, and nodded. Sure, there was rum in it, but that'd probably do the lad good, in his state.

"Here ya go. Drink slow." He pressed the rim of the pitcher to the half-elf's lips and watched him drink greedily. After four swallows, Koybur tilted the pitcher back.

"Easy now. Don't want ya gettin' sick. Best have somethin' ta ballast that load. Here." He plucked a slab of roast pork from a platter and fed it to Ghelfan a bite at a time. "Better?"

"Yes. More to drink, please."

"Sure, lad. Looks like you could use it."

"My, my. What a shambles this is."

Bloodwind's smooth baritone startled Koybur, but he refused to let it show, continuing to feed Ghelfan.

"And Mister Koybur has come up from town to help us attend to our guest. How very thoughtful."

"You let him die of thirst and you'll have no more ships like *Hippotrin*." He fed the last bite of pork to Ghelfan and let the half-elf drink deeply of the pitcher. He glanced over his shoulder and, having prepared himself for what he might see, did not gape at the gossamer finery Cammy wore. It was a far cry from the gingham and pigtails she wore the day Orin and Peggy Flaxal met their end, the day she had been stolen away by Bloodwind. Now she was clad in a gown that displayed her as an object of desire. *Dressed like a sultan's whore*, he thought.

"Oh, I don't think any *permanent* damage has befallen Master Ghelfan," Bloodwind said, escorting Cammy to the head of the table and taking the one unoccupied seat. Camilla stood at his shoulder. "He simply had to learn a lesson last night, one that I'm sure he has taken to heart. But you, Master

Koybur, why are you here? It was my understanding that you did not want to be part of the family I plan to create here."

"I don't," he stated flatly, knowing Bloodwind would be shrewd enough to detect an outright lie, "but I want to be near Cammy, and she's chosen to be part of this. I don't like it, but I'm not gonna leave her."

"Well said." The pirate captain reached for a small brass bell and rang it.

A flood of servants swept into the room, rousing the sleepers and carrying away those who could not be stirred. They cleared away the partially eaten feast, and brought in a silver blackbrew service and a platter of toasted cheese, fresh bread, butter and mango preserves. In moments three place settings of fine white porcelain had been set. Bloodwind beckoned Camilla and Koybur to sit.

"Please, Mister Koybur, join us for breakfast," he said as Camilla settled into the chair to his left, as graceful and serene as a tropical bird coming to roost.

"What about him?" Koybur asked, indicating Ghelfan with a nod.

"Master Ghelfan has but to say one simple phrase and the ropes will be forever removed from his wrists. He knows the words that will free him. It is his choice to remain a prisoner."

"You'd best rethink yer options here, lad," Koybur told the half-elf, patting him on the shoulder. "You'll get no ballads sung fer yer noble defiance here." He rounded the table and limped toward the other end where Bloodwind and Cammy sat. He stopped briefly, regarding the empty chair for a moment as if it were more dangerous than an entire island full of pirates—which, of course, it was.

Koybur sat down and dropped the white linen napkin into his lap.

"Blackbrew, Master Koybur?" his host asked, lifting the silver pot.

"Don't mind if I do, Captain. Don't mind if I do."

CHAPTER THIRTY-SEVEN

Ships in the Night

"SOME BLOODY SEAMAGE I am," Cynthia muttered, helping Chula and Paska pull the swamped outrigger up onto a broad beach.

She had discovered that the orchestra of wind and water was not to be conducted by a neophyte. Wind, chop, current, tide and swell all struck at once, and every time she tried to concentrate on one element of the mix, the others played havoc with her makeshift sail or the small craft's low freeboard. After losing their improvised sail, masts and all, to an errant gust, she concentrated on the sea alone. This was easier, until they approached the next island.

As they passed through a narrow cut in the reef, a breaker appeared from nowhere to dash them hard from astern. She never even felt it coming. If not for the craft's remarkable stability, they might have capsized, but Chula simply laughed and dug his spade-shaped paddle into the water, driving them forward on the next wave.

With the boat safe, Chula grabbed their possessions and tossed them on the sand. Paska started bailing the water out of the craft, chattering away at him in an admonishing tone, obviously blaming him for their whole predicament. Chula only grinned, nodded, and continued drying out their equipment.

Cynthia stripped out of her sodden garments and hung them on a driftwood log to dry. She thought it strange how quickly her ideals of modesty had changed. She still couldn't imagine stripping down to her scanties in front of someone like Feldrin, but with Chula and Paska it seemed natural. When she turned back Chula was trotting away down the beach, his bow and club in hand, while Paska continued complaining to no one in particular.

"Hey! Where's he going?" she asked, not really expecting a coherent answer, but knowing no other way to get the girl's attention. Paska simply looked up and made a dismissive gesture, her scathing diatribe never slowing as she continued bailing.

"Well, I hope he comes back soon," Cynthia said, her gaze drifting around the wide beach and the forbidding jungle, wondering if any other tribes lived here and just how friendly they might be. She sat down in the shade of a driftwood stump, the bleached white roots arrayed above her like the bones of some deep dwelling sea monster. Eventually, the soft sand, warm sun, and the hypnotic roar-hiss of surf soothed her into a peaceful sleep.

≈

One knock on Brelak's cabin door and Rowland entered, grinning widely.

"We've raised the smoke of Fire Isle on the horizon, sir. We're on course. Speed's a steady fourteen knots."

"Bloody fine. Thanks." The waning light through the deck prisms shone down on a thick black book and a chart beneath it. He scratched notes on the chart while keeping his place in the book with a finger. Sighing, he rubbed his tired eyes and said, "Could ya light my lamp and send down another pot o' that poison you call blackbrew?"

"You should sleep some, Capt'n. I know yer wound as tight as that catapult bolted to the foredeck, but you won't be much good in a fight if you don't get some rest." Both concern and frustration colored Rowland's tone.

"Not bloody likely. I'll sleep when we make the Fathomless Reaches. Call me fer the midnight watch."

"Aye, sir." He left, closing the door softly.

"Bloody privacy's what I really need, ya mother hen," he muttered, referring back to the leather-bound tome. The book had come aboard with Cynthia's man Brolen, who had said it was her father's journal, but that he didn't think she'd mind him putting it to use, under the circumstances.

"Bloody amazin'," he muttered, examining the hand-drawn renderings on the journal's pages. The information here would be worth a king's ransom to any captain plying the waters of the Southern Ocean. The book showed many details of the undersea that Feldrin had never known nor cared about. Notations of "Undine-home" and "Bunodosoma grove" left him scratching his head, but the details of depths, currents and tidal forces throughout the cuts of the Shattered Isles were priceless.

"Who the hell's Whuafa?" Rowland asked, putting the blackbrew pot into its gimbaled cradle.

"What?" Brelak looked up and glared at the interruption. "Don't you ever knock, Row?"

"I did. You didn't answer, so I came in, thinkin' you'd fallen asleep, which you should be doin', not drinkin' more of this stuff." The cook filled the captain's cup and scowled back. "Sorry I interrupted."

"And what are you talkin' about, anyway? Who's who?"

"Saw the name Whuafa there in that book, and wondered if you knew who it was, is all. Didn't know anybody lived out on Vulture Isle."

"Vulture Isle? What the..."

Brelak inspected the drawing once more, finding the bit Rowland was referring to, a tiny notation in a flowing hand that read:

Whuafa's people, Southeast coast.

Ware the Others, northeast highlands.

"So who the hell is Whuafa?" he wondered aloud, sipping his blackbrew as Rowland shrugged and left the cabin.

≈

Cynthia drifted awake to the smell of wood smoke and cooking meat, a warm bed of sand that conformed to her shape perfectly, and the light breeze that played over her skin in a delicate caress. She opened her eyes slowly, smiling at the subdued azure of the evening sky.

Evening?

She sat bolt upright, hitting her head on the low fronds that had been placed to shade her from the sun. Chula and Paska sat silently tending a driftwood fire surrounded by skewers of sizzling meat, utterly unconcerned that she'd slept through the entire day.

"Bloody hell!" She levered herself up and snatched her dry clothes. She pulled her chemise over her head, but it rasped painfully over her sand-covered skin. She growled as she stripped off the garment and began brushing herself off. Sand and salt clung everywhere, an abrasive mixture which, on top of a slight sunburn, left her itchy and frustrated after several minutes of futile effort.

She sat back down and sighed. "There's got to be an easier way."

She brushed at her sandy legs with her sandy hands, but the sugar-fine granules adhered to her skin like iron filings to a lodestone. Eventually, the soothing roar-hiss of the surf intruded on her thoughts, the call of the sea drawing her to the crystalline waters of the lagoon.

"I could just take a bath, but then I'd be..." A crazy idea clicked into her mind. She stood and headed for the water.

"Shambata daroo!" Paska chimed, smiling and rattling off several more sentences, gesturing to their fire and the food.

"Paska. Chula." She smiled at them, but walked right past, down the beach and into the warm crystalline water.

Swimming had not been one of the skills she'd been taught as a young lady, but as she waded forward she felt the sea surround her and every motion became easy, smooth and *right*. In moments she moved comfortably through the deep water, willing the sea to buoy her up, push her along, and rinse away all the sweat and sand that clung to her skin. She ruffled her hair and surfaced, creating a small wave to carry her into shallow water. Finally free of sand, she strode forward until she stood in ankle deep water.

"Now, let's see if I can..."

Cynthia closed her eyes, feeling the thin film of the sea covering her skin chill in the breeze. But the water was still part of the sea; all she had to do was send it back where it belonged. *Back down*, she thought, willing the water away.

A rippling wavelet started at the crown of her head and coursed down her skin, leaving no trace behind. She opened her eyes and shook out her dry hair, laughing and grinning as she strode ashore. "Well, maybe I'm a seamage after all."

She shook out her sandy clothes and joined her friends, smiling at their slack-jawed stares. Chula muttered something, and Paska snapped an admonishing retort. The meat proved to be some type of bird and two spiny lobsters which, accompanied by fresh fruit and water from one of their skins, sated her deliciously. When they finished, however, the sun hung only a hand-span above the horizon—she had wasted the day.

Then Chula began loading their meager gear into the dugout.

"Chula. Stop! It's getting dark. We can't go now."

He said something she didn't understand, gestured toward the sky and the open sea, and continued to load their gear. Paska also helped, evidently agreeing with him.

"No! Not until morning." Cynthia grabbed Chula's arm, but he just smiled at her, nodded, and continued. Paska gently pulled her aside, motioning to the flat hard-packed portion of the beach. Here she took a stick and drew some simple pictographs. The first was a disc with rays radiating in all directions; under it she drew several lines of sharply peaked waves. Next to that she drew a crescent moon, and several lines of lesser peaked waves. The meaning was clear—the seas were calmer at night.

"Yes, I know, Paska, but we can't see." She pantomimed squinting into the distance.

"Na, na..." Paska made a waving motion overhead, and pointed to the crescent moon pictograph. "Daroo, daroo!"

"The moon? You think the moon is bright enough?" She thought about it for a bit and realized that Chula and Paska certainly knew what they were doing. Besides, sailing at night had never impeded a merchant captain, unless the waters were dangerous or unknown.

"Okay," she decided, trying to swallow her trepidation. "Okay, we go now."

Less than half an hour later they were paddling along the leeward side of the island, heading northwest inside the lagoon. As the last light of day faded, they paddled through a break in the reef and into open water. The trade winds were indeed less powerful at this hour, and the swells had diminished correspondingly. She reached out with her mind to the sea around them and calmed the waters further, urging the tiny craft gently forward.

"So far, so good."

Each time she used her new skills she learned more, often the hard way. Calming the water didn't tire her physically, but it required her constant concentration. As she became distracted by the beautiful bluish luminescence trailing behind them, she felt the control slip away. A rogue wave slapped the side of the canoe, splashing her with a warm spray, as if to chastise her for forgetting her duty. She relaxed once again and expanded her mind to encompass the ocean surrounding the small boat.

Ahead, the plume of Fire Isle lit the sky in a ruddy glow. Three other islands, dark by comparison, could be seen on the horizon. It would be several hours before the waning moon rose, but the active volcano shone better than any lighthouse, and the stars glowed brightly overhead.

"Okay, Cynthia," she told herself, gripping the sides of the canoe and feeling the power of the sea around them, "let's see if you can do more than make waves and dry yourself without a towel."

She slipped her hands down into the warm water, and felt the power of the sea swell under them. She called to the power, shaping it carefully and letting it build. A wide swell formed behind them, high enough to block out the island they had just left. The tiny craft rose up and raced down its face. Chula whooped in glee, digging his paddle hard into the water while Paska steered their nose down the wave, using her paddle like a rudder.

Cynthia adjusted the speed of the wave delicately, keeping track of the other waves coming in at oblique angles, flattening them one by one. In short order they reached the perfect speed, the canoe sliding down the wave with only occasional paddling by Chula, and only minor steering from Paska. Cynthia found that she could maintain their course and speed with little effort, adjusting from time to time for changes in the swells and chop. She immersed herself in the power of the sea, letting it envelop and course through her.

"Thank you," she whispered, though she didn't know exactly who she was thanking, her father, Odea, or the sea itself.

Maybe, she thought soulfully, *they're the same thing.*

CHAPTER THIRTY-EIGHT

Chula's Choice

CYNTHIA WOKE TO THE high-pitched buzz of wings. She waved her hand to shoo Mouse away, but it turned out to be nothing but a monstrous mosquito. Wakefulness and memory returned: Mouse was gone and she was somewhere in the Shattered Isles.

When exhaustion forced them ashore in the early hours of the morning, Cynthia curled up in the bow of the outrigger and tried to cover every exposed bit of flesh with her threadbare garments. The giant mangroves protected them from the sun, but also harbored a whole population of biting and stinging insects.

She successfully swatted the offending bug, but the motion only seemed to attract more. A glance through the canopy showed the sun at its zenith edging behind a looming column of cloud. She adjusted her clothing and watched the cloud billow, and realized that it wasn't a cloud at all, but a plume of volcanic smoke.

"Plume Isle," she said, sitting up and looking around. A line of human skulls prominently displayed atop bamboo poles along the length of the beach confirmed her suspicions.

"A ruse to run off visitors," she said, wondering just how many rumors of cannibals had been fostered by Bloodwind and his pirates. She had to admit, it was an effective deterrent. "Nobody in his right mind would go ashore with that as a welcome."

She peered up at the jungle-clad mountainside, looking for any sign of the island's true denizens, but the canopy was impenetrable. She had little doubt that Bloodwind had lookouts.

"Lucky we weren't spotted," she muttered, moving to ease herself into the water to evade the ravenous insects.

"Shambata daroo," Chula said sleepily, his voice pitched low. He rattled off something that sounded like a question then said a single word that she knew all too well. "Pirate." He punctuated the word by pointing to the skull-decorated beach. "Pirate imba. Shambata daroo na eriki. Pirate."

The meaning seemed simple enough: this was the home of pirates, and she should not go walking around, or swimming around for that matter. She had to admire his economy of words.

"Yes, Chula. Pirates." She swatted futilely at mosquitoes, hastily donning her grimy clothes. "We go?" She made a motion as if paddling, then pointed to them all and then out to sea. "We leave?"

"Na, na!" He pointed up at the sky, at the sun, and shook his head, voicing and pantomiming his worry that the sun would show them to the pirates. The hissing motion he made while passing his thumb across his throat needed no translation.

She had just about resigned herself to a day sweltering in the shade of the mangroves swatting bugs, when a thought came to her: this would be the only opportunity to find anything out about Bloodwind's home base. It would not be easy talking Chula into letting her look around, but they had all day. If they were careful and kept to the dense undergrowth, she felt sure they could get in and out without anyone the wiser.

≈

Orin's Pride cut a flawless line parallel to the outer reef of Vulture Island no more than a hundred yards from the razor-sharp coral. They had rounded the Fathomless Reaches and now planned to run a zig-zag course up the archipelago, cutting between the islands while the light of midday gave them perfect visibility.

"Lookout! Tell me what ya see, man! I'm not a bloody mind reader!"

Feldrin's impatience with the inexperienced crew had become a silent joke among the seasoned sailors. He tried very hard not to show his temper, but most of the landsmen were afraid of him, which was just as well.

"Uh, there's a coral reef about two boat lengths to the right, er starboard, Capt'n. It runs straight ahead. No sails on the horizon. No sign of anyone ashore."

"Bloody lubbers," he muttered, ignoring the smirk from the helmsman. "Give her a point to leeward, Jacob. I don't trust that landsman to spot a whale in a ballroom, let alone a coral head. Horace, would you *please* climb up there an' give that lubber a once over on the finer points of lookout duty?"

"Aye, sir." He scampered up the ratlines to join the lookout.

"Rowland, gimme my glass." He held out his hand and the bronze telescope popped into his palm.

"Marta's got some fried pork sandwiches and toasted cheese made up for ya, sir," Rowland said, concern adding a timbre to his voice.

"Bloody fine. Bring it up on a tray with another pot of blackbrew. I'll eat on deck." He brought the glass up and swept the western horizon from south to north, his jaw clenched as he strained to catch the faintest glimpse of a sail. His eyes had rarely left that horizon since they made their northerly turn, but they had yet to see anything but whitecaps.

"Here's your lunch, Captain!" Marta's cheery tone cut through the clatter and chatter of the deck like a cutlass through linen. "Now tuck in before the cheese gets cold. I put a cup of ale on the plate to wash it down. Blackbrew'll be half a moment as I just put the kettle on."

"That'll be fine, Marta. Thank you." He did not lower the glass, and did not take his eye from the horizon.

"Ahem."

He ignored her. She was getting as bad as Rowland. In fact, he thought the two were in cahoots.

"Captain, if you don't eat this right now, I'm going to bank the stove fires and refuse to feed the crew their midday meal until you do." Her tone had gone from motherly to shrewish. "The word *mutiny* comes to mind."

"Bloody mother hen," he muttered, lowering the glass and taking one of the sandwiches. He ate mechanically, chewing and swallowing without really tasting the spicy pork and sharp cheese. Marta watched every bite. He drained the cup of ale and placed it carefully back on the tray. "Thank you, Marta. Please bring the blackbrew up when it's ready."

"I will if you promise to get some sleep tonight. I wouldn't give a good God's damn, except that your pacing is keeping me awake." She scowled and descended the companionway, not waiting for his answer.

Feldrin hadn't really heard her scolding, for he was already scanning the horizon again, searching for any sign of the ship that had taken Cynthia Flaxal away from him.

≈

Chula had a problem.

The Scimitar Moon would not listen to him. She had insisted on leaving the boat, though she could not tell him why; she knew this was the home of the pirates, and knew they would kill them if caught. What she evidently did not know, and what he couldn't make her understand, was that the evil witch watched the beaches, and no matter how careful they were, the blood drinker would know they had intruded.

Chula could not physically restrain her, for she was the Scimitar Moon; she was his mistress. He could only follow and try to protect her when the pirates attacked. He told Paska to stay with the boat and be ready to flee when they returned. For once, the combative woman did not argue.

"Come back with her, Chula. Just come back," was all she said. He reluctantly took his war club, bow and knife, and followed his mistress into the jungle.

The Scimitar Moon might be able to move wind and water, but she knew absolutely nothing about moving quietly through the jungle. This, at least, he could do something about.

"Quiet!" he hissed as she stepped into a pile of dry leaves. He pointed to the leaves and shook his head, making a low "ssst" sound. She seemed to understand this, and did not complain when he took the lead, pointing at the places he put his feet, and making it clear she should follow exactly where he stepped.

They climbed slowly, keeping to game trails and remaining fairly silent. Finally, they reached a real trail near the top of the ridge. Chula stopped, motioning for her to crouch down. Her white blouse and blue skirt were almost as bad as the noise she made, so keeping her out of sight seemed the best course.

He waited and listened, knowing the trail would be dangerous.

She whispered something he couldn't understand and tugged at his breechcloth. Surely she didn't want to do *that* right now!

She pantomimed crossing the trail and continuing up the ridge. She wanted to look over at the pirate stronghold.

"You are crazy, woman," he muttered, unable to dissuade her. He made motions to keep low, which she seemed to understand, and they inched forward.

The boot prints on the trail were obvious and recent. Several men had come this way in a hurry. He stopped again and listened, but heard nothing. A wall of foliage edged the other side of the trail, broken only by a gap where the game trail resumed. The ridge top was only another twenty strides beyond. Maybe they *could* make it. He nocked an arrow and nodded to her.

They crossed the trail in four strides, ducking into cover on the other side with only a slight rustle of leaves.

Chula crouched and waited. Nothing but the twitter of birds and the distant roar of surf reached his ears. He nodded to the Scimitar Moon and led her up the game trail to the crest of the ridge where he got down on his belly and crawled up to the edge.

Four hundred feet below, two ships sat upon the hard black sand of the pirate shipyard. Four more bobbed at anchor in the deep bay, and one, red sails furled on her yards, lay at the wide stone pier. Another of a type he'd never seen floated at the dock near the shipyard.

"*Hippotrin!*" she hissed, though the word meant nothing to him. "Six ships ready to sail, and two in dry dock. Holy hell, look at the shipyard!"

"Ssst!" he hissed, making calming motions, which seemed to help. She kept muttering, lower but still audible, until finally she made it clear that she had seen enough. He had seen enough at the first glance: a village of pirates, eight ships, and the channel through the giant mangroves and the reef beyond, all indelibly imprinted on his mind.

They inched away from the edge, rose and descended to the trail. A quick glance in each direction and a hasty moment of listening confirmed that they were still undiscovered. He gave her a nudge and stepped out into the open.

The crack-whir of a crossbow and the shocking impact of iron-tipped hardwood slamming into his shoulder sent Chula tumbling into the underbrush. Consciousness fled for a moment, but a scream reached through the haze of shock and pain. The men who had shot him had taken the Scimitar Moon.

In a flash of pain and rage, Chula knew exactly what he had to do.

≈

When Cynthia saw Chula fall, she thought how silly it was for him to trip. Then a hand grabbed her hair and another snaked around her waist. She screamed involuntarily, both with the realization that Chula had not tripped, and the knowledge of who had hold of her.

She kicked and gouged and scratched, reaching over her shoulder, hoping to find her assailant's eyes. Others moved in, grasping at her arms. She lashed and bit, unsure how many there were.

"Here! Stop that ye little—"

"Hold 'er, Parik!"

"I am, damn ye, but she's go' claws like a—"

"Hey, look out! That—"

With a crack like an axe biting into wood, the grip went slack. She pitched forward, rolling to look back. The pirate who had held her fell to his knees, then toppled forward into her lap, his skull peeled back above his vacant eyes, his lifeblood surging forth in torrents. For a moment Cynthia could only think to get out from under the pirate's twitching corpse.

As she scrabbled away the haze of panic cleared and she saw Chula fending off five more pirates. His war club wove in whirling arcs, his obsidian knife in his bloody left hand. The head of a crossbow bolt protruded from just below his left collarbone. The pirates advanced in an arc, easily fending off his attacks with their cutlasses.

Steel met stone as Chula blocked a thrust that would have disemboweled him, but the obsidian knife snapped at the hilt. He was overmatched, wounded and outnumbered; he would be dead in moments unless she did something.

The fallen pirate bore a number of weapons, none of which Cynthia

knew how to use. She'd never been in a fight in her life, let alone a sword-
fight. There was one thing, however, that would draw their attention away.

"Hey, you motherless pigs!" She picked up a rock and threw it, managing
to score a hit on one of the pirates. She reached for another, and backed
down the trail as their attention turned to her. "Chula! Run!" But he did
not run, and took the opportunity of her distraction to smash his club into
the sword arm of one of his assailants. The man went down, gripping his
shattered forearm.

"Jorry, Vic! Get the girl. We'll finish this heathen."

"Chula!" she screamed, trying to make him understand. This was her
fault; she would not have his blood on her hands, too. "Na! Na! Paska! Go
to Paska!" She flung her stone, turned and ran down the trail, two pirates
hot on her heels.

≈

Crazy woman! Chula thought as he watched the Scimitar Moon dash
away. Why hadn't she slipped into the bushes while he had the pirates' attention? Now he would die for nothing.

With that thought, the last words she screamed came to him: Paska. *Paska...*

No, I will not die, he decided, sidestepping a thrust and lashing out with
his club to rake the shards of obsidian along the man's arm. The pirate
screamed and dropped his sword, but the one whose arm he'd broken
had one of the strange sideways bows. He could not defend against that.
Another scream from down the trail told him the pirates had caught the
Scimitar Moon. There was nothing he could do to save her now, but he
would not let the Scimitar Moon die without a fight. He would go to the
chief! Yes, he would go and bring back the whole village to kill these pirates
and take her back!

But to do that, he had to live.

He ducked into the brush at his back and flew down the game trail as
only one born to the jungle could. He heard the crash and yells of men
behind him, but knew they would never catch him. The trail that had taken
them an hour to climb flew past in a mad ten-minute dash. A crack and
whir past his ear told him his pursuers were still close. He hoped Paska was
ready to go when he got there.

"Go, Paska!" He hit the beach running flat out, yelling for her to get the
boat into deep water. If he could just reach the water, he had a chance.

He didn't hear the crack-whir this time; he only felt the smashing blow
to his leg that sent him sprawling to the sand. His breath came out in an

anguished cry as the fall drove the first bolt back through his shoulder.

He heard them approach as he pushed himself over onto his back. Fire lanced through his shoulder and leg as the bolts hit the sand, but he managed not to scream. His war club still hung from his wrist by its leather thong, and he brought it up, though he couldn't push himself up with his other arm. All he could do was lay there and let them come.

"Finally gotcha, you slimy heathen pig," one of them said. The words were unintelligible, but the meaning was clear enough. The man stepped forward, cutlass at the ready. "Now yer gonna pay fer Parik, and it's gonna hurt."

"Just run 'im through an' be done wi—"

The pirate's words ended in a gurgling gasp, and the man standing over Chula turned.

Paska stepped past the man whose throat she'd cut, plunged the obsidian dagger into the second pirate's belly, jerked it to the side and stepped back. The man looked dumbly down at the pile of intestines at his feet. The cutlass fell from his hand as he clutched his eviscerated stomach, crumpling to his knees. She ended his horrible screams with another slash of her knife.

Then the scolding began.

"Where is the Scimitar Moon? I knew you would lose her! Is she dead, or did they take her? Here, take that one's sword while I tend to this. Now get up! I can't paddle that boat alone!"

During her rant, she picked up the first one's cutlass and economically decapitated the corpses. She then took the severed heads and stuck them onto two of the conveniently placed bamboo poles on the beach. By the time she finished, Chula had managed to get shakily to his feet, though the bolt in his thigh stabbed him with every move.

"You can't walk with that sticking in your leg, Chula. By Odea, must I do everything for you?" She knelt, cut the head from the bolt in his leg and jerked the shaft free before he could protest. The clothing from one of the dead pirates made a serviceable bandage, though he was still bleeding. "I will take the other one out when we get into the boat. You will die from fever if we don't get home soon, so you will have to paddle fast. I will help. Come on."

He just smiled and accepted her help to the boat. He knew he could not argue with her. He didn't even want to. He just kept smiling and thought, *What a woman*, while they paddled through the narrow cut into the open sea, headed southeast toward home.

CHAPTER THIRTY-NINE

Old Enemies and New Friends

"WE GOT 'ER FOR ya, Capt'n!" one of her captors crowed triumphantly, dragging Cynthia up the steps of Bloodwind's palace. She hung from her bonds, doubled over and gasping for breath, bruised and exhausted from fighting every step down the mountain. "Some savage killed Parik, but the others're after the heathen. We'll have his head on a pole soon."

"They are wrong, my captain." A woman's sultry voice brought Cynthia's attention to a pair of legs clad in leathers and silks. "Your men are dead. The native and his woman are beyond the reef."

"No matter, Hydra." A hand gripped Cynthia's hair and wrenched her upright.

The curse on her lips died as recognition kicked her in the stomach. The face had aged, but the voice was the same; it was the voice from her nightmares, the one that laughed while her parents died. Memory of that moment snapped into her mind: standing at the rail of *Peggy's Pride* in bloodstained stockings, watching the ship with blood red sails drift away. He stood at the taffrail beside a ballista, the weapon that had killed her parents, his laughter searing her soul like a glowing hot sword in her heart. Now, as she stood face to face with the man, her long-nurtured hatred burned so brightly that it consumed her. Only the rope cutting cruelly into her wrists kept her hands from his throat.

"Thanks to your skull sentinels we landed the big fish." He stepped up to Cynthia and smiled broadly, thumb and forefinger tracing a line down her bruised jaw. Her teeth snapped just short of taking a finger, and his laughter burned her like hot coals. "Well, well indeed, Miss Cynthia Flaxal, so very spirited. We were worried you'd been lost at sea. In fact, several of my men told me that very thing. How ever did you manage to save yourself?"

"Yes, how *did* you survive?" Yodrin asked from behind Bloodwind.

Her eyes swept the group before her for an instant. She ignored Yodrin and the red-headed whore draped over Bloodwind's arm. Koybur earned only a scathing glare. For a moment her gaze met that of the one he had called Hydra, and her insides turned to ice. Those eyes shone fathomless black, as if something stared at her from behind dark, false windows, something hungry and not at all human. She looked away quickly, centering her hatred upon Bloodwind.

"I was rescued by a pox-ridden sea hag. She said she was your mother."

"Delightful, delightful. And so very ladylike. I imagine the natives showed you an easy time of it with such feminine wiles to barter. Is that how you made your way to my doorstep, by laying with all of them?"

Her spittle reached him easily, the surprise on his face worth the clout she received from the man holding her arms. She was not, however, ready for the dagger that suddenly hung before her face. Cynthia realized that she had just done something very stupid; this man could make the rest of her short life a sea of agony.

"Someone bring me a pair of pliers. I think this fishwife needs her wagging tongue shortened." Laugher rang around the crowd, but the request proved to be no joke, for a pair of pliers was quickly thrust into Bloodwind's waiting hand. Cynthia's eyes widened in terror as the knife and the pliers were held up to her lips. "Now someone hold her still."

"She's of no use to you if she can't speak, my captain," the redhead beside Bloodwind said smoothly, drawing his attention long enough for Cynthia to swallow and clench her jaw against the rough fingers trying to pry her mouth open.

"Hmmm, perhaps you're right, Camilla. But I think something must be done to instill the proper courtesy. Turn her around."

Before Cynthia could voice a protest, the pliers closed around the smallest finger of her left hand and pain exploded up her arm. She screamed through clenched teeth, collapsing against her bonds, but the men dragged her upright and turned her back to face him as her screams devolved into a whimper.

"Let this be a lesson to you, Miss Flaxal." Bloodwind held her severed finger up before her tear-streaked face, then cast it aside. Hydra's eyes followed it like a dog's following a thrown stick. "You've got nine more lessons, then we start on your toes." He held the bloody knife up before her eyes. "Do you understand me?"

"I understand you," she said through clenched teeth, fighting back the urge to vomit.

"Good." He cleaned the knife on the lapel of her blouse and returned it to its sheath, then took a step back and held up his arm for his woman. She came forward to take it. "Bind her hand—she's bleeding on my steps—and chain her in a cell, but no liberties. Nobody touches her but me, understood?"

Murmurs of assent filtered through the crowd as someone wrapped something around her bleeding hand. Bloodwind and his entourage turned away, but three eyes followed her progress into the palace. The sympathy in Koybur's ruined visage struck a thousand memories in her mind; all the years he'd spent teaching her everything he knew about sailing and ships.

She forced the memories aside. They were nothing but lies. She could not read the red-haired woman's face, but something in it nagged at her memory as her captors dragged her into the palace and down to the dungeons.

≈

Feldrin shot out of his bunk and reached for the dagger at his belt before he realized that he wore no dagger, no belt, and no pants. He wondered briefly what had shattered his sleep when another cry rang out, barely audible, and Horace's harsh call answered.

"Heave to, Mister Rowland. Rig a harness and put someone on the boarding ladder. Bosun, bring an armed party amidships."

He was into his trousers and out of his cabin before the last words reached his ears. He emerged onto a deck lit by the subdued glow of a spectacular sunset. They were on a westward reach, but Horace had hove to just upwind of a small outrigger canoe.

"What's this about, Horace?" he asked, squinting down at the two dark-skinned figures in the small craft. One was a woman clad only in a breechcloth, which drew some laughs and cat calls from the crew, but the other, a man, sat slumped over his paddle. A broad swatch of cloth over his shoulder and another around his leg were both stained the color of the sky.

"Don't know as yet, sir. Couple of natives, but the man's hurt and the woman's got a cutlass."

"Cannibals?"

"They don't have the look."

"I think I can understand a word er two of what she's sayin', Capt'n," Rowland said from his position at the wheel. "She keeps pointing to the bow of the ship and sayin' somethin' about the moon."

"The moon?" Feldrin looked over the side at the small craft. The woman had not shut her mouth since he came on deck, continually gesticulating and crying out. "She crazy?"

"Maybe, but... Wait a second. Sword moon? What the hell?" Rowland called out a few halting words in that same strange language, and the woman fell silent. Then he said a few more, and the woman answered. "Holy Odea! She's sayin' 'scimitar moon!' You remember Cynthia's medallion? She's pointing to the figurehead, Captain! They've seen her!"

"Rig a harness! I want 'em aboard right now! Horace, I've got the watch. Row, talk to 'em and find out what they know. You there! Rig a lift and bring that canoe aboard. I want someone to go over it with a lantern and bring me any scrap of anythin' you find." He looked around for something, then swore. "Rowland, have Marta get hot food for 'em, and a cup o' rum wouldn't hurt."

Sailors scrambled like monkeys in a burning house; in moments Rowland sat on a tarp with the two, talking and offering them hot blackbrew spiked with rum while Marta examined the man's leg wound.

"The woman says the pirates took Cynthia. Says she and the man *belong* to her, and were takin' her north to the big land, the mainland I guess, but they stopped on Plume Island, and the pirates took her."

"Plume Island? So that's where they're holed up. Bloody, bloody hell and high water! We got 'em!" His fist met his palm with a report like a jibing sail. He looked at the dimming sky, then at the northern horizon. "We're due ta meet *Winter Gale* tomorrow evenin' just south a Plume Island. We'll meet up an' send a runnin' message up the isles."

"Wait, Cap'n. She's sayin' somethin' else. They found her on their island, Vulture Isle as near as I can guess, and they want to go there. Says the chief'll bring the whole village to get the *Scimitar Moon* back."

"Bloody hell." He remembered the notation on the chart that Rowland had been interested in. "Whuafa's people…"

The native woman's eyes shot open at the name, and she rattled off something so fast that Rowland had to ask her twice to slow down before she understood.

"She says yes, they *are* Whuafa's people. The one who knew the Flaxal. I think they mean Orin Flaxal, Captain."

"Odea's green garters," he muttered, chewing his lip. Calculations flashed through his head, distances, tides, currents, and the intensity of the trade winds. "Set a course sou'-sou'west, helmsm'n. Lookout! Well done spottin' that boat. Watch fer the reef to the south. As soon as we're clear, give a call." He turned to Horace. "Soon as we clear that reef, I want sou'-sou'east, an' I want every single stitch o' canvas aloft. If we're not dippin' a rail on the down-roll, I wanna know *why.*"

"Aye, sir!"

The great wheel turned and the ship rounded to the south. Crewmen tended their sheets and braces under the boatswain's delicate encouragement, and in moments *Orin's Pride* plowed south-southwest, throwing spray from her bow on every rolling wave.

≈

Straw rustled at Cynthia's feet, stirring her from a fitful slumber. She kicked at the sound, hoping to scare the rat away. She'd already been bitten twice. They smelled blood, and wouldn't be dissuaded easily.

"Fssst!" she hissed, glaring at two beady little eyes staring at her from the darkness. "Come closer and I'll kick your little rat brains out," she warned, shifting her legs to a slightly less painful position.

The rattle of keys and a flare of torchlight heralded the one thing she least expected: visitors. The real surprise came when Koybur limped into view with Bloodwind's red-haired companion at his side. The jailor joined them, looking nervous.

"You can go now," the woman told the turnkey, holding out her hand. "I'll return the keys on our way out."

"Oh, I can't let you have the keys, Miss Camilla. I was told ne'r ta let 'em leave me side."

"Well, then unlock the door and you can come back later to lock it. We're here to talk to the prisoner and I don't want to do it through bars. She's hardly a threat chained to the wall."

"Aye, that'll do. Jus' give a whistle when yer ready." He rattled the key in the lock and opened the bars a hand-width. "Have a care, now."

"Thank you," the woman said as the jailor ambled off. When the outer door thudded closed, her two visitors edged into the tiny cell.

"Here, I brought you a blanket. It's not much, but it's softer than stone." The woman helped position the folded blanked under Cynthia's backside, easing the pain of the hard floor.

"And I managed a bit from the kitchen." Koybur pulled a small sack from under his tunic, handing it over to his young companion, who withdrew a half loaf of bread, a wedge of cheese and an earthenware bottle.

"Why are you doing this?" Cynthia asked, eying them both suspiciously before taking a bite of bread. She thought about refusing, but any kindness at this point, even from Koybur, was welcome. "After what you did, why do you care what happens to me? And who *are* you?" she asked the woman, accepting a bite of cheese and a drink from the bottle. It was water, clean and cool.

"You don't remember," the red-headed woman said, her voice a little cold. "You knew me when we were girls. We used to play sharks and mermaids with that little sprite in your back yard."

"What the..." *Bloodwind called her Camilla!* Realization struck like a hammer blow, a thousand dim memories of her childhood rushing back in a muddled haze. "Cammy? I thought you were dead! Wait! Koybur, you told me your daughter died at sea."

"For more'n a year, I thought she had. Then I got a note sayin' *he* had her, and I'd do what he said, or she'd be worse'n dead." He stared at her for a while, letting it sink in. "Maybe you understand a bit better now, Cyn.

I don't 'spect you to forgive me, but maybe you understand."

"You've been here fifteen *years*?" Cynthia tried to accept it: a childhood friend thought long dead, in fact stolen away by the man who had killed her parents. "How did you... I mean, you're not in chains, so you must be..."

"Free?" Camilla asked, her tone harboring the anguish of a decade and a half of slavery in that one word. "I don't know what free is anymore, Cynthia. I was his slave so long I forgot what else I could be. I did what I had to do. He thinks he loves me. I don't know if he really does, if he *can* love, but it's the only chance I have to survive."

"Oh, Cammy. Gods, I'm sorry." She couldn't believe she was saying this, chained and mutilated, a prisoner, apologizing to the mistress of her captor for having to live a life of slavery she knew nothing about and couldn't have changed if she had. But the apology was heartfelt. She could not imagine surviving so long at the hands of someone like Bloodwind.

"He promised if I helped him get one of your ships that he'd let me take Cammy away, but now..." Koybur's tone held no apology. "I came here to take her away, an' now Cammy tells me that ain't gonna happen. But we can stay here."

"Nice," Cynthia said, a little venom creeping into her tone. "You trusted *him*? I thought you had more *sense* than that, Koybur."

"I had to do somethin', Cyn. Maybe we're not free, but at least we're alive, and together. I just came down here to explain, is all. I owed you that much. After all the years, I mean, you was like family to me." He looked miserable but he held his daughter closely, his hard-won prize.

"What about Ghelfan? Is he here?"

"Aye. Bloodwind's workin' the poor feller over pretty hard. He don't let him alone much. Won't be long before he cracks, I think."

A long silence hung between them as Cynthia finished her meal. She thought long and hard, wondering if she dared tell them what she was, what she could do. She decided silence would be best at this point, but could not let the opportunity pass to try one last gambit.

"Before you go, do me one last favor, Koybur. Arrange for Bloodwind to bring me down to see *Hippotrin*."

"Why?" he asked. Koybur was no fool. He knew she would make no idle request at a juncture like this. "What'll that accomplish?"

"When Ghelfan gives Bloodwind what he wants, I become superfluous. I just want to see her, before I die." She didn't know if he'd believe the lie, if lie it truly was. Getting aboard *Hippotrin* with Bloodwind would bring her close enough to the sea to use the only weapon she had. With any luck, she could kill them all and sink the ship as well.

"I'll see what I can do, Cyn, but I can't make any promises."

"I wouldn't believe you if you did," she said, meeting his stare one last time before they called the jailor and left her in the dark.

CHAPTER FORTY
Blood Dawn

HYDRA DID NOT DREAM, but the bloodlust, the hunger of the demon within her, often plagued her sleep. She stirred, muddled visions and memories not from her own mind blurring into her semi-conscious thoughts. Half awake, half mired in the mind of the demon, she saw mists, and in the mists... Fire... Steel... Blood... Oblivion.

And laughter...

She woke up screaming.

≈

"Gods-damned mists," Pel muttered, rubbing his hands and squinting to the east. The first glow of dawn had shown an hour ago, but the sun's disk had yet to pierce the eastern horizon. He hated squinting into the mists that hung in the caldera in the calm of dawn; it gave him a headache. The reef and the mangrove channel would be in deep shadow until after the sun broke the horizon.

Finally the first rays of dawn changed the colors around him from muted grays to vibrant greens and browns. He sighed deeply; his relief would be here soon.

"Oi there, Pel! You ready fer yer mornin' bracer?" a boy's voice called from around the first bend in the trail.

"Zat you, Tim?" Pel smiled; Tim was a good lad, and would make a fine pirate.

"Aye." The skinny boy strode up the trail, a kettle and bundle of bread and cheese balanced in either hand.

"Come and share a cup wi' me."

"Right!" He put the bundles down on the big flat rock and stretched his skinny frame, focusing his sharp young eyes far to the west, then closer. "Wha'sat?" he asked, pointing down into the dimly lit shadow of the island, just beyond the reef.

"What?" Pel shaded his eyes from the morning sun and looked. Two faint vertical shafts pierced the mists like dead trees above a winter snow. But they were moving. "What the..."

The heat of dawn permeated the air, and the mists began to recede. As they did, the square topsails of a merchant galleon emerged at the bases of those bare shafts, its fore and main masts.

"It's a ship, lad. And closer'n one oughta be. You run down an' tell—"

"There's another!" Tim shouted, his fervor overriding caution. "An' that'n's comin' up the channel!"

"Holy..." Pel's oath trailed away as the mists receded further and the triangular topsail of yet another ship materialized, this one even further up the channel and cutting a smooth line between the hedges of giant mangroves.

He reached for the ivory horn at his hip and brought it to his lips. The first note split the air for a count of three. He paused to take a breath then sounded another blast like the first, then another breath. He continued until nine blasts had sounded.

"You best run, Tim. We're under attack."

Tim sat down on the wide flat stone at the very peak of the mountain and stared at the ships as the older man ran down the trail toward Blood Bay. He gazed out over the mists, seeing the ships more clearly now. Clouded memories arose—another life, his father's smile, the crack of a whip... and tears welled up in his eyes.

≈

"Fire! Blood! They come!"

"What the hell?" Bloodwind bolted out of bed, the dagger from the night table in his hand. As his mind cleared of sleep, he recognized Hydra's distinctive screech.

"What is it?" Camilla asked, rolling up and reaching for a nightgown.

"Nothing, I'm sure, my dear. Just Hydra on a rant. I don't know what's gotten into—"

The door to his chambers shattered into a thousand splinters. One of his guards landed amid the wreckage and skidded to a stop, his chest a mass of broken bone and torn meat.

"Touch me and die," Hydra seethed at the other guard before stepping through the obliterated portal.

"What in the name of all Nine Hells is going on, Hydra?" Bloodwind traded the dagger for his cutlass. "Have you lost what shreds of sanity you ever possessed?"

"Death comes to you, Captain Bloodwind. It comes through the mists this very hour!" One craggy finger pointed past him toward the fog-shrouded cove. "The ships of Southaven have found you!"

"Ships? What—"

A horn sounded through the thick air, the nine consecutive blasts that designated an attack.

"Impossible!" He strode to his balcony and peered into the mists. The silhouettes of four corsairs at anchor and *Guillotine* at rest alongside the pier were clear enough. Then a long bowsprit edged from the gap in the mangroves, its raked foremast following behind. He stared slack-jawed at the dozens of launches and dugout canoes following in the ship's wake, each crowded with figures.

The crews of the corsairs were responding with the same lethargy, stumbling on deck to stare in wonder at the ship entering the cove. Some shouted warnings, others threats and calls to arms.

Orin's Pride turned gracefully to present her broadside and a storm of arrows raked the nearest corsair, *Black Guard*. Men screamed and fell as the captain shouted to cut the anchor free and raise sails. They never got the chance, for a small cask flew in a high arc from the foredeck of the schooner. Just before impact it exploded into a blinding shower of white-hot fire. Before Bloodwind could cry out, the entire ship erupted in flames. Pirates leapt into the water, some burning as they swam, some foundering and sinking, but still burning.

Orin's Pride rounded the blazing wreck, her bowsprit aimed straight for the pier and *Guillotine* as a second ship emerged from the hidden channel.

"Rouse everyone!" Bloodwind yelled to his guard as he snatched up a shirt and trousers. "We'll form up at the palace steps and get to *Guillotine*." The guard dashed off. "Camilla, put some clothes on. You'll be coming along. Hydra, prepare yourself. Your powers may turn the tide."

"I need blood, Captain." Her dark eyes drifted toward Camilla.

"Take his." He pointed to the dying guard. "I'll have the house slaves brought to you."

"Very well." She dropped to her hands and knees, her mouth gaping wide. Needle-sharp teeth plunged into the man's neck. In moments it was over. She rose and wiped the gore from her lips as Koybur and a dozen guards surged into the room.

"What'n high hell's goin' on, Bloodwind?" Koybur hobbled to Camilla, who had donned a gown. "There's a ship burnin' in the harbor!"

"It would appear that Feldrin Brelak has found us, and that he has mustered a sizable force." Bloodwind finished buckling his boots and sword belt. "No matter. We'll cut them to pieces and take the other ship to replace the one they destroyed. Come on!"

Guards, servants, slaves and a number of officers and crew joined the group as they headed for the entrance to the palace. Yodrin and the entire crew of *Hippotrin* met them on the steps.

"Three ships at least, Captain," the assassin said calmly, pointing toward the prow of *Syren Song* as it edged into the cove. "*Hellraker* and *Blackheart* are engaging. *Cutthroat's* short handed and can't make sail. *Black Guard's* a loss. They're armed with some variation of the lightkeeper's gift I told you—"

"I've seen it," Bloodwind cut him off, gesturing toward *Winter Gale*, which had taken a tack north toward the shanty town. "They're landing! We've got to get to *Guillotine* before they set her afire."

"Yer a little late on that'n, I think," Koybur said, pointing toward the big corsair tied to the pier. As they watched, *Orin's Pride* turned from where her lower hull had been hidden behind *Guillotine*, and a small missile arced toward the larger ship. This cask exploded on impact, lighting the sky with white streamers of flame and catching the entire rig on fire in an instant. Men and debris rained into the water around the doomed ship.

As they all gaped in shock, *Winter Gale* lobbed a missile high over the line of boats landing on the black sand beach, right into the center of the shanty town. The cask exploded, raining sheets of white flame down among the ramshackle buildings and setting the entire town ablaze.

Bloodwind stirred from his shock and began barking commands. "Yodrin! Get Ghelfan. He's in the feasting hall. Meet us back here with as many fighters as you can find. We'll escape on *Hippotrin*. Hydra, do something about that damned ship! You, Tommy, go get me the Flaxal woman. They'll not set us afire with her along. Go!"

Yodrin and Tommy ran into the palace while Hydra stepped forward, raised her arms and forced the sea to her will.

≈

"Holy mother of sea and storms! What the hell is that?"

Everyone aboard gaped at the horrific shape rising up out of the water behind *Orin's Pride*. A saurian head the size of a wagon formed up on a sinuous neck and turned toward the tacking ship.

"Magic!" Rowland's assessment seemed unnecessary, considering the thing was made entirely of water. Then its mouth gaped wide and he yelled, "Captain, it's going to—"

"Hard alee!" Brelak joined Rowland at the wheel, pulling hard over as the great glistening sea serpent vomited a torrent of water at the ship. *Orin's Pride* lurched as thousands of gallons of sea water thundered against her hull and deck, knocking everyone flat. Some were swept kicking and screaming over the side or lay senseless, crushed under tons of water. Brelak and Rowland lost their grip on the wheel, and the ship slewed away from the pier.

"Bring her about!" Brelak cried, crawling back to the wheel and pulling her hard to port. "Get her headsail sheeted in!" The ship rounded slowly in the light wind, stern toward the swirling seawater serpent.

Horace's bellow shook the air. "Rig lifelines and harnesses! Secure for heavy weather! Hatches dogged tight!"

"Captain! Look out!"

Brelak didn't know where the warning came from, but he ducked and clutched the wheel, turning to look over his shoulder at the towering beast of magic and water that bore down on them.

"Hang on!"

The great maw gaped wide and crashed into the ship's transom, enveloping the entire afterdeck in a wall of semi-solid water. The ship lurched forward with the force of the impact. Brelak was flung to the deck like a rag doll as *Orin's Pride* shot forward. He rolled to his feet, spewing water and clamoring back to the wheel, but too late.

The ship ground to a halt upon a sand bank to the north of the pier, her bowsprit projecting almost to the beach. He looked around, but the magical beast was nowhere to be seen.

"We're hard aground!" Rowland shouted, regaining his feet and helping him up. "Bloodwind's got some kind of mage at work, Capt'n. Look!"

He turned as the magical serpent formed again, this time near *Syren Song* as she tacked toward the shipyard. Two corsairs had cut their anchor rodes and were getting under way, while the third remained tethered in place, unable to man her sails. If the serpent drove *Syren Song* ashore on the far side of the cove, she would be of no use.

"We've got to find whoever's conjuring that thing!" Brelak took in their situation at a glance: the ship's bow rode high, hard aground, her mainsail hung in tatters, torn from luff to leech by the force of the attack. "Horace, kedge her off. Launch skiffs and run the anchor out astern. Get that mainsail replaced."

"Captain! Look! It's Bloodwind!"

Feldrin looked where Rowland pointed and his hand drifted to the haft of the boarding axe at his belt. A tight knot of figures stood upon the steps of the palace carved into the side of the mountain. One was indeed Bloodwind, and another he recognized instantly as Koybur. In front of them stood a woman, her arms raised toward the cove as if in supplication.

"Damn if that ain't his witch. Boarding party, with me! Rig a cargo net over the bow! Horace, get the *Pride* off this damned sand and land her at the pier."

"Aye, sir, but isn't that... Captain! Look!"

His eyes darted back to the knot of figures as the one person he sought most stumbled down the steps in the hands of a pirate. "It's Cynthia. Come on!"

≈

Cynthia woke to the rattle of keys and a wave of overwhelming nausea. For a moment, she thought she was back aboard *Winter Gale*, but the chains on her wrists and the ache of three days in a dungeon reminded her quickly of her situation.

"Here, gimme them keys!"

"Not on yer life, Tommy. You ain't no captain!"

"You'll bloody gimme them keys, 'er you'll be eatin' yer own liver!"

"Oh? And who's gonna—Uhhh!"

Keys rattled again as a man approached the barred door to her cell. Her nausea subsided slightly, as if a raging hangover ebbed away to only a minor irritation. The man tucked a bloodied cutlass under his arm and started trying keys. Cynthia watched, wondering what was going on. The lock finally clicked open and he pushed the door aside. He went to work on her manacles without a word, trying smaller keys.

"Who sent you?" she asked, thinking the question her safest gambit.

"Shut yer mouth a'fore I lose my patience and cut you out'a these damned things instead'a findin' the damned key."

She shut her mouth.

The locks finally clicked open and he grabbed her by the hair. "Up, wench!"

"Ow! Damn it, my legs are numb, you dolt! Give me a moment." Her protests went unheeded. When her legs really did prove shaky, he simply pulled harder. Halfway up the stairs, another bout of nausea struck her like a kick to the stomach, doubling her over and sending her to her knees.

"Up, you lazy cow!" He punctuated his command with a kick that sent her sprawling, bruising her arms on the steps. He grabbed her collar and hoisted her up without breaking stride, forcing her forward. "I got no time fer foolishness."

Sunlight blinded her as they emerged from the palace, but the clamor of battle and the acrid smell of smoke gave her an accurate picture of what was going on. Bloodwind's secret base had been breached. She blinked and squinted, and almost toppled over at the sight of *Syren Song* being attacked by a sea drake made of nothing but water and magic, its maw spewing a column of water as thick as a man's chest. Men clung to rigging or hid behind bulwarks as the ship veered off course into the shallows.

Then she saw Bloodwind's sorceress and nausea rose in her like a tide. The bodies of four slaves lay around her, their blood smeared across her arms and face, running down her neck in rivulets. Bloodwind's men held two more screaming wretches, food for her power.

Cynthia's knees buckled. She could feel Hydra's corrupt magic forcing the sea to do her bidding. The sensation of that malevolent force bending the sea to its will felt like a personal violation.

"Yer gonna have company right quick, Capt'n," Koybur said, drawing her attention from her misery. He pointed to the bow of *Orin's Pride*, where men swarmed down a cargo net slung from the bowsprit. At the forefront, Feldrin Brelak waded ashore, a boarding axe in each massive fist.

"To *Hippotrin*! Now! We can't wait on Yodrin any longer." Bloodwind grabbed Camilla and led them forward, thrusting another slave at his sorceress in passing. "Come on, Hydra. You'll have to eat on the run."

Cynthia managed to walk, the nausea subsiding as the sorceress paused in her corrupt manipulation of the sea, but the sight of the creature feeding on the hapless slave left her gagging. The woman's mouth stretched impossibly wide, rows of black needle-like teeth visible for an instant before she ripped a hole in her victim's throat. Cynthia turned away in disgust.

Bloodwind urged his guards toward the shipyard where *Hippotrin* lay at the dock. The area was quiet, the workers having not yet made their daily migration from the shanty town. A guard crew manned the schooner, and they were keeping the few small craft straying in their direction at bay with crossbows and the ship's two ballista. *Syren Song* lay heeled over, her hull resting on an oyster reef near the mangroves.

They would reach *Hippotrin* unopposed.

CHAPTER FORTY-ONE
Fight or Flight

"HURRY!" BRELAK YELLED, URGING his force forward at a reckless pace. They met some opposition: knots of pirates from the palace and an occasional bow shot from Bloodwind's retreating group. They were gaining, but far too slowly.

An arrow whistled past his ear and a man behind him yelped in pain. His landing party had been supplemented by native forces. Chula and Paska stalked at his sides, both clad only in loincloths and crimson paint.

Orin's Pride had sailed past Plume Island at the dark of the moon two nights before, packed to the gunwales with the majority of the tribe and towing a string of outrigger canoes in her wake. Before they met with *Winter Gale* and *Syren Song*, Chula provided detailed drawings of the cove, the defenses, and most importantly the channel through the reef.

Brelak spared a glance over his shoulder at *Winter Gale* and the burning town. The galleon tacked sluggishly in the light air, a victim to the two corsairs cutting nimbly around her, just beyond range of her catapult but well within striking distance of their ballistae. The pirates learned quickly.

Ahead, Bloodwind's group reached the dock and clamored aboard *Hippotrin*. Dock lines fell into pieces under their cutlasses, and the ship's jib shot up the forestay to pull them away. A weak hail of arrows landed among Brelak's force as they mounted the dock and raced forward, but the gap was already too great to leap.

"Grapples! We should'a brung grapples!" Brelak waved his men to cover, but stood and glared at the ship. Fifty feet separated them; it may as well have been leagues.

"Cowards!" he bellowed, brandishing his boarding axes. "Come back and fight, Bloodwind!"

"Perhaps another day, Master Brelak! Until then, accept this with my compliments!" The pirate captain turned a massive ballista toward the dock and fired.

Feldrin didn't have time to react, dodge, or even turn to evade the wrist-thick bolt of steel-tipped hardwood. He felt a jerk, and a line of pain across his shoulder. A quick look brought a rueful grin to his lips. Only a thin cut showed through his torn shirt; a foot to the right would have killed him.

"You talk better'n you shoot, pirate!" he bellowed across the widening gap, but Bloodwind just grinned and sketched a mocking bow before turning to bark orders to his crew. More sails unfurled into the freshening breeze, and *Hippotrin* pulled away.

"Less talk, more action, Feldrin," he muttered to himself, turning to join his squad of fighters. "Back to *Orin's Pride*. We've got to get her off the sand!"

"Captain! We got problems!"

He looked to where a crewman pointed, and gritted his teeth. A tight knot of fighters descended the steps of the palace, Yodrin in their midst. Behind the traitorous captain, the half-elf Ghelfan hobbled between two burly guards.

"Bloody hell! After 'em before they can get out the pier. We can't let one of them corsairs pick 'em up!" They raced back the way they'd come, but again, arrived behind their quarry.

The knot of pirates hastened onto the pier and out toward the burning hulk of *Guillotine*. On the water, one of the corsairs disengaged *Winter Gale* and tacked around toward the pier. The pirates reached the end of the long stone structure and stood with their backs to the water, cutlasses bared and ready as Brelak's force charged into them.

With a scream of challenge and a clash of steel, wood and flesh, the two forces met. Brelak knocked the cutlass facing him spinning away with one of his boarding axes, and clove through half a dozen ribs with the other. The man fell, but another thrust his blade at Brelak's throat. Chula knocked the pirate's blade up and away, and Paska sliced across his stomach with her captured cutlass, all the while loosing a steady stream of language that sounded suspiciously like criticism.

"Push 'em hard! Watch that corsair!" Fifteen feet separated Brelak from Yodrin and Ghelfan, but the corsair was closing fast. The burning *Guillotine* blazed hot on their left, but there was enough room beyond her transom for the corsair to pass. In seconds they would be close enough for the assassin and his prize to jump to safety.

"Down!"

The call came too late as a ballista bolt ripped through his crew, killing one and maiming another in passing. The wounded man fell into the crimson-stained water between the burning ship and the pier, and screamed anew as a dark shape took him from below. Battle and blood had called the wolves of the deep. Anyone who fell in the water would be devoured, alive or dead.

Another pirate fell at Brelak's feet. One step closer—ten feet and two rows of defenders separated them. Brelak seethed in rage as he noted Yodrin's calm demeanor; the pirate looked back and forth, gauging the approaching corsair and the proximity of his foes. In his left hand he firmly grasped the collar of Ghelfan's shirt.

Brelak parried another thrust, smashed his fist into the man's nose and hooked his other axe into his opponent's groin. Another quick glance at Yodrin and his heart sank; they would not reach the assassin in time. The corsair's bow swept past the end of the pier, and Yodrin turned to make the leap that would save his life.

Gale force wind rose from nowhere, slamming into the corsair's taut sails. The ship's masts groaned as they were pushed over by the gust. The hull lurched away from the pier in a violent yaw that plunged the ship's leeward rail into the bay. Spars snapped like kindling as the masts were hammered into the water. Men tumbled into the sea and screamed in horror as sleek shapes converged on them from below. The water in the corsair's wake ran red, her barnacle-encrusted hull exposed as it passed, too far away for Yodrin to leap to safety.

Brelak howled in triumph, smashing a pirate's face with the haft of one axe while hacking through the wrist of another. The defenses were melting away, and Yodrin could not escape. For the first time, Brelak saw fear in the assassin's eyes.

≈

Cynthia grimaced in pain as the rough hemp cinched tight, binding her to *Hippotrin's* starboard mainmast shrouds. The pirate grinned at her, his bearded visage an inch from her face. She turned away, and chance brought her gaze to the forces of Feldrin Brelak and Yodrin clashing on the pier.

It all struck her in an instant: the approaching corsair, the lines of combat, and Yodrin watching it all, readying himself to leap with Ghelfan to safety.

"No," she muttered, calling all the strength she could muster and reaching out with her will. She pleaded with the winds and felt the sudden response, the ethereal joy of the air as it came to her call. It slammed into the corsair's sails, heeling the ship over, ripping sails, cracking spars and snapping lines. She held the wind against the sails until the ship passed the pier, then released it, thanking the wind and feeling its answering elation. The ship righted, but her rig was in tatters, her crew decimated. Then a scream rent the air, the most inhuman sound ever to reach Cynthia's ears. It was Hydra, and she was in pain.

≈

"It's over, Yodrin!" Brelak called out, hacking aside a cutlass and felling the pirate who wielded it with a blow that clove him to mid-sternum. The last man between them fell away in a welter of blood. Three pirates stood beside the assassin, horror painting their features as they realized they were trapped between fire, steel and shark-infested waters. "Hand Ghelfan over, and we'll take you alive."

"To kick at the end of a yardarm? Not likely, Morrgrey." Yodrin leveled his cutlass at Feldrin's eyes and laughed. "You'll walk away, or your friend Ghelfan goes for a swim. You may have won the fight, but there's no prize for you."

"My prize is yer head, Yodrin. Killin' Ghelfan won't save you. Drop yer sword or die."

"Or I kill your precious shipwright then cut your fat throat."

Brelak raised his two gory boarding axes and grinned. "I thought you were more the type for stabbin' a man in the back, like yer friend Karek. Yer facin' a blade, now."

"Better a blade than a rope," Yodrin said. He pushed, and Ghelfan toppled backward.

Before they even heard the splash, Yodrin lunged, but Feldrin was ready, and the cutlass skittered along the haft of his axe. The Morrgrey's counterstroke met a dagger, which kept the axe from hacking through the pirate's stomach. Two of the pirates next to Yodrin went down, overwhelmed by the rush of Brelak's men, and the third fell wounded into the water. Screams of horror and agony rent the air, but none could spare a moment to see how Ghelfan fared.

Yodrin faced four weapons: Brelak's two axes, Chula's war club and Paska's cutlass, but the assassin knew his business, and his own blades blurred in lightning parries and thrusts. He cut a line across Paska's torso with the tip of his sword, adding more crimson to her body paint, then turned another of Brelak's blades with his dagger and ducked under the sweeping arc of Chula's club. His dagger raked the Morrgrey's knuckles, and he blocked a killing stroke from Paska, who seemed undeterred by the gash in her breast.

Chula swept his club low—too low for Yodrin to parry—and it cracked into the half-elf's ankle. The obsidian spike on the end of the club fractured bone, and Yodrin tottered backward.

Horror contorted the assassin's features as he parried another axe stroke, his balance ruined and nothing behind him but water and blood. He dropped the cutlass and snatched the bloody haft of Brelak's axe, teetering at the brink on his one good foot, his broken leg dangling uselessly. For a moment, everything stopped, Yodrin's terrified eyes locked with those of his nemesis.

"I saved your life in Tsing, you know," he said, grimacing at the pain in his leg.

"I wondered 'bout that," Feldrin said with an utter lack of pity. "Figgered you did it to put yourself in good with Cynthia. No suspicions'd fall on you after that."

"But I *did* save your life!" Another horrible scream from over his shoulder ended in a gurgle, and all hope fled his features. "A blade, if you please. Better than that."

"Who said you had a choice?" Brelak's blade separated the assassin's hand from his arm. Yodrin toppled back in a spray of blood, his features registering only surprise as he fell.

Brelak stepped forward as the assassin splashed into the water, then stood in shock at the sight of a huge shark closing in. The creature measured five strides from nose to tail, and it rolled over slowly to take Yodrin. The assassin's scream split the air as the beast shook him like a rag doll. Then it was over. The animal swam away with half its prize while the other half bobbed lifelessly once, then sank, right next to where Ghelfan treaded water.

"Hold my legs!" Brelak yelled, lunging forward with one boarding axe, trying to hook the shipwright's collar. He came up short. "Further!" he commanded as four strong men grasped his ankles.

The blade hooked cloth, and he drew him in.

"Now heave!"

Men groaned with the strain, but managed to haul the weighty Morrgrey and the stunned shipwright up onto the pier. The two of them lay there for a moment, gasping for breath as Paska cut the half-elf's bonds and gag.

"Master Brelak, your timing is flawless." Ghelfan rubbed his wrists and smiled. "Though I haven't a clue why the beast didn't eat me, I can't say as I'll argue with its culinary preferences."

"Never question yer own luck," Brelak said with a grin, standing and helping the half-elf to his feet.

"Captain, look! *Hippotrin's* near out the channel!"

One glance told him the tale: *Winter Gale* tacked sluggishly after the one corsair still under full sail, which had broken off and headed for the channel behind *Hippotrin*. Boatloads of natives and sailors from *Syren Song* were clamoring aboard the crippled corsair, whose remaining crew were vastly outnumbered. *Orin's Pride* still lay hard aground.

"We've got to get the *Pride* off that bank. She's the only ship that can catch *Hippotrin*! Come on, lads!"

"You'll forgive me if I sit this one out, Captain," Ghelfan said as the group turned to race down the pier littered with dead and wounded. "I'll see what I can do for these men."

"Have a care, Ghelfan! You'll have company soon enough." Brelak gestured toward the broad black sand beach where the force from *Winter Gale* had finished with the disheartened populace of the shanty town. The ground looked like a slaughterhouse floor.

"Fare well!"

Ghelfan knelt near a man with a bleeding head wound and began tearing his shirt into bandages, feeling nothing more than lucky to be alive.

≈

Hydra's inhuman wail rang in Cynthia's ears as she watched Ghelfan fall. She could feel the hunger of the great predators cruising under the surface of the lagoon. Blood had called them, and in their small minds, anything that moved the wrong way in the water meant food. Then she recalled Whuafa's words about his first meeting with her father: "Sent dat shark away wi' a wave of 'is 'and."

Maybe... She stretched out her feelings and knew instantly that she had no way to tell the sharks to go away. Her link was with the sea itself, not its denizens. So how could her father have sent a shark away?

Without actually touching the water her senses were dampened, as though trying to feel something through a layer of cotton. She did, however, feel the vibrations of the ships moving through the water and the thrashing of more than a dozen swimming men. This thrashing, even more than the blood, was what frenzied the sharks.

Maybe that's it, she thought, feeling her way around the kicking shapes. It was easy to find Ghelfan; his arms were tied. He was staying afloat by kicking his legs and bobbing up and down, catching a breath every time his head broke the surface. This sent out fewer vibrations than the wounded men around him, but still enough to attract the predators. Cynthia asked the sea to insulate him, to absorb those vibrations, to make him invisible to the circling hunters.

Ghelfan vanished to her senses. One instant he was there, the next gone. The big predators cruised right past him. She felt something hit the water close by where he had been, and the huge animals reacted. A high-pitched scream drifted over the water.

"Someone is wielding power, Captain Bloodwind!" Hydra's voice sounded strained, as if suppressing fear or pain. Cynthia hoped it was pain.

"What do you mean? Who?" Bloodwind paused in his ordering of the ship's crew, his features wrinkled in concern.

"I know not who. Perhaps there is a shaman, or a priest of Odea among them. It matters not. They wield no power I cannot counter."

Oh yeah? Cynthia thought, relieved that the witch could not pinpoint the source of her opposition. She might be a seamage, but a knife would still end her life readily enough. She glanced around the cove as *Hippotrin* slipped into the channel between the towering rows of mangroves, and took in the positions of the other ships. Sailors struggled to free *Orin's Pride* and *Syren Song*, and she knew just how to help. She felt the open sea outside the reef, and asked it to come to their aid.

Hippotrin slowed as the tide turned and water flowed like a river up the channel into the cove.

"What in the name of the nameless serpent just happened, Hydra?" Bloodwind swore as they drifted perilously close to the leeward reef with the opposing flow. "What game are you playing?"

"This is not my doing! The shaman calls the sea to his aid!" She clutched her abdomen, her skin shriveling around the corners of her mouth as she grimaced.

"Well, do something about it!" He barked orders to his helmsman, cracking the man across the back with the flat of his cutlass. "*Orin's Pride's* the only ship that can catch us. If they get free of that sand bank, they'll be after us."

"Very well, Captain, but I will need sustenance to wield such power."

Bloodwind cast about the deck. His last remaining slave cowered in the lee of the low cabin, her hands bound securely to a cleat. He cut her free and thrust her at Hydra like a scrap of meat. "Here. Take her, but stop that ship!"

≈

"The tide rises!" Horace cried as Brelak and the others climbed aboard, soaked and bloodied. "Rowland, get the wounded below. Captain, somethin's bringing the tide in like a mill race. Do you feel it?"

"Aye!" He braced himself as the ship rocked on her keel. "And somethin' knocked that corsair flat right when it was set to pick up Yodrin. Man the capstan! Get us off this shoal and set sail!"

"What do you think? I mean, could it be Cynthia? You think that Whuafa feller was tellin' the truth?"

"Chula said he saw her make water move, an' that they rode a single wave fer a whole night. If she can do that, maybe she can make the tide rise." The ship lurched and the men on the capstan cried out as the load on the anchor rode went suddenly slack. *Orin's Pride* wheeled around, her bow pulling free of the sand. "Cut that cable! We don't have time to retrieve it. Set all sails! Horace, make for the channel. Seamage or no, we're gettin' Cynthia Flaxal back!"

CHAPTER FORTY-TWO

Odea's Chosen

"NOW WE WILL SEE who is the stronger," Hydra said, rising from her repast. Cynthia cringed at the gruesome spectacle. Hydra either no longer cared about her appearance, or hadn't the power to maintain the illusion. Skin hung in flaccid folds around the bloody smear of her mouth, her hair a gray-green mat of oily tendrils plastered flat on her skull.

Cynthia realized that woman was a witch—not a sorceress or mage, but the bride of a demon from one of the Nine Hells. She'd heard the tales of such creatures, those who traded their souls for power. The tales always ended poorly for the witch. She hoped desperately that they were true.

As *Hippotrin* cleared the outer reef and jibed to the north, hands like claws gestured toward the sea behind them and Cynthia felt the corrupt power swell like a swarm of maggots writhing through her. Nausea doubled her over to retch onto the deck. This brought laughter and some comments about weak sea legs from the crew, and a sidelong shake of the head from Koybur. She forced herself upright, squinting into the morning sun at the ship emerging from the wall of giant mangroves, and felt Hydra force the sea into a massive wave.

Cynthia reached out with her senses, feeling the ship, the hull, the sails. A grim smile touched her lips. She turned away and did nothing.

The wave rose behind them, sweeping toward the shore, gaining in height and momentum with every yard it traveled. It crashed over the reef and swept up the channel, a wall of killing force towering half the height of the hapless craft's mast.

"Hydra! No! That's *Hellraker!*" Bloodwind's warning came far too late for the witch to do anything but gasp in horror.

Hydra stared wide-eyed into the rising sun as the mountain of water lifted the ship up and over the reef, sweeping it into the mangroves. The corsair's sleek hull struck the unforgiving coral with a thunderous crack of splintering timbers, her masts felled, her sails shredded and her keel broken. The waters receded, carrying a slick of corpses and flotsam, leaving the broken ship high and dry.

Bloodwind raged at the witch, his cutlass at her throat, but her stance did not waver and her eyes showed no fear. With the crew's attention focused elsewhere, Cynthia extended her senses once again, feeling her way up the channel. She smiled as she felt *Orin's Pride* ease over the diminished remnants of the destructive wave and continue on under full press of sail.

"*That* is *Orin's Pride!*" Bloodwind bellowed, his cutlass pointing to the schooner's distinctive bowsprit as it nosed from the gap in the mangroves. "*That* is the ship you must stop, Hydra. Is that clear? That ship and that ship only! Do it now!"

"I have not the strength. Something opposes me, saps my power." Her shoulders slumped with the strain of commanding the sea so violently. "I must feed before I use my powers again."

"You've fed your last, witch. I'm out of slaves. You stop that ship, or we have to fight them hull to hull outnumbered two to one."

"If I expend my strength without sustenance, we all perish." Her voice had taken a tone as cold as death. Cynthia looked eagerly toward Hydra, hoping beyond hope that she had gone too far, that her power would consume her. Then those pitiless eyes turned toward her, sending a chill down her spine. "I cannot raise another wave without blood. The blood of the get of Orin Flaxal would give me much power."

"And if you fail again, there is nothing to keep them from using that fire catapult on us. No, Hydra, she is our protection, and I'll not sacrifice any of my crew to sate your thirst. If you cannot use your magic, we'll just have to do this the old fashioned way."

Bloodwind turned to his crew and began barking orders to set more sail and jettison any unnecessary weight. He adjusted their course to a more northerly heading as they rounded the last reef of Plume Isle, pointing them straight into the tangle of reefs and shoals of the Shattered Isles. *Hippotrin* responded like a thoroughbred, leaping forward, her sails taut with the wind hard on her beam.

Cynthia squinted to the south and saw *Orin's Pride* trimming her sails to follow.

Now, she thought, her spirits rising with the motion of the sea under her feet. *Let's see what we can do.* She eased her senses into the sea around them and increased the pressure on *Hippotrin's* hull. Hopefully Hydra would not detect such a subtle use of power, but the pressure would slow them. *Orin's Pride* sailed only a mile or so behind, and with Feldrin Brelak at the helm she did not doubt that he was bending every spar to catch up.

≈

"We're gainin', Capt'n," Rowland said, lowering his glass and grinning up at the dour Morrgrey. "We'll have 'em by mid afternoon."

"Aye, and I wonder why. With that sea witch aboard, you'd think we'd be fightin' a headwind." He looked through his own glass, accepting a cup of blackbrew from Marta with his bandaged hand. "Looks like he's leadin' us right through the narrow bits. Put yer best lookout on the foremast, Horace. Row, bring up the charts and the black book from my chart table. I'm gettin' the feelin' I'm bein' led into a trap."

"You know these waters as well as anyone. Why worry?" Horace barked orders and a sharp eyed youth scampered up the ratlines.

"I thought I knew 'em, too, until I read Orin Flaxal's journal. Makes my charts look like a two year old's scribblin's."

"So what's the plan when we catch them?" he asked, his voice pitched low enough that only the helmsman and a few others could hear. "Bloodwind has at least one of them ballista on that ship. He could set our sails afire before we get close enough to grapple, and we can't use the fire catapult with Cynthia aboard."

"I'm wonderin' how many bolts he has left fer that thing. The guards who were aboard during the attack fired quite a few. I don't think *Hippotrin* was ready to set sail, so they're probably short on provisions, too." He accepted the black journal from Rowland and began flipping through pages as the charts were laid out. "I'm thinkin' to get close enough for him to take a few shots at us, but far enough to make his aim difficult. When he runs out of bolts, we close the gap."

"And if he gets lucky and catches our foresail afire?" Rowland asked.

"We cut it free and raise another. We've a spare for every sail on the ship, and enough canvas to stitch half a dozen more." He found a page in the journal that gave details for the intricate maze of reefs north of Plume Island. "There. That's where he'll try to run us aground. Somewhere in there."

"Looks like a real meat grinder," Rowland said, squinting at the drawings. "I can't believe the detail Flaxal put into this. How do you suppose he got all these soundings?"

"Don't know. I just hope they're accurate."

"And if they ain't?"

"Then we've got bigger problems than a few flamin' ballista bolts."

≈

"They're gaining on us." Bloodwind lowered his spyglass and moved to the helm. He took careful bearings of three different points on nearby islands, considering them for a moment before telling the helmsman, "Half a point to windward."

"Aye, Capt'n!" The crew responded, trimming the sails to take best advantage of the new heading.

"They shouldn't be gaining on us," he muttered. "Identical ships, identical sails, and we're the lighter by far. Why are they gaining on us?"

"The sea is against us, Captain Bloodwind," Hydra said, one craggy hand clutching her abdomen. "I can feel the power that opposes us. It drags at our hull like a growth of weed and taxes my strength. Someone on that ship wields power."

Bloodwind's eyes narrowed at her then swept across the deck, gauging his crew, their mood and their loyalty. He glared down at the ballista mounted upon Hippotrin's poop deck; there were only four more bolts for it, and the one on the bow had none. These he would save for his last defense, or for Feldrin Brelak if the opportunity presented itself; four bolts would not keep *Orin's Pride* at bay.

"Tommy, call 'em together." In a few moments most of the crew stood facing aft, forty-five strong and not a faint heart among them; everyone but the helmsman and the lookout above.

"We are in battle, lads and lasses," he began, drawing his cutlass and pointing it toward *Orin's Pride* while pacing back and forth across the deck. "That ship carries a wizard, and right now he's usin' magic to slow us down. When they catch up, they'll either board us with twice our numbers, or stand off and lob one of their fire casks onto our deck. Hydra can destroy them, but she needs blood to feed her magic."

He whipped around without warning and brought the pommel of his sword down on the back of the helmsman's head, felling the man and grabbing the wheel before the ship could veer off course. The massed crew stared wide-eyed, shocked into immobility.

"I did that to save our lives," he bellowed, leveling his cutlass at the massed crew, "just as I would order any of you to lay down your lives in battle. This *is* battle. Either we fight back, or we burn." He nodded to the unconscious man and said, "There's your blood, Hydra. Don't waste a drop."

As she fell on the man, murmurs ran through the crew. They had all faced death in combat, but being fed to a witch was something else entirely. Bloodwind ordered another man to take the wheel, but did not put his sword away. He knew they would not mutiny, not yet, but he dared not show weakness. They were, after all, pirates.

"Reef! Two points off the port bow."

The call from the lookout broke the tension and brought a smile to Bloodwind's lips. "That's your target, Hydra. We'll pass within bowshot of that reef. Put them on it."

"Yes, my captain," she said, her grey-green tongue licking the last of the gore from her lips.

≈

"Reef off the port bow, Captain! We'll clear it by two boat-lengths on our present heading."

"That'd be Hobart's Reef, accordin' to this chart," Brelak said, marking their position and taking a quick sighting of the nearby headlands. "We're right on the mark."

"A lee shore. How comfortin'." Horace's sarcasm would have flowed out the scuppers if it had been as palpable as it was audible.

"Relax. Deep water fer a mile east. Take her up a point if you want. Tell Rowland to make lunch, somethin' special for the whole crew. We'll have a fight this afternoon, one way or the other." He turned to leave just as a hysterical call sounded from the foremast lookout.

"Rogue wave!"

"Hard a starboard!" Horace and Brelak shouted as one, both realizing intuitively the trap they were in.

The wave bore down on them from windward, a sheer cliff of water rising out of nowhere. It towered as tall as their mast, capped in plunging white. Even if they could bring the bow into the wave, the ship would be flipped backward onto the reef, if not crushed outright by the weight of water.

"I bloody knew it!" Horace raged, shooting orders for the crew to haul on all sheets as they came into the wind. "All hands, hang on for your lives! Get these below!" Without waiting for anyone to obey, he scooped up all the charts and Orin Flaxal's black journal and pitched them down the companionway, then slammed the hatch and dogged it tight.

A sudden gust of wind and thrust of force on their stern caught everyone by surprise. *Orin's Pride* surged forward, rounding up into the wind, her bowsprit pointed at the wave like a spear.

"Shambata Daroo!" Chula cried, clutching a shroud and thrusting his war club at the wave and laughing like a fiend. Paska took the more prudent approach of crouching behind the mainmast, though her voice also rose on the wind with the call.

"They think Cynthia's helping us!" Rowland cried, lending his weight to the wheel along with Brelak and the helmsman.

"I think they're bloody right! Look!" He nodded to the wave bearing down on them. "It's thinning out in the middle!"

They could see light through the center portion of the wave. With their sudden burst of speed, hope rose in their hearts.

≈

Cynthia clutched her hands behind her back, ignoring the wave of nausea and the pain of her mangled finger, willing herself into the sea. The force of the witch's magic was staggering. Without actually touching the water, she knew she could not counter that much raw power. She could, however, help *Orin's Pride*.

"Someone fights me!" Hydra cried, raging at the sea to crush the ship. "Someone helps them!" She fell to her knees and screamed her venom at the sea, whipping the wave forth.

The intensity of hatred welled up inside Cynthia like a tide of filth filling her until she thought she would scream. "Please," she muttered under her breath. *Please just a little... less... water... right... there.*

It felt like asking a man under torture to please help her dull the knife being used to part his flesh. The more she poured into the effort, the more Hydra fought her, and the more corrupt power poured into the sea.

All eyes save Cynthia's were locked upon *Orin's Pride*. Considering the strain on her features, this probably saved her life. She did not need to see; she *felt* the pursuing ship ride up the base of the massive wave until her deck inclined halfway to vertical, wind and water pushing her forward at Cynthia's urging. Hydra had meant to smash the wall of water down onto the broad side of the ship like a hammer upon an anvil. But with Cynthia's aid they had turned the ship fully so that they met the wave head on; instead of an anvil, the hammer struck the tip of a spear.

Orin's Pride impaled the wave, her bowsprit and foredeck knifing through for the main hull to follow. Her momentum continued to carry her up as the wave swept past, leaving the entire ship airborne for a moment before she drove back down into the sea, burying her bow into the calm behind the wave. She bobbed up, decks awash, some canvas in tatters and some spars snapped, but her main rig intact.

Cynthia eased her breathing, opened her eyes, and then wished she hadn't.

Hydra had fed again.

≈

"Man overboard!" Brelak bellowed as the schooner's bow plunged down the mountain of water. He'd heard the fore topmast part, and knew the lookout had not made it to the deck before they hit, but the ship itself had passed through the wave with miraculously little damage. "Get her bow around, Horace. Lookout aloft! Watch for another wave."

"Aye, sir. Man in the water dead astern!" Horace grabbed a coil of line tied to a cleat on the taffrail and threw it toward the floating shape. "I still don't like that lee shore. We're dead if that witch puts another wave on us right now."

"I know. We'll circle once for survivors then get away from this rock. You there, cut that wreckage away. Topmen, get aloft and clear that broken yard! I want a new fore-top on her right now!"

Orin's Pride came around in a tight circle, dragging lines in the water, but only one man could be retrieved; three others had vanished. As they resumed their former course, a call came down from the new lookout.

"Captain! *Hippotrin's* turning! She's tacking!"

"Tacking? That don't make any sense at all!" Brelak pushed through the men struggling to bring a new spar up from the hold and braced himself on the foredeck, raising his glass to view the distant ship. As the lookout had said, *Hippotrin* had tacked. She was headed southeast, sacrificing much of the lead she had gained.

"What's he thinkin'?" He lowered his glass and called aft, "Row! Get my charts! Horace, plot a course after 'im."

"Aye, sir!"

Orin's Pride turned upwind, beating toward the northeast, cutting the gap to her quarry as their courses converged.

≈

"Odea preserve us," Cynthia muttered, shocked into immobility at the sight of the thing that was Hydra, but not, as it fed on a fallen man.

The man's chest had been flayed wide open, ribs torn as if by the claws of a great cat. Hydra crouched amid the gore, hands coated, her deformed face dipping down to slaver amid the pulsing flow. Her mouth stretched impossibly wide, a circle of needle black teeth.

Camilla screamed at the spectacle, drawing everyone's attention before turning away to bury her face in Koybur's shoulder.

"Makin' bargains with monsters, Bloodwind?" Koybur turned his daughter away from the sight. "I don't know what yer thinkin', but that's no sorceress. It ain't even human."

"Hydra! What in the name of—" Bloodwind took two steps toward her, then stopped. The pirate upon whom she had fed was Tommy, his personal guard.

"I needed blood, Captain." She rose from her gory repast, shook herself once, and slowly regained a vaguely human aspect. "If I had not taken this man, we would have perished."

He opened his mouth to argue, but a cry rose from aloft, "Somethin' in the water ahead, Capt'n! A school of dolphins or tuna, maybe. Somethin' ain't right!"

"What new curse is this, Hydra?" he asked rhetorically, turning to stare into the water ahead. The sea a quarter mile off their bow churned white with a thousand splashing shapes.

"The power I have expended has brought them," Hydra said. "They are Odea's chosen. They come to oppose me. Give me blood now, Captain, or we will all be dragged down to their domain."

Bloodwind looked at the roiling sea ahead, at the flashing fins of a thousand merfolk rushing toward his ship, tridents and lances held high as they broke the surface in graceful arcs. Cynthia smiled thinly at the fear in his eyes.

They come for you, Bloodwind, she thought. *They come for you and the beast you have been using to torture the sea.*

"Bring her about! Close haul the main sheets! Drop that fore tops'l!" Men scattered to do his bidding and *Hippotrin* answered, rounding up and crossing the point of wind. He looked at the approaching school, then at their course and speed. "Bowmen to the taffrail! Keep them off our hull!"

As crossbowmen lined up at the stern and began firing into the school of merfolk, he glanced at the opposing headlands facing him. To the south loomed the craggy face of Ataros Isle, her barren slopes cruel and unforgiving; well to the north stood Minos, less forbidding, but without a single passage or cove; between them lurked a maze of coral and rock ready to rip the bottom out of any ship trying to pass through. He knew these waters well, and he knew where he could sail that no one would dare follow.

"We need speed, Hydra," he said, gauging the angle of the wind.

"Feed me or die, Captain. Your choice is simple."

As if in answer, one of the bowmen at the taffrail screamed and fell thrashing on the deck, a trident transfixing his abdomen.

Bloodwind looked to Hydra, his lip wrinkled in distaste. "Take him, but make it count. I'll not sacrifice any more of my men for you."

She silenced the man with one pass of her hooked fingers. Her maw opened again, gaping to close over the horrible wound in his throat. He thrashed and kicked, but his blows landed without effect.

As the man died in Hydra's chill embrace Cynthia felt the creature's power swell. The sea at the stern of the ship built in a pressure wave, pushing *Hippotrin* forward. With the wind on her other side, the ship heeled steeply with Cynthia now on the low side of the deck. Water surged up through the scuppers against her feet.

"Yes," she said, luxuriating in the feel of the sea. She urged the water up to play over her tired, aching legs, and the sea answered.

"We're beatin' 'em!" a man cried, pointing aft. "We're leavin' 'em behind!"

Hippotrin surged forward, sails straining, pulling away from the murderous school of Odea's chosen, and Cynthia Flaxal let Hydra aid the ship. She knew now where they were going, and she knew what would be waiting for them.

CHAPTER FORTY-THREE

Blood of the Hydra

"She's cuttin' between Leviathan Shoal and Raven's Reef!" Brelak said, scanning the tumultuous waters between the ships and tapping the narrow gap on the chart. They were closing the distance, but there were still repairs to be done on the damaged rig. "That gap ain't but about a stone's throw wide, and the tide's runnin' with the trades. It's gonna be a mill race in there."

"More like a death trap, with that witch throwin' rogue waves at us," Horace said, as he scanned the sea between the two ships. "What's that rough patch of water off of *Hippotrin's* stern? Looks like a school of fish."

"Lookout there! What's off their stern?" Brelak's call brought every eye on the ship forward. After their near capsize, everyone's nerves were drawn tighter than the jib sheets.

"It's a school o' them fish folk, sir! Damn big one, too! Looks like they're followin' 'em."

"What the hell? Merfolk? Why would they be followin' *Hippotrin?*"

"Who knows what mer think? We should cut to the north." Horace pointed to the calmer waters to the north of Leviathan Shoal, some four miles distant. "It's wider and the current won't be so bad. We'll make up the time not having to fight it."

"And if he tacks back to the south, we lose him completely. He could duck behind any one of these islands. I've played that guessin' game one too many times. Hold your course, Rowland; half a point upwind of his transom."

"Aye, sir, half a point, right at 'em." Rowland leaned on the wheel, sighting along the compass and grinning like a madman. "Right at the bastard."

≈

Cynthia bit her lip in trepidation, wondering if she had made a dire miscalculation. Her first thought had been to stop Bloodwind from escaping. But as she watched Hydra feed on yet another sailor—this one felled by the uncanny aim of a mer harpoon—she revised her priorities.

There's the real threat, she thought, watching the woman-thing's obsidian eyes as they followed everyone on deck. Hydra bristled with power, but still she hungered. Bloodwind might wield her like some kind of foul weapon, but his petty greed paled in comparison to the burning horror that hid within that husk of flesh. That hunger could devour them all. That was the threat Cynthia had to neutralize first. Bloodwind would come later.

Despite having fed, Hydra had not increased their speed. She kept them ahead of the murderous school of merfolk, but hoarded her power, saving it for the conflict she knew would come.

She knows where the true battle will take place, where the sea is strongest, Cynthia realized, guarding her own strength. With her feet doused in a constant flow of the sea her power was doubled, yet she held it tightly in check. She could slow the ship enough to allow the merfolk to catch them, but they would swarm over the rail and slaughter everyone aboard. Cynthia could not control their indiscriminate hatred, and though she felt sure she would be spared, Camilla and Koybur would not. She wondered why she cared about the man who had brought about this entire ignominious tragedy.

"So many lives, Koybur," she said, her voice lost in the rush of wind and sea. "So many lives for one..." She paused as she considered her words. What would she have given to save her mother and father, or her grandfather, or even her grandmother? Would she have set such a plan in motion for the chance to be held in her daddy's arms once again, as Koybur now held Camilla?

"Yes," she said finally, a different type of salt water wetting her cheeks. She let the tears flow unchecked. "Yes, Koybur." And though her voice was drowned by the cacophony of their passage, his one good eye turned to her. She nodded and smiled, and the surprise on his tortured features almost brought a laugh to her lips.

He knew.

She could feel the gap between reef and shoal approaching even without extending her senses into the sea. The hull shuddered as tidal current gripped *Hippotrin* like a giant hand, slowing their progress.

"Steer for the southern reef, and keep her nose into the current," Bloodwind told his helmsman. "We'll have to tack to get through, but not until I say or we'll end up on the rocks!"

"Aye, Capt'n," the man said, keeping one eye on his heading and the other on his commander's sword. The entire crew gave Bloodwind a wide berth, none wanting to be Hydra's next meal.

Now, Cynthia thought, easing her thoughts into the sea, willing the racing current to turn slightly as it met the egress of the narrow channel. She asked the wind to match that turn, faster, and *faster*, to pull at the surface of the sea. The turn in the water created a void, which created a backwash, which made the turn more pronounced.

More wind, more turn, more water, she pleaded and the river of tidal flow turned fully back onto itself. The sky above the narrow channel darkened and coalesced into a bank of swirling clouds.

The water between the opposing reefs was very deep, and the weight of that much water turned back on itself formed a massive whirlpool, but Cynthia asked the sky to come down and play with the sea, and the two joined in a cacophony of forces. The sea leapt skyward, and the sky came down to urge the sea into the heavens.

Sail through this one, you bastard, she thought, letting her power feed the growing vortex.

"Waterspout!" the lookout called, pointing as the whirling mass of air and water coalesced only three boat-lengths ahead. It broadened and thickened in the span of a few heartbeats, filling the entrance to the channel, pulling the surface into an ascending arc that became a tornado of seawater. Burgeoning clouds swirled, darkening the sky in a sudden storm, lightning flashing at its center.

"Turn the ship!" the helmsman screamed, but Bloodwind countermanded the panic with a swipe of his cutlass. The man fell at Hydra's feet, clutching his gaping abdomen.

"There's nowhere to turn!" the pirate captain bellowed, taking the wheel himself. "Rocks to the north and south, and that school of monsters behind us? We sail through this, or we perish!" Then, in a lower voice he said, "Take him, Hydra. Take him and get rid of that thing!"

"Yes, my captain."

Even before the witch descended upon the dying man, Cynthia felt the crushing weight of her foul energy slamming into the sea, beating against the natural flow of the waterspout. A countercurrent began to run against the edge of the vortex, and along the line of conflicting flow, the sea became a wall of ripping white spray. But Hydra only commanded the water, not the winds. She had no way to counter the tornado of air that Cynthia had called to merge the sea and the sky into one.

Cynthia intensified her call to the sea and the air, pleading with both to maintain the merger of forces. Hydra rose from her gory meal screaming her rage and pain at the opposing power. Hate like a wall of fire slammed into Cynthia through her contact with the sea. The water ahead of the ship boiled, and the waterspout constricted ever so slightly.

"No! Please!" she cried, not realizing she spoke aloud.

"Sail on!" Bloodwind commanded, steering straight into the swirling vortex.

Hippotrin struck the line of conflicting flows and staggered like a drunken sailor, heeling sharply to port, then careening hard to starboard as she raced forward, her sails cracking with the howling wind. The deck inclined steeply as their course turned to accommodate the tornadic winds. Spray from the waterspout lashed against them, making it difficult to breathe.

"Loose the sheets! Let her luff or we'll roll over!" Bloodwind's bellow cut through the panic that would have destroyed them. The pirate crew reacted without thinking, without fearing, and without knowing their peril. He pulled the wheel over, steering into the vortex where the winds would press more astern instead of rolling them over. He could not sail past the waterspout without jibing, which would tear the booms off in this wind. He could escape the winds if he could sail around the maelstrom. Speed was his weapon, and *Hippotrin* was careening through the water so fast her bowsprit cut the waves like a knife.

"Now! Haul her sheets!" He pulled the wheel hard over in the opposite direction and the ship began to turn away from the waterspout. Canvas cracked and filled, pushing them even faster. With enough speed, they would escape the waterspout's grasp.

"Gods damn, but that bastard can *sail!*"

Cynthia stared at Koybur, astonished, and knew he was right. Bloodwind was a master, *Hippotrin* his instrument. But their momentum would not be enough to escape the clutches of Cynthia's will. She shifted the vortex so the tornado of sea and sky moved parallel to the ship, pacing them in the opposite direction they had intended to go. They were racing at top speed right toward *Orin's Pride.*

"NO!"

Hydra's scream ripped the very air around them and snapped Cynthia's concentration. The witch sat in the gore of her repast and shriveled as if the beast within her, finding no other source to sate its hunger, fed on the very vessel that kept it contained. Hydra reached out to a passing seaman, but the man cowered away; none would come close to Bloodwind or his sorceress for fear of becoming her next victim.

"Feed me, my captain!" she shrieked, turning her bulging eyes to Bloodwind, but no man strayed near enough for him to murder. He stood alone at the wheel, unable to leave the helm unattended without sending them straight into the waterspout's center.

"No! No, you can't!" Hydra cried out, though no one stood near enough to have earned her protest. The hag clutched at her head as if in great pain, and a line of black fluid ran down her face from her matted hair. "Give me blood!"

Her dark eyes, now mad with terror, raked the deck, but none were near enough to be devoured—none save Cynthia, who stood tied to the shrouds.

The witch lunged, her mouth gaping in a whirlpool of black teeth. The attack startled Cynthia into immobility long enough for the hooked hands to grasp her shoulders and that horrible mouth to near her throat. The ship lurched, but the attack commanded all of her attention. Breath like a ton of rotting meat slammed into her as that maw opened to end her life.

Something fell between them in a flash of steel, and one of Hydra's eyes erupted in a gout of black ichor.

The witch's scream ripped into Cynthia like a spray of needles, but a high-pitched cry of victory lifted her heart from the depths of horror into the light of day. The cry came from a very bedraggled seasprite perched upon her breast, one hand clutching a stolen dagger, the other her scimitar moon medallion.

"Mouse!" Cynthia cried, hope warming her from scalp to toes.

"Die, Odea's favored!" A hand like the tentacle of a vile squid reached for the seasprite, but he yelped in fright and flipped over Cynthia's shoulder. The hand grasped Cynthia's medallion instead, and a flash of ice-blue lightning blasted it into a stump of charred meat.

Hydra reeled back with a shriek that shivered the air, clutching her blackened hand.

"It is *you!*" the witch hissed in a voice no longer even remotely human, her remaining eye wide with recognition. She reached for Cynthia's throat, hooked nails biting deeply. "The blood of a seamage!"

Cynthia gasped for breath as Hydra's mouth stretched into an orifice of bristling teeth. As the mouth neared she felt Mouse sawing madly at her bonds, but she knew they would not part in time to save her.

"Nice comp'ny you keep, Bloodwind," Koybur said as he plunged a cutlass into the creature's back.

Hydra's remaining eye widened, not in pain, but in absolute horror. Her grip on Cynthia's neck fell away, her body twitching spasmodically as that black void of a mouth gaped and slavered to form words.

"No! No! Please!" Her back arched impossibly, as she reached back in an attempt to wrench the blade free, but Koybur would have none of it.

"Please *this*, you hacked up piece of hagfish meat!" He twisted the curved blade savagely, working the tip deeply into her.

The wound in her back gaped wide, but instead of a torrent of blood, six ropy tentacles wormed their way from the gap, each tipped with a bifurcated hook. One wound around the cutlass and Koybur's one good arm, while the other five lashed out to encircle Hydra. Ten hooked digits grasped the edges of her screaming mouth and pulled, peeling the husk of flesh back from the demon that had been imprisoned within.

A mouth like that of a huge lamprey emerged from the ripping sheath of dead meat, black teeth dripping venom, the sloped head sporting the eyes of a giant squid. The beast's roar split the air, hammering Cynthia with a palpable wave of hate and hunger. The cocoon of human flesh, rent and oozing, pulled away in a wet, ripping mass, landing at the thing's splayed feet like a noisome pile of discarded rags.

The tentacle that held the cutlass pulled the blade free, and bent Koybur's arm around until bone snapped and sinew parted. The old sailor's scream echoed his daughter's as the creature turned the newly freed blade on its owner. One thrust buried the cutlass to the hilt and flung Koybur across the deck, slamming him against the mainmast. Koybur hung there, impaled on the cutlass, gasping for breath, unable to even grasp the blade that had pinned him.

Then the beast turned its attention toward the seamage.

Cynthia's scream tore at her lungs, her terror so great that she almost did not feel the bonds on her wrists part. One tentacle encircled her neck, a slimy, cold mass of gray-green scales. It peered at her as if she were a delicacy perched on a fork.

"Now you die, Odea's minion," it growled, drawing her close.

The hilt of a dagger pressed into her numb hand. Reacting instinctively, Cynthia buried the blade in the demon's torso. It looked down at the wound and another tentacle encircled her arm. She twisted the blade but it seemed not to notice. Instead, it pulled the dagger free of its body and bent her arm while lifting her from the deck by her neck.

Mouse leapt from her shoulder to bat at the thing's eyes with his tiny fists, but another tentacle snatched him away. A cry tore from the little sprite's mouth, so high-pitched that even the beast cringed. The answering roar left Cynthia gaping in panic as the tentacle brought the struggling sea-sprite toward its black maw like a tidbit.

"No!" Cynthia cried. She grabbed at the slimy limb, her hand slipping down its length until the two of them grasped the struggling sprite.

The tentacle holding her wrist and the knife bent until the blade pointed at her own stomach, inching toward her skin. Remembering Koybur's fate, she struggled to open her hand, to drop the blade, but the tentacle had wrapped around her fingers.

Cynthia called out desperately to the sea for aid. A geyser erupted at her back, dousing the entire ship in a salty wave, hammering against them, but the beast that held her did not notice.

The tip of the knife pricked her stomach, and she gasped sharply. Her eyes watched as the blade pushed slowly into her flesh, inch after inch of cold steel, stealing the air from her lungs with waves of agony. The beast's horrible laughter rose as its slavering mouth neared her face. She closed her eyes against it, feeling her life bleeding away. Something jerked her hard, and through a haze of pain she felt herself falling.

≈

"Bloody witch!" Bloodwind cursed as he sighted down on the embattled pair and pulled the ballista's release.

The bolt of iron and hardwood struck the creature low, impaling it against the bulwarks. It thrashed on the bolt, flinging Cynthia Flaxal over the side. As her torn body hit the water, the waterspout collapsed upon itself. The weight of the water released from funnel cloud fell like a tidal wave, tossing the ship like a toy. As the deck finally stilled, the creature ripped itself free from the ballista's shaft, howling in rage, tentacles writhing as it turned toward the new threat. Bloodwind stared in awe as the massive wound in its abdomen closed.

Curse of the Gods, he thought. *What manner of creature has Hydra released?* But it bled, and if it could bleed, it could die.

"This isn't good!" He drew his cutlass and ordered the ballista crew, "Load it again, and make this one count."

The captain of a nation of pirates stepped forward and leveled his blade at the mass of squirming tentacles. "Hydra! Enough!"

"Hydra is gone, Captain Bloodwind." The voice nauseated him, its power a wall of visceral hate. "And I am unlikely to thank you for helping her keep me imprisoned for half a century."

"I'm not askin' for your thanks, beast. I'm *tellin'* you, this is *over*! Now stand down, or I'll have you spitted like a hog on feast day." He glanced over his shoulder toward the ballista, but his men were still cranking the heavy weapon's cocking mechanism. The rest of his crew gripped weapons, lining up around the creature in a loose formation. *Not a faint heart among them*, he thought, pride swelling his hopes. This, at least, was a threat they could face.

"The only way this is going to end, Bloodwind, is with your heart in my stomach." A tentacle lashed out farther than he thought it could reach, but Bloodwind had survived on little but treachery and betrayal for two decades. His cutlass flashed and the tentacle's barbed tip fell onto the deck. The severed piece dissolved in a noisome puddle, but the other end quickly grew another double-barbed hook.

"Boarding pikes!" he commanded, and a dozen iron-tipped shafts thrust forth. Tentacles grasped several, but many more struck home. It roared and snapped the pole arms, leaving the iron heads lodged in its body.

"Crossbows!" A dozen shafts buzzed past the waving arms to pierce the beast to the core. This onslaught affected the creature less, its grey-green flesh closing up over the feathered shafts as if absorbing the bolts.

"Cutlasses! With me!" Bloodwind lunged forward, sweeping aside the writhing arms in sprays of black blood. Men screamed as hooked tentacles grasped them, pulling them into crushing embraces or the beast's murderous teeth.

"Ready, sir!" came a call from the poop deck.

"Ballista!" he cried, and his men flattened themselves onto the deck. A blazing shaft of hardwood slammed into the thing, dousing it in burning pitch. Where blades and arrows had caused it only minor pain, fire sent the creature into an agonized frenzy.

"Forward!" Bloodwind cried as he waded in, hacking at tentacles until he could bury his cutlass in the thing's bloated body.

≈

Cynthia felt herself falling through rose-colored water, shafts of light stabbing down from the surface through clouds of crimson.

Pretty, she thought, the pain ebbing with her lapsing consciousness. Something twitched in her hand, and she saw poor Mouse, coughing up little bubbles, trying to breathe. She opened her hand and his little body floated away, hopelessly crushed. As he drifted free he looked toward her, his face twisted in astonishment.

I'm sorry, my dear little friend, she thought, reaching out to him. *Sorry it ended like this.*

Something large flashed past, and Mouse was gone.

She blinked, coughing against the pain in her stomach, finally realizing that the crimson clouds were blood—her blood.

Another shape flashed past, too fast to see details, only a glimpse of silver scales. Shapes moved at the edge of her vision, circling, closing, drawing near enough to see.

Then a hundred hands grasped her all at once, and she felt herself being carried down into the depths.

≈

The burning demon writhed, howling in agony, pierced by a score of blades, black ichor spraying from a hundred wounds. The tentacled arms had been cut short too many times to regenerate, and still the creature spat hate at them, a thousand curses in all the languages of the Nine Hells. Finally, it toppled forward, reaching out one last time, burning and gibbering, to grasp at Bloodwind's legs.

"Die, you useless hag!" Bloodwind drove his cutlass into its eye, forcing its loathsome head down to the deck. A crewman with a boarding axe chopped at the thick neck until the head came free.

Gouts of black and green oozed from the severed neck, hissing on the hardwood deck.

"Over the side with it!" he ordered, heaving the severed head into the sea.

Pirates cheered and surged forward, levering the disgusting corpse over the side, watching it sink in their wake. Then their ardor faded as they beheld the mass of glittering shapes swimming beneath *Hippotrin's* hull.

"Prepare to repel boarders!" Bloodwind shouted, cringing as his much-diminished crew took up station along the gunwales. Between Hydra's insatiable hunger and the battle with the beast, their number had been cut by half. And though they had turned back onto their original course toward the narrows, *Orin's Pride* bore down on them, closer now than ever.

"Captain!" The helmsman cried, pointing. "The reef!"

Bloodwind barked orders, walking past Camilla without even noticing her kneeling on the deck, clutching her father's maimed body. He looked forward, expecting to see the line of breakers marking the shallows. What met his gaze left him astonished beyond cognizant word or thought.

"Holy mother of..."

The sea ended less than two boat lengths ahead, a razor-cut line of nothing but rocky sea bottom several hundred feet below and exposed coral reefs on either side, a bare canyon waiting to engulf them if they sailed off the edge.

"Hard over! Helm alee! Slack sheets!" Sails flapped as *Hippotrin* swung around to the north, her bow coming up through the wind.

The hull shuddered as if a thousand hammers pounded into it from beneath. They slowed and stopped, perfectly still, the wind directly on their bow. At first, he thought they had run aground, but the northern reef stood a boat length from their bowsprit. *Hippotrin* floated in irons, held as if stuck in stone, unable to fill a single sail, with the dry canyon of the channel yawning less than a stone's throw from the starboard bow.

"What in all the Nine Hells?" Bloodwind swore as he strode to the rail and looked down. Beneath the surface, hundreds of merfolk surrounded the ship, the points of their tridents and lances thrust into the hull, holding *Hippotrin* fast in place. "Odea's chosen..." he muttered, shocked beyond the ability to show any further surprise.

As he stared, something shot out of the water like an arrow, missing his face by scant inches as it soared skyward, leaving a glittering trail of sea spray and stardust. It arced down and flew over the deck, straight as an arrow and blindingly fast.

"A seasprite! What in the names of all the serpents of the deep?"

It shot past him again, close enough to jerk several hairs from his beard in passing. It cackled in glee and snapped to a stop, hovering just out of reach, showing him the fistful of red hairs. It made a face and several very rude gestures before shooting off so fast he did not see which direction it had gone.

"You've plundered your last merchant, Captain Bloodwind," a soft voice said from the taffrail, drawing everyone's attention like a magnet.

Cynthia Flaxal stood there as if she had materialized from thin air, a puddle around her feet the only clue that she'd been tossed over the side like a rag doll only minutes before. Her clothes hung in tatters, a huge tear where the dagger had been thrust exposing her bare midriff. But no wound gaped there, no blood flowed, not even a scar marred her flesh.

"Have I, indeed?" he asked, the wonder on his features subsiding as his ire finally centered once more upon something solid, something he could fight, someone he could kill. "I think not, Mistress Flaxal. Take her!"

Wind and sea exploded over the ship's transom, swirling around her in a tight column, fluttering her threadbare clothes but leaving her untouched. With a wave of her hand, tornado-driven sea lashed across *Hippotrin's* deck, casting pirates into the water as if cleansing the ship of an infestation of rats. Where they splashed, the water boiled in a bloody froth.

After a few moments, the torrent of Odea's fury subsided, and only two people stood on *Hippotrin's* deck.

"I think so," Cynthia said as she stepped forward, a slick of seawater carpeting the deck at her feet—her connection to the sea.

He looked around, blinking dumbly. He stood untouched, his cutlass still in his hand, and she only four short strides away. He could kill her if he struck quickly. He had killed one demon today, why not two? He only had to get a bit closer.

"I don't understand, Mistress Flaxal." He shrugged, letting the sword droop loosely at his side. "If you had this much power, why not destroy all of Blood Bay? Why not sink the entire island, for that matter? Why the charade? Why leave me alive at all?"

"Because I want my ship back," she answered, her voice tight with control. "And I want to take you back to Southaven. I want you to face the families of all the people you've murdered."

She had changed, he realized. Something about her was different from the woman who had fallen over the side. Perhaps the merfolk had done something to her. Perhaps she was no longer really human, or even alive. He hid his fear behind a chuckle and a sneer.

"How very noble of you. I'm rather surprised, though." He took a step to the side as if beginning to pace and turned, half a step closer. "You disposed of my crew readily enough. Why not exact your revenge on me personally?"

"Because there are others who need it more than I."

"Families of dead sailors you never knew? I don't believe it."

"Well, maybe there's one I know personally." She shrugged, ignoring him as he crept another half step forward.

"Like who?"

"Like me."

Camilla's voice caught him completely off guard, and he turned in surprise. She stood there trembling, her tear-streaked face as lovely as ever, but her mouth was set in a hard line he'd never seen before. The seasprite sat on her shoulder, still holding its fist-full of red hairs. It grinned and blew the hairs at him, then made an odd little "ssst" sound, drawing its tiny thumb across its throat.

"I don't—"

His cutlass clattered to the deck as all strength suddenly left him. He looked down at Camilla's hand, the one holding the dagger... the dagger she had thrust into his heart.

She let go and backed away. The blade's hilt twitched with the last fluttering beats of the organ she had not thought he possessed.

"But... I... *loved* you..." he said, falling to his knees.

"But I *didn't!*" she said, revulsion seething in her voice as darkness closed around him.

EPILOGUE

Seamage

Rough stone warmed her bare feet as Camilla strode to the end of the pier and raised a hand in greeting.

"Ahoy, *Orin's Pride!*" she called as the stately schooner tacked smartly, setting a course for the pier. Feldrin Brelak grinned broadly and waved.

The schooner tacked once more, approaching at a steep angle before turning upwind, backfilling her sails and drifting broadside up to the wide pier. Men clad in little more than loincloths and shell jewelry ran to catch dock lines and make them fast. In less than a minute the gangplank slapped down and the Morrgrey captain strode ashore.

"Don't you ever haul cargo anymore, Feldrin?" Camilla asked, accepting his huge embrace.

"I *am* haulin' cargo," he said, releasing her and grinning. "Horace dropped off a load of metalwork at Keelson's, and about twelve-hundred-weight of bronze fittin's for the yard here. He didn't have time to deliver it, so I offered."

"Good! I'll tell Ghelfan. Dura will have a crew down here to help you unload." She wasn't fooled by his explanation. Horace would have added only a few days to deliver the fittings himself. Feldrin made landfall at Plume Isle whenever he had an excuse.

"Bloody fine." He looked around the harbor, formerly Blood Bay—now Scimitar Bay. To the north, where the shanty town once cluttered the beach, huts clustered against the jungle-clad hillside. To the south, the old pirate shipyard had been completely rebuilt, and at the dock, two former corsairs rested placidly beside Ghelfan's graceful little smack *Flothrindel*. "The place's shapin' up nicely. Them fellers work like a nest of termites when they're got real tools and someone like Dura to tell 'em what to do."

"You don't know the half of it," she said, guiding him up the pier toward the palace. Bloodwind's former lair had been cleansed and rebuilt from the inside out, every remembrance of the pirate eradicated. "She's teaching them dwarvish."

"Dwarvish? You gotta be kiddin' me!" He laughed long and hard, and Camilla welcomed the sound. "And how's Ghelfan?"

"Happier than a clam at high tide. He's got the keel laid for the new ship, and the wood for framing is being cut. They don't have a proper sawmill yet, but he's making do."

Feldrin squinted at the new building as if he could pierce its walls to see what progress had been made on the new three-masted schooner. His gaze drifted back to the towering stone edifice carved into the mountainside.

"Is she here?"

Camilla didn't have to ask who he meant.

"Somewhere, I think. I'll have Chula find her for you."

"No need," he said, smiling and patting her shoulder. "If she's here, I'll find her. I'll be stayin' 'til mornin' at least. Rowland's got a hold full of provisions fer ya. Said he'd cook you a proper meal."

"Tell me he brought beef, and I'll kiss you."

"Some, but it's salted."

"I don't care if it's on the hoof!" She stretched up on her tiptoes and kissed him on the cheek, enjoying his blush. "You know your way around, Feldrin. If you want to look for her, your best bet's the south beach. She's usually there in the afternoon."

"Thanks, Cammy. I'll be back fer supper."

He stepped off the pier and strode across the beach toward the trail-head. Camilla watched him go, wondering, as she did every time he visited, if he would ever truly find what he was looking for.

≈

"Feldrin!"

His head snapped up at the two dark figures running down the trail toward him.

"Chula! Paska! Hello!" Embarrassment darkened his already-dark features as Paska wrapped her long arms around him and kissed him soundly. Chula embraced him also, and seemed unperturbed at his wife's display of affection. He would never understand their proclivities, but that didn't make him like them any less. They'd stood side by side in combat, baptized in blood and fire. Petty differences meant little after a bonding like that. "You see Cynthia? Shambata Daroo?"

"Ya! She swim. Skull beach. You go see her." Paska latched onto Chula's hand and pulled him down the trail toward the shipyard. "We go. You stay night, ay? I got frien' for you, Morrgrey man! She big woman! Big like you!"

"Another reason to sleep on *Orin's Pride*," he muttered, waving as they trundled off.

Feldrin continued the long climb and the steep descent down the other side of the ridge to the south beach—Skull Beach, the natives continued to call it, but there were no skulls on the beach anymore. All of Hydra's foul magics had been removed, all her curses and traps banished. Plume Isle was clean now, home to the Scimitar Moon, the seamage of the Shattered Isles.

He paused in the shade, enjoying the breeze that rustled the palm fronds overhead while his sharp eyes scanned the beach. There were footprints aplenty, but no sign of Cynthia. He sat on a fallen log at the head of the trail; if she returned to Scimitar Bay tonight, she had to come this way.

Feldrin's eyes were sagging with the warmth of the day when a tiny blade thunked into the wood beside his leg. It quivered there an instant before a streak of stardust circled once around his head and Mouse dove in to snatch up the tiny weapon. The little seasprite snapped to a hover two inches in front of Feldrin's nose, striking a fearsome pose, his tiny sword held at perfect guard position, his new crystal-gossamer wings a blur. The merfolk had made him whole again, as they had Cynthia.

"Hello, Mouse. I surrender." Feldrin grinned in response to the sprite's elaborate bow. The little fellow had taken on quite a swashbuckler affectation since aiding in the demise of the most notorious pirate of the Shattered Isles.

"Have you seen Cynthia?" Feldrin asked as the sprite lighted on his knee and sheathed his tiny cutlass, a gift from Dura for his bravery. He nodded vigorously, pointing to the lagoon and pantomiming holding his breath and swimming under water. "Aye, that's what I thought. Out with her new fish-folk friends, ay?" The sprite nodded again and sighed. Feldrin knew how he felt.

A splash and a flash of silver at the shallow cut through the reef caught his eye.

Tarpon, he thought, but another splash and a glimpse of bright orange changed his mind. The water rippled with wakes as several submerged bodies charged through the gap into the shallow lagoon. They swirled around one another like a pod of playful dolphins, a streak of silver occasionally breaking the surface, and less often, a flash of orange. Feldrin stood as the cavorting merfolk approached the beach.

When they reached the shallows, Cynthia left her mer escort and broke the surface to wade ashore. Feldrin waved and left the shade, walking slowly to mask the eagerness he felt at the sight of her. He marveled how the sea had changed her; not much outwardly, though the sun had darkened her skin and lightened her hair, but inwardly. The sea had enriched her, giving not just power, but confidence and peace as well. Cynthia had become a different woman from the one he'd fallen in love with, the woman he had risked his and others' lives to rescue, but he found he loved this new Cynthia even more.

He watched as the water rippled away from her, leaving hair, skin and clothing perfectly dry. He never tired of that spectacle, though he'd seen it dozens of times now. Her sarong, the flash of orange he'd seen from afar, flapped in the wind, exposing enough long, tan leg to warrant indecency had they been on the mainland. But they were on Plume Isle, Cynthia's home, and she dressed how she liked, when she dressed at all.

"Hello, Feldrin." She stopped a stride before him, then stepped up to give him an awkward kiss and quick hug before stepping back again. The clean scent of the ocean in her hair made him wish he could touch its silken waves.

"Cynthia," he said, letting her name linger on his tongue. The silence between them spoke volumes. As if to break that tension, Mouse flew to her shoulder to tickle her ear, and streaked away with a peal of high-pitched laughter.

"How is *Orin's Pride* treating you?"

"Well enough, thank you, or should I say, thanks *to* you." Cynthia had given him the ship outright as a prize for coming to her rescue. Feldrin was his own master, a truly independent merchant—though he still flew the new Flaxal pennant, a white scimitar moon on a field of blue—and captain of one of the fastest ships riding the seas.

None begrudged Cynthia's gift to Feldrin, nor her claim to the island, especially since she had been so generous in her rewards. She had granted a large portion of Bloodwind's vast fortune to the captains and crews of the three ships engaged in the assault of the pirate stronghold. *Syren Song* and *Winter Gale* sailed away with their hulls full to bursting with contraband, as well as an embarrassing bit of gold. Feldrin had refused both gold and plunder, having an entirely different reward in mind. When that failed to materialize, he'd accepted *Orin's Pride*.

Not quite a fair trade, he thought, nodding to the lagoon behind her. "Your friends are waving goodbye."

"Thank you." She smiled and turned, raising a hand to the school of five merfolk who bobbed head and shoulders out of the water, each holding a webbed hand high in farewell. The small troop dove, their broad tails lashing the water into a white froth. "They're a possessive bunch, but they mean well."

"Possessive? You mean they'd keep you down there if they could?"

"Meaning, they're jealous." She turned and reached out to take his huge hand in hers for a brief eternity. He caressed her odd grip, bereft of the finger that the merfolk could not renew. "Like many of my friends."

"I'm not jealous, Cynthia," he lied as their hands parted. "I'm just not comfortable with 'em, that's all."

"Few are," she admitted, shrugging. To the local sailors, her friendship with the mer merely added to her growing mystique as seamage. For Cynthia, there were other benefits. She withdrew a red-leather book from the folds of her sarong to show him. "But they are good friends, and they've helped me immeasurably in understanding this!"

"Orin's log? I thought you could read it fine now." Feldrin turned up the beach toward the long climb back over the ridge.

"Read it, yes," she said, keeping pace with him as she flipped through the pages. "Understanding it is something else entirely. The language is theirs; just because I can read the letters doesn't mean I can translate it."

"Why'd yer father write a journal in the merfolk language?"

"Tradition, I think. That and to make doubly sure no one else could read it." Cynthia gave him a sidelong, conspiratorial glance. "It's more than just a log, Feldrin, and more than just a bunch of spells, though there's a good bit of both in it. Most of it," she shrugged, "I can't even begin to tell you about, not because it's a secret, but because you just wouldn't understand. I wouldn't have understood it myself a few months ago."

"No need," he said. Magic held no lure for him. Feldrin was a man of the sea, a sailor—his interests lay in the natural, not the supernatural. He didn't give a damn about anything he could not hold in his hands, read on a nautical chart, or see in the sky.

Well, he thought, following her up the steep trail in silence, *there is one thing I can't hold in my hands that I care about.*

When they reached the ridge-crest trail, she stopped, looked up at the sky, then back at him. Turning, she started toward the summit instead of down toward Scimitar Bay.

"Where we goin'?" he asked, though he followed without pause.

"The plume's low today, and I want to show you something. Something I think might help you understand."

The trail steepened toward the end, and they were breathing hard when they finally emerged from the jungle and climbed the last bit of bare ground to the long, flat stone at the mountain's peak.

"Mistress!" a boy called, jumping to his feet and running to her. He knelt, his hand on the dagger at his belt, the other clutched to his chest. "No hostile ships in sight, Mistress. Only *Orin's Pride* has approached, but I see her master's already found you."

"That's fine, Tim. Relax. We're just here to have a look around. Why don't you show Mouse the trail you found down to the caves on the north shore."

"Yes, Mistress!" The youth sprang to his feet and dashed away, the seasprite flittering about his head.

Feldrin knew Tim's story; abducted and seduced by Bloodwind less than a year ago, he'd never really come to grips with being set free. Many of the young ones had fared worse, continuing to fight alongside the pirates even after most had surrendered. Some like Tim had adopted Cynthia as their new mistress, despite her unwillingness to accept their service.

She stood on the flat stone and turned in a slow circle, her eyes scanning the horizon. Feldrin didn't know what she sought, but he followed suit, turning to take in the vista. A few distant sails dotted the indigo blue between the islands, while arcs of white denoted where reefs lay close to the surface. To the southeast, the smoke from Fire Isle hazed the sky. Minutes passed as they admired the view; when he finally turned to her, he could see the adoration in her face.

"I wanted you to see it, Feldrin, all of it."

"It's impressive, all right," he said, startled at the emotion in her voice. "Yours. All of it."

"More than I ever wanted. Maybe more than I can manage."

"Na. You got yer friends to help you with it. The Shattered Isles're free now. No pirate'd dare ply these waters."

"You're right," she admitted. "I've given the ship building over to the Keelsons, Ghelfan and Dura, and Cammy's a natural for keeping me organized. She's even learning the books; oh, and she loves the children. Did you know she's planning to start a school? You should ask her to tell you about it. She's going to dedicate it to... Koybur..."

They both fell silent, remembering their friends—Finthie Tar, Vulta Kambeo, Rafen Ulbattaer, Morris Keelson, and Koybur—who had not lived to share the dream.

"And what about you?" Feldrin asked as he stared steadily into the distance. "What will you do?"

"Me?" Cynthia snorted a laugh and shook her head. "I have so much to learn! I thought I was doing well on my own, but the mer have shown me how little I really know. Most seamages start learning as *children*. They tell me my powers are strong, but right now that only makes me dangerous; kind of like a child with a really sharp knife. I've got years ahead of me before I can even attempt some of the incantations in my father's log."

"Mistress of Ships, Seamage of the Shattered Isles with two whole nations of allies, one above the water and one below, who don't particularly like one another, and now all this magic to learn, too? Sounds like you'll be busy."

"More than busy," Cynthia admitted. In a quieter tone, she continued. "Do you understand, Feldrin? Do you see why... what I need to do right now?"

Feldrin nodded, not trusting his voice. He had avoided this conversation, knowing how it would play out. Her life held no place for devotion to anything but all those things he'd just listed. No room for family... No time for love.

"We both have so many duties and responsibilities," Cynthia said as she looked into his eyes. "And we both know the truth of it, don't we?"

"The truth?"

"The sea, Feldrin. We both know her."

"Aye, we both know her...and love her." He turned to gaze at the ocean and took a deep breath of the heavily scented air. They both loved the sea, and that love would always lie between them. He tasted salt on his lips that had nothing to do with the ocean. "She's a harsh mistress."

"Harsh, aye, but *only* a mistress," Cynthia insisted. She tugged at his hand to bring his attention back to her. "The mer reminded me today of one other responsibility I have, one that I hope you might share with me, once things settle down."

"What might *that* be?" he asked skeptically. How could he share her responsibility to them?

Cynthia smiled at him, a mischievous expression that caught him off guard.

"They reminded me that the mer rely on the seamage as much as the seamage relies on the mer, so it's my responsibility to provide them with something."

"And what's that?" he asked, cocking one dark eyebrow.

She pulled him even closer to whisper in his ear.

"An heir."